LANTERNS ON THEIR HORNS

LANTERNS ON THEIR HORNS

RADHIKA JHA

Beautiful
Books

First published 2009.

Beautiful Books Limited
36-38 Glasshouse Street
London W1B 5DL

www.beautiful-books.co.uk

ISBN 9781905636655

9 8 7 6 5 4 3 2 1

Copyright © Radhika Jha 2009.

Cover design by Studio Dempsey.
Typeset in Sabon by Ellipsis Books Limited, Glasgow.
Printed and bound in the UK by CPI Mackays, Chatham ME5 8TD.

Acknowledgements

No book is written absolutely alone, especially this one. I would like to thank Mr Ashok Thapar and Anna Thapar in Madrid for helping me learn about Spanish cows and bullfighting toros; Joselito and Pepe for making me see toros bravos not as animals but as the human soul; and all those at BAIF for showing me the mechanics of artificial insemination in cows. I would also like to thank Dr Steve Newman and Dr Ian Lane for their valuable information on cows and cattle rearing, and Vinnie for teaching me the names of trees in Madhya Pradesh. What errors remain are the result of my persisting stupidity. I thank the staff of Ahilya fort, Maheshwar, for helping me find 'Nandgaon', and Mr. Richard Holkar, for giving me a honeymoon gift of four nights in Ahilya fort; not only was the book one result, so was my daughter.

The manuscript itself would never have come close to publishable if Lisanne Radici, Laura Susijn, Simone Manceau and, of course, my father had not read it first and given me their valuable comments. To them I owe a debt of gratitude that cannot be repaid. Also to Karthika, for her editorial comments and a conversation about cows, long before the book had begun, that gave the book its title. And to Jonathan Wooding, whose gentle questions made crucial changes possible. Also to Simon, for seeing that cows were not what it was all about. And to Paul and Jai and Amaya, who bore the brunt of my forgetfulness and sudden disappearances.

'Gau' is the Sanskrit word for cow. It is also the word for the first ray of light, the eldest child of dawn. The nature of light is to move. That may be how the cow got included in the family of words rooted in the verb 'gam', for 'gam' means to go. Like its ancestor, the first ray of light, the nature of the cow was to move and therefore it had to go somewhere. But the 'somewhere' is what it forgot and in time there grew to be a difference between simply 'going' and 'going somewhere'.

PROLOGUE

MANOJ

The Jaipur-Mumbai Rajdhani was twenty minutes early so Manoj decided to do a little sight-seeing before he went to see his prospective in-laws. He stepped out of the railway station and immediately a taxi pulled up.

'Where do you want to go?' the driver asked.

Manoj thought about it. 'Take me to the Gateway of India,' he said.

The taxi set him down in front of a tiny park dominated by a giant statue of a turbaned man on a horse.

'Shivaji Rao,' the taxi driver said proudly. Manoj didn't respond. He was staring at the giant stone doorframe just behind the statue.

Manoj wasn't impressed. It was too solid, too plain. As if the architect had been in a hurry and on a tight budget. But he walked up to it anyway. Then he looked beyond the empty gate and amazement filled him. He'd never seen the sea before. It looked like an immense bedsheet. On its wrinkled surface, several oil tankers and cargo carriers with wedding earring shaped cranes on their decks could be seen. He saw a sailor, no more than a dot on the deck waving at him, and suddenly the immensity of what he was looking at made him dizzy. An idea blossomed inside him: that what he was seeing was not his future as it had been in the crowded lanes of Jaipur, but another better one, one that could only exist in a place like Mumbai.

1

He heard the click of a camera and turned around to see an attractive blonde tourist armed with a big black camera in a half crouch not far from him. She was trying to photograph the fat grey pigeons that crowded the pavement, too lazy to fly away. He began to examine her closely, doing to her what she was doing to the pigeons. She was not young, he decided, closer to forty than to thirty. But she had abundant blonde hair just like the naked women he sometimes watched on the internet. His eyes slid downwards, piercing the semi transparent material of her trousers. He could almost tell the colour and texture of the skin beneath, wonderfully pale and suspiciously free of underwear. She moved closer and closer to the pigeons, her camera held before her like a weapon. The sight excited him almost more than he could bear and he forced himself to look away.

He noticed that there were others interested in her too. A beggar boy, a peanut seller, a honeymooning couple, and a thin young gigolo in sunglasses and tight blue jeans, were all staring at her with varying degrees of curiosity and calculation. Suddenly the little beggar boy leapt forward and grabbed her bag. Manoj gave a shout of warning and stuck his foot out in front of the boy. The boy went sprawling across the pavement. Manoj jumped on top of him and grabbed the grubby hand holding the bag. But the boy's fist was like a small vice and there was nothing Manoj could do to free the bag. So with his other hand he grabbed the boy's collar. But the boy wriggled like an eel and Manoj heard the sound of rotten material tearing. At the same moment the boy turned his head and bit Manoj's hand. Manoj yowled in surprise and let go. The boy then headbutted him viciously in the stomach and dashed away, upsetting the peanut man's tray and basket in the process. The tray wobbled wildly and slowly tipped over, sending the peanuts flying up into the sky. Then gravity asserted itself and the peanuts began to fall. For a fraction of a second, everyone just stared at the falling peanuts, fascinated by the sight of such extravagant waste. Then pandemonium broke out as tourists, gigolos and beggars got down on all fours, scrambling for the peanuts. Seeing the bag lying forgotten not far from him, Manoj grabbed it.

'Here is your bag,' he said, handing it to the woman a little breathlessly.

She smiled, showing perfect white teeth. 'Thank you.'

Manoj took her outstretched hand, feeling as if he were entering a lovely place. 'No, no. It was my pleasure to be of help,' he replied carefully.

She disentangled her hand and dimpled up at him. 'You Indians are really so polite.'

Twenty minutes later Manoj was sitting opposite the blonde goddess in a giant wicker chair under an equally giant fan that whirled with a certain pompous vigour. How did one get into bed with a foreign girl? he wondered. The porn films always began after that bit was done.

'So what brings you to Mumbai?' he asked tentatively.

'It's a long story,' she said.

'I am sure it is interesting and worth hearing then,' Manoj replied courteously.

She smiled. 'Though I behaved like a stupid tourist today, actually I come to this country a lot,' she began in heavily-accented English. 'In another life I think I was born here. But in this life I was born in Spain I am afraid.'

'Spain?' Manoj said hesitantly, racking his brains for something he could say about the country. 'Bullfighting?'

'Yes, bullfighting still happens. Do you know Guru Gangadhar Mishra?'

'Oh.' A sigh of disappointment escaped Manoj. He couldn't compete with a guru, he was just a boring old MA (History). Everything he knew about sex came off the internet. Foreign disciples of gurus were known to be perverts.

'You know Guru Gangadhar Mishra then?' she asked eagerly. 'He has a big ashram in Benares.'

Manoj shook his head. She too looked a little disappointed but then brightened as she told him about the guru. 'He is a great, great man, and he can heal people, with just the touch of his hand. Like Christ. When I met him he told me, "Come to India; in India even a poor man feels rich enough to share his little bit of bread." So I came.' She looked away, her face growing dreamy. 'Everything that is India is in his face. I stayed with him in Benares for six years.'

'Six years?' What about your family? Manoj wanted to ask.

'No one in my family knew where I was,' she said, smiling naughtily as she answered his unspoken question. 'I was free. They were very worried at first; they thought I must be sick or had died. In a way, I had done both. For the person I was, the sick unhappy person my family and friends had known, had been killed by the swamiji's first stare, and the real me, the one no one knew, had been pulled out by the force of his third eye. You are Indian, you know about the third eye. But when I go back to my family – because in the end they hired a detective and found me – they do not understand at all. My uncle came and he made me go back. I was very very sad, but I made my uncle promise to help me return. And he did. So now I am here again.'

'And you will go back to the Ashram then? When?' Manoj asked anxiously.

'Not immediately. First I have business here.'

'What business?' Manoj asked eagerly. 'I too have business here.'

She laughed again then grew serious. 'In my guruji's ashram, we had one hundred cows. Their milk was used to feed many, many widows and children. I made my guruji put me in charge of them. You see, I know cows. My family has nearly ten thousand. I grew up with cows and I love them. I did my best but Indian cows don't give even a third of what our cows do. Every day we had to make the poor go back hungry; there was not enough for all of them. When I had to leave I asked my guruji what he wanted from Europe. "Why should I need anything from Europe? I have everything I need right here?" he said to me.

'"But there must be something, Guruji," I insisted. He laughed then his face became serious. "Daughter," he said, "I saw on the TV in your country they are killing cows for their flesh. That is a terrible crime. For the sake of your people, save those cows and bring them here. We will look after them."' She stopped and sat back with her hands on her knees like a schoolgirl. 'For seven years I have been working to fulfil my guruji's wish.'

'And?' Manoj asked.

'And now I wait for the cows to arrive tonight,' she answered triumphantly.

Manoj stared at her in disbelief. 'You are bringing foreign cows to India?'

'Yes,' she said simply.

Manoj said nothing. He looked up. Somewhere in that sky the colour of her eyes, a plane full of cows was hurtling towards them.

Then he looked into her eyes, seeing the promise in them. 'I am called Manoj. Manoj Mishra,' he said, 'and you?'

'Durga,' she replied simply. 'That is the name my guruji gave me.'

When Manoj got to his prospective in-laws' opulent apartment in North Mumbai, they'd given up on him.

'Who are you?' the dark-skinned servant girl who opened the door asked insolently.

'I am Manoj Mishra. Your sahib is expecting me,' he replied haughtily.

She began to shut the door in his face. 'Hey, wait a minute.' He grabbed the door, wondering how the daughter of a colonel of the Indian army put up with such a strange servant.

'Pratima beti, who is it?' a sweetly feminine voice called from somewhere inside.

Manoj froze.

'No one, Maa.' She glared at him from under bushy black eyebrows. Manoj's empty stomach somersaulted. He stared hard at the small, dark woman his mother had chosen. He had taken her for a servant, but this was Pratima herself. She was not pretty by any stretch of the imagination. He felt relieved.

High heels clicked on polished marble, accompanied by the scent of jasmine and the swish of silk. 'Hai Ram!' his prospective mother-in-law exclaimed. Mother and daughter stared at him in silence and Manoj became painfully aware of his dishevelled state.

'I just came, I . . .' he whispered, his throat suddenly dry. 'I came to say sorry. . .'

'Sorry for what?' Mrs Pandey gave a tinkling laugh. 'We were worried silly. Mumbai is such a big city. Come in, come in. Now you are here. . . We will call your parents immediately. They were so worried too. I was just speaking to your mother – she was crying. We called the police but they were useless. "Madam, he must be dead by now," they said. "The streets of Mumbai are dangerous."' She smiled at him warmly. 'I am so glad you are not.'

At the mention of his mother, Manoj's resolve melted. He allowed himself to be led down the narrow passageway into the large L-shaped living room.

They sat him down on an overstuffed sofa facing the sea and the dark, badly-dressed daughter served him tea and samosas. Mrs Pandey chattered on about his mother and what good friends they'd been in boarding school. He listened dully, feeling the inevitable close in.

The interrogation began like a bullfight in which neither side really wanted to participate. 'So tell us about you, beta, what do you do?' Mrs Pandey asked.

'History MA, Jaipur University,' Manoj replied dully, 'working on a PhD on Indus Valley civilisations outside of the Indus Valley.'

But Sudhakar Pandey, ex-captain of the Indian army and scion of Mumbai industry, angered by what had in fact been a three-day silence without explanation, suddenly cut him off.

'History? What kind of a fool studies that? A young man should be thinking about his future not the past.'

'History teaches us who we are. Without knowing who we are, how can we make a decent future?' Manoj replied patiently. He'd had this type of conversation over a thousand times in the last eight years with his family.

'You mean to say you don't know who you are?' Captain Pandey asked incredulously.

'I do, I studied history,' Manoj replied tiredly, not wanting to argue. 'The point is, does modern India know? Look at this city, the richest place in India, what does it have to compare with Jaipur's palaces? If commerce told us who we were then this city should have been the most beautiful city in India.'

Captain Pandey bridled. 'Look Mr Historian, don't try to judge what you don't know. You think I don't know who I am? Look around, does this look like the house of a loser? Would I have been able to become a millionaire if I didn't know who I was?'

Millionaire. The word whipped up the anger lying dormant inside him. 'If you Mumbaiwalas knew who you were,' he spat, 'would your children run off to America the moment they got a chance? These expensive Mumbai buildings you are so proud of are filled with old people.' He stopped suddenly. 'I'm sorry, I shouldn't have said that.'

But to his surprise, instead of being angry, Captain Pandey chuckled. 'At least you look under the surface of things and you can argue,' he said gruffly. 'That's useful in business.'

Then came the crucial question. 'So what are your plans for the future, young man?' Captain Pandey asked.

'I want to work for society. I want to end poverty,' Manoj replied distractedly, thinking of Durga waiting for him at the hotel. He'd told her he was going out to buy a newspaper.

'And how will you do this? Politics?' Mrs Pandey asked encouragingly before her husband could say anything.

'Politics?' Manoj laughed. 'Politics won't cure poverty. My plan is simple, and therefore it cannot fail.'

'And what is that?' Captain Pandey asked. 'A lot of people have tried to end poverty and have failed, you know why? Because unless people help themselves, no one can help them. Some people are weak, others stupid, others lazy, and still others poor.'

'Darling, let the boy speak,' Mrs Pandey interrupted him.

Captain Pandey stopped mid-sentence. 'You are right darling, I should let the young genius speak. What is your plan, genius?'

Manoj licked his lips. He saw the future, dark, warm and inviting, like the space between Durga's legs.

'Poor people can't cope with technology. They are illiterate, they don't understand complicated things,' he began. 'We have to give them something simple, something they can understand.' He took a quick look at them. They were both listening, so he continued more confidently. 'What all poor people do know how to do is take care of animals.' He shut his eyes and thought of Durga, of the shape of her lips, the light in her eyes as she spoke. 'My plan is to import foreign cows who give twenty-five times more milk than our Indian ones, breed them here and give them to the poorest of the poor in our villages.'

At first all they could do was goggle at him. Then Captain

Pandey began to laugh. 'Oh, that is the funniest joke I've heard this year.'

Manoj stood up. Captain Pandey and his wife watched him, relief and anxiety in their eyes. He saw a chance to have the last word. 'I made a mistake coming here,' he announced quietly. 'What can people like you know of a poor man's problems? To do that you need to have imagination, and for that, you need to know history.'

He turned on his heel and walked towards the front door. No one stopped him. But when he got to the door he saw there were seven different locks on it. He was staring at the locks helplessly when Pratima arrived. She must be relieved, he thought. Wordlessly she began to open the locks. When the last one was undone, she turned and faced him. 'I believe you,' she said fervently. 'You will be a great man some day – just like Gandhi.'

CHAPTER ONE

THE COW

Each day the cow went with the herd.

In the morning the little creature with two feet and soft hands would come to the thatched barn where she lived, open the gate and take her out to join her companions. She would then move in a cloud of dust, to the tinkling of cow-bells and the soft clopping of hooves in the dusty village lane, the reassuring sense of sameness all around her as two feet guided the herd into the fallows to graze. There were no untidy stops and starts; she just flowed with the others, the fore-knowledge of fresh grass a tickle in her nostrils.

When the fields around the village dried and the earth hardened, the herd was forced to go further and further afield to find food. The cows left earlier and returned later, but hunger still wandered through their many compartmented stomachs. They grew thin and their once tight and glossy skins hung about them like old shawls. But in spite of the long futile marches, the cow drew comfort from the fact that the day's routine remained roughly the same and there were always little hands and gentle voices to come back to.

But as the sun continued to blaze from a cloudless sky the ponds dried up and even the early morning dew vanished as soon as it touched the ground. The cow's skin began to itch and became as brittle as paper. Cracks appeared where insects would feast, creating sores that oozed a smelly liquid that tasted awful when she licked it. Still the herd went out each day, bound as much by habit as by blood, even though each and every animal knew that the sap in the trees had retreated to their cores and all that was left on the surface was dead.

Then the herd began to dwindle. It happened at night, a few at a time. A roaring smelly thing came and parts of the herd went away leaving behind a silence that didn't get filled. Each time it happened the ones left behind would bellow sadly and the animals in the truck would reply, their calls growing softer as the truck pulled further and further away. The next day none of the herd would eat for a while. Then hunger would force them to pack their sadness away and concentrate upon the emptiness in their stomachs.

And so it went on. The sun watched the earth like a jealous lover, burning away the few clouds that came. And with each rainless week the herd grew smaller.

At last there was no herd left. The cow knew her turn had come when they didn't take her out that day to graze. Little Hands brought her grain, straw and some smelly wilted greens in a bucket. That evening the cow had an entire half bucket of water to herself. She waited for the smelly, noisy one to arrive. But it never came. Instead, just before dawn Old Two-legs appeared with Little Hands. They fed her more grain and sugar and the little one clung to the soft folds around her neck, wetting them with something hot that stung a little but brought welcome relief to her itching skin. So the cow stretched out her tongue and licked the child's face. She tasted salt. She licked it again, eagerly. More came and she continued licking, growing almost happy. Then Old Two-legs untied her and walked her out of the silent village, Little Hands still clinging to her neck.

At the edge of the village Little Hands stayed behind, and it was only her and Old Two-legs. They walked across the dried fields, the empty river bed, into the dead forest. They walked for two days by the light of the moon, stopping to sleep only when the sun grew too hot to continue. But the cow was happy. They were looking for the herd, and they would find it.

On the third day they found water – a tiny green pool, thick with algae and almost undrinkable. But the cow went in gratefully and lay in it, and the soft cool mud eased the sores on her back and belly. Old Two-legs squatted at the base of a tree and watched. Their eyes met and the knowledge that there was no herd to join cut through her like a knife. Old Two-legs was the first to look away. He got up and called to her softly. In his hands she smelled something familiar and yet unfamiliar. He asked her to eat it, and because he was all that was left of the herd, she obeyed.

The opium did its work well. In its dream the cow's mouth moved, full of the taste of the sweetest, freshest grass it had ever eaten. Her ears twitched – keeping time with the clop of four thousand and four hooves. Her skin felt pleasantly cool and she no longer felt hunger. After twenty hours, she awoke to find that Old Two-legs had gone.

For the first time in her life the cow was utterly alone.

Forests are quiet places. But only during the day. At night, they became noisy thoroughfares, alive with rustles, coughs, grunts, alarm calls, the whoop of bullfrogs, the crack of a falling branch and the occasional roar. Each sound is amplified by the night so that a leopard scratching its claws on the bark of a tree or a wild pig digging for its favourite roots can sound like a herd of feeding elephants. The cow was afraid. Each time a new sound reached her ears, she would peer around, ears and eyes straining to find its source. But darkness gave the sounds grotesque disguises and fear played havoc with her senses.

Towards dawn, the forest grew calm and she managed to fall asleep again – only to wake, petrified, as the ground beneath her began to tremble. A herd of elephants had taken over the clearing and was busy eating its way through the surrounding vegetation. She had never seen any creatures so huge, so powerful. They reached up and tore young trees out of the ground as if they were blades of grass. Beside herself with terror, she called out to the herd to save her but no one, not even Old Two-legs, came. So she cowered in the thicket of lantana until a thin grey light announced the morning. At last the elephants had eaten enough and moved on. Silence returned and once more the cow found herself alone.

Being alone was new. From the time she was born, creatures similar to her had surrounded her. Now a nameless dread loosened her bowels. It was of a place to which cows went alone. It made her want to run, but she did not know where. So she took a few steps forward and then broke into a shambling trot.

Going somewhere was very different from going with the herd. It was much harder. But she persisted, driven on by that nameless dread. Eventually it became easier and she slowed to a walk. The forest ended and she came upon a road. The surface was smooth and easier on her feet, and it seemed to be going somewhere too. It smelt strange and new, and that reassured her. All evening and well into the night she followed the road. She ate little and soon felt desperately thirsty. She turned to the road for an answer, but the road stretched in front and behind her as straight as Old Two-legs' stick. Eventually the thirst made her so tired that she lay down beside a haystack on the side of the road and slept.

She awoke to the sound of hooves, the smell of dust and the trembling of the earth. A herd! She struggled to her feet. On the horns of the leaders and on those of the animals at each end were strung lamps that bobbed up and down, to make a moving river of light. In the dim light of the lamps she saw red daubs of colour on their foreheads. They were thin, so thin that they resembled the two-legs running beside them; so thin that their cheeks were hollow and their hip bones jutted out; so thin that their massive horns felt too heavy for their bodies. In spite of this they were magnificent creatures and the cow would have been proud to attach herself to them. But the smell stopped her. It was not only the smell of exhaustion. There was something more, something she instinctively recognised. It was the smell of fear. It hung over the herd like a pall, their constant companion. She staggered over to the bushes beside the road. From their safety she watched the herd. She was sure they had smelt her too, as she stood half-hidden by the side of the road. But not a single head turned. Their fear was too powerful. They too were going somewhere, and that somewhere was a place they dreaded.

And so the animals moved past in an endless stream – hundreds of them – till the last one was gone and all the cow could see was the lights on the horns of the tail-enders. When they had disappeared over the horizon, she walked out into the middle of the road and bellowed loudly, giving voice to the sorrow that had invaded her, willing them to turn back, to follow her into the forest. But not one head turned around. They were a herd, accustomed to being together and moving together, even towards the place they feared the most. The cow returned to her place beside the road and lay down once again. But sleep evaded her for the rest of the night.

Close to morning her fear abated and she was able to move again. She fell into a rhythm. From time to time she would forget that she was going somewhere, and stop and look around. Then she would remember and move on. During the day the road would be busy with roaring smelly things of all sizes, rushing along at speed. They never stopped, so she learned to ignore them. Perhaps because she looked as if she was going somewhere, no one interrupted her solitude. She would dream often of the cows with lights attached to their horns, and twitched uncomfortably as fear of the silent place they went to in the middle of the night invaded her. Sometimes she would wake up and lie silently, longing for the dawn, longing for an end to her solitude. Most of all she longed for the touch of a cool wet snout, a rough tongue and soft hands.

One day she smelled other animals and sweet river grass. She quickened her pace and the scent grew stronger, until she came to a marshy pond. It was all that remained of what must have once been a large lake. There, scattered in and around the pond in the still damp mud, was a small herd. They were well nourished, with fleshed-out haunches, rounded bellies and soft faces. Among them were several calves. They were being washed by three small two-legs.

The sight of the animals was like a magnet. The cow paused, overcome by indecision. Here was a herd in which she sensed the contentment she had known. All of a sudden going somewhere felt heavy and tiresome. She turned towards the water shyly.

But as soon as she entered the water the other animals moved away. Hurt, she stayed a little way away, keeping her face to them in the hope of some sign of acceptance, if not welcome. But the herd did not respond. Instead it moved by gradual degrees towards the far shore, mothers nudging their curious offspring in front of them. The cow waded out to the middle of the pond and waited, but the herd ignored her. So she waded onwards to the opposite shore where the grass was greener and smelt sweeter. Before she settled down to eat, she began to clean herself. Perhaps it was the smell of the road that had scared them away.

The herd continued to behave as if she did not exist. At dusk the little two-legs began to round it up. She was tempted to join it but hesitated, torn between the longing for safety in their numbers and the fear of rejection. A fleeting memory of

Little Hands came to her, of salt tears and small arms encircling her neck. If the two-legs accepted her, she reasoned, the herd would too. So she waited. At last a little two-legs in ragged shorts noticed her. He was the smallest in the group but had the largest stick. He came racing towards her, waving his stick. She prepared to run, but instead of driving her away he jabbed her with his stick, pointing her towards the herd. Apprehension turned to relief and she rushed to obey.

Her relief was indescribable. Once again she was with a herd. They came to a village in a cloud of chalky white dust. As they walked down the central pathway, the smell of cowdung fires enveloped her. She felt giddy with the familiarity of it all. But as they moved further into the village the herd began to melt away, going their separate ways to their homes, the two-legs trailing behind. Not knowing what to do, the cow kept walking. By the time it reached the far end of the village, she was alone again, so she stopped.

'Are, whose cow is this?' a raucous voice behind her called. Looking back she saw a small bunch of little two-legs looking at her.

'I have never seen her before. Maybe she is a junglee cow. Let us take her to the headman.'

'No, no, let's chase it out. Let us see how fast this fat cow can run.'

The cow felt a stone hit her. Then another and then another, each accompanied by the piping, jeering yells of the little boys. She began to walk, but they followed her. The boys came closer and the stones got bigger. She felt a sharp stabbing pain and swished her tail to remove its cause, but it got worse. She paused to turn and lick the spot, and tasted her blood. She began to run.

Then she was outside the village in the wilderness in the gathering dusk and there were no more voices, no more stones. For a while she stood there, mooing loudly in protest, but heard only silence. The moon, bright, golden and full, rose over the fields turning the walls of the village huts to mottled silver. The cow bellowed hoarsely one last time, and plodded away. She was tired. Her body ached and the wound pulsed and burned. Blood oozed from the ugly gash. She kept licking it but more came.

Then the reassuring bulk of a forest loomed over the horizon to the east and, remembering another forest, the cow turned abruptly and headed towards it. The same instinct that had made her run now told her that when she stopped she had to find cover. Behind her the afterglow of sunset was snuffed out by clouds that spread rapidly to cover the sky. A tongue of lightning lit the gloom. She heard a dry crack, like a giant twig being stepped on, and behind her a lone tree burst into flames. Then came a drum roll of thunder. Still she kept going, not even bothering to glance back.

At last the tall trees closed over her. Inside the forest, there was a breathless silence. Even the patter of raindrops was muted, muffled by the large leaves overhead. With the last of her strength the cow climbed a steep escarpment to her left and came to a clearing. A huge thorny kair tree dominated it, its overhanging branches almost touching the ground. She crawled quickly underneath the tree, the thorns once more opening her wound. In its dark dry centre, she at last collapsed.

It rained for two days. By the time it stopped raining she had a fever. Despite her constant licking, the wound on her flank was badly infected. She felt a terrible thirst but was too weak to get up and find water. So she lay under the tree, her mind in a haze. When the goat arrived, she imagined that the herd had found her. When the man arrived she thought it was Old Two-legs come to send her away in the smelly thing, to the place to which cows went alone.

CHAPTER TWO

RAMU

The goats knew that another storm was coming, and didn't want to be out in it. It was different in the village. There the peal of thunder would be robbed of its terror by the everyday sounds of dogs barking, barn doors banging in the wind, and people hurriedly closing their doors and windows. And when the rain came, it would announce itself with a shushing hiss as it lost its way in the straw of thatched roofs. In the village the goats could always seek shelter in a barn, or in the lee of a friendly wall. But it was afternoon, and Ramu had taken them out to graze. So they swallowed their fear and walked determinedly into the fields that bordered the forest.

But as the sky darkened and the wind rose, their unease grew. The hunger in their bellies was sated, so they began butting Ramu in their friendly way, urging him to take them home. But Ramu was lost in thoughts of his wife. She was more beautiful than any woman he'd ever seen: her eyes huge and dark, her nose slim and short, her lips like a boat in full sail. But it wasn't just her face that made Ramu ache all over. It was the way her body was sweetly curved and rounded in all the right places, the way her deliciously long and thick hair moved like a nest of blue-black snakes when she turned her head. The previous evening she had slapped his dinner down before him. 'Your food,' she'd said with a scowl when he'd stared at her darkly beautiful face. He'd looked down at his plate, hastily dipped a piece of chapatti into the vegetable and popped it into his mouth, almost spitting it out an instant later.

'What is it?' she had asked challengingly, a small smile hovering at the back of her almond-shaped eyes. 'You don't like my food?'

'Water, give me some water,' Ramu had gasped, his mouth on fire.

'You get it,' she'd replied, smiling victoriously.

Ramu tugged at the cloth around his neck. His wife grew more and more incomprehensible with each passing week. Yet it had been her family that had sent the matchmaker to Nandgaon. And she had married him knowing he could give her nothing – for the matchmaker had to have told her family all about him. Ramu shook his head again. He just couldn't understand it.

As was his habit, Ramu drove the goats towards the river. At first the goats followed him, because he was their familiar, trusted herder. But when there was a crack of lightning followed by a deafening peal of thunder, and the rain burst on them in torrents, Natthan Lal, the headman's lone billygoat, who was the leader of the herd, took charge and turned towards the forest, quickly climbing the escarpment which marked its beginning. The other goats followed and within seconds Ramu found himself alone, his shouted commands lost in the growing din of the storm. Knowing that he could not climb the escarpment the way the goats had, Ramu circled around it and took the long way up, a threadlike path down which rainwater gushed with such force that he was almost knocked off his feet several times. Each time he got his breath back, he cursed Natthan Lal and the other goats.

But when he got to the top, his anger evaporated. The goats were all there, spread out across a grassy meadow protected by giant arjun trees. But his relief was short-lived. A quick count showed that Natthan Lal was missing. Cursing loudly and fluently, he scanned the edges of the meadow. On the far side he saw a thicket of kairs, and just a little way inside it Natthan Lal's wagging brush of a tail. With an exclamation of relief he crossed the clearing and called out to the goat. 'What are you doing there, you ungrateful wretch? Come out. We have to go home.' But Natthan Lal refused to move. He was standing unnaturally still. Then his rump moved as he pushed himself deeper towards whatever was inside. His curiosity aroused, Ramu tried to follow but found himself entangled in the thorns that were the kairs' natural defence. Slowly, and with mounting irritation, he pushed the thorny branches aside and edged deeper into the clearing at the centre of the thicket. By then it was almost pitch dark. But just beyond Natthan Lal, he could make out the shape of the large, dark creature that had aroused the billygoat's insatiable curiosity.

At the same moment his nose was assaulted by the smell of decay, and he heard an uneven, rasping pant coming from the animal. His blood froze. A tiger? And him trapped in a bed of thorns, unable to move! But no sooner had it come than his fear passed. Had it really been a tiger, Natthan Lal would have given the warning and run away long ago, taking the herd with him. It must be some other animal, he concluded, and from the smell it seemed it had been there for a while, and was probably wounded. He felt for the short lengths of sugar cane he usually took with him to chew on as he watched the goats graze, and threw one towards the shape. After a few seconds, he heard the sound of chewing. He reached into his pocket and took out another piece but, on an impulse, threaded his way further into the thicket and held it out in the palm of his hand.

The dark shape moved, and a pair of mournful almond eyes set in a delicate white face turned towards him. He felt a rough tongue scoop the sugar cane out of his hand. He drew back in surprise. A cow? What was a cow doing all by itself in the forest? Ramu's heart rate returned to normal. He took another length of sugar cane and gave it to the cow. Again the tongue came out, but he did not draw his hand back. Instead he reached out to pat the creature's dimly-perceived head.

This time it was the cow that jerked away. It tried to hiss a warning, but a low moan escaped it instead. Pity stirred within Ramu and he reached out again. This time the cow did not pull back and allowed him to pat its forehead and move his hand down to fondle its face.

The cow's nose was hot and dry, and its breathing laboured, he noticed. It was probably very sick. Either he had to do something for it or get the goats away. As he was trying to decide, Natthan Lal took matters into his own hands, broke free of the kair and ran off to join his companions. Torn between duty and pity, Ramu gave the cow one last look, threw the last of the sugar cane towards it and crawled out. He would take the herd back and return as soon as it stopped raining, he rationalised.

But it rained all night. Rivulets became torrents and paths became mudslides. Ramu knew he couldn't return, but found it hard to sleep. His thoughts kept returning to the cow. What does it look like? he wondered; what is the matter with it? Where has it come from? Why is it alone? She appears young, so why did her owner let her go? The questions chased themselves around his head until, towards morning, he fell into a dream-laden sleep.

The next day, when Ramu returned to the meadow, the cow had moved a little further out into the clearing under the canopy of kairs. A stray beam of sunshine made a halo around her long delicate face. Ramu was able to admire the domed elegance of her head and the translucence of her mango-shaped ears. The goats, after sniffing her curiously, lost interest and scattered across the meadow. Only Natthan Lal stayed by the cow, licking her wound worriedly and glancing at Ramu as if to say, 'Do something.' Ramu got up then and went into the forest. He found two large undamaged teak leaves and turned these into a cup with the help of a twig, then rushed down to the river to fill it. When he returned to the clearing he placed it before the cow and quickly backed away. In the now verdant meadow he collected an armful of grass and scattered it before the cow. When the goats had eaten he gathered them for the trip back to the village. At the edge of the meadow he looked back. The cow was watching them warily, the grass lying untouched before her.

But the next day when he returned, the grass had been eaten and the cow was sitting up, looking in their direction as though she'd been expecting them. Ramu reached into his pocket and his hand closed around a fistful of sugar cane and some millet he'd put there especially for her. In the days that followed, it became a routine. When Ramu arrived she'd be watching the point where the path came into the meadow. Her expression wouldn't change as he scattered the grain mixture before her. Then she'd wait until he retreated to the middle of the meadow before touching the food.

At last the day arrived when the cow let Ramu touch her again. He had made her a special mixture of grain, sweet river grass, sugar cane and a few medicinal herbs to fight the infection. The goats, used to his actions, went foraging further into the forest as he scattered his offerings before the cow. As soon as he'd finished, barely giving him time to step back, she rushed forward and buried her nose in the food. He watched her quietly, then went to fetch water. When he returned she didn't even look up. He put the water down beside her and slowly stretched out his hand. Cautiously he began to scratch her behind the ears. Then he scratched the soft folds of skin that garlanded her neck. Her skin was surprisingly cool and he felt her respond to him. He began to lengthen his strokes, exploring her shoulders and scratching her stomach and ribs, always using the fleshy parts of his fingers. She let him touch her, but looked the other way as if he was touching someone else.

It rained for two whole days after that and the goats were kept inside. Ramu, confined to the village, felt restless, unable to concentrate, thoughts of the cow interrupting his every task. Had the herbs done their work? Had the wound healed? Or had the rain inflamed the wound even further? On the third day, he woke up at dawn to blue skies and birds gone mad with joy. He got up and quickly collected his things. Without waking his wife, he rushed over to the headman's goathouse and collected the goats.

But when Ramu arrived at the clearing the cow was nowhere to be seen. Disappointed, he walked around the glade looking for her, even crawling some of the way under the kair tree in the hope of finding her hiding there. When he came out, the forest seemed deafeningly empty. Not knowing what else to do, he sat down and began to play his flute.

That's how the cow found him, entering the meadow from the direction of the stream. The wound had healed and the cow had known it was time to leave. And yet, something made her want to stay. When she heard the flute she turned and listened, the music like gentle hands rubbing the pain out of her wounded flesh. Then she uttered a soft grunt, shook her head once as though she'd made up her mind and turned around.

When the cow finally came closer, Ramu fumbled in his pocket for the grain he'd stored there, took out a few handfuls and scattered them by his feet. The cow hesitated, watching him intently. Then she came forward in a rush as if she were trying to scare him away. A few inches short of him, she stopped, dropped her head and began to eat the grain by Ramu's feet. After a while Ramu stopped playing to watch and the cow looked up questioningly. So he played some more. Then he put the flute down and let his fingers find her head.

Man and cow stayed like that for a long moment. Then, as Ramu was about to pull away, the cow leaned forward and put her head on his shoulder. Ramu went absolutely still, feeling the heaviness of the cow's head, the sweet warmth of her breath on his cheek. Never had he felt so close to anyone before. He thought of his wife, imagining the cow's softness and warmth was hers. Then the cow licked his nose with her rough tongue and his little fantasy melted away. Laughter bubbled inside him and suddenly he felt certain that the cow belonged to him and that he belonged to the cow. 'Oh you beauty!' he exclaimed, hugging her tightly.

When the time came to take the goats home, the cow followed him.

CHAPTER THREE

LAXMI

While Ramu was discovering his newfound love, Laxmi, his wife, was sitting in the verandah of their mud-walled hut counting the grains of rice in the wickerwork tray in front of her. She did not know why she was doing it. Had Ramu been a rich landowner, there would have been many other things to tend to. There would have been large storage bins of rice in the granary behind the kitchen to keep free of pests, bottles of pickles to put out in the sun, chickens to feed, children to tend to, clothes to get washed and utensils to stack.

But a poor man's wife did not have much housekeeping to do. There was also not much to cook. So, after making dal and the single vegetable they ate every day, she would find herself with time on her hands. Counting the grains of rice seemed as good a way of passing the time as any other. But it was not as easy as it seemed. For she did not choose the easy way of letting them drop one by one from her fist. She was trying to count the grains as they lay on the tray. And that was not easy to do for they seemed to flow into one another.

The task was made harder by the fact that much of the rice was broken. So how many broken grains made a whole grain? She laughed out aloud, imagining her namesake, the goddess Laxmi, creator of wealth, sitting cross-legged on the floor in all her finery, trying to solve the riddle. Just as suddenly, her laughter died and she threw the rice from her violently, the little bits scattering all over the hut.

When it catches the light an unbroken grain of rice tossed in the air can look like a tiny sleeping baby. Her father had shown her that, at harvest time, when the women came to the threshing floor to winnow the newly de-husked rice from the chaff. They were so quick and so expert at it, that to the little child she'd been, it had seemed that it was raining babies. And indeed, for Ramdas Athawale it did rain babies for a while, almost one each year. But only girls. And each girl added to the weight of the dowry that he would, one day, have to pay. When she was born the women in the room had begun to wail. Their cries were so loud that they drowned out her furious screams of protest at having to leave the safety of the womb. The clamour made her father rush in, fearing the worst. 'Is she all right?' he had asked, looking towards his wife.

'You've had a girl,' they had told him gravely, when they stopped to draw breath.

'Yes, yes. But is the mother all right?'

'She is fine,' they had assured him, almost as an after-thought.

Ramdas had gone over to his wife's bed and held her hand tenderly. With the edge of his gamchha he wiped the forgotten beads of sweat off her forehead. His aunt tapped him on the shoulder. 'She'll be fine in three months, then you can try again. What shall I do with the girl child?'

'What do you mean what shall you do with her?' Ramdas had cried. 'You will do nothing. She is mine.' And he took the newborn from his aunt's outstretched arms and told the rest of the women to leave. With his own hands, he washed her, something he had never done for his other children, marvelling at the strength and fullness of her limbs. He stared at her perfectly-formed lips and thick dark curling hair, her luminous skin and thought, I shall call her Laxmi. For a child this pretty can only bring good fortune to her family. The next year they had a boy. This was the story her father had told her while they watched the women de-husking the rice.

Perhaps because of that unexpected beginning, Laxmi remained her father's favourite until the end of his life. Even in death, he refused to be parted from her. Laxmi found a picture of the goddess clasped in his dead fist when she was cleaning him up and dressing him in white for the cremation. In the picture the goddess was wearing a crown and garland, and held lotuses in her hands. Jewels dripped from her ears and glinted on her belt. The garland was made from large champak flowers and her lips were an inviting crimson, as was her bindi. It was an alluring image. Just the kind that would inspire confidence in a package of pesticide.

After that day, whenever she thought of her father, it was the picture of the goddess in his hand that she remembered most vividly. She never managed to see him in her dreams the way her mother and sisters did. So the most important question she would ever want to ask in all her life remained unanswered: 'Did you not pause to think when you saw the picture on the packet? How could you have looked at it and still wanted to die?'

She had been told the answer to that question more than once, but could not bring herself to accept it. Ramdas Athawale had committed the sin of greed. The village moneylender's wife had been the first to point a finger. Then everyone in the village was saying it, first in whispers then aloud. What else but greedy is a farmer with ten acres of land who tries to produce as much as a farmer with twenty-five acres? 'It is a sin to covet your neighbour's Kismat,' they would mutter darkly. Naturally the goddess had become angry. Who was Ramdas to try to force her to give him more wealth than she deemed necessary? Laxmi, the goddess of wealth, was after all only a subordinate form of the all-embracing goddess, Bhudevi*. Laxmi heard it all, but

* earth mother

27

refused to accept it. A slow rage built steadily in her heart as she grew older. Rage is usually destructive. But not always. On the day that Laxmi first heard the remarks the villagers were making about her father, she made herself a vow. She would redeem her father's reputation in the village. She would show that he had not been moved by greed but by an understanding of what was possible with the new methods of farming.

On his visits to Mandleshwar, fifteen kilometres away, Ramdas had listened carefully to self-confident strangers talk of tubewells, of chemical fertilisers that were a hundred times more powerful than their manure-based khaad, and of the new, miracle strains of wheat and rice. What he had failed to find, with his limited resources, was a source of water on his land. When the bank's loan was exhausted he had gone to the moneylender, the very one whose wife was the first to accuse him of greed. It was the sixty per cent interest rate the moneylender charged that had killed him. For although the money enabled him to find water and sink a tubewell, the seeds of 'miracle' Kalyan Sona wheat he bought from a seed merchant turned out to be useless. Death was the only way to save his family.

Laxmi was determined to fulfill his dream, even though the moneylender had taken two thirds of their land in repayment of his loan. This determination carried her through secondary school, then college in Mandleshwar, and then an agricultural polytechnic. When her mother's money ran out, she had gone to the principal of her college and asked him for help. He arranged a scholarship for his brightest student, and the foundation that came to her aid took her through the rest of her education. By the time she was twenty-five, the women in her village looked at her with something between dismay and horror. She had become a creature apart. 'Who is going to marry her?' they would ask her mother in hushed tones when they sat around the open cooking fires in the women's courtyard in each other's homes.

Laxmi was at the bank when her marriage was arranged. 'No, we cannot give you a loan,' the bank manager had been telling her for the umpteenth time. 'Headquarters has asked us to be very strict this year. Your father was a defaulter. No loans to defaulters.'

'But I am not a defaulter,' Laxmi replied.

'Or defaulters' families,' he corrected himself.

'But we have ten acres of good land, all we need is twenty thousand rupees in order to tear out the useless sugar cane and plant soyabeans and mustard,' she cried, hoping that telling him her plan would convince him.

'I don't care what you need, you are lucky the bank didn't take your land and sell it. If it hadn't been for me. . .' He paused, blushing. 'Anyway, I did what I could. But I am just a bank employee, I can only give money when I am sure it will be returned.'

'But it will be returned, just as soon as the harvest is sold. And you know that my father failed only because he was sold fake seed by the seed merchant. If the seed had been genuine, we wouldn't have needed this loan.' And my baba wouldn't be dead, she thought.

The bank manager went red and he began to shout. 'Excuses, excuses, if only this hadn't happened, if only the rains hadn't failed, if only. . . Can't you people understand this is a bank not a charity? What am I supposed to tell my superiors? That you were stupid enough to buy bad seeds with the money I gave you?'

'But I'll pay it back,' Laxmi replied doggedly. 'You know my brother is in the army. Even if the rains fail, he can pay your money back. It's a crime to let good land go to waste like this!'

The manager softened. He sighed. 'Don't talk to me about crimes, beti, I've seen more than my share of them.' Then, as if he was afraid of softening, he stood up, suddenly towering over her. 'But it isn't your land, it is your mother's and brother's land. You have no share in this.'

Laxmi looked at him, surprised. How could he say that? He knew how hard she had worked on the land, how after her baba, she was the one who knew it best.

'Now go home beti,' he said gently, knowing he had won, 'or you will miss the last bus.'

When she returned, her mother hugged her tight for the first time in many years.

'It's all arranged,' she said.

'What's arranged?' Laxmi had asked stupidly.

'Pugli, your marriage,' her mother had answered, smiling. 'At last I will be able to hold my head up.'

Laxmi looked at her in surprise. In the days after her baba's death Laxmi would have done anything to make her mother smile. 'But Baba wouldn't have wanted it,' Laxmi burst out, wiping the smile off her mother's face. 'How can I get my degree if I get married now? Just six months more, Maa, and then I will be able to get a job as a lecturer. And then even the bank won't be able to refuse me a loan.'

'Loan-shoan besharam. Chhodo tumhare baba ke baatein. If he hadn't relied on loans, we wouldn't have been here today.' She looked down at her bare hands and Laxmi's eyes followed. The gold bangle, the only piece of jewellery her mother hadn't already sold, was gone. Nothing more was said.

She was pulled out of her reverie by the creak of the courtyard door. 'Look what I have brought you,' Ramu shouted from the door. Laxmi looked up, relieved. He had returned early. 'Come out and see what I have brought you today, Laxmi, devi,' Ramu called again from the angan. Laxmi didn't answer. Her eyes went to the chinks in the thatched roof. A peace offering! Did he think she was so naïve? Did he think she had not noticed? Like lightning striking a dead tree, anger raced through her body. I am not your Laxmi and I am certainly no goddess, she wanted to scream. How long did he think he could hide from her what the entire village already knew?

The women had been talking about Ramu at the ghat that morning when she arrived. As she walked past them, they stopped hurriedly and looked at her the way they would have at a leper. As soon as she passed the talk began again, but in whispers. 'Well, well, look who's come to join us today?' she heard someone say. 'Wonder what could have made her come? Maybe she is missing her Ramu.'

'Ramu does not seem to be missing her,' she heard another voice say. This provoked a snicker of laughter. Laxmi's hands curled into fists but she kept them by her side. Women without pride fought and scratched each other. She would not give them that pleasure.

'Look what I found in the forest, Laxmibai. It is a gift from the Devi herself,' Ramu said excitedly as he entered the hut.

'You keep it,' Laxmi muttered. He laughed, a joyous big sound.

'Come,' he said, taking her hand.

She pulled away and he didn't insist.

'Come Laxmidevi, if only to see what I have brought you,' he said, turning away. In spite of herself, her hand reached out to him. But he was already outside. Cursing under her breath, she followed him.

'There, look,' he said, pointing towards the south-west corner. 'You didn't believe me, did you?'

'Believe what?'

'That the Devi would look after us.'

She followed his pointing finger and saw it glowing faintly like a neon tube against the darkness of the animal house.

'I wanted to name her Laxmi after you, but we can't have two Laxmis in the house,' he joked.

Laxmi continued to stare at the animal, unable to believe her eyes.

'Is this what you have brought me?' she said to him at last.

The joy leaked out of his face. 'I found her in the forest,' he stammered. 'The Devi gave her to us, to you. It is not a very big gift, I know, but it is better than. . . than. . .' he began to stutter.

'Than nothing?' Laxmi suggested softly. 'All you have ever given me is nothing.'

His features crumbled, then he pulled himself together. 'Do you not remember what you said to me the night we were married?' he asked.

Laxmi looked at him in silence. The night they were married? Of course she remembered. How could she forget that night?

The bus had dropped them off around eight in the middle of a ghost town. 'Where. . . where are we?' she'd asked nervously, gazing at the crumbling walls that surrounded them.

'This is old Nandgaon, the road ends here,' he'd answered. 'Our village is on the other side.' He had a surprisingly sweet voice, she noticed. 'Other side of what?' she'd asked suspiciously.

'Of the river,' he'd replied. 'But don't worry, the boatman is waiting for us.'

'The river?' she'd asked, surprised. 'What about the road? Isn't there a bridge? How do people get in and out?'

He shook his head. 'There is no road. It ends here.'

Laxmi had been dumbstruck. What kind of a village was not connected to a road? Khargaon had had a fully metalled road connecting it to Mandleshwar since before she had been born. The idea was so preposterous that she thought he was joking.

But the boat was waiting for them, unmistakeably real.

'Are, Ramu, what have you brought back from the town this time?' the boatman called out when he saw her huddled behind him.

'Nothing for you Dada, nothing for you,' Ramu had replied, helping her on to the boat. 'This is my wife.'

The oar slipped from the old boatman's hands. 'Married? But how? When? Why didn't you tell us instead of sneaking into the village like a thief?' he demanded. 'We'd have prepared a proper welcome for your bride. What is her name? Where is she from?'

'From Khargaon. And her name is Laxmi,' Ramu had answered.

The boatman pushed off with his pole and the slim vessel had slipped easily into the midnight water. No one spoke, each wrapped in their own thoughts. To Laxmi, it was as if they had entered another world, one made of rock and water and a hard unforgiving silence broken only by the slap of oars hitting water. Seized by a premonition that her husband was not all he seemed, she turned to ask him why there was no road to the village when all of a sudden a huge clapping sound shattered the silence and a large white bird rose out of a clump of reeds. Laxmi's body jerked backwards in fright and immediately her husband's arms had come around her. She leaned back gratefully and the moment was lost. She'd looked instead at the opposite shore, wondering why it never seemed to get closer. Then she realised that there were no lights visible anywhere.

'The village is hidden behind the trees, you can't see it,' her husband had whispered into her hair.

'It's so dark. How is it that there are no lights?' Laxmi had whispered back.

'Because there's no electricity,' he'd replied.

'No electricity at all?' Laxmi had been shocked. All the villages she knew had the wires, even if the electricity only came at midnight.

'Who needs lights at night?' the boatman had said, suddenly

entering the conversation. 'The night is for sleeping.'

'But surely your headman must have insisted?' she had asked curiously.

'Our headman didn't want electricity either. He has a generator, which he uses only when there is a puja or a marriage in the village,' Ramu replied.

'So he has light but no one else does,' Laxmi had remarked.

But the boatman would have none of it. 'Our headman is a great man,' he corrected her gently. 'We may not have light but we have everything we need. No one starves in Nandgaon, no farmer commits suicide and no child goes without milk.'

Then they were at the other bank, and further conversation became impossible. Ramu grabbed her small bundle and leapt on to the shore. Then the boatman helped Laxmi out carefully, slipping a small tightly wrapped parcel into her hand. 'A small gift to welcome you,' he'd whispered into her ear, his breath smelling of rotten teeth and betel juice.

When they entered the village the moon had hidden itself behind the trees, cloaking the village in darkness. They walked down a winding dusty lane between the blank outer walls of houses and low mud walls that hid sheds and vegetable patches. Nothing moved. Nothing disturbed the darkness. Not a child coughed, not a dog barked. It was so quiet that Laxmi felt sure that the man beside her could hear the frightened beating of her heart. But when they reached the centre of the village the moon reappeared briefly and Laxmi had stared in delight at the painted facades of the houses. The village had ended abruptly even as her mind still grappled with the beauty of the village centre. The lane they were on became a footpath but her new husband continued to lead her on, through tall stands of whispering sugar cane until they came to a recessed doorway tucked into a crumbling mud wall. 'We have arrived,' he told her with simple pride, pushing open a worn and scratched wooden door. Inside was a courtyard, bare except for a small neem tree. To her left, the adjoining wall ran down to a modest thatch-roofed house that was clearly the living quarters. At right angles to it, facing the perimeter of the courtyard, was a much smaller hut. Both had wide verandahs facing into the courtyard. 'The bigger one is the house,' Ramu said, sensing her question. Not meeting her eyes, he hurried up the steps to the house. Laxmi was left alone to familiarise herself with her new home by the light of the stars. It looked extremely small, with no windows and a tattered curtain hanging across the doorway. But perhaps the other rooms were directly behind and in better condition, she told herself. The silence was unnerving, and Laxmi felt a stab of unease. Why was there no one to welcome her to her new home? Ramu, she had been told, was an orphan. But where were the aunts and uncles who should have performed the Griha Pravesh ceremony? Where were his relatives and friends? In her own Khargaon the entire village had come to the bus stop to bid them goodbye.

A feeble light began to glow inside the house: Ramu had lit a lantern. So she hurried towards it eagerly, determined to make the best of her new life. But at the door of the hut a cry escaped her. In all her life she'd never seen a room so bare. A single rolled-up razai and two pillows was all it contained. On the window sill above it, Ramu had placed some flowers in a small earthenware bowl. That was the only spot of colour in the room. Her hands had clenched into fists, making the parcel she'd been holding rustle. She opened it and saw within a handful of salt and three chillies, the gifts of the poor.

Suddenly the shape of the rest of her life had become startlingly clear. Yet a part of her refused to accept it. So she'd asked, 'Where are the animals?', her voice rising sharply at the end of the question.

He'd looked ashamed and stared down at his feet. The silence lengthened, till she understood that there were no animals. Sensing the dawn of realisation in her, Ramu looked up at last and said: 'There are no animals. This is all we have.'

'Why did you marry me then?' she'd cried, merciless in her grief. 'Why did you not tell me?'

'I know this is only a single animal, but we can keep her in the cookhouse. In time she will have children, and they in turn will have children, and one day we will have a herd, like you. . . used to have,' Ramu explained lamely.

Laxmi stepped off the verandah and walked up to the animal. 'Do you really believe I would want such a creature?' she asked cruelly.

The 'creature' looked at her warily. One ear was ragged, a chunk of empty space where there should have been skin. 'Look, the ears are too big, they belong to the Mahesar family. For the rest of her, she could be anything,' she said coldly, like a buyer. 'It is a creature of mixed blood.'

The cow turned its head and looked at Laxmi steadily as if it knew what Laxmi thought of her. Laxmi pretended not to notice, continuing her mock inspection.

Suddenly it all became perfectly clear and her heart inflated with rage. This pathetic creature was the cause of her humiliation. This was the thing that filled her husband's eyes with joy each morning. A strange animal sound tore its way out of her throat. She looked away. Then when she felt she could trust her voice again she looked him full in the face so he could see the scorn on hers. 'This is a junglee,' she said accusingly. 'You should have left it in the forest.'

CHAPTER FOUR

GOVINDA

The Kamdhenu Institute for Rural Development (KIRD) was spread over an area of fifty acres, roughly a hundred kilometres south-west of the Mumbai-Pune highway. Once upon a time it was a wasteland where only the poorest of the poor took their cattle to graze. Now several kinds of hi-tech buildings were housed on its sprawling campus – laboratories, class-rooms, offices, two canteens, a semen-freezing centre, a biogas plant, staff apartments and bachelor dormitories, cattle sheds, goat pens, fodder warehouses, vegetable gardens, greenhouses, orchards, a silkworm factory and a dairy. In spite of this, a third of the land was thickly forested, and there was even an artificial lake in its midst where members of the KIRD team went boating on Sundays.

But none of this was apparent to Manoj and Pratima, their senses blanketed by the dust of the road. As far as they could tell, the world they were entering was all beige and sepia, like a nineteenth-century photograph. Manoj eyed his new wife curiously. She seemed so calm. Every once in a while, when something they passed caught her interest, her face lit up and for a brief moment, she looked almost pretty. What kind of a woman was she, he wondered, to marry a man with no pros-pects who she had met once, and, willingly leave a city like Mumbai? He looked at the semi-arid landscape flashing past – bare of all but the most rudimentary of habitations, a few stunted trees and thorny acacia bushes. What on earth did she find out there to make her face glow?

When they entered the gates of KIRD their senses were jolted to life by the abundance of fresh, carefully-watered greenery.

'Here we are – the Kamdhenu Institute for Rural Development, KIRD for short, your new home,' their well-dressed and unusually good-looking driver announced, stopping in front of a steel and glass building. 'Sorry about the rush, but Manikbhai, our Director, wanted the car by noon.' He lowered his voice confidentially and added, 'He is leaving for Amsterdam today.'

Amsterdam. The word sounded alien and exotic. 'Does the Director go to Amsterdam very often?' Manoj asked curiously.

'Oh yes, all the time. All our top people travel,' the driver boasted. He opened the back door of the jeep and pulled out their bags.

They got out and looked around them curiously. Through floor-to-ceiling glass windows they could see an imposing entrance hall that could have come out of a European design magazine. The flooring was of Italian marble; large archways in the lateral wall led to passages punctuated by office doors. At the entrance to the passageway on the left a discrete sign on the wall read 'Mahatma Gandhi Library'. A little to the right, to the rear of the entrance hall, a broad chrome and glass staircase rose to the first floor. But it was what was behind the glass wall directly in front of them on the opposite side of the hall that took their breath away. In the triangular inner courtyard, on the far side of a narrow exquisitely-kept rectangle of grass, was a sight that stunned them into silence.

It took them a few minutes to realise that what they were looking at was actually the wall of the adjoining building. For, far from looking like a wall, it looked like and was in fact a vertical garden. A small door, also of plate glass, led into the courtyard and husband and wife rushed over to get a better look at the wall. A discreet sign beside it gave the wall a name: Living Wall.

From close up it was even more fantastic – with about a dozen species of plant growing vertically out of the wall itself. 'It makes me feel dizzy,' Pratima whispered, 'as if I were looking down at a tropical forest from a low-flying plane.'

But Manoj was preoccupied by something else. 'Are those real birds calling to each other from behind the greenery, d'you think?' he asked Pratima.

Before she could reply, the driver's deep voice boomed across the courtyard. 'You are looking at the Director's favourite child,' he said, coming up to them.

'It is. . . beautiful.' Pratima's voice was raw with wonder.

The driver's voice warmed in response. 'Our Director is a great man. Do you know, since he made the living wall, we have had three times as much money coming in to KIRD? Foreign tourists come here just to take photos of it, all the way from Pune and Mumbai. We let them take pictures for free but only after we give them the tour and tell them what we do to fight poverty. And they open their wallets happily.'

'But, but where. . . how?' Manoj stammered, unable to understand how the plants could grow against gravity.

'Our Director is always on the look-out for good ideas. And when he finds one, he won't rest until he has found a way to make use of it. This one came from Paris,' the driver explained.

'From Paris?' they exclaimed simultaneously.

'Yes. Our Director was there for a conference three years ago. He was driving by a river at night, you know there is a river going through almost every city in Europe? What is it called, the Paris one? Reine Seine, something like that, and as he was looking out of the window of his taxi he suddenly saw a forest growing from the front of a glass building. Any other person would have thought "how marvellous" and driven on, but our Director made the taxi stop and he got out. He returned the next day to see it again in the sunlight, and thanks to our good luck, the great French artist that had made it was there himself pruning the plants. Our Director plied him with questions and ended up asking him if he would make a wall for us at KIRD. The artist knew all about the third century B.C. murals of Ajanta and the Kailasha temple at Ellora; he had been wanting to visit them for a long time. It did not take him long to say "yes". He told our Director what materials to get and promised to come and make it. Manikbhai returned straightaway and began. The visitors' centre, that is the building you see on the other side, was just being built. He made the workers tear down the wall and start again. He got them to make fresh bricks and these were not to be burnt. Instead he got the workers to add a little cement to the clay, press the bricks in a hand press and leave them out to bake in the sun. When the artist arrived we thought he was crazy too – because he had green hair just like his plants, and he had painted the fingernails of his two little fingers green too. But when the artist saw what our Manikbhai had prepared for him, he said, "There is nothing for me to do, you have done it all pretty well by yourself."' The driver paused and looked at Manoj and Pratima triumphantly. 'That's the Director for you. A great man if ever there was. See the green and copper-coloured sunbirds in there? They are real too.'

They looked at the wall again, at last seeing the birds that had been calling to each other from inside the foliage. Pratima reached out and squeezed her husband's hand. 'I'm so glad we're here,' she whispered.

But Manoj didn't reply. To him the wall was more than just a beautiful object, it was a sign that he was in the right place. A weight rolled off his chest and for the first time he could think of his abandoned PhD without pain. What use to the future was a PhD in history when the present itself was changing so fast? People had never bothered to learn from history in any case. He was glad he would be doing something useful at last, something that would directly change people's lives.

'So when do we see the Director?' he asked eagerly, turning to the driver.

The man shrugged his shoulders. 'The Director never meets trainees when they arrive. He says it is a waste of time. He will only meet those who stay.'

'But. . . but surely it would be possible for us to meet him for a few minutes? We've come a long way,' Manoj insisted.

Suddenly the warmth left the driver's face. 'You don't choose to meet the Director, he decides when he will meet you,' he said coldly.

'A month? That's too long,' Manoj exclaimed.

'Don't worry.' The driver slapped Manoj familiarly on the back. 'You have a lot to learn. The month will be over before you know it. Now let's get you registered.' He thrust out a large, surprisingly hairy hand. 'I'm Doctor Pandey by the way. Head veterinarian at KIRD.'

A siren jerked Manoj out of an exhausted sleep at six the next morning and simultaneously he realised that the electricity was off. Pratima stirred next to him.

'What time is it?' she asked, 'and why is it so hot?'

Before Manoj could reply, Dr Pandey's head appeared at the bedroom window. He rapped loudly on the windowpane and made signs for them to let him in.

'Hurry up, hurry up. Prayer time,' he said, as Manoj opened the door. 'You have five minutes. If you aren't at the visitors' centre by the time the second siren goes off, you'll be made to clean the cattle sheds.'

'But. . . but it's only six fifteen,' Manoj protested.

But Dr Pandey was already walking away.

They made it to the Living Wall as the second siren went off. Dr Pandey was waiting for them.

'Hurry, hurry,' he said impatiently, turning and marching down the corridor without waiting to see if they were following.

They rushed after him, bursting through the double doors at the end just as the siren stopped.

They found themselves in an enormous airy hall with a high sloping ceiling. The silence was deafening. Lines of people in white were filing solemnly past the far end of the hall. Sunlight coming through the narrow floor to ceiling windows turned the people into blocks of pure white light.

'Isn't it lovely?' Pratima whispered, grabbing her husband's hand.

'You find everything lovely,' he whispered back, frowning. 'It's weird, that's what it is.'

They caught sight of Dr Pandey beckoning anxiously and joined him in the queue.

'Why aren't you wearing the clothes I gave you?' he whispered.

'Because you didn't tell us we had to wear them first thing in the morning,' Manoj whispered back.

'But it is obvious. No one prays in ordinary clothes.' Dr Pandey's eyes flashed with annoyance. 'Since it's your first day you will be forgiven but make sure you remember tomorrow.'

'Why?' Manoj asked promptly. 'I always pray in ordinary clothes.'

Dr Pandey placed a finger on his lips in answer. 'We talk afterwards. This is the Hall of Meditation. Tune your thoughts into God.'

Manoj and Pratima stared hard at their feet and tried not to laugh. They shuffled forward slowly along with the others. Everyone here looks like a pundit or a widow, Manoj thought suddenly, except that they all look terribly satisfied with themselves.

At last they came to their goal, a pagoda-like thing built of tiles and wood that was unmistakeably shrine-like. The inside was decorated like a stable with paintings of two strange-looking black and white cows, each with a calf beside them, a baby Krishna who could easily have substituted for a baby Jesus, a figure of a woman in a Maharashtrian sari and a man wearing the triangular Congress topi on his head. On the other side of the cows was a bald, bespectacled Mahatma Gandhi, his wife Kasturba and a man with a long flowing beard whom Manoj didn't recognise. As they went past the tableau each person knelt and bowed with folded hands. Manoj felt a little shocked. This was supposed to be a secular, scientific organisation. But he did as the others had done, touched his head to the first step, and rose, swearing to himself that he would never do it again.

Afterwards Dr Pandey took them to the canteen for breakfast. He introduced them hurriedly to several of his colleagues who smiled at them vaguely and then went back to their discussions. The silence of the meditation hall seemed to linger in the hushed discussions and serious expressions of the others. Dr Pandey led them to a table at the far end of the hall. Almost instantly a waiter in a sparkling white pyjama kurta appeared with three plates of steaming poha.

'Eat, eat,' Dr Pandey said, smiling at them benevolently. 'Our Manikbhai is very particular about the standard of the food in our canteen.'

And indeed the poha was delicious, the grains of pressed rice melting in their mouths, the coconut and coriander on the top fresh and fragrant.

Manoj closed his eyes in delight. If only Pratima could learn how to cook like this. He decided to say nothing yet about his plans. When he finished his poha his good humour had returned. He looked across the table at Dr Pandey's handsome face and decided to tease him a little.

'So, Doctor, as a man of science, can you explain to us poor newcomers what exactly was the meaning of the ritual we just witnessed?' he asked.

Dr Pandey looked surprised. 'What ritual? You mean the morning prayer meeting? That is no ritual. Everyone is free to pray the way he or she wants to pray.'

'But they all have to be there at the same time and wearing the same white uniform?'

Dr Pandey began to look uncomfortable. He wasn't used to being questioned. 'It's not a uniform,' he said with a tinge of asperity. 'Nobody is obliged to come either. We like to be together in the morning. When the Director is there, we have discussions about the future, about problems facing KIRD, we share our thoughts, our experiences. It is quite secular I assure you.'

'But what about the "temple"? You people pray not only to the gods, but to humans as well,' Manoj insisted. Again Dr Pandey looked blank for a second. Then his face cleared. 'Those are there for remembering why we do what we do. They are not people outside us, they are a part of each of us, they are inside all of us. Our Director says that every Indian has inside him Krishna, the symbol of love energy, the Mahatma who is the symbol of sacrifice energy, and the farmer, who is the symbol of pure labour energy. These three energies create the universe.'

'Love, sacrifice, labour? Aren't you a man of science? Don't you want to be a part of the future?' Manoj sneered.

Dr Pandey frowned. 'I don't see your problem. Science is for solving problems, God is for giving hope. Without hope, there is no future. Where is the contradiction?'

'And why the uniforms?' Manoj shot back.

'Oh, we only wear them in the morning for the Hall of Meditation. Our Director's idea. It is to remind us that before God and before our own conscience we are all naked, all equal,' Dr Pandey snapped.

Manoj realised he'd gone too far. 'When do we see the cows, Dr Pandey?' he asked.

Dr Pandey took the olive branch. 'As soon as you both finish, I will take you on the grand tour.'

'I feel like a foreign tourist already,' Manoj joked. Then, seeing the look of consternation on Pratima's face, he said no more.

The first stop on the grand tour was the library. 'Public computers, books and magazines. Next door there is an auditorium where we have film screenings twice a week and cultural programmes every month. Many famous singers have come here – Anup Jalota, Bhimsen Joshi. Even if we are far away from the city, we have the best that a city offers culturally. And we have clean air.'

'So you don't miss the city, Dr Pandey?' Pratima asked, suddenly joining the conversation.

'Oh no, not at all. We have everything here – nature, culture, community.' Dr Pandey smiled at her knowingly. 'Cities are for those who love only money.'

Manoj felt a pang of irritation. They were from the city. What did that make them in Dr Pandey's eyes?

'And when do we see the cows?' he asked again, his voice sharp.

'Soon, soon, young man.' Dr Pandey's attention was once more on Manoj. 'Everything in good time. First, the laboratories.'

They continued down the broad corridor, walking beneath portraits of the heroes of the Indian freedom struggle on one side and different breeds of cow on the other. Seeing what they were looking at, Dr Pandey said, 'Nothing here is without purpose. These portraits on either side reflect the theory of KIRD.'

'And how is that?' Pratima asked curiously.

'In KIRD everything has a purpose. First, one needs inspiration. Where does inspiration come from? From God. How does it come? Through prayer and meditation. And how does one go about making inspiration a reality? By emulating our role models.' Dr Pandey paused and looked at Manoj, waiting to be challenged. But Manoj said nothing. He was impatient to get to the animals. Disappointed, Dr Pandey turned away and continued to walk down the corridor. Behind Dr Pandey's back, Manoj looked at Pratima and raised his eyebrows. She gave him a quick smile and squeezed his hand. Dr Pandey continued with his lecture.

'Next comes the body which must be nourished before it can work. Hence the cafeteria which you have already seen. Then comes knowledge, for without knowledge inspiration cannot be put into practice. How does knowledge come? Through research, the library, which you just saw, was created to nourish all aspects of a man's brain, not just his knowledge of science. Hence we even have a fiction section and a poetry corner.'

'How wonderful,' Pratima murmured, and was rewarded with a very seductive smile. Then Dr Pandey grew serious again. 'After the research comes the testing – the laboratory.' He stopped suddenly before a pair of steel doors and knocked imperiously. The doors opened immediately and they were shown into a small anteroom where they were made to put on lab coats, white cloth envelopes over their shoes and gloves on their hands. Lastly, small masks were tied over their mouths. Thus equipped they were shown through another set of steel double doors into a giant, brand-new laboratory. Manoj stopped and stared. Before him were two rows of gleaming white work-stations, each with a computer, a bottle of water and a small earthen vase with a single flower. Everything was spotless and tidy. Just beyond the computers were lines of gleaming stainless steel workstations, each with a sink, two racks of test tubes a microscope, a monitor and a printer. Manoj gulped. Never had he seen such a high concentration of expensive machinery. He felt as if just by being there he had separated himself from

India and had entered the future. A rush of adrenaline made him want to snatch the clipboard away from the white-coated man nearest to him. Instead, he did nothing, contenting himself with watching them minutely as they went from computer to microscope and back again, solemnly noting things on their clipboards. Soon he would be a part of them.

Then Dr Pandey was at his elbow, pulling him along to the area where the test tubes were. 'The section closest to us is the semen-testing area. Here we test the semen we collect for motility and vigour,' Dr Pandey explained.

Manoj had no idea what motility was, but he wasn't going to show it. 'Yes, yes, of course,' he said, nodding vigorously.

But Pratima was more honest. 'What's motil. . .whatever?' she whispered to Manoj.

'I'll tell you later,' he replied tightly, frowning at her.

'It means we count how many little wiggly fish-tailed sperm the bull releases and then we measure how fast they swim,' Dr Pandey explained, smiling. 'You women have no problem, you release a single egg that just sits there and waits. It is for the male sperm to swim upstream in a liquid that slowly poisons them. And then even when they have swum up to the egg, their problems are not over. The egg resists. It fights back. Its shell is a very powerful defence mechanism. The poor sperm has to knock its head against that thick hard shell till it breaks it down. Otherwise it dies. It's all or nothing in nature – winners take all, losers lose it all.'

'Do they really swim?' Pratima asked, her eyes wide with wonder.

'Didn't you take biology in school?' Manoj snapped, feeling irritated because she was giving Dr Pandey a chance to talk to her of such intimate things.

'Oh yes, very fast,' Dr Pandey answered, ignoring Manoj. 'If they don't find an egg in which to embed themselves, in seventy-two hours they are dead. And there are twenty million of them, and only one egg. Quite a cut-throat competition. That's why we study the sperm – to see which ones are possible winners. Much depends on how fast they can swim. Here, I'll show you.' He grabbed Pratima's hand and made her bend over the shoulder of a white-coated lab assistant. The assistant obligingly moved away and let Pratima look into the viewer. Dr Pandey leaned over her and whispered into her ear as he fiddled with the knob on the side of the machine. Suddenly she cried out excitedly, 'I see them, I see them.'

Hearing her excited cries, Manoj wanted to kick her for making a fool of him in front of the entire staff of KIRD. And to kick himself, for allowing Dr Pandey to stick his skinny body into his wife's soft behind. He turned away, wishing he had the courage to pull the doctor away and beat the hand-someness out of his face. Instead, he walked off, wandering over to the huge bay windows on the far side of the lab.

There, on the other side, the India he was familiar with presented a stark contrast to the room he was in. He looked at it with relief. The yard had a hard mud floor, blood red like the soil of the region, and scarred wooden fencing decorated with twists of barbed wire. It had the temporary yet ancient look of all the public spaces he'd ever seen – the wooden posts were stained with mud, betel nut juice and urine, cardboard boxes, plastic pans and containers of all sorts turned the corners into garbage heaps. To the right was a gate. Behind the first enclosure was a second and a third, and behind that was a long brick building with a tin roof and wall painted dark green. Suddenly the gate at the far end opened and a short, dark and extremely hairy man wearing gumboots and a rubber apron walked casually towards the main enclosure right in front of the laboratory. He looks like an animal himself, Manoj thought, feeling pleasantly conscious of his own relatively untenanted pale, wheat-coloured skin. Maybe that was why Pratima's family had accepted him, he mused, feeling superior. His wife's skin colour was far closer to the hairy little man's than to his.

Outside, the object of Manoj's regard was rummaging amongst the debris in a corner. He straightened up, tucking what looked like a small hot-water bottle under his arm and Manoj, getting a closer look at his face, was shocked to see that it bore a deep pink scar almost three inches long that began at his right eyebrow and ended by his lip. The gate opened again, distracting Manoj, and a young bull was led into the yard. Manoj took his eyes gratefully off the man's face and examined the animal instead. He was surprised at how small it was. If these were the future of India, he thought, that future wasn't very bright. The man re-entered his frame of vision, walking boldly up to the animal and throwing a black rubber sheet over it, which he then fastened under the creature's belly with a buckle. He then led the animal across the yard and fastened it to the railing not far from the window with steel handcuffs. He scooted quickly under the rubber sheet and blew a whistle.

'It's quite complicated, isn't it? Is this your first time?' a high, slightly nasal male voice just behind Manoj asked.

Manoj turned around sharply. In front of him was one of the tiniest men he'd ever seen. Thin and wiry, with a thick black moustache covering his weak upper lip, the man stuck out his hand and gave Manoj a smile that was boldly sensual. 'I'm Prakash, second year. Laboratory technician. You're new aren't you? On the grand tour with Pandey I see. You have a nice wife.' The little man licked his lower lip suggestively. 'I am in B-4, bachelors' quarters, that is. Come and see me if you want to have fun. No wives allowed though.' His eyes flicked to Pratima, and Manoj wondered briefly how the man knew he was married. 'Why has that man gone under the bull?' he asked.

'Because he has to protect the poor animal,' Prakash replied with a titter.

'Protect him?'

'Of course, from Govinda.'

'Govinda?'

Prakash laughed again, but this time threaded into the edges of his laughter Manoj detected fear . . .and respect. 'Govinda is our star. A fighting bull from Spain, which is why he likes to play rough. Just wait, you'll see.'

Manoj's mind clouded with memories. He stared out of the window at the small animal tethered to the fence. Was that one of the animals Durga had brought with her? How had it ended up at the Institute? He shook his head. It couldn't be.

As if he could read Manoj's mind Prakash said, 'Govinda was given to our Director for free by the director of customs at Mumbai International Airport. The brute had injured four other animals and almost killed two men. But being a good Hindu the Director could not bring himself to kill it.' Manoj stared at the small animal before him. It looked so docile, so utterly harmless. How on earth could it have inflicted so much damage?

The gate opened again noisily and Manoj gasped.

The animal that had just been brought in looked like it was a prehistoric beast, possessing the same wide, powerful shoulders and huge chest ending in the heavy knuckled forelegs of its mammoth ancestors. Manoj couldn't see the animal's rear for the animal was facing him, staring directly at him. In comparison to its enormous shoulders, the animal's head was small, with bloodshot eyes that seemed to look at the world with innate suspicion. The face, though somewhat small and squashed-looking with a pig-like snout, was rendered noble by a pair of giant horns curling back on either side of the animals face like a judge's wig. As if he were tired of being stared at, suddenly the bull dropped his head and rushed forward. The two men holding the animal were forced to let go and he entered the yard at a gallop. He circled the barricade twice as if he were establishing his ownership of the place. Then he turned and came straight at the window, stopping barely six inches away from the window, and glaring at Manoj inside. Manoj stepped back quickly and looked around for something behind which he could hide.

'Don't be scared,' Prakash told Manoj. 'Govinda is only looking at himself. He is very vain and does it every day. He cannot see inside, the glass is one-way only. He'll turn away in a minute.'

Somewhat reassured but not totally convinced Manoj stared at the bull's fantastically alien features, trying to read his mind. Where had such a creature come from? he wondered. And how did he feel being trapped in hot, dusty India. For even without being told, Manoj had instinctively known that the creature in front of him did not belong there. Then, just as Prakash had predicted, Govinda did an about-turn and charged into the centre of the yard. Then it let out a long ululating cry and brought its giant horns smashing down on the ground again and again.

'My God, what is he doing? He'll hurt himself!' Manoj cried.

No one answered, too absorbed in their work, used to the spectacle outside.

Clods of raw red earth flew up into the air and fell like rain on the creature's shoulders. Or like a shower of blood, Manoj thought, trembling. He felt a bond with the animal and the thought came to him, that in fact it wasn't the animal that had been looking at its image in the reflecting glass, but Manoj who had just been given a glimpse of himself as he would have been if he had had the fortune to be born in another, richer country. For here was a creature that had been made to put fear into all that came before it, a creature that was meant to rule the earth. And yet it was forced to do the opposite, to surrender its future into the hands of puny little men with microscopes. Manoj felt the stirrings of compassion and some-thing else which he couldn't put a name to. His fear vanished and his entire being shook with indignation at the injustice of it. Men were not meant to steal the seed of a creature as mag-nificent as this. It was wrong.

'It's very exciting, sperm collection, don't you think? Are you from the animal side or the social side?'

Manoj didn't understand what Prakash meant. 'What do you mean?' he asked him coldly.

'I think you are from the animal side. You look it,' Prakash continued staring admiringly at Manoj. 'I like that side too, but I am not strong enough for it. You have to be strong and good with your hands to control a creature like that.'

Manoj tried to ignore him but the lab technician simply wouldn't stop talking.

'You have to be very strong to master that brute there,' Prakash said happily in his high female voice. 'Do you know, he already killed one of his keepers. The others we had to double their salaries to make them stay.'

Shut up! Manoj almost snarled, wanting to concentrate on Govinda. The bull had moved from the centre of the enclosure to a trough not far from the other tethered animal, from which it was eating hungrily.

'You see the cloth on the smaller male? That is full of the sex scent of a female in heat. The big one has weak eyes and is guided by his nose. After Govinda finishes, he will turn and mount his friend. Then whoop, out comes the hot-water bottle, and sperm collection is completed.'

'But why a male? Why not simply get a cow inside?' Manoj asked.

Prakash giggled again, his eyes shining behind his spectacles. 'Because this is the one Govinda chose. It is his special friend. Govinda doesn't like our Indian females. I told you, he is a brute.'

'But why not just give him an injection or something?' said Manoj.

Prakash gave Manoj a condescending smile. 'You can't fake an erection yaar, not even on an animal. That is why sperm collection is the most difficult and dangerous part of our job.' He giggled. 'And it has to be done manually.'

'So he and the other one are friends?' Manoj asked, not quite able to believe what he was seeing.

'Oh yes, very good friends. Secret pillow friends,' Prakash sniggered. 'At least they would be if they were allowed to see each other outside the ring.'

'What ring?' Manoj asked.

'That place there where they are is the semen collection ring.'

From the long green barn, a worker entered the yard on the other side of 'the ring', a pail in his hand. Manoj assumed the pail contained more food but was surprised to see the man lean over the rails and throw the pail, which only contained water, straight in the black bull's face. The animal let out a roar that shook the glass windowpanes and charged the fence. The worker scuttled back to the barn and disappeared behind its doors. Govinda ran at the fence again. It shook but didn't fall. Govinda was about to charge the fence a third time when suddenly from under the legs of the other animal, the man that had been hiding there leapt out, a dirty red blanket in one hand and a rubber hot-water bottle with a funnel-shaped tube attached to its mouth in the other. He ran in front of Govinda, waving the blanket. Manoj held his breath.

'Now comes the exciting part. They must make him angry first. It builds up the sex feeling inside the animal,' Prakash, the lab technician, commented knowledgeably, giggling like a girl. His voice went up an octave as he added, 'Sometimes I wonder what it would be like to be there inside with the big one.'

Disturbed by the lab technician's remark, Manoj moved away.

In the yard Govinda had turned around to face the intruder, snorting warily. But the man didn't pay any attention to the warning. He danced in front of the bull again, waving the red blanket wildly, and then slipped to the side where Govinda couldn't see him. Govinda grunted and pawed the earth some more then went back to the trough. Just as he was about to eat, the little man picked up a lump of earth and threw it at him. Govinda turned and the man danced up to him, waving the blanket in his face again. Manoj, his eyes fixed upon the animal's face, didn't notice the men outside reach in and jab the bull's rear with a pointed stick until suddenly, Govinda leapt into the air, and turned so quickly that Manoj gasped, awestruck by the speed and grace of the movement. Govinda charged the part of the gate behind which the men stood. They moved back, shouting defiantly. The man with the blanket danced after Govinda, suddenly throwing the blanket over the the bull's head.

The animal came to a thundering, panting halt. He shook his head uncertainly, took a few steps in the man's direction and stopped. The man dodged to one side of the bull, his arms reaching for the blanket. But the wind must have changed because Govinda turned also and was once again facing his opponent, snorting and pawing the ground. The blanket fell uselessly to the ground and suddenly there was fear in the man's body. But he was a brave man and obviously from a poor background, and so the survival instinct in him was strong. He began to run for the gate, right past the bull. But Govinda was faster. He tossed his head and managed to pick up the man with his horns in a single move. The man flew into the sky like his blanket had and then fell to the ground right beside the blanket.

A collective groan escaped those watching from inside the

laboratory and Manoj suddenly realised that he wasn't alone – at least half the laboratory's white-coated technicians were standing behind him.

'What will he do now?' he heard a woman's voice ask. No one bothered to reply. Later Manoj realised that the woman who'd asked the question was his wife. He looked at the bull and then at the man and shut his eyes.

Outside in the yard Govinda walked over to the man and placed his forelegs on either side of the man's body. Another gasp went through the crowd of spectators inside the lab. Manoj opened his eyes. The man had grabbed the blanket and pulled it over him – in the vain hope that it would protect him. Manoj felt sorry for the man, imagining what it must feel like to be face to face with death.

'Look at Govinda's erection; I have never seen it so big.' Prakash's squeaky voice, though barely above a whisper, sounded loud and intrusive to Manoj.

But indeed it was amazing. Pure red, eager flesh thrust out from a thick ebony base. The animal's sex was huge, ramrod straight and so swollen it was almost painful to look at. To Manoj's fascinated eyes it looked less like a sexual organ than a thing to be adored and worshipped. Awe-inspiring, a thing far more ancient than the bull itself, far more beautiful than any puny human organ. Looking at it, he was convinced that mankind's salvation consisted in the worship of that incredible organ. Then a movement under the blanket distracted him. The man was still alive, of course. Then it was as if the blanket had taken on a life of its own, reaching towards the source of all that aggression and unfulfilled desire and grabbing it firmly. Govinda let out a grunt of surprise then stood stock still, back and neck tense, muscles twitching in anticipation.

Two arms emerged from the blanket. One held the rubber hot-water bottle, while the other grabbed the base of the Govinda's penis firmly and began to squeeze and pull alternately. Manoj watched in fascination as the man's hands danced along the length of the bull's penis, a dance in which daring soon gave way to confidence. Govinda's eyelids drooped. His body began to tremble with pleasure, ripples running from his hind-quarters up towards his massive chest. In the laboratory people cheered and then they all returned to their work as if nothing had happened.

Eventually only two people remained by the window, Prakash the lab attendant and Manoj. Had Manoj been aware of it he'd have left too. But he was far away. For in his head he was no longer Manoj but all three of them: Govinda, powerful, dangerous but ultimately tamed by the small, weak little man; the man, weak, vulnerable and victorious; and himself, the helpless witness of a forbidden act.

Such was his state that he never realised when the whole thing ended. He never saw how the man wriggled out from under the animal clutching the hot water bottle triumphantly to his chest. Long after the helpers led the now docile and exhausted bull away, Manoj remained glued to the window, his mind unable to let go of what he had just witnessed. Until at last, Pratima found him, and led him gently away.

CHAPTER FIVE

THE MAKING OF
A SUPERCOW

Manoj soon grew used to his new life. There was a simplicity to it, and a sense of purpose. He understood why the others looked so contented. Everything they did had a concrete result. Nothing was superfluous. But while the others prayed to the nation, to their Director or to the cowherd Krishna, he preferred to pray to the giant black bull that people in KIRD had christened Govinda. In his mind, Manoj called him Ganja, the bald one, after the four inches of deep red flesh that crowned the bull's erection.

But long before he could go anywhere near Ganja, Manoj was first made to learn about the other parts of the insemination business. He learnt that what he had seen Govinda undergo was called 'milking' and was the most dangerous and difficult part of the entire process – and the least technology intensive. After a sire had been milked, his semen was carefully numbered, tested and classified as 'A', 'B' or 'C' grade semen. C-grade and some B-grade semen was quickly sold off – either to private dairies or to the government insemination centres. 'The A-grade stuff we keep for our own experiments,' Prakash the laboratory technician told him, pointing in the direction of a menacing black door with 'Do Not Enter' written in silver letters. Once labelled, the semen was transferred into a big machine much like a soda-bottling machine, the only difference being that tall glass vials were used rather than bottles. A conveyor belt carried the glass vials to the machine where a syringe-like nozzle injected 0.050 to 0.075 millilitres of liquid semen into each one. Computers kept a check on the amount of sperm in each glass tube after which they were put into slotted steel racks and parked in multi-storeyed storage vats. Liquid nitrogen was then pumped into these vats freezing the semen for posterity. The liquid nitrogen was so cold that if it touched human skin, the skin would instantly burn and die. In an amazingly short time Manoj became as good as any laboratory technician and could manage the whole process of sorting and storing himself.

After the semen had been frozen it was kept in giant walk-in refrigerators until the KIRD staff were ready to go on a 'raid'. 'A raid is what we call the field insemination programme, the most important part of our activities here at KIRD,' Dr Pandey explained. Then the doors of the giant freezers were opened and the glass vials containing the semen removed. Each member was given three milk cans filled with semen rods, which he tied to his Enfield motorbike like an ordinary milkman. 'Which is why a KIRD milk can is called a "disguise",' Dr Pandey explained. 'So for a raid, our staff put on their disguises, and go in search of suitable cows. When they return, the number of glass straws that remain in the milk cans are counted and destroyed. In this way we keep a score for each full-fledged raider and at the end of the year, the one with the maximum hits is named the "king" of KIRD.' He winked, slapping Manoj on the back in a man-to-man sort of way.

The raids were the highlight of life at KIRD. Only a handful of the trainees made it through the rigorous training process to become full-fledged inseminators. An inseminator's first successful raid was an initiation and didn't take place until the trainee had completed a whole slew of preparatory exercises, which included mundane but unpleasant tasks from cleaning the cow sheds to manipulating the computers that kept track of sperm counts and matings to conducting village surveys, and doing in-depth person-to-person interviewing. In these tasks Manoj easily surpassed the other trainees, but the real thing he knew was the raid. Prakash the lab technician with the knowing eyes had tried and failed five times before he had given up. So Manoj waited nervously for his turn to come, listening with dread to the stories the others told when they got together at the clandestine bar behind the bachelors quarters to drink home-brewed alcohol (for KIRD was ostensibly a ' dry' campus in the Gandhian style).

Unlike the other trainees who were eager to become full-fledged inseminators, either because the pay was much better or because they couldn't wait to show what men they were, Manoj was quite content with his duties as a trainee. His encounter with the Spanish Durga had revealed to him the hole in his core which made him bend like a blade of grass each time the wind blew too hard. He did not feel like a man. For what man would have abandoned a beautiful blonde stranger who was madly in love with him in a hotel room in Mumbai? What man meekly accepted the wife his parents had chosen, and demanded a dowry as well? And so he was content to worship the maleness of others, like Govinda the Spanish fighting bull, and the Director, Manikbhai.

Every morning Manoj got up at five and by quarter to six, with the sky still a pearly grey and the vegetation yet to take on its daylight colours, he was in the animal sheds. There he helped the local boys clean the stalls and prepare the animals for milking. There were two sheds, large and airy, more like airport hangars than animal pens. In one were kept the young mixed breeds and the pregnant females. In the other were kept the purebreds. The milking was entirely automated. The lactating females were taken inside a special room, fondly called the glass cage by those who worked there. Here udders were attached to tubes and the pumping machines were switched on from the control room. Then with a whirr and *chsht* the machines came alive; brightly-coloured pistons moved up and down over rubber tubes linked to the cows' udders. The rubber nozzles at the ends of the tubes clenched and unclenched like hands as the pistons pumped air into them and then sucked the air out, squeezing the milk out of the animals.

Sitting behind the wall of glass in the control room, Manoj watched the computer diagrams fill with blue light. When the milking was over, the machines stopped and a number began to flash on the computer screen. This was the amount of milk produced in the milking. Then Manoj would press a key and a menu would appear. He'd press another and the computer would spit out a series of statistics such as fat content and water content, a grading of the quality of the milk as well as a list of uses and places it could be sent. Manoj would then decide how the milk would be disposed of and press another button on the computer. There would be a sucking sound, and the machines would send the milk collected to the appropriate refrigerated container. A few minutes later the computer would come alive with numbers – giving exact measurements of the amount of milk harvested, its quality and where it would eventually go as well as the amount of money they would make. He loved the machines – for they made the future seem so certain, so easy.

But it wasn't as if Manoj disliked the manual side of his work in the dairy. Quite the contrary. Cleaning the stalls, the sharp smell of cowdung filling his nostrils, the animals shuffling and snorting all around him, he felt the other side of him, the humble-servant-of-an-idea side, swell and grow. As he entered the stalls, brush and hose in hand, he was their slave, their priest, their keeper. As he ran his hands along the fat bodies of the foreign Jerseys and Friesian-Holsteins, he felt awestruck by their foreignness, by the sheer abundance and wealth they represented. But the knowledge that they were delicate and fell ill easily made him feel tender towards them and clean their homes with special care. And yet, even as he worked the stalls of the others, it was Govinda he was thinking of, Govinda he was caring for, and seducing.

But try as he would, Govinda would not let him get more than a few feet into his stall. For Govinda, like a true royal, only allowed the man with the scar to touch him. But Manoj would not give up – even though each morning when he would arrive at Govinda's large enclosure at the end of the barn, the bull would simply turn his back to Manoj and ignore him, refusing every little tit-bit Manoj offered him.

Then one day, almost five months after he had first visited the bull, Govinda didn't turn away. Instead, the bull's small eyes, which held a hint of tragedy in their depths, never left Manoj's face. Manoj leaned over the fence, staring back blissfully. For a long moment neither moved. Then, just as Manoj felt himself begin to melt into the shiny black depths of Govinda's eyes, without warning the bull charged the fence. Manoj jumped back, stumbled over his cleaning equipment, and fell in a tangled aching heap right on top of his pails and brushes. Anger filled him as he realised that the bull was teasing him. Pulling himself up, Manoj reached for the gate. He was not going to let the bull make a coward of him. With trembling fingers, he undid the wire.

The bull was so surprised that it took a step back. It didn't have much respect for men, though some it had learnt to fear. Then it struck the earth with its powerful hooves and when even that didn't frighten the man away, it lowered its head and charged. Manoj shut his eyes, deafened by the thud of those heavy hooves on the packed, rock-hard earth. Time slowed. Manoj felt his life flash past – everything he had done until then – and he acknowledged how useless it had all been. No-one except his mother, he thought distantly, would miss him.

All of a sudden, the ground stopped vibrating like a drum

and in the ensuing silence, Manoj could hear his heart beating louder than he'd ever heard it. He opened his eyes a chink. Govinda grunted – his breath, hot and grassy, grazed Manoj's face. Then the bull moved to his trough and buried his face inside.

Manoj backed away as unobtrusively as possible, leaving behind the little offering that had been sitting securely in the hollow of his sweaty palm all the while.

Perhaps because Govinda sensed Manoj's adoration, or perhaps because the animal wasn't really a killer after all, after that he allowed Manoj to enter his enclosure and though he ritually charged Manoj each time, in a few weeks, the giant animal was letting Manoj clean his massive shoulders, take his temperature and rub him down with hay. After he'd finished, Manoj would sit in the semi-obscurity of the animal pen, and talk to Govinda. The barn would be empty and silent as all the others would attend the morning prayers. 'You are the one,' he would confide to the bull, 'you are the one that makes my life worthwhile. I will never leave you.' Then Manoj would tell the silent animal of his dreams, his plans for the future and for Govinda, promising to rescue him from the indignity of having his precious sperm stolen from it day after day. Eventually he would tear himself away, heart raw and lacerated, bathe, change, grab the newspapers and go straight to breakfast.

Five weeks after Manoj arrived Manikbhai Godhawale, the Director, returned. Manoj felt his presence even before he saw him. He felt it that morning in the urgency that had suddenly invaded everyone's movements, from the lordly inseminators walking around in their lab coats to the lowly cowshed cleaners. For once Manoj rushed through his tasks, finished feeding the animals early and rushed to change for prayers. When he arrived at the prayer hall it was filled to the brim.

'Where is he?' Manoj asked a fellow trainee.

'In the front, on the dais.'

Manoj craned his head to try to see the man. All he could make out was the Director's back. He was short, and below the white Gandhi hat, he was bald.

After the prayers, the Director stepped on to the stage. At last Manoj could see his face. It was an unremarkable Gujarati face, square, with slightly puffy cheeks, prominent cheekbones and a huge hooked nose. In contrast to the generous proportions of his other features, his lips were thin, and he had practically no chin at all. But when he began to speak, Manoj immediately forgot about the way he looked.

Manikbhai spoke about his trip to Europe, the enthusiastic response he'd received, the journalists that had interviewed him, and the concrete result that had come of the trip – more foreign cows, this time for free. And not the low or even medium level cows, but the best. Manikbhai himself had gone to each prizewinning breeder's home and begged for a child from his best animals. And such was the goodwill towards India, that the Dutch and Danish farmers had agreed. Then he'd met the King of Sweden who had given him a cheque. Manikbhai whipped out a piece of paper from behind his back and held it up in the air. 'This is a cheque of one million kroner. The king gave me this money, one billion rupees, to help the poor.'

Though his words were anything but poetic, Manikbhai's speech nevertheless exercised a mesmeric power over his audience. People began to clap. Faces brightened, shy smiles appeared on faces that rarely smiled, eyes shone and the normally sombre hall took on an air of celebration. For Manoj, listening to him for the first time, the effect was electrifying. Manikbhai's words wrapped themselves around Manoj's heart, transporting him into a future that seemed not just achievable, but foreseeable. Never had Manoj felt such clarity emanating from a man. For the first time since he abandoned Durga he felt the darkness that had enveloped his heart lift. If Manikbhai could turn a wasteland into a world-famous institute, then surely, he Manoj, could root out the cowardice curled like a snake in his heart? An image of Govinda blossomed in his mind and he felt another surge of hope.

But when he was finally called to meet Manikbhai, he never got a chance to ask about the bull.

'Come and sit,' Manikbhai had said, coming around his giant desk to put a fatherly arm around Manoj's shoulders. 'I don't think we have met, yes?'

Manoj, somewhat taken aback, managed to stammer, 'That is correct, sir. I am Manoj Mishra. My wife and I arrived the day you left.'

'That's right, of course. Then you must be my dear friend Sudhakar's new son-in-law.' And the tiny bit of reserve that had begun to develop inside Manoj melted away.

'How are you settling down, beta?' Manikbhai leaned into him as if he were eager to hear his response.

'Very well, thank you. This place feels like home already.'

'Good.' Manikbhai chuckled and sat back, pleased. 'And your father-in-law, he is well? You know, he is one of my oldest friends and one of KIRD's trustees. We know each other from our college days.'

'Oh.' Manoj sat back in disappointment. The idea of his square and hairy father-in-law with his gold chains and crystal bar being one of KIRD's trustees filled him with disgust.

But Manikbhai seemed to read his mind. 'Organisations are hungry animals. Like politicians, they are in constant need of money. It helps to have rich benefactors.' And he winked.

Manoj was utterly charmed. Before he quite knew what he was saying, eager words began to spill out of his mouth. 'Since I have been here, sir, I have heard the inseminators talk of the difficulty of getting the villagers to let them inseminate their animals. Well, sir, I thought of a way of making it easier.'

Manikbhai nodded but said nothing, his face neutral, listening.

'We have so much milk, sir, from these foreign cows, half of which we can't even sell. Why can't we give that milk to the villagers in order to convince them? We could have a two-pronged approach. First we set up a dairy in a village and we distribute milk free to the poorest families. This way we nourish the next generation of the poorest of poor Indians, feed their brains so to speak. Then, we explain about the insemination and how it works. And we let them decide, and we charge money for it.' By the end his words were tumbling over each other in their eagerness to be heard.

Manikbhai was silent. He began to stroke his chin. After a few strokes he looked up. Manoj gasped. Manikbhai's eyes were no longer soft and warm and welcoming. 'How long have you been here, young man?'

'Six w-weeks, sir.' Manoj felt his face grow hot.

'Six weeks, and you have never been to a village even. Yet you claim to have found the fatal flaw in our program?'

'Not flaw, just improvement, sir.'

'Spare me your pretty words. I am not a fancy city boy, I am a peasant,' Manikbhai snapped.

Manoj's cheeks felt as if they were aflame.

Manikbhai continued. 'Six weeks and you have the audacity to come in here and teach me. Do you know how long the training programme here is?'

'Yes sir, nine months.'

'Yes, nine months, the time it takes for a baby to be born. And you have done just one eighth of it.'

Manoj wanted to apologise and leave right then, but the image of the ebony-coloured Govinda forced him to remain where he was. 'Sir, I know I am young and inexperienced, but could we not try my idea as a pilot? I would be happy to go wherever you send me, set it up myself. I have been studying the dairy here. Dr Kewalramani can tell you sir, there is nothing in the machines or the operations side I don't know. I even know how to repair them.'

Manikbhai laughed suddenly and clapped him on the shoulder. At the same time he shook his head, as if to rid himself of his anger. 'You city boys are all the same. You just want the easy life. And you want it today. You cannot wait, can you?'

Manoj felt his heart leap. But Manikbhai's next words made it fall again.

'Your father-in-law warned me about you. But I told him I could handle you. I have faith in young people, you see. Eventually they fall in line with their elders. Now go, go and finish your course, do the exams, qualify, and come and see me when you are a full-fledged inseminator.'

Manoj knew he'd been beaten and when he next saw Govinda he felt he had to apologise to him. 'I will get you free, I promise,' he told the bull. 'It will take a little longer, that's all.'

One night, by the time Manoj got to the clandestine bar (called the laboratory by those who frequented it), the others were already on to their second or third drink. There were nine men altogether that evening – five trainees, Dr Mundkur, Dr Vijay Kumar, Prakash and, of course, Dr Pandey.

'Ah Manoj, come in, come in.' Dr Pandey said, waving a half full glass at him. Manoj came forward timidly and sat down on the only free stool available, a rickety plastic thing a little away from the others. All along the walls were stacked racks of glass beakers and test tubes. Beneath them, on the stainless steel counters, were Bunsen burners and ceramic bowls, the kinds found in any high school laboratory. Charts on the walls explained the basic elements and their molecular compositions. Blackboards with scribbles indicated that during the day the room was indeed used as a classroom. In a corner an electric fly catcher made crackling sizzling sounds every few minutes when a fly met its end. Manoj stared down at the glass in front of him, wondering yet again how it was made and whether it really was safe to drink.

'Don't just think, drink, Mishra. You'll see, it will take you straight to heaven,' he remembered Dr Pandey shouting across the room to him the first time he'd come.

The drink was delicious – both fiery like whisky but tasting of cream, neither sweet nor bitter, but somewhere in the middle. Cautiously he'd taken a second sip and when that was part-way down his throat Manoj decided that in fact, Dr Pandey was absolutely right. It was the best alcohol he'd ever tasted. 'My God, what is this stuff? We should market it,' Manoj had cried enthusiastically as he finished his glass.

'Spoken like the true son of a shopkeeper,' Dr Pandey had said, not looking at him. 'Eh Mishra, can you justify why any old drunk with a few rupees in his pocket should have access to this magic potion? The splendours of this earth are only for the chosen.'

But a month later, the remark still rankled, adding a sour note to a drink he was fast becoming addicted to. It was true that his father was a small industrialist and that despite the Mishra surname adopted by some upwardly-mobile ancestor, Manoj was no Brahmin. Was that how they still saw him? he wondered. A surge of anger brought him to his feet then left him stranded. Not knowing what to do he helped himself to more of the drink sitting invitingly on a stainless steel counter in a large glass beaker. Prakash, the lab technician, giggled.

'It's delicious, who made it this time? Doctor Pandey, you?' Manoj asked.

'Don't ask who made it young man. In this campus, there are no intellectual property rights,' Dr Mundkur replied.

'I made the "milk" this time,' Dr Pandey eventually said,

wiping the tears of laughter from his eyes, 'and it's part cream, part fermented rice wine, part fermented sugar cane juice and a few other secret ingredients you would rather not know about – at least not yet.' He winked at the others.

'Some sacred bull semen, for example,' the tiny lab technician called out, giggling.

Manoj looked at Prakash with dislike. He wondered how the others tolerated such an obviously effeminate man in their midst. But for some reason they didn't seem to mind him at all, and judging by the number of laughs his interjections received, he was actually popular.

The conversation resumed. 'We were just talking about the last raid when you came in,' Pandey confided to Manoj. The trainee whom Manoj had interrupted resumed his narrative. He had just been promoted to full inseminator and was describing his first day in the field. He told his story well, making the others laugh as he described how he'd lied to the farmer whose cow he had inseminated.

'I told him that the government was giving out prizes to those who agreed to try out the miracle seed,' he said. 'I pulled out a bunch of forms from my knapsack, rubbed my pen all over his thumb and made him press it down at the bottom of each sheet. I then wrote down his name and the name of the village in the blank spaces. I told him that he would shortly receive a money order from the government and a postman would come to deliver it. Actually they were my own application forms for a ration card. I didn't have anything else that looked sufficiently official. In any case, I knew that he could not read.' The others laughed uproariously and even white-haired Dr Mundkur permitted himself a small dry smile.

Then Dr Kumar described his first insemination: how first his fingers, then his hand and then half his forearm had gone into the cow. 'She had the largest vagina of any damn woman I have ever known. You could have stored all your gold inside it,' he concluded amidst peals of laughter. Manoj did not find the story particularly funny. He suspected that the others had heard it before and wondered why they found it so funny. The conversation moved on to other topics, funding, foreign trips, politics.

Manoj took no part in it, sitting quietly on his stool and drinking steadily. 'Here, pour me some as well before you finish it all off,' Dr Mundkur asked, holding out his glass. Manoj refilled it quickly and handed it back. Dr Mundkur smiled in a fatherly way, his white beard wagging. 'So how are you liking KIRD, young man? I heard you have a rich father-in-law and a rich father. So what are you doing here?'

Suddenly all eyes were on Manoj. And yet, Manoj couldn't help feeling that the question had already been discussed and an answer arrived at which he was only meant to confirm. Yet he felt grateful to Dr Mundkur for giving him the chance to explain himself.

'I may be the son of a shopkeeper,' he said, smiling self-deprecatingly, 'but my father is not rich.' He paused for effect, then added, 'but my father-in-law is. In fact, he is filthy rich.' He waited till the laughs died down. 'Making money was never my ambition. I want to be a part of something larger, to be a part of history like all of you. I want to be the motor that makes India grow rich.'

There was a short silence when he finished, and he looked from face to face, seeing respect mixed with scepticism. Perhaps he'd overdone the last bit, he thought ruefully.

'The motor that makes India grow rich? What do you Mumbaiwalas know about development? You are city people yaar, you only know how to make money,' Dr Kumar said scornfully,

Manoj replied carefully this time. 'Actually I am from Jaipur not Mumbai, and I couldn't agree with you more. Mumbai may no longer be called Bombay but it is still not a part of

Maharashtra or even India. If anything, Mumbai belongs to the sea. Maybe one day it will float away and join America.' He laughed and looked around expectantly. But no one joined him. There was an icy silence, the Maharashtrians in the group looking decidedly put out.

But Dr Mundkur quickly intervened. 'Ah, Jaipur,' he breathed. 'The pink city, a truly Indian city. Beautiful, beautiful. They should never have stopped building like that. An authentic Indian city. Have you seen it, Pandey?'

Manoj breathed a little easier and cast Dr Mundkur a grateful glance.

'Actually sir,' he said, addressing Dr Mundkur, 'Mumbai and KIRD have one thing in common.' He paused and looked around the room. They were all listening. Even Dr Pandey was looking intrigued. 'Uniqueness. Though my wife and I have only been here a short time,' he continued, 'and against both our families' wishes, we are very happy and cannot imagine being anywhere else. This place is like this drink, absolutely original.'

'Hear, hear.' They all clapped, and Dr Pandey came over and slapped him on the back. 'Good man, good man. Well said.'

Everyone in the room raised their glasses and drank to him. Manoj found himself wishing he could make the moment last forever. There was something pure and intoxicating in being in the company of men. He took another long draught of the 'milk'. The others smiled approvingly and many did the same. Then Dr Mundkur spoke again. But this time there was something new in his voice, something bitter and dissonant.

'Change? Develop? Sometimes I think only the gods can change this country. After all, what has changed after all these years? Villages have become dirtier and more crowded. Old Shiva temples have been abandoned and new ones to Rama have been built. But has that purified their minds? No sir. Those villagers' minds have remained the same, narrow and superstitious. And our work? Has it become any easier? You would have thought that it would have become easier with our success. But instead we have now to fight other NGOs for money, to prove ourselves on paper, on television, in the newspapers. Who cares about the truth? They have turned us all into babus.'

They all nodded in agreement. Dr Mundkur was the most senior inseminator in the team and had more stories to tell than the rest of them put together. It made his pessimism all the more powerful.

He took another gulp of his drink, draining his glass to the bottom. He banged it on the table, making the other glasses shake. 'No, I tell you,' he roared, 'these ungrateful villagers only make it harder each year. When I started, we paid them two rupees for letting us inseminate their worthless animals. Today we have to pay fifty. You would have thought that by now they would be paying us. But no. They are smarter than us, those villagers. Education gave us ideals and that made us weak, vulnerable. These villagers, they have no such illusions. Therefore they are stronger than us. In the end, they will win. We will not convert them, they will convert us – to their temples and their unchanging view of life.'

Manoj caught the trainees and doctors exchanging glances.

'But you don't regret what we are trying to do, surely?' one of the other three trainees, a man with buck-teeth and glasses, asked.

'Regret? I am too old to regret anything,' Dr Mundkur exclaimed. 'But more and more I have begun to believe that it is not the countryside that has developed but KIRD. Instead of our two worlds moving closer, KIRD's development has meant that we are living in a different time zone from them. In their world time moves in circles, in ours it moves in a straight line. How can the two survive together? One will have to destroy the other. If they win, then everything we are trying to do becomes null and void, and we may as well all go and become bankers and teachers. If we win then we are not developers, we are destroyers.'

'Their world will be destroyed in any case. Whether by us or by the USA. We cannot go back. Better us, I say, than the Americans,' Dr Vijay Kumar rumbled.

Suddenly Manoj felt emboldened to say what had been uppermost in his mind for the last few days. 'But why can't we just give the villagers the milk? No poor family would refuse the gift of milk that would develop their children's bones and their minds. The new India would then be born naturally wouldn't it?' Manoj asked eagerly, looking around the table.

A hostile silence greeted his question. Several of the men shook their heads.

'We are not here to give the poor anything. Charity is bad, it makes people weak. Charity is what the government hands out. We are here to make the villagers strong, self-sufficient,' Dr Kumar explained gently. 'Let them organize the fodder. It will do them good to work, give them less time to drink and fight. If you'd ever stuck your toe into a village you'd have seen that the big problem they have is knowing what to do with their time. Alcoholism is rampant; they are totally degenerate.'

The conversation had taken a dangerous turn so Dr Pandey intervened. 'Have you heard,' he asked, winking at the trainees, 'Champion has fallen in love. He has become so generous with his seed that now it is just raining down on us.'

'Really? Who with?' a trainee asked.

'Chamki the donkey,' Dr Pandey replied and everybody burst into uneasy laughter.

'Are, Pandey, that is an old story,' Dr Kumar said. 'Don't you know any new ones?'

Again everyone laughed, more freely this time. But Manoj

didn't laugh. He knew the story and knew it for what it was, a distraction.

'Does it happen often, a bull falling in love with another species?' one of the trainees asked afterwards.

'Not often but it happens,' Dr Mundkur replied. 'Usually though, they fall in love with those who look after them. You have to be careful. In fact I remember one case. . .' and he began on a long and rambling story.

Manoj's mind wandered. He thought of Govinda, 'the Spaniard' as some called him. Would Govinda fall in love with him? What would that feel like? He stared at his drink, seeing the semen whirling inside it the way one saw it in the lab. He put his drink down on the table, feeling sick.

'These foreign cows are just milk producing factories,' he heard Dr Kumar say scornfully. 'They have had the brain bred out of them and are probably as stupid as their masters. Our Indian cows are a thousand times smarter but don't like to work hard. We mix the two and that is how we can make the supercow.'

'But your supercows are foreign,' Manoj could not resist pointing out.

'No, only in the beginning when we took the foreign seed and implanted it in the womb of an Indian cow. What is born is a hundred per cent Indian miracle. No one thought it would work.'

'But the seed is foreign. So how can the cow be Indian?'

'Because the womb is Indian. The seed is only accidental to the process of giving birth. Only in the West do they lay such emphasis on it. The survival of the seed depends entirely upon the womb; it is the womb that gives life to the seed and not the seed that gives life to the womb. Just like our western capitalist masters, if they cannot find a virgin womb to embed themselves in, like the sperm their culture will be extinguished.'

Dr Pandey got up abruptly, his chair falling over in the process. Everyone turned to look at him. 'You know what the problem with this party is? It is too serious.' He grabbed the beaker sitting in the middle of the table and refilled it from a large glass container. Then he came to each man in turn and solemnly refilled his glass.

Eventually it was Govinda that cleared the way. On the morning that Manoj went out into the field for the first time to do some interviewing, Govinda, whose regular keeper was on his annual leave in the village, took a dislike to the replacement, and while the unsuspecting boy was cleaning out his trough, charged him from behind and chased the boy out of his territory. Then, as a means of further showing his displeasure, he destroyed the feeding trough, and not satisfied with that, began to run at the fence around the enclosure. The bull broke it down eventually and escaped into the thick grass beside the lake.

When Manoj returned late that night, he learnt what had happened and was beside himself with joy. The very next day he went straight to the Director's office. This time he had carefully planned what he would say.

'My training is almost finished, sir,' he said stiffly. 'I would like to leave with your blessings. My ambition is to work in the field for a few years, to learn more about village India.'

'Excellent, excellent, beta,' Manikbhai said absently as he studied a map of the world. 'I have been invited to speak in Iceland. Do you know the name of its capital?'

'No I don't, sir,' Manoj said impatiently. 'I just want to ask you for a favour before I leave.'

'What kind of favour?' Manikbhai asked looking directly at Manoj for the first time, his eyes wary in his shopkeeper's face.

'Yesterday Govinda almost killed someone again. I am the

only one he will really allow to handle him. When I leave it will only be a matter of time before he kills someone. So let me purchase him. I will pay you whatever you ask. Full market price.' Manoj knew very well that Manikbhai had got the animal for nothing, everyone did. And yet the price Manikbhai named made his jaw drop.

'Thirty-five thousand rupees?' he squeaked. 'That's crazy.'

Manikbhai said nothing. 'You decide and let me know next week when I return from Iceland. Now I must leave. I have a plane to catch.'

But Manoj chose not to leave KIRD. The look on Pratima's face when he told her of his plans for them and Govinda, and his request that she get her father to part with thirty-five thousand rupees told him that no matter how they presented it to her father, he would never agree. So instead, Manoj chose to bide his time and finish the course first.

And so he graduated from the sheds to the laboratories. He learnt to extract the semen from the bulls, to grade it and freeze it, to transport it and, in the carefully controlled environment of the Institute, to inseminate the cows that resided there.

Govinda was captured and brought back, but would allow only Manoj to come near him, for the man with the scar, returning after a month, had been forgotten. So Manoj continued to clean Govinda's stall, brush and feed him, and eventually, to extract his semen. Every time he did that he would whisper, 'I am sorry Ganja, it is not much longer now. The Director knows that I want you and he knows that without me you are worthless. I will make him part with you.' Govinda would calm down and look back at him, as if he understood. Manikbhai continued to go on his foreign trips and come back waving cheques and bank drafts, and everyone continued to meet for prayers in the morning.

Then one morning Manoj was awakened by a sharp rat-a-tat-tat on the bedroom window. It was Dr Pandey again, but wearing an unusually solemn look on his face. 'No classes today Mishra. Come to the "laboratory" after prayers, and do not tell anyone where you are going.'

In the laboratory the rickety wooden table and plastic chairs were nowhere in sight. Nor were the glasses and beakers of 'milk' with which the trainee inseminators and professors lit up their evenings. When Manoj got there most of the trainees had already assembled. So had Dr Vijay Kumar and Dr Mundkur. Even Prakash, the lab assistant, had found his way in. The look of unholy anticipation on his face was unsettling.

Dr Pandey wasted no time. 'You have been here almost a year and your course is coming to an end. Soon you will be fully qualified inseminators. But all of your knowledge is only theoretical. You have never been in the field, never been tested. So it is time you went out on a raid.'

'Tested?' one of the trainees protested. 'What is there to test? We know how to inseminate the cows, and have done it several times here. Some of us even know how to make the bulls part with their semen.' He looked across the room at Manoj, and a few of the trainees snickered.

'But you have yet to meet the Indian farmer on his soil,' Pandey said, portentously. The three professors exchanged glances, and the first hint of a smile began to appear on Dr Pandey's solemn face. Manoj realised that this was a pantomime that they had enacted several times before. 'You have yet to find out how difficult he is to persuade.'

'Yes, yes,' Dr Pandey hurried on, raising his hands, palm outwards, as if to forestall dissent. 'You have heard us speak of it often during our evenings here. But you have still to experience it first hand; you have still to learn guile and deceit, for that is what you will need to overcome his stubbornness and suspicion.'

'But why?' the trainee persisted. 'Surely the farmers have heard of the dairying revolution that is sweeping the north? They must know that crossing their cows with exotic breeds can increase their yield of milk ten-fold?'

'They have heard, but they do not believe,' Dr Pandey replied. 'The north is an alien land to them. Not even one in ten of them has been further than the nearest market town. And try as they will, they simply cannot understand how a cow can give birth to a calf without being mounted by a bull. To them what we are proposing is no different from magic. They want to believe in it but cannot bring themselves to.'

'But surely,' the trainee, who Manoj now remembered came from Kanpur, remonstrated, 'they must have some idea of what the hybrid cows are capable of. Your trainees have been going out to the villages for years.'

'But each village is virgin territory. And remember, for the farmers the link between the visit of the inseminator and the milk yield of the calf is not as obvious as it is to you and me. The calf must first be born, and grow to maturity before it starts lactating. Almost three years must pass therefore before the link can be established. That is a long time. Then some farmers have been known to take out "insurance" by crossing their cows with a local bull during the same heat. Then alas, some cows have died during the calving, and villagers have been quick to blame their deaths on the adoption of new-fangled ways.' Dr Pandey gave a theatrical sigh and shook his head. 'Anyway,' he concluded, raising his head and glancing around the room, 'you have now to go out and be tested. The next few days will be your agnipareeksha.' He turned towards Dr Vijay Kumar, who solemnly took up the refrain.

'Over the next ten days, four of you will go out every day with cans of frozen sperm and inseminate the cow of every farmer who is willing to give the new techniques a try. From each you will ask permission to cut a tiny part of his cow's tail off to bring back as proof of your success. This is not officially part of the course. So you will tell no one where you are going.'

Dr Mundkur nodded his head sagely and smiled. Manoj suspected that the entire escapade was his brainchild.

'In the vehicle shed are four motorcycles,' Dr Vijay Kumar concluded. 'You have three days to learn how to ride them. The first batch will go out on Sunday.'

CHAPTER SIX

THE INSEMINATION

Manoj was lost. For miles he had seen nothing but rocks and scraggly Kair trees hugging the degraded land. Overhead, the noon sun was a fiery eye that turned men into pygmies. There was not a soul in sight. For the first time in his life, Manoj was absolutely alone, and the realisation sent icy fear up his spine. If he hadn't been so tired he might have dwelt more on the feeling, but he was bone weary. He had been riding the heavy Enfield all day and his legs ached like those of a long distance runner.

It had been easy on the national highway. The tarmac had felt as smooth as skin, and the Enfield had purred like a cat between his legs. The milk cans that contained the small vials of semen, cocooned in their beds of ice, were reassuringly cold against his calves. The sun, the wind, the sky, the endless swathes of ripening wheat and sugar cane on either side of the road, even the garishly-painted trucks, all seemed to exist for the sole purpose of teasing his senses back into hungry life. He felt his spirits lift for the first time in months. At last, he was free, doing something that mattered. And he was far, far from KIRD. The steady throb of the engine spread from his groin to the furthest reaches of his body.

But as the motorcycle ate up the highway, his exhilaration had begun to give way to anxiety. The villages on either side of the road had bristled with TV antennae and satellite dishes; their streets were crowded with motorcycles, trucks, even the odd car. The fields were busy with tractors, and whenever he stopped, the silence would be chopped into tiny pieces by the plopping of tube-well motors. He had even spotted a yellow combine harvester idling under a mango tree. He slowly became aware that he had seen almost no bullocks in the fields, and no cows being herded into the fallows to graze. There were, in fact, very few fallows.

Enquiries at several villages along the road had confirmed his fears. The people would simply ask, where was the space for keeping cattle? 'Are sahib, gai rakhne ke liye jagah kahan?' Those who still kept them had surrendered them to the dairy cooperatives for stall feeding and artificial insemination. Their milk now came in packets. So, as morning turned into afternoon, he decided to leave the highway and go down the unbeaten tracks that led to the villages in the interior. That was when his troubles began. For if the villagers along the highway had no need for his services, those in the interior seemed never to have heard of them. Most met his assertions, that he could make their cows bear calves without first being mounted by a bull and that the calves born of this strange union would yield more than ten times as much milk as their mothers, with blank disbelief. Some thought he was a liar and braggart, typical of the young men the towns were spawning in these days of Kaliyug*. Others eyed him with deep suspicion, and wondered whether this was not an elaborate scheme to steal their best cow. 'We have no cows,' the headman of one Harijan† hamlet told him blandly. 'We scrape a living by working in the Thakur‡ fields. You give us the cows and we will do everything you say. In another hamlet, the headman tried to

* Age of Kali, the third and last age of humans on earth, according to Hindu belief.
† lowest caste
‡ landowner caste group

convince Manoj to marry his eldest daughter.

And so it was that he had not performed a single insemination when the path ran out. He was still riding on slowly, weaving through scrub and bushes in search of a track, when a large speckled stone turned into a fat bird that flew straight into the air from under his front wheel, forcing him to brake sharply. The motorbike wobbled wildly and the engine coughed twice and died. Manoj got off, cursing loudly. In front of him, the land rose gently, blocking his view. With a last burst of desperate energy, he pushed the bike up the slope to the top. He was on the top of a low cliff. Below him a broad river flowed placidly through a wide river bed. Otherwise, all he could see was rolling hills dotted with scraggly trees, interrupted here and there by dark ribs of rock. He felt an intruder. But as he was turning the bike around, he caught sight of dun-coloured walls. He hesitated. 'One last try; one last village,' he promised himself, 'then I will feel I have done my best.' He kicked the bike back to life and turned to the right along the top of the escarpment. The village was further away than it had looked, but when he crested the final rise his breath caught in his throat.

In front of him there stretched an unbroken line of ochre coloured wall over which could be glimpsed tiled roofs unmarred by satellite dishes or TV antennae. Above the roofs tall trees flowered in the full abandonment of spring. To the right, the low hilltop on which the village stood sloped away in a patchwork quilt of terraced paddy fields, mango orchards and fallows verdant with juicy green grass, which stretched to the edge of low bluffs that marked the edge of the river. The water was edged with sedge and wild grasses, decorated with pink, turquoise and yellow wildflowers. As he was admiring the scene, he heard what sounded like the low rumble of distant thunder and the meadows filled with animals racing joyously towards the village. In the lead were the bulls, powerful awe-inspiring creatures with long, curving, massive horns more than a foot long. Their blue-black bodies gleamed with good health and around their necks were garlands of river grass interwoven with white flowers. He stared at the beasts in disbelief, for they were easily the most magnificent creatures he'd ever seen outside of the Institute. This is the place, he thought excitedly. I have found it!

Proof came when he entered the village, for the walls of the houses were covered with the most intricate portraits of village life, done in a naïve childlike style but with great attention to detail. A delighted smile painted itself across his dusty face and he barely noticed the little children who pointed, screamed and hid when they saw him. On one wall a river sported many-coloured fish, boats bobbing on its wavy surface. Adjacent to it, a herd of cows with large human eyes wandered over a flower-studded meadow. On the other side of the street, on a beautifully whitewashed wall, a single enormous banyan tree doubled as a tree of life sheltering peacocks, wild animals, flowers and children. On yet another wall, cows and humans played Holi with a gorgeously midnight blue Krishna. At the corner of another street, fishermen cast their nets towards the sun as flocks of geese and ducks flew up from the river's edge.

Each wall was different. Each told a story. He stared and stared at them, unable to tear his eyes away. Amazement gave way to excitement and a sense of anticipation.

As he ventured further into the village, his delight kept growing. Every house was exquisitely maintained, their facades whitewashed, the verandahs neat and carefully plastered with cowdung and clay, the arched niches in the walls, designed to hold lanterns, decorated with little motifs. Outside every door was placed a welcoming pot of cool well water. No election posters or graffiti disfigured the walls. The cleanliness wasn't limited to the houses; the street was just as well maintained, the drains neatly covered and the road swept clear of debris. No plastic was visible on the street, and even the occasional paan stain looked aesthetic. This was the way all of India should have been, he thought. Maybe it was the way it once was.

At the same time he couldn't help noticing that though everything was exquisitely maintained, the village seemed poor. There were no electricity poles, and he could see no signs of piped drinking water. None of the houses he'd passed had cement or steel in them and they had very little wood as well. There were no shops, no cars or even motorcycles, and no tractors. The silence breathed peace.

The lane he had been walking down ended in a square. Around it the houses were older and built more closely together. Many had dispensed with protective outer walls and faced the street from behind wide verandahs. This was, Manoj quickly realised, the heart of the village. The square had taken shape around the intersection of the lane with a much wider thoroughfare which was clearly the main street; it was full of people. Young women balancing loads of firewood on their heads were hurrying home to light the evening fires. Older men were walking slowly up and down, nodding to each other, or sat on benches and doorsteps, hookahs by their side, waiting for their daughters-in-law to bring them tea. Harassed-looking mothers were sweeping their doorsteps or walking over to neighbours' houses on suddenly-remembered errands, a feeding infant tucked under one arm. There were children everywhere, playing hopscotch or gulli-danda, moving aside only when the odd cow or goat or chicken marched confidently through the centre of their game.

Stepping into the busy street Manoj felt at a loss. Where should he begin? It was already early evening, and only the very old and the very young seemed to have time to spare. Just then a voice called out from behind him, 'Rama, Rama Sahib.'

He turned quickly. The speaker was a middle-aged peasant with gold earrings and the most guileless smile Manoj had ever seen. He was sitting on a doorstep a paintbrush in his hand. Manoj walked up to him. Snow-white eyebrows and thick moustache caught the evening light and illuminated a face burnt a deep mahogany by the sun. It took Manoj almost a minute to realise that the man was blind in one eye.

'Aap kahan se aayein hain, Sahib?' The man asked politely but directly where Manoj had come from, turning his head at an angle so he could look at Manoj out of his good eye.

'I am from Jaipur,' Manoj replied, giving the man the name of his birthplace. He didn't want to scare him off by mentioning the Institute.

The man's eyes widened in disbelief. 'Then you have come a long way and must be tired. Sit and have a cup of tea with me.'

Manoj hesitated, looking at the busy street. But the sight of a steaming cup of tea on the bench beside the villager reminded him that he hadn't eaten all day, so he nodded his acceptance. The man called for a charpoy to be brought for the guest and himself and stood politely until Manoj was seated. Then he sat down and took up his paintbrush again.

For a while neither of them spoke, the man absorbed in his work, and Manoj content to watch him painting, marvelling at the one-eyed man's skill. Then, after a while, Manoj's eyes wandered to the street and were caught by a tall slim woman walking along slowly, carrying three pots of water and a bundle of wood as if they were no heavier than a stack of hay. She wasn't veiled and though she saw him staring at her, the firewood on her head and pots in her arms prevented her from covering her face so he could feast his eyes upon it at leisure, taking in the symmetry of her straight little nose, her small perfectly bowed lips and large almost jet black eyes set under strong straight eyebrows that gave strength to an otherwise unreal, almost film star beauty. Suddenly his chest felt light and happiness bubbled inside it, making him smile involuntarily.

Seeing this, the man turned and followed the direction of Manoj's gaze. 'You seem to like our village and its inhabitants a lot,' he said, his good eye twinkling.

'It is beautiful,' Manoj answered with feeling, tearing his eyes away from the woman reluctantly, 'the most beautiful place I have ever seen. Its people rival the forest's most beautiful flowers.'

'The beauty is in your eyes, Sahib; this is just a poor village,' the man replied, looking pleased nonetheless. 'You must have far more beautiful things in the city.'

'No. The city is an ugly place,' he replied absently, remembering the mildewed, poster-laden, urine-stained walls of the houses in Khandwa. Somehow the memory didn't upset him though. If anything, it only increased his sense of wonderment. Could anything equal the richness of the gold of the early afternoon sun warming baked mud walls and sun-bleached tiles, and turning the dust that hung in the air into gold? He was struck again by the unhurried grace of the people moving in the street. They were like actors on a filmset waiting to be turned into a film, he said to himself. He smiled again, admiring his own eloquence. It was the effect of the village, he thought; its beauty was inspiring.

'Sahib, why have you come here?' The directness of the question startled him. He looked quickly at the man's face but he saw only respect and curiosity there.

'I have come to help,' he replied warily.

'To help whom?'

'All of you. The village.'

'To help us? How?' The man put his paintbrush down, looking intrigued. But there remained something about his body language of the adult humouring a young child that Manoj found irritating.

'To make this village rich,' he said bluntly, wanting to chase that doubt away.

The man's good eye widened in surprise. Then he looked down at his feet and said, 'That is very kind of you. You have come all this way from the city to tell us this? That is good of you.'

'Not to tell you, but to show you how,' Manoj went on strongly. 'I have rarely seen such a beautiful place. And yet, you are so poor. It is not right.'

The man looked apologetic. 'What can one do, Sahib, it is in our fate to be poor – as it is in yours to be rich.'

'That is not true, I am not rich. But no one is destined to be poor. Those days are gone. Many things are possible today that we could not have dreamt of only a few years ago. Your village deserves to be rich. I sense such richness of spirit here already. Why should you remain poor when science can so easily make you rich?' he said passionately.

Disbelief, then confusion, chased each other across the villager's face. 'How could we become rich?' he asked.

'If you have a cow that is on heat just now, I could show you.'

The man looked surprised but didn't question him further. Instead he shook his head regretfully. 'I am a poor man. I have just one cow, and she has not been fertile for three years.'

'Oh.' Disappointment stabbed at him. He would have liked to help this man.

Tea arrived, in small clay cups, on a wickerwork tray. It was brought by a demurely-veiled woman who Manoj assumed, was the man's daughter-in-law. The tea was rich and creamy. A fragrant aroma of cardamom and ginger wafted from it. He accepted a cup eagerly. It was delicious. 'This is the best tea I have had in a long time,' he told the man enthusiastically.

The man's smile lit up his face. 'You are very kind.' He put his untasted cup down on the bench beside Manoj and asked, 'Would you like another cup?'

'No, this is enough for me. You must let me know when your cow goes on heat.'

'Ah but this milk doesn't come from our cow,' the man replied, smiling but still a little wary. 'It is our headman's milk.'

'Your Patel's milk?' he asked, bewildered. 'He sells you this milk?'

'No, Sahib.' The man laughed. 'I am a poor man. I could not afford to buy it. He gives it to us.'

'Gives it to you? In exchange for what?' He was stunned.

'For nothing, Sahib. Because he is the Patel and he has too many cows,' the man replied simply.

Manoj digested the information with difficulty. Why would a headman give away his milk?

'Our Patel is a great man,' the man continued, as if reading his thoughts. 'He would help you with your project, Sahib. You must go and see him. He has many cows.'

Manoj did not answer. He did not want to be rude to his kind host, but his experiences with other village headmen had not been encouraging, so he was reluctant to confront yet another. He stood up, thanked his host and asked him if he knew of anyone else who was poor but had a cow on heat.

'I don't know, Sahib. There must be many,' the man replied honestly. 'Everyone dreams of owning cows here. If you go to the right there,' he said pointing down the main street to the west, 'you will come to the houses where the big people live; they have many cattle. You should go and see them.'

Manoj gave up. The one-eyed painter was obviously too much in awe of the headman to be of any use. He made his excuses quickly and proceeded up the street.

As Giridhari the painter watched Manoj push his heavy motorcycle up the road, the polite smile faded from his face. He shook his head. The outside world seemed to be getting crazier and crazier with each passing year. Thank God the headman would soon find this man and send him and his motorcycle on their way. Such madness could be dangerous. Especially because the man had seemed so sincere.

As Manoj made his way in to the heart of the village, he passed gorgeously-painted houses, each a little bigger and more elaborately painted and wondered if the one-eyed artist had done the paintings on them. People nodded to him, some smiled and then respectfully lowered their eyes. He came to another intersection. A tiny general store was set into the wall of a large house where three streets curled around an enormous banyan tree. On one side of the tree was a broad platform seven feet wide and almost three feet high. Several young men were gathered around the tree drinking tea and listening to a running commentary on a cricket match on an ancient radio. The sight of the radio jolted Manoj. In this village the voice of the commentator sounded alien and intrusive.

Catching sight of him, the young men invited him to have a cup of tea with them. Manoj was about to refuse when he thought better of it. They seemed less unworldly than his first host, and there had to be at least one cow on heat owned among them, he thought. He parked the motorcycle on one side, and immediately three of the young men detached themselves from the commentary to come and look at its powerful clean-cut lines. 'This is an Enfield, isn't it?' one of them asked. Manoj realised that the dust of his travels had completely cloaked the logo on the fuel tank, and nodded. 'We do not see many of those here,' another said admiringly. The others nodded. 'We don't see any motorcycles, for that matter,' the third one laughed. 'No one likes to leave the road.'

The roar of an excited stadium crowd overlaid by the rich chocolate voice of the commentator put an end to further conversation. The three rushed back to the radio and Manoj followed. Immediately a steaming cup of tea was placed in front of him.

'I am looking for a cow in heat,' he shouted over the noise of the radio.

'Why? Do you not have the money for a wife?' one asked.

A chorus of laughter followed. But it wasn't unkind. A young man offered him a beedi*, which he declined. Another turned the radio down.

'So what brings you to our village, Sahib?' the one who'd given him his seat asked politely.

'I have come to help the village,' he replied carefully.

'Help us? How? Do we look like we need help?' Their friendliness had acquired an edge of suspicion.

Manoj ploughed on, heedless of the drop in temperature. 'I want to help you become rich.'

The warmth continued to seep out of their eyes as they glanced at each other and then at him. But Manoj didn't see it.

'Shall I tell you how?' he asked eagerly.

Taking their silence for an answer he began to explain the basics of what he would be doing. 'You see those milk cans there?' he began. 'They are full of injections. I put one injection inside a cow that is on heat, and the resulting calf gives five times the milk of the mother,' he ended. 'Simple.'

He sat back and looked at them expectantly. But there were no smiles, no eager yeses.

'But what would we do with the extra milk?' a young man asked, waving his teacup in the air. 'No child goes without milk in our village.'

'You can sell it of course,' he replied.

'Sell it?' The man looked puzzled. 'To whom? We even give this old chaiwala free milk, isn't that right, Baba?' He looked towards the owner of the shop as he spoke. The old sadhu nodded.

* indigenous cigarette

'To other villagers, to the towns,' Manoj replied impatiently.

'Ah yes, the towns.' The young man nodded politely.

'You could sell the milk in the city even – it is not so far away.'

'Ah, the city. But surely they have their own cows in the city, being so much richer than us?'

'No, they don't.' He tried to keep the irritation out of his voice. 'You've been to a town surely, and you've seen how little space there is.'

'Where are you from, Sahib?' one of the young men asked.

'From Jaipur,' he replied automatically.

'Jaipur. That's far. What are you doing so far from your home? Don't you have cows there?'

'Of course we do, but . . .' he stopped. 'The point is, do you want to be rich or not?'

'Are you rich?' a man with a handlebar moustache asked.

'I? No.'

'Then how can you help us to become rich?'

'Because I have the education, and the science,' he replied.

'Are you a politician?' a squint-eyed youth asked innocently.

'No. I am not,' he replied tautly.

'You sound like a politician. You want us to give you our cows first, then you will show us how to make money.'

'But I don't just talk, I do,' he snapped, banging his empty glass down in front of them.

He tried to ignore the laughter that followed him up the street. So much for the younger generation, he thought disgustedly.

He continued through the village, stopping and asking at every small house if they had a cow on heat. But everywhere he went he was first made to sit down and drink a cup of tea while the entire family inspected him, and then told, 'No, no animal on heat.' How could it be, he wondered, that in a village this big there was no animal that was ready? And yet they were all so welcoming, so open in their curiosity and eagerness to tell him about their village that he somehow felt embarrassed even imagining that they were lying to him. 'Are you sure none of your animals are ready? You could make a whole lot of money, build yourself a new house, buy a car even,' he asked somewhat desperately. Back came the reply: 'No sir, we are sorry. But why don't you go and see our headman? He has the largest number of cows in the village.'

At last, as the light began to fade, he decided that he had better see the headman after all. If there was one person who would understand the importance of what he could do for them, it was the headman.

'Where is the headman's house?' he asked.

'The Patel's house?' They looked surprised. 'It is at the other end of the village, Sahib, you have to go back the way you came. Look for the house with the eyes.'

'The eyes?'

'Our headman's eyes are everywhere, like God's eyes,' a young boy with the shadow of a moustache on his upper lip replied.

So he turned around and went back through the village and sure enough, at the opposite end, barring the road, he saw a large black gate with two eyes, somewhat asymmetrical, painted on either side. Behind it was a large, rambling multi-storeyed house. He went up to the gate. The eyes looked straight through him, focusing on a point somewhere at the back of his head.

He knocked on the gate with a stone. 'Patelji hain? Is he in? I need to speak to him, I am a doctor,' he shouted. The eyes stared through him and beyond, unimpressed.

'There is no sick person here,' a woman's voice replied from behind the gate. A volley of hastily muffled giggles followed her words.

'I want to see his animals,' he corrected himself hastily. 'I have something very important to tell him.'

'He is not here. And there is no sick animal in the village either,' the same strong feminine voice replied. From somewhere behind him an animal mooed loudly, provoking another cascade of laughter. This time the laughter lasted longer and was louder.

He gave up. 'But can I at least have a drink of water?' he shouted.

In almost no time at all the door opened. A young boy, obviously a servant, with the wide innocent stare of an idiot, appeared with a glass of buttermilk and a plate of glucose biscuits.

'Thanks.' He took the glass of buttermilk and slipped a ten-rupee note into the boy's hand. 'Tell me, where is your Patel?' he whispered.

The boy's hand closed into a fist and he looked around nervously. But the road was deserted so he whispered, 'He is in the fields.'

'Show me the way, I have to speak with him. It is important.' He returned the empty glass and grabbed the boy's arm before he could disappear inside.

The boy didn't struggle; he just stood still, looking at the ground.

'Don't worry, he will want to see me. I promise he won't be angry,' he whispered.

'Follow the road that way,' the boy mumbled reluctantly, his eyes flicking to the road to the left of the tree and then to the money in his fist. The boy pulled free and ran back inside.

Manoj got back on his bike, ignoring the curious eyes raking his back. The houses dwindled and soon he found himself amidst fields once more. The road was high and he could see a long distance on either side of the road. But it soon became narrow and badly overgrown so he parked his bike and continued on foot. He came to a field of sugar cane and saw a tiny track carved into its heart. The track ended before a partly broken-down boundary wall. He stared at it in disbelief. The wall was in ruins and yet he could hear snatches of song and the sound of bangles coming from behind it. What was the headman doing in such a place? he wondered. Was it the house of his mistress? His eyes travelled the broken-down unpainted wall to the doorway made of straw and twigs and rags. It didn't look the kind of place a patel would keep a mistress – even if it was far from the village.

He pushed the reed door and entered, startling the woman inside. Even as she pulled her sari over her head to cover her face, and ran to the verandah of the house at the far side of the courtyard, he had time to notice that her clothes, though worn were spotlessly clean, and her ankles and wrists were slim and shapely. She was wearing silver anklets which tinkled as she ran. Even though she had partly covered her face so all he could clearly see was her lush full-lipped mouth, he recognised her as the woman whose gait he had admired on the main street.

'I'm sorry. Someone in the village told me I would find the Patel here,' he stammered.

She shook her head violently and pointed to the entrance. He turned to go, not wanting to embarrass himself further. Then he saw the cow tethered to the trunk of a neem tree in the corner of the yard.

At first his brain refused to register what he was seeing. This was not one of those statuesque animals he'd seen on the meadows earlier that evening, it was a desi cow of indeterminate parentage, one of the millions he had seen on his travels across Maharashtra. The animal yawned and licked its rear lazily. She was not particularly large. He noticed an ugly scar across her hindquarters. All of a sudden he knew that this was the animal that the boys at the tea shop had been pushing him towards all afternoon. He understood their admonitions to go and see the headman, the barely-suppressed giggles from inside the headman's house – someone had obviously gone ahead to warn the family – and the dispatch of the retarded child to the gate to make their message credible. He wondered if, at this very moment, the entire village wasn't guffawing with laughter, and felt himself go hot with rage and humiliation.

The beauty of the woman before him and everything his eyes had feasted on during the course of the afternoon turned rancid in his stomach. But with the anger came a renewed determination. Manoj swore to himself that no matter what, even if he had to return to this godforsaken village twenty times he would impregnate at least one cow here. But not this one! He glared at the junglee specimen before him. The animal, unperturbed, began to lick its rear once again. It was then that he noticed the swollen pink flesh around its vagina and the wetness seeping on to its legs.

He looked at the cow more closely. A smile spread slowly across his face. This cow was a potpourri of breeds but it had the long body and short legs of the Ongoles, and did he detect the lyre-shaped horns of the Thari? That could explain her small size, he thought. If that were so, her calf would give its owners a huge surprise. Why not? he thought. Why on earth not this one? Why not flood this miserable hovel with milk, and turn it into the richest house in the village? It would be he who would then have the last laugh. He walked up to the cow and gave her hind-quarters an exploratory rub. The cow looked back at him enquiringly but didn't move away. This one would not be about the supercow, he thought, making up his mind; this would be revenge.

He turned impulsively toward the woman, but the verandah

was empty. 'Could you please give me some water, I'm thirsty,' he called out towards that empty doorway.

After a lengthy pause the woman emerged with an earthenware bowl containing water.

'I see you have a beautiful cow,' he told her insincerely.

She made no reply, pouring the water from a little pot into the glass instead.

After he'd drunk his fill he said boldly, 'I am a cow doctor. Your cow is very healthy. You are obviously very fond of her and look after her well.'

After the barest pause, she nodded.

'I can see that she is in heat. So why have you not crossed her with one of the bulls in the village?'

For the first time she looked him directly in the eye and spoke. Her voice was musical, and, to his surprise her accent was that of an educated woman. 'We asked everyone. But no one wanted a calf from a junglee cow.'

'In that case perhaps I have come at just the right time, for I can help you,' he said. 'I can give your cow some medicine that will give her a calf that will give twenty times as much milk as a normal cow.'

She looked up and smiled for the first time. It was the gentle smile of a mother humouring her child. It made him feel instantly embarrassed.

'You mean artificial insemination, don't you?' she asked. It was his turn to register surprise.

She looked around her, at the irregular patched-up courtyard walls, the sagging door, and the beaten earth floor, and said, 'Don't believe everything you see.'

What Laxmi didn't tell Manoj was that from the moment she'd seen him sitting in front of Giridhari, the painter's house, she'd known exactly what he was and why he was there. Three years earlier her father had had some of his best cows 'treated' by just such a one. He had read about the process in a newspaper and visited the newspaper office in Indore, asking for the inseminator's address.

'You're going to have an ice-cream factory in this backward old village,' she had teased her father when, on her return from college one day, her sisters had excitedly described the visit of the man on the motorcycle.

'Of course, I am. How did you guess?' her father had replied, pulling her long thick braid. 'And I will become very rich selling ice cream, not just here but all over our state.'

'Nothing good will come of this,' Laxmi's mother had grumbled, seeing the two of them smiling conspiratorially. 'You've gone against nature and this time you will be punished.'

Laxmi remembered how her father's face had grown dark. He'd pulled out some money and given it to her mother. 'Instead of cursing us, why don't you go give this to that blood-sucking pujari of yours and tell him to do a puja for us. I am only trying to do what's best for our family. The calves that our cows will give birth to will be very special. They will give thirty times as much milk as an ordinary cow.'

'But don't our cows give enough already?' her mother had replied in perplexity. 'They give more milk than any other cows in the village. Why do you always want more?'

Laxmi had only to shut her eyes to see her mother's face as it had looked then. She had always thought of her mother as a brave woman. But that day, she'd seen something new in her face. It was fear.

She never saw the results of the inseminator's work. Three months into the calves' pregnancy the bank notices began to arrive. Her father had laughed them off at first. The new cotton plants from the American seeds were tall and leafy, their stems thicker than any others in the village. Six months into the calves' pregnancies, her father killed himself. The cotton bushes were tall, almost double the normal height, their branches thick and pulsing with life. But there were no pods. The plants were tumours, sucking the life from the earth, converting water, fertiliser and labour into weeds. And the heavily pregnant calves were all sent away in the middle of the night.

Now Laxmi looked up and the expression on her face scared Manoj. 'Go and get your tools, I will prepare her,' she said, nodding at the cow.

Speechless, Manoj headed for his bike.

When he returned, she was waiting in the verandah and the cow was hobbled and tied securely to the tree. 'This will only take a minute, but effects will last you a lifetime,' he babbled, putting the milk canister down and pulling on his rubber gloves. Quickly he twisted open the lid of the milk can. Steam burst like a cloud from it. He reached in and pulled out an icy tube filled with the frozen semen. Drops of condensation frosted the outside instantly. It felt like an icicle in his hand, an icicle, he reflected, that was waiting to burst into life.

He approached the cow nervously. He could hear Dr Pandey of the Institute in his head. 'The first time is always the hardest. Like with a woman, you have to be in sympathy with the animal. A kick from a cow in the wrong place and you can say goodbye to your future. And remember, cows don't have words to keep a man at bay, they only have their feet.'

'So should we tie it up, sir?' one trainee had suggested.

'Wish one could do the same to women,' another added in a low voice.

'Depends upon you. It's better to make friends of course, but if you do choose to tie her up, then make sure her feet are tied first. For they are very strong creatures,' the good doctor had replied.

Manoj looked at the cow. Thank God it was hobbled. He grabbed a fistful of gur* mixed with grain and moved closer.

* Type of sugar made from molasses, also known as jaggery.

The cow seemed to know he'd come for her. She looked back at him and didn't move. He fed her the sedative-enriched jaggery – the 'date rape drug' as it had been affectionately called at the institute – then waited. After a while the cow began to look sleepy. Manoj began to whisper sweet nothings and stroke her hindquarters rhythmically, conscious of the woman watching from the verandah. After a few minutes, he put his forefinger and middle finger inside the cow. He wiggled them to check the tension. She was relaxed inside. He wiggled his fingers some more.

'Just pretend she's a woman yaar. It's easy,' Prakash the lab technician had told him after his maiden 'ride'. 'Remember we're the hell's angels. Cow or woman, they're all the same: just love power and authority. She'll look back at you when it's over and if she could speak I swear she'd be saying, "More, more, give me more."'

Manoj had laughed dutifully with the others, but had not really been amused. For him, sex and birth were miracles. The fact that they had succeeded in controlling the timing and circumstance of the miracle did not make either of them any less amazing.

He looked at the cow's delicate haunches, caught and lifted her tail and pushed the glass tube deep inside. She jerked a little, not liking its coldness. He slapped her hard a few times on her buttocks, thinking of the way the village had humiliated him. She grunted and tried to move away, almost breaking the glass syringe. That brought him back to his senses and so he continued more gently, alternately stroking and slapping as he had been taught. Then he blew hard into the syringe to make sure all the semen was inside, and pulled it out. As he was putting the empty tube away, his eyes met the woman's. Hastily he dug into his pocket and pulled out ten rupees. 'Here, keep this,' he said, walking quickly up to Laxmi. He thrust the money into her hand. Her face became a kaleidoscope of emotions: surprise, anger, humiliation, then shame. She looked down and closed her fingers.

'It's OK, you'll see. You'll soon be rich,' Manoj whispered hurriedly. Even to himself, he thought, he sounded unconvincing.

She said nothing, staring down at her closed fist as if it was an alien object.

'Thank you, thank you,' he babbled as he hurried towards the door, feeling as if it was her he'd just raped instead of the cow.

He had barely walked a hundred yards down the path when he saw a man approaching carrying a bundle of fresh grass. Something told him the man was the owner of the cow. He looked the other way, avoiding eye contact.

'Are pardesi*, were you visiting my wife? Are you her brother then?' the man called out. He was not as handsome as the woman but had an open, kindly face and pale grey-green eyes.

'No, I am not,' he replied frostily. 'I have business with the Patel. I was told he could be found here.'

The villager laughed uproariously. 'Who could have told you a thing like that?' he said at last. 'This is his sugar cane field all right, but he never comes here. I look after it for him.'

He felt the cold hand of certainty clasp his heart. So he had guessed right after all. He looked up and found the villager still standing in front of him, looking concerned. 'Are you all right, Sahib?' he asked. 'You look unwell. Why don't you come inside and eat with us? You must be hungry.'

Manoj stared at the man. All he wanted was to get on to his bike and escape. 'No, I must go,' he said sharply.

'Are you a doctor, Sahib?' the villager asked suddenly, not moving out of his way.

'An animal doctor, of sorts,' he replied.

* foreigner

'I have a cow. Please come and see it before you go, Sahib. I found it in the jungle very sick with a wound in its thigh that was badly infected. It was very ill. Our village is so remote no doctors ever come here so I tried to fix it myself. Please come and see if it is all right now.'

'No, no, I can't. It is late. I have to go,' he said weakly.

'Please, Doctor, Sahib, it will only take a minute,' the man begged.

The woman was surprised to see them. Surprised and agitated. He could tell from the way she gripped the pillar of the verandah. He looked to see if the man had noticed. But the man had gone straight to his cow and was bending over it, caressing its head and ears.

'I've come to see the cow,' Manoj said loudly. 'I am a doctor.'

She turned abruptly and went into the house. He walked over to where the man was still petting the cow.

'She is my luck, you know,' the villager said without turning. 'Ten days after she came back with me the headman fell down the stairs and sprained his foot. When I fixed his sprain, he promised he'd fix my wall. All because of her.' He rubbed the cow's small rump lovingly.

Manoj wondered how any man could love such a useless animal. 'In the forest? How lucky. The gods must have left her there for you,' he said insincerely.

'Absolutely. I too feel she is a gift from the Devi.' The villager's face clouded over. 'The villagers, they wanted me to get rid of her. They said she was barren, old, useless. But they were wrong. A miracle happened four days ago. This old junglee that everyone swore was barren came into heat.'

'You should mate your cow quickly then,' he said perfunctorily, wanting to leave.

The villager gave him a grateful look. 'I too feel that. But no one will let their bulls mount her.'

The animal bellowed softly. The villager looked at it distractedly. 'Look how sad she is. She wants to be a mother, I can feel it.'

Suddenly Manoj had an idea that made him smile. 'I can help you,' he told the man. 'I can give your cow an injection that will make a beautiful healthy calf.'

'A calf? Without being mounted by a bull?' The villager hesitated, looking embarrassed. 'I don't understand. . .'

'It's a very simple technology,' Manoj explained quickly. 'I have injections with me which contain very powerful medicine. All I have to do is put it inside your animal.'

He waited.

'I don't know. . .' The villager looked torn.

Bangles clinked. His wife appeared magically behind him. She pulled at her husband's sleeve, and took him inside. At the doorway, she threw Manoj a grateful glance.

By the time they re-emerged, he was pulling off his gloves. This time he hadn't thought of revenge. He hoped the sperm would take. They were a beautiful couple. They deserved to be rich.

The woman had an earthenware glass in her hands, which she offered him, her face impassive. Taken on its own, without the ubiquitous tea, the milk tasted even better than he remembered, the fragrance of flowers and fresh grass perfuming it. It was probably the most delicious milk he had ever drunk, he reflected dreamily; creamy, with a faint echo of earth coming like a surprise after the grass and flowers. They could brand it under a special name even, it was so good.

'You people are right, you do have the best cows in the area. It's a pity your Patel wouldn't meet me. Maybe next time.' He raised his empty glass in a silent toast. The woman took the glass from him and walked away. The man didn't understand. 'You should meet our Patel, Sahib, he is a great man,' he said earnestly.

CHAPTER SEVEN

THE HEADMAN

About the time Manoj was slipping his icy tube of surprises into the cow, Gopal Mundkur, the Patel of Nandgaon, awoke as he always did. The sun had just hidden itself behind the giant neem tree at the entrance to the house, blanketing his khaat* in shadow. Above him the sky was a deep and invincible blue. A tall glass of almond milk lay on the floor beside him, perfuming the air with the scent of cardamom and saffron. The deep wooden-beamed verandah was quiet, stretching endlessly on either side. He stretched lazily, feeling the flow of blood quicken in his limbs, enjoying the relative peace of the moment.

As he had grown older evening had become his favourite time of day. Separated from the morning by a refreshing two-hour nap, the evenings would often find him feeling young, and alert, something that no longer happened to him in the mornings. For day sleep was untroubled. At night, demons crept into his dreams wearing the familiar faces of the dead. 'You are growing old, that's all,' his wife would have told him had she still been alive. 'Your bad deeds are catching up with you. You should go on a pilgrimage to Kashi.'

Kashi. That was another one of his regrets. He'd never taken her there though she'd asked him several times. 'Who will look after the village if I go to Kashi?' he'd always told her.

* jute string bed

After his wife's death, the demons of sleeplessness had become stronger and more and more dawns found him grumpily pacing the verandah in front of his bedroom.

But this evening, as he reached for the glass of milk, he felt wonderfully young and full of hope. The steadily-increasing hum of voices on the other side of the gate told him he was needed. He looked across the courtyard towards the big wrought-iron gate. Through the gap in the centre he could see the people sitting on their haunches outside. Some had genuine problems; others came just to see him, seeking his blessings for the marriage of a son or daughter, or his opinion on what to plant the next season. Many came simply to see justice done and to reassure themselves that the village, their universe, was being properly taken care of. He smiled, knowing exactly what they would be seeing: his eyes – painted on the panels of the gate – watching over them. He had the eyes painted after the flood of '79 when he moved the village from its old location to its present one on the other side of the river, because he wanted to reassure the villagers that he was looking after them, protecting them, always. Many had questioned the wisdom of his decision at the time. People moved, but villages didn't. Villages, like temples, were a part of the eternal order of things. But the headman had stood firm. They had to get as far away from the road as possible, he insisted. For though he had managed to force the government to take the road away from Nandgaon, one day he knew, the government would bring the road back. And with the road would come all the evils of the town – for roads made men dream impossible dreams. Which was why the village had to be protected – not just from the outside but from itself as well. Finishing the last of his milk quickly, Gopal stood up and walked stiffly into the inner courtyard for his evening bath.

In the last thirty-five years his routine had never varied. In the small enclosure where he had installed the handpump, his daughter-in-law had already placed a brass bucket and matching lota* and a small bar of Lifebuoy soap. Over the wall was draped his muslin towel, a starched and crisply pressed kurta and a snow white pleated dhoti. Gopal entered the enclosure and worked the hand-pump until the bucket was full. Then he removed only his kurta and sacred thread, placing the latter carefully over the top of the wall, and started ladling the water in the bucket on to himself. When he was thoroughly wet he soaped himself vigorously through the now wet muslin dhoti and washed himself again. Then he dried himself with the towel and taking the crisp new dhoti in both hands, encircled his waist. Then, and only then, did he let the dripping wet daytime dhoti, now soaped and washed, drop at his feet. Swiftly tying the new dhoti over his still damp waist and legs he pulled the fresh kurta over his head, slipped his feet into his wooden slippers and clumped his way to the pooja room. There he chanted the gayatri mantra, oldest of all mantras, sang Om Jaya Jadadisha Hare in praise of the formless, timeless, all-knowing one, and anointed himself with a tikka of the devout follower of Shiva. Then, and only then, did he return to the world and its troubles, seating himself on the verandah and waiting for those outside to be let in.

On the other side of the gate, Dayanand Kharde stared at the blood-stains on his dhoti, torn between shame and hope. It was not his blood, but that of his son. Dayanand was a quiet, unassuming man. All his life he had tilled the family fields with his three elder brothers, accepting without murmur whatever share they thought fit to give. But it was his own two tiny fields, the ones he'd been given as dowry by his father-in-law, that were his pride and joy. Though the land was stony and tended to get waterlogged in parts, Kharde and his wife, and

* Small brass vessel with a spout.

later his sons, had toiled day and night on them to produce a respectable crop year after year. Then, a few weeks ago, just as he was about to plant his new crop of millet and lentils, he arrived at his fields to find that his neighbour, Ram Manohar Athare, had turned the path through Kharde's best field, that led to Athare's own, into an irrigation channel, making one half of Kharde's land waterlogged and the other a desert. When Kharde had plucked up the courage to ask him to move the channel elsewhere, Athare had abused him and beaten up the messenger, Dayanand's eldest son. Kharde had found him in the field an hour later, still unconscious. His son had only just regained consciouness before Kharde had left. Looking at the bloodstains Kharde almost got up and left. Why wait for justice when at home his axe was sharp and eager? He got up, but even as he did so, the gates opened and he was ushered inside.

'Dayanandbhai, what can I do for you?' the headman asked warmly, hiding his surprise. Dayanand Kharde had never come to see him before. Dayanand began hesitantly to tell his story. When he'd finished and dared to look at the headman's face, the headman was looking furious. 'Where is Ram Manohar? Go and call him here immediately,' he shouted to one of his servants, and turning to Dayanand he added, 'Dayanandbhai, have some tea while we wait for the mouse to arrive.' The crowd laughed nervously as a servant led Dayanand Kharde to a bench beneath a honeysuckle bush at one end of the verandah.

The headman continued to deal with the other plaintiffs. Some wanted advice about what to grow next season. Others wanted a small loan, or a promise of help in finding their sons and daughters a suitable bride or groom. Dayanand sipped his tea solemnly and watched the headman listen to each man's problems. What a great man he is, he thought. For twenty-five years, he has listened to his people every day, never missing out a single person.

A man was brought in and Dayanand stood up. He recognized the pockmarked angry face only too well. It was a face that had taunted him morning and evening for three months. All of Nandgaon knew that Ram Manohar Athare was an alcoholic, a cheat and a bully. And yet, no one had helped Dayanand with Athare. Now, seeing the man cringe before the headman, Dayanand felt as if a huge burden had been lifted off his shoulders. He looked gratefully at the headman.

'Are you still beating your wife?' Gopal said conversationally, when Athare was brought in front of him. The headman was referring to the last time Athare had been brought before him.

Athare looked scared. 'Are, Patelji, how can you even think such a thing? I treat her like a devi though she has the mouth of a witch.'

'And your mouth? Clearly it isn't much better.'

'But he was the one who allowed me to make the path. How does it matter if I cut a channel in the middle for water? The path is still there,' Athare whined.

'One more lying word from you and I will personally break your teeth,' the headman hissed, suddenly losing control. 'You will apologise, seal that irrigation channel immediately and then, if you are very nice to Dayanandbhai, perhaps he will show you where you can make another. Now get out of my sight.'

Athare retreated, beaten. The others cheered. Some might have wished in their hearts that the headman had hit him, for no one liked the man, but they all saw that what the headman had done was to ensure that there would be no feud between neighbours. Dayanand's face broke into a relieved smile. 'Thank you, Patelji. I will send you my very best pumpkins immediately. I have two that are as big as young calves,' he stammered, touching the headman's feet. The headman blessed him automatically but his face remained severe as he thought of the departed man. Ram Manohar Athare was a troublemaker; the problem was far from resolved. One could fix a land dispute but not a man's character.

Next Chhannu Mahadev walked up the steps, a tall gangling young man in tow. Chhannu Mahadev was a tribal, the leader of the small community that lived on the edges of Nandgaon, working in the villagers, fields and distilling alcohol for a living. The father of five sons, a thing that should have made him walk tall, Chhannu Mahadev always looked worried, for four out of the five had run away to the city. Gopal looked curiously at the young man, who met his gaze frankly, eyes bright and intelligent. It didn't take much guessing to see that the latter was his son.

Chhannu Mahadev fell at the headman's feet. 'Patelji. . .' His voice broke and the tears he'd managed to keep at bay for so long suddenly began to flow. 'This is my son, Patelji, he has come back.'

'And which son is this?' the headman asked, wanting to postpone the inevitable.

'The third one, Patelji. He was in Nagpur and then in Pune, but now he is returned,' Chhannu Mahadev replied.

'You know the rule,' the headman replied, a little more gruffly than he had intended to. 'Those who leave cannot return for a holiday. They must stay. This one has already returned once and then gone away. Tell him to go, he is no longer your son.'

Chhannu paled. They all knew the penalty for those who ran away from the village a second time – the parents of the boy had to cut off their hair and observe a full thirteen days, mourning, as if the son had died. 'Yes, of course, Patelji,' he answered quickly, 'but he is ill and doesn't want ever to go back to the city. He hates it and its ways.'

'That's what he says now, but he should have thought of it before he ran away.'

The young man fell at Gopal's feet, his hands wrapping themselves tightly around the headman's ankles with a strength born of desperation. 'No, no Patelji. I can't go back. I want to die here. The city takes a man's heart and grinds it into the dust. I want to stay here and look after my parents. Forgive me, forgive me.'

Over the young man's head Gopal's eyes met those of Mahendra, his right hand man and the latter nodded slightly. Immediately two hefty servants walked up and pulled the young man and his father away, still sobbing. The crowd parted to let them depart, their faces sober. Almost all of them were fathers. The headman found that his own eyes were moist and his head had begun to throb. He looked away, his eyes falling on the silent goat tied to the rice husking stone, the goat Chhannu Mahadev had brought him.

They had been listening to the radio when it happened. They'd been listening to a cricket match when an excited voice had suddenly interrupted the commentary to announce that the Americans had landed on the moon.

'Why would anyone want to land on the moon?' Vilas Rao had asked. 'Isn't the earth good enough for them?'

'Must be a mistake,' Govind Rao had replied.

'Crazy.'

'I doubt it's true.'

'How could a man get to the moon?'

'In a plane?' Govind Rao suggested.

'What kind of a plane? Have you seen one?' Vilas Rao scoffed. 'No such thing exists. I tell you it is a lie.'

'Shh, wait, I think there's more,' Gopal told them, leaning forward to turn up the radio.

They all went silent. The radio crackled and hissed and spat. And then, very faintly, words emerged. But the words sounded far away and they were in English, so they had listened to the strange language without understanding what it was saying or where it came from.

No one had noticed the bright red ball roll past.

'What is he saying?' Vilas Rao had demanded.

'Why can't he speak in a language people can understand?'

'Those were the words of the first man on the moon,' the announcer said clearly in Hindi.

In the tea shop there was total silence.

'Those filthy land-hungry Angrezs! Now they've gone and put their barbarian feet on the face of our moon. Who do they think they are?' Vilas Rao was the first to speak.

In the distance, wrapped in a cloud of dust, a truck moved ponderously towards Nandgaon.

'Someone should teach those bloodsuckers a lesson. They mustn't be allowed to grab everything they see. One day they'll come here and take our land too,' he added, and the others nodded silently.

Gopal Mundkur said nothing, but in his heart he was thrilled. Unlike the others he'd been to Mumbai, had lived and worked there. He had seen aeroplanes and cars and double-decker buses. He had seen Americans, looked them in their blue eyes as he handed them their train tickets.

'Gopal, you are very quiet. What do you think?' Vilas Rao had asked.

'It is not that I don't agree,' Gopal had replied slowly. 'But the road to the moon has been opened; it's only a matter of time before everyone will use it. How can you stop that?'

'What road? You think one day people will be driving around in trucks on the moon? The sun's got into your head,' Vilas Rao had scoffed. 'Besides, the moon belongs to the gods, it doesn't belong to humans in trucks. Terrible things will come of this. The gods won't forget.'

'Shh. Listen, it's the Prime Minister,' Govind Rao had interrupted him, leaning into the radio.

The radio crackled, spat and cleared its throat.

'Turn it up Gopal,' Vilas Rao, the eldest, had ordered.

No one saw the child suddenly spot his beloved ball resting in a pothole in the middle of the highway. Nor did they see the smile of joy that lit his face as he turned and trotted sturdily out into the middle of the road on his short plump legs.

On the radio the Prime Minister was congratulating the brave American astronauts. 'No one will forget this day. The world has shrunk and grown at the same time to include the stars. Mankind's future has grown bright. . .' The rest was swallowed by the screech of brakes and rubber as the truck swerved and tried to stop at the same time, the horrified driver seeing the little child too late.

Gopal Mundkur swallowed. Even thirty-eight years later the memory still hurt like a fresh wound. 'It is fate. Your child was too good for this world,' the elders had said to him. 'Look, your wife is already five months pregnant. Soon you will have another son to replace the one you have lost. That is God's way.'

Gopal had listened to their words in silence and pretended to be comforted. But in the depths of the night, he had allowed himself to cry. It was all his fault, he admitted to himself. He was the one who had mocked the gods the day the Americans had touched the moon, he was the one who had dreamed in secret that a man could be bigger than his fate. The gods had known, and they had punished him.

'Take that goat away,' he cried and immediately two servants untied the animal and led it away. 'Don't kill it, give it back to Chhannu,' he ordered. He looked hard at the crowd of expectant faces, reminding himself that it wasn't for one person that rules were made, but for the entire village. But Chhannu was a good man – a good worker, a good husband, a good chief, a good father. How he wished he could have done things differently! He called Mahendra to his side and whispered in his ear, 'Have someone tell him that his son doesn't have to leave until he is well. But the boy should not go into the village.'

'Next,' he called, banging his stick on the ground. He looked with relief at the man entering the gate, his lips curving upwards in the beginnings of a smile. Of all the men in the village, Darbari the barber was probably the one he liked most, and trusted least. For Darbari was too intelligent for his lowly station in life, and he was always in debt. As children they had studied together under the same tree and as young adolescents they had wrestled together though Darbari was by far the better wrestler. Darbari was followed by his two youngest sons, the twins Sushil and Samir. He looked frail and sickly – except for the thick head of salt and pepper hair that refused to go white. 'They just won't stop fighting, Patelji,' he complained. 'I can't control them so I want you to punish them.' The headman looked at the two boys and then at Darbari. 'Send them to me; I need help for the sugar cane cutting. I will make them work like bulls, and if that is not enough, I will tie them to the plough instead of my bulls,' he said loudly. Darbari's face split into a huge smile. 'Thank you, thank you. I knew you'd do what's right, Patelji.'

At last there was no one left. The ache in Gopal's head had grown until it seemed like a giant boulder was pressing into his brain. 'So, that was easy,' Gopal said trying to ignore the pain. 'Seems we have a happy village today.'

'Nandgaon is a contented village, Patelji, because of you,' Mahendra, replied from behind.

'You flatter me, Mahendrabhai.' The headman laughed shakily. 'Perhaps Umno Devi is looking our way.'

'Being an ungodly citywala, Patelji,' Mahendra replied,

laughing, 'I have no faith in your Umno Devi. It takes a man to understand men, and to keep order.' Mahendra was referring to Chhannu Mahadev, for he knew that Gopal was feeling bad about it. Gopal smiled gratefully at his best friend. He had learnt early on that as headman the only person one could trust was a man from the outside. Mahendra was the one thing that Gopal had brought back with him from the city. He was an accountant by profession, a middle-class native of the city – until he'd become an addict. They had met in the crowded compartment of a Mumbai suburban train. Mahendra, who at the time had just become a heroine user, had tried to pick Gopal's pocket but the latter had caught him in the act. Mahendra had done his best to escape but the compartment was so packed with bodies that neither had been able to move. So they'd travelled the entire way from Mumbai Central to Andheri holding hands like lovers. At the station when Gopal had dragged Mahendra out of the train in order to hand him over to the police, Mahendra had fallen at his feet begging Gopal to let him go. He'd promised to do anything Gopal asked of him in return and so Gopal had taken pity on the man. Together they'd gone to a nearby restaurant and Mahendra had told Gopal his story. After that Gopal had accompanied him to a nearby dealer and bought him his last hit of heroine. Then he brought Mahendra back to Nandgaon.

'And your hand also, Mahendrabhai; without your work here, there would be no order in Nandgaon,' Gopal said fondly. 'Not one of my sons knows half as much about the village as you. Come, let us go inside.'

But as usual, Mahendra refused, mumbling that he had work to do. And so the headman levered himself up with the aid of his stick and went into the smaller courtyard where four charpoys had been laid out in the centre in anticipation of the evening's visitors. Gopal settled himself comfortably on one of the charpoys. The evening sky was indigo now, and the servants rushed around the courtyard placing oil lamps in the niches in the walls. The lamplight illuminated a host of familiar faces – sons, daughters in law, granddaughters, grandsons, nephews, nieces, great-nieces. All of them seemed so happy and contented, so confident that nothing terrible could ever happen to them. Normally the sight warmed his heart, but today he felt disconnected from his family – as if his memories themselves had become a trap, separating him from them.

When he was made the headman after his father's death, he had sworn he would protect Nandgaon. And yet, in spite of all his efforts, the filth from the cities still managed to find a way in. Every week a salesman on a motorcycle arrived promising unimaginable wealth with little effort. Some of his people fell under the spell of those men, and they suffered. Only last month Vasantrao Amrate had been the latest victim, losing his entire crop of wheat because the fertiliser he'd bought had burnt away the roots. Of course, the slick, smooth-talking salesman had forgotten to tell him that the fertiliser required double the water and if the plants didn't get that, the fertiliser would burn away the roots. Vasantrao had been horrified when the headman told him.

'But I told the man I was going to use it on my poorer fields, those that got little water and therefore gave me little yield,' he had exclaimed. 'I showed him the fields.'

Gopal had said nothing, not wanting to increase Vasantrao's rage. 'Here,' he'd offered, 'take this grain with you and come back tomorrow with your bullock cart.'

'B-but Patelji, I c-can't.' Vasantrao had begun to cry, the relief in his face bringing smiles of approval to the faces of those who had been there then.

It wasn't only the salesman with their miracle grains and fertilisers, but the government as well who'd become thieves. Nowadays not a season passed without some government official coming to them with some scheme to steal their land. Gopal smiled wryly, remembering how six or seven years ago, a new Block Development Officer (BDO) had arrived in Nandgaon and informed him that every family would have to give up a little bit of land because the government was going to put in a piped water supply system so that each family would be able to turn a tap and get water in its own house. 'No more handpumps,' he had said triumphantly, as if no other explanation were needed. But the headman knew what had happened in other villages. Though Nandgaon was effectively cut off from the world, he had kept up with the world all the same, making frequent visits to the district headquarters in Khandwa and listening carefully to what people from other villages had to say.

'Where will the water come from?' he had asked innocently.

'From the river, of course,' the BDO had answered condescendingly. 'We will make a small dam about three kilometres upstream and feed the water into a piped water system. The pipes will carry the water to your homes. We have already picked a perfect site. The river narrows and deepens into a natural pool because of rocks. All we need to do is build a little wall between the rocks and place feeder pipes in it.'

Gopal had pretended to be impressed. 'How much will all this cost?' he had asked submissively.

'About fourteen million rupees,' the BDO had answered promptly.

'But that is a huge sum,' Gopal had said, pretending to be aghast. 'A hand-pump in the aangan* only costs fifteen thousand rupees to install. We have only a hundred and forty families in the village and a third of them have hand pumps already. The rest can have one too if you only give us fourteen lakhs.

* courtyard

That is one tenth of what you are proposing to spend. Now what will our share of this money be? Or are you going to do it all for nothing?'

'The government will provide most of the money,' the BDO had replied. 'You need to raise only ten per cent, and you can give it through shram daan*. We will need quite a lot of labour for the project. In any case,' he had added, 'the project is not for your village alone, but for the entire block.' Gopal knew that this was the main reason why the BDO was here. There were ninety-three villages in the block; all but a few of them lay downstream of Nandgaon. The piped water system could not be laid if the village did not give up some of its land.

'I think it is a wonderful idea,' he had said after what he hoped was a long enough pause. 'I will put it before the panchayat. But you must realise, Sahib, that I am only their servant. I can push them to accept the project and I will, but it is they who will decide.'

That had been the end of it! The BDO had come a few more times and had even sent for him when he lost his patience. But there was another election and he and his party were thrown out of power.

His eldest daughter-in-law Savitribai arrived with another cup of tea, putting an end to his ruminations. She was carefully and expensively dressed as usual. 'You came early, that is why your tea wasn't ready,' she said a little breathlessly. 'There is no one left?'

'No. No one. We have a contented village this evening,' Gopal replied, echoing Mahendra's words.

'Of course, Father-in-law,' she agreed readily. 'Thanks to you, the goddess Laxmi herself smiles upon us all.'

* free labour

115

She cast him a speculative look from under her eyelashes as she knelt down to light the mosquito coil near his feet. No one had shared his bed for eight years. He had to want a woman sometimes. What if he married again? She could not bear the thought of another woman ordering her around. She would not have minded sharing his bed, but he had never even given her a second glance. Was he truly the man of iron the villagers believed him to be? Somehow Savitribai doubted it. All men had a weakness. It was a woman's job to find it.

Gopal watched his daughter-in-law's long, red-tipped fingers as she lit the match. Flattery made him uneasy, especially when it came from a woman. Though she had never done anything to displease him or to bring shame upon the family, he could not bring himself to like his eldest son's wife. Her words and actions were always designed to please. But the showy way in which she dressed gave lie to her actions. Savitribai must have sensed some of what her father-in-law was thinking for her good-looking face with its carefully applied lipstick paled. 'Can I get you something else, Patelji?' she asked, careful not to look directly at him.

'Have my hookah readied,' he ordered gruffly, taking the cup from her and sniffing at the fragrant liquid. But it was still too hot to be drunk and so he set cup and saucer down and waited for the tea to cool. His son Gajendra should have chosen a better wife. As she turned away, he glimpsed the gleam of gold around Savitribai's waist. So, the cunning woman had managed to wangle yet another piece of jewellery out of her fool of a husband, he thought wryly.

A dry cough made him turn. 'Ram, Ram, Patelji, may the gods always bless you and your family, may Laxmi Devi herself fill your rooms with gold and your fields with grain,' Bicchoo said unctuously. The headman frowned. It was unlucky for a gambler to wish a man luck. Bicchoo had to know that. Though Bicchoo was quite a close relative, being his eldest sister's son, the headman had never been able to bring himself to like him. For Bicchoo's specialty was always knowing or guessing, long before anyone else, what was going on in the village. And yet his information, like the curved tail of the scorpion which gave him his nickname, had a sting, or else was somehow tailored to serve a purpose of which Bicchoo was inevitably the beneficiary. For example, it was Bicchoo who had told the headman about how sugar cane was making the farmers in the surrounding villages rich beyond their wildest expectations. The headman had cross-checked when he had next visited Khandwa and indeed Bicchoo's information had been right, so he dug up his best field and put sugar cane in there instead. The next day, Bicchoo arrived and asked for a loan. The headman was forced to give it to him and of course, he still hadn't seen a penny of it.

'You again, what do you want?' he said gruffly.

Bicchoo smiled his famous smile. 'Patelji, I want only what is best for you and your family.'

'Naturally, who but me would give you money?' he said sarcastically.

'How can you say that, cousin? I just want to share with you a story.'

'Ah, just a story? Since when has a story earned money?' the headman asked, intrigued. This was a novel approach.

Bicchoo's face broke into a smile. 'You are most kind to listen to a man like me, cousin. But I am afraid that the story of my misfortune will bore you who are so favoured by the gods. Perhaps it would be better if I went away.'

The headman laughed. 'And you are favoured with the sweetest tongue of any man born in this state. Come on, let me hear it.'

Bicchoo sat down on the top step. 'I was ploughing my field, Patelji Sahib,' he began politely, 'with Gauri and Raja. They are good animals, mukhiya Sahib. Well mannered, courageous, humble and strong.'

'Yes, yes,' he cut him off. 'I gave them to you as a wedding gift, don't you remember? It is a wonder you haven't gambled them away yet.'

Bicchoo opened his eyes wide, he understood the game. 'What are you saying, Patelji? I would never do that. Even we gamblers have our pride. But I don't gamble for myself, I do it for my family. And only on sure things.'

'Yes, of course.'

Bicchoo sighed theatrically. 'I am just unlucky, Patelji. It is all my mother's fault – she had to send me into this world on amaavasya* night.'

'Indeed,' the headman agreed, 'it was most unkind.'

'You think so?' Bicchoo asked doubtfully, the headman's willingness to agree unnerving him more than a shouting or even a beating would have.

'Of course, what man can fight against fate?' the headman said, enjoying himself. 'Now tell me what happened.'

He returned hesitantly to his role. 'Of course, forgive me, it is just that my tongue is slower than my brain; no, my brain is slower than my tongue, I think.' He began to speak very fast. 'I was ploughing the north-west end of the field with Gauri and Raja when a tiger erupted out of the forest and ran on to the field right in front of us. I shut my eyes, convinced we were facing our end. Then before I could do anything, Raja, our dear sweet docile Raja, let out a roar and leapt at it, pulling Gauri and me along. We flew across the field like Indra in his chariot, and then the plough hit a stone, and I went flying out of my seat and hit the earth. Everything went black. I thought I was dead, then my eyes opened and there was Raja, and Gauri still attached to the cart. The gods had been kind, I thought, and I said a quick prayer. When my eyes opened I

* new moon

118

saw the plough. And then, I began to curse the gods and curse all animals too, though I know I should not have. But what could I do, the plough was broken.' He paused for effect. 'I am just the world's most unlucky man.'

The headman remained silent for a long time, savouring the growing discomfort of the man before him. 'Where is it?' he said finally.

'Huh?' Bicchoo looked startled.

'Where is the broken plough?' the headman repeated. 'Show it to me and I will give you the money for a new one.'

'The plough? I haven't brought it with me.'

'Then go and get it, stupid.' He gave the man a gentle kick to emphasise his words. 'Hurry up.'

'Oh yes, the plough. Of course, how silly of me not to bring it,' Bicchoo babbled. He stood up reluctantly, turned and began to walk to the gate. Suddenly he stopped, then turned back. 'Patelji,' he said, his face a tragic mask, 'I just remembered, the plough, it was stolen.'

'Stolen?' the headman asked, hugely enjoying himself. 'How is that? Who could want a broken plough?'

'The hyenas stole it. You know what thieves they are,' Bicchoo replied, sweating visibly.

'Oh, the hyenas. Of course, I should have thought of that. They would want a plough to clean their teeth, am I not right?'

Bicchoo nodded eagerly. 'I wondered why they wanted the plough myself. You are so clever, Patelji.'

Gopal stood up. 'Get out,' he roared, banging his stick on the ground. 'Do you think I have become so old? I already gave you money for your plough last week. Do you think I have forgotten? Get out of my sight, you miserable liar, or I will have you beaten up.'

Bicchoo backed away. 'I'll just get it, of course I will,' he stammered. But he knew he was beaten. After a few steps he turned and ran to the safety of the gate.

The headman sat down once more. For a few minutes he just sat there, both hands clasped tightly around the head of his cane. Suddenly a laugh shook his frame. 'Hyenas,' he gasped. 'What will the man think of next?'

But by the time the first of his nightly guests arrived, the slight depression that had dogged him since the time he'd woken up had returned.

'You're looking very serious this evening,' Vilas Rao remarked, his grandfatherly face looking concerned. After the headman, Vilas Rao was the richest man in the village but unlike the headman he had never left Nandgaon to see the world, contenting himself with managing his family's extensive holdings and fathering innumerable children. The two had been friends almost since the day they were born, playing as toddlers, for their mothers had been close friends, stealing mangoes, learning to swim, playing hookie from school and hiding in the fields, breaking the girls' water pots with their slingshots and wrestling together. And where Gopal led, Vilas Rao, lacking the imagination and intelligence of the former, was content to follow. The relationship was cemented once and for all when Gopal married Vilas Rao's sister. The marriage, which was arranged by their respective parents, made sure that there would never be any feud between the two most powerful families in the village and so the entire village had approved heartily. What surprised everyone was that the two men's friendship became stronger than ever after the death of the headman's wife. No one, least of all Vilas Rao himself, had appreciated the depth of Gopal's love for his best friend's sister. The headman gave a start and smiled wanly. 'Oh, it's you.'

'Yes, it is me. Who did you think it would be?' Vilas Rao, older than the headman by ten months, sat down with some difficulty.

'I don't know. I was just thinking. . .' the headman said

dismissively.

'Don't think too much. At your age, it can only harm you. Get married again, to a very young juicy girl.'

'At our age?' The headman raised an eyebrow.

'Why, at our age one doesn't think at all. One becomes a young man again. The women love it.' He chuckled as he remembered something. Then he looked at the headman and lowered his voice. 'You should have seen me last night,' he said proudly. 'The new tantric doctor who moved into Tiger Baba's cave last year has some very special medicines. He gave me some and wah! I became a tiger myself.'

The headman laughed. 'That is your wife's magic not the medicine's. Not everyone is lucky enough to have a young, beautiful wife.'

'But you could have one easily. You are young still and handsome,' Vilas Rao persisted, pointing to his own snow white head, 'and your hair is still grey.'

But Gopal knew he wasn't young any more – and didn't particularly mind. The thought of a pair of critical young eyes looking at his body made him shrink. 'And how is the gaumata?' he asked, changing the subject. Gaumata was the village's nickname for their only tractor, used mainly to transport the sick – animals or people – to the hospital.

'Almost ran over a goat today. Don't understand why people can't look after their animals better.' Vilas Rao stopped suddenly, looking stricken as he remembered the headman's first son. 'I'm sorry,' he mumbled.

For a few seconds the headman didn't reply. 'I think you should go and get that brake repaired soon,' he said when he felt in control of his voice.

'Of course, tomorrow, how stupid.' Vilas Rao tugged at his moustache, relieved. 'I heard the price of milk is going to fall,' he added, changing the subject yet again.

The headman shook his head. 'That is what they always say

when they buy our milk. It is the only way they can justify their ridiculously low prices.'

'But this time it will happen,' Vilas Rao insisted. 'It wasn't the government dairy people who told me. The man who told me worked in the sugar factory. He said that the dairy cooperative had just offered to buy the sugar factory.'

'What?' The headman sat up, startled. 'You mean the Khandwa sugar mill? But it has been making losses for years.'

'Precisely. But people say that Rajnath Patel has contributed a crore to Rameshwar Chauhan's election fund and in return the Dairy Welfare Cooperative Society will buy the mill. So milk prices will have to fall.'

'So now the farmers will have to pay themselves for the sugar cane they produce?' The headman gave a bitter laugh. 'In from one pocket and out the other. What a world. Thank God we don't have to be a part of it.'

'But what about your sugar cane? What will you do with it?' he asked.

The headman shrugged. 'Burn it, probably.'

Vilas Rao looked worriedly at his brother-in-law but was saved from having to think of something to say by the arrival of the priest, Saraswati Rane. Once upon a time, the pundit had been as good a wrestler as the headman but today even the most wildly imaginative of men would have been hard pressed to see the wrestler inside that smooth flabby chest. Saraswati Rane's face had changed too, Gopal reflected as he watched the village priest approach. The years had whipped the flesh off his face, hollowing out his cheeks and making his well-cut lips almost non-existent. Now his nose preceded him, rising beaklike from between close-set eyes ringed with dark circles. And, though he was a vegetarian, he always had bad breath. Gopal sighed, remembering Saraswati Rane's radiant face when together they had taken the wrestling trophy out of the hands of neighbouring Kesarigaon.

Beside Saraswati Rane limped his cousin, Jaiwant Rane, the village schoolteacher. He too had been a great wrestler, some said even better than Gopal himself. Like Gopal, Jaiwant Rane had lived outside Nandgaon. But while the headman had failed the test for the army because of his weak eyesight and had joined the railways instead, Jaiwant Rane had passed and was accepted into the army. Then one day he had returned to Nandgaon – minus half a leg. He claimed a Pakistani bullet got him when he was fighting on the Siachen, the world's highest glacier, but Gopal suspected that Jaiwant had shot himself in the knee in order to escape that icy hellhole. In the railways he had met many with similar injuries who had been given jobs there. Those men had told him about the glacier and how the air was so thin that it made men starve themselves to death.

'Radhe Shyam, Ram Ram.' Saraswati Rane, wrapped in his pristine white dhoti, his chest bare except for the sacred thread, his head bald except for the tiny knot of hair that marked his caste, greeted them. His sharp eyes took in those who were already assembled there and then he asked, 'Has Govind Rao not arrived yet?'

The others looked uncomfortable.

'Not yet. He must be helping Sushilabai close the shop,' Vilas Rao replied.

'It isn't right for a high-caste man like him to have a shop,' the priest remarked, looking slyly at the headman.

The headman pretended not to have noticed. In his heart of hearts he agreed with the priest but Govind Rao was a friend, even if he wasn't at all popular, for his shop was twice as expensive as the city shops and when people borrowed money from him, he charged much more interest than the headman. But Gopal knew that Govind Rao's behavior, though astonishing in a man of his caste, wasn't his fault. It ran in his family.

Many was the time that Gopal's father, then Patel of Nandgaon, had had to intervene in order to get Govind Rao's father to return a piece of land he had illegally taken. Yet, despite the bad blood between the families, when Gopal's first son had died, Govind Rao had made a point of visiting Gopal every evening, much to the amazement of the others. Eventually, the others had grown used to having him amongst them. 'Unfortunately a village cannot survive on food and prayer, Punditji; it needs its oil and soap and sweets,' he said lightly. 'Anyway, here he comes now.'

Govind Rao arrived, out of breath as usual. He sat down heavily on the charpoy that was reserved for him and wiped his face with the edge of his gamcha. 'I am growing old,' he said sighing heavily. 'I can't move as fast I used to.'

'When did you ever move fast, Govindbhai?' Vilas Rao teased.

The others burst into laughter and even Govind Rao joined in good-humouredly. Of all those present, he was the one that looked the most like a wrestler gone to seed. Yet Govind Rao had never struck even a fly in all his life. As a child he had been the fattest boy in the village. But his weight had been balanced by his kindness and generosity – until he'd married Sushilabai. She was as thin as he was fat, and her love of money was as great as Govind Rao's love of good food.

'How is Sushilabai?' Saraswati Rane asked. 'She doesn't come to our kirtan any more.'

Govind Rao looked uncomfortable. 'Of course she will come. She has not been well lately.'

Satisfied, the pundit turned on the headman next. 'What are your plans for Gangaur Puja this year? Have you asked the kirtan singers yet? And what about a new sound system? The one you hired last year was useless. Surely there is a better one to be found in Khandwa?'

The headman laughed, shaking his head at the same time.

'Saraswatibhai, the festival is six months away. You just got a fistful of money out of me today, and already you are thinking of new ways to take more?'

But the pujari only laughed. 'I am a servant of God, Gopalbhai,' he said. 'I can't let you replace him, no matter how efficient you are.'

The others, surprised by the priest's audacity, looked at the headman anxiously. Vilas Rao hurriedly asked him a question. 'Gopalbhai, was that Bicchoo I saw hanging around the gate? What did he want this time? I can't understand how you put up with him.'

The headman laughed. 'He tells good stories, that's why. He makes me laugh. The man is wasted in Nandgaon. He should be in Mumbai, writing stories for movies.'

The others looked relieved. 'What story did he tell this time?'

'Lies, you mean,' Jaiwant Rane interjected sanctimoniously.

The headman ignored him. 'Ah, this one was in a class of its own,' he said, leaning forward and rubbing his hands together. 'He tried to get money out of me for a lost plough.'

'A plough?' Vilas Rao exclaimed. 'How can you lose a plough?'

'The hyenas took it,' the headman replied, his face poker straight.

The others burst into laughter – even Saraswati Rane, the priest, and Jaiwant Rane, the schoolmaster. When they stopped, Vilas Rao begged the headman to tell them the whole story and they all laughed again. Then servants brought more food and a contented silence descended upon the group.

'I have a story,' Gajendra Mundkur, the headman's eldest surviving son, said. Everyone turned to stare at the man. Gajendra hardly ever spoke, especially not in front of his father and his friends. None of those present could remember when they'd last heard him say more than two words.

The headman himself was perhaps the most surprised. 'Go on then,' he said gruffly, not looking at his son.

Now that he had their attention, Gajendra's fair skin flushed with excitement. 'This afternoon,' he began nervously, looking at his father, 'while you were sleeping, Father, one of those salesmen you are always warning us against came by,' he paused looking deliberately at each person, 'pretending to be a doctor. He asked to speak to you, said he wanted to talk to you about our cows.'

'What! We don't sell our cows!' the headman interrupted him, feeling embarrassed that his son should betray his greed in front of his friends.

'I. . . uh. . . that is exactly what I thought, Father. So I sent him away,' Gajendra agreed, licking his pale lips nervously.

No one said anything, politely waiting for Gajendra to continue. But when he didn't, Bicchoo, who had quietly sneaked inside under cover of darkness, asked, 'And did he go away?'

'He did,' Gajendra replied eagerly. 'I sent a servant out who told him my father was at Ramu's.'

'Ramu's? Why Ramu's?' the headman asked.

'Because Ramu has a very fine cow,' Gajendra replied, straight-faced.

A moment's astonished silence followed. Then Vilas Rao laughed, followed by Govind Rao and the others. The headman was the last to join in, as he struggled to master contradictory emotions – pride at the way his son had handled things, dismay that he had not been consulted. 'Well done,' he said at last, looking at his son, 'you did well.'

'Your son is smart, just like his father,' Govind Rao added sincerely.

CHAPTER EIGHT

THE MAKING OF AN INSEMINATOR

The return to KIRD went smoothly. Luck travelled with Manoj and at each crossroad or fork in the path he took the right turn. Nevertheless, when he finally hit tarmac, he was relieved. Bike and biker flew across the smooth skin of the road. As he neared the Institute, he began to feel elated. The night air was cool against his skin. A giant moon smiled down upon him from a silver and velvet sky. He remembered his mother's voice warning him: 'If you fall down too often you will end with a face as pitted and scarred as the moon's.'

He hadn't fallen down much as he'd learnt to ride the Enfield – though at first he hadn't liked the machine at all, finding it bulky, smelly and incredibly unwieldy. By the time his turn came to go out, he'd mastered it sufficiently to know he wouldn't fall off. The grounds of KIRD had been bathed in an almost supernatural light when he left for his initial raid. When he returned, dawn had already begun to lighten the sky. But in the darkness of his pocket lay half of a cow's tail, the talisman of his failure and source of his reborn shame.

He had roared around the administrative buildings past the animal sheds where his bull Govinda slept, not wanting to face the moment when he would have to bring the tail out. But they were waiting for him in the 'laboratory' with glasses in their hands – trainees, colleagues, teachers, friends. So he went in, and lied. 'Yeah, it was just as you said, really easy.' He hoped his voice was steady. 'Nothing to it.' He did not tell them about the village and the pathetic creature he'd inseminated. He did not tell them that he had given another villager a hundred rupees to let him cut off the bottom half of his cow's tail. He'd broken the glass reeds containing the rest of the semen on the ruins of a temple in a field of peas.

To his surprise they believed him. Dr Pandey had been the first to raise his glass in a toast. 'Congratulations, welcome to the Hell's Inseminators club,' he had said. Since then Manoj had lived a lie and the lie had slowly soured every moment he spent at KIRD until at last, his training completed, he asked permission to leave.

Manikbhai had been genuinely surprised. 'But why Mishra? I have had really excellent reports on you. In fact, I was going to tell your father-in-law so myself. I leave this afternoon for Mumbai and we are meeting tonight for dinner.'

'Thank you,' Manoj had mumbled, 'that is very kind. It is not that I don't want to do this kind of work – I do. But I feel that my services will be better appreciated just over the border in Madhya Pradesh which is so backward still. KIRD has done its work too well here.'

Manikbhai was not immune to flattery and so he forgot his original question and just beamed. 'Aha, we have turned you into a true Hell's Inseminator, I see. Before you leave, make Pandey teach you how to make our special "milk".' Encouraged, Manoj brought up the subject of Govinda. But this time he said it was because he wanted to set up a small branch of KIRD himself.

Manikbhai had been most generous. He'd sold the animal for just ten thousand rupees. With Govinda packed into the back of a pick-up truck they said their goodbyes and left for Khandwa. Manoj vowed he would never touch 'milk' again.

Khandwa was a provincial headquarters and market town for

the surrounding villages. Manoj had chosen it because it was in a relatively backward part of Madhya Pradesh, on the border with Maharashtra, and living was cheap. But the farmers had discovered the new long staple cotton, and there was a palpable air of affluence which he hadn't noticed the first time he'd stumbled upon it. As soon as they had arrived, Manoj had begun work on the dairy, buying the materials himself, haggling with the wholesale merchants, the contractors and the suppliers. In less than two months the land had been cleared and the building materials bought and paid for, the workers hired and the foundations begun. Then Pratima had had her stupid idea of a havan.

'What is wrong in getting the gods' blessings?' she'd argued hotly.

'Nothing wrong. But it's expensive. And I hate giving money away for nothing,' he'd replied.

She hadn't replied but the look she'd given him spoke volumes: the money, it said, wasn't his really, it was hers, the last of the enormous dowry her industrialist father had given him. He'd looked away and said no more.

And so the preparations for the havan began and grew more and more burdensome with twenty priests and a goat and gifts for all of them, and a feast for the workers for which special Brahmin cooks had to be hired. Eventually Pratima had announced that she was ready and that the havan would take place that Sunday. She'd forced him to wake early, bathe, shave and dress in the fine silk dhoti she'd bought him. And once he'd sat down beside the pundit, he'd felt that maybe the gods did have some part to play.

But in the middle of the puja, the police had arrived, arresting him and confiscating everything on the site. When he was released, the site was all tied up in yellow tape and he was drowned in fines and legal notices from the municipality. He tried telling the police he'd applied for the licences four months earlier through a lawyer, but they wouldn't hear of it. Eventually Pratima had saved him. She'd gone to see the deputy commissioner and though she steadfastly refused to tell him what she'd told the man, the very next day he had been freed. The lawyer of course had taken his money – their money, he corrected himself, for after all they were still living on Pratima's dowry – and disappeared. So Manoj went back to roaming the countryside on his Enfield. He searched in vain for his perfect village, but no amount of questioning revealed the slightest bit of information about the whereabouts of the place as he'd forgotten its name and all he could remember were the paintings on the walls.

'Paintings on walls, Sahib?' The villagers had looked at him with polite puzzlement. 'In our parents, and grandparents, days all the villages had them. Today, who has the time?'

One night when Manoj returned to Khandwa after yet another fruitless day of wandering, he found the house was in darkness. That surprised him, for Pratima always turned on all the lights in their house at the first approach of night. A house that was called Asha Kutir had to have lots of light spilling out of it, she always said, for otherwise how would it give hope to others? Personally he thought the darkness suited it better, hiding its boxy outline and peeling façade.

He opened the garden gate and climbed the steps to the porch. It was locked. He knocked. No answer. So he went around the side to the main door. On it was taped an envelope. He tore it open. Inside the envelope was an invitation, and the house key. The mystery had resolved itself. He knew where his wife had gone.

The invitation had come a week ago. It was more of a summons than an invitation. *Deputy Commissioner Choudhury and Mrs Helen Choudhury request the pleasure of your company at a dinner.* It was badly typed on cheap paper. But the letter had Ashoka's lions in red on the top and 'Deputy Commissioner's Office' typed on the top left-hand corner – that's all Pratima had cared about. She'd been so proud of the invitation she'd propped it on the dining table so they could look at it as they ate. He had sneered at her, calling her a snob and a social climber. She'd hung her head but that hadn't stopped her from going out and buying a gift for the deputy commissioner's wife and a new kurta and shaving kit for him. In his heart he was both anxious and relieved. He needed the deputy commissioner if his dairy was ever to function. He showered and shaved quickly, then dressed himself in the kurta she'd bought him.

The deputy commissioner's house was a square brick structure painted the ubiquitous ivory colour of all government buildings. But the garden was well looked after and full of flowers. The lawn itself was cut in two by an impressively broad driveway in which an official-looking white Ambassador, complete with aerials and red flashing light, was parked.

The white back of the uniformed servant led him through a small hall with a staircase at one end, through a door on the right and into a large square room. There was a fireplace built into one wall. Manoj wondered fleetingly which architect had dreamed this up for a town where the mercury seldom went below fifteen degrees Celsius.

There were seven people in the room, three men and four women. The women were sitting in a tight little group, his wife in the middle looking very uncomfortable. The men were standing by the mantelpiece, drinks in hand. Another white-robed waiter was busy refilling the glass of one of them, a khadi kurta-clad, moustached man who could only have been a politician. Manoj took a deep breath. In spite of himself he was a little overwhelmed by it all, the Kashmiri carpet, the servants, the stiff government-issue furniture and especially the people. He'd never met either a politician or a bureaucrat this important before.

A short hairy man detached himself and came up to Manoj. 'So you are our newest troublemaker? Welcome to my humble house,' he said humorously, looking back at the others. He looked exactly like his voice, businesslike but reassuring. Dressed casually in a pale blue safari suit, he nonetheless had a very expensive gold watch and a ruby ring on his left hand. Manoj took all of this in as the deputy commissioner was saying, 'We didn't think you were going to join our poor dinner party.'

Manoj looked down, shamefaced. 'Sorry sir, I got lost in the countryside. Many roads that are marked on the map are actually non-existent.'

Deputy Commissioner Choudhury scowled. 'Rubbish. The roads are all there, you just got lost, that's all. You shouldn't blame the roads. Anyway, better late than never, eh? Come, have a drink and forget about it. What is your poison? Whisky? Gin? Rum?'

'Thank you, but I don't drink,' Manoj replied. 'Some water will be fine.'

'Water?' The deputy commissioner's puffy face looked put out. 'All right,' he said grumpily, then ordered, 'Ek soft drink le ao,' in an unnecessarily loud voice.

He introduced the others. The tall man in white kurta pyjamas was a local congressman and the other man, also in a safari suit, was a lawyer. Choudhury didn't bother introducing Manoj to the women sitting on the other side of the room. Pratima, looking tense and miserable, gave him a relieved smile but he ignored her, focusing on the men around him.

The congressman gave Manoj a polite smile while the lawyer accorded him only the slightest of nods. Though they were curious about him, they'd been briefed by the deputy commissioner already. Social workers were troublesome people, always sticking their nose into what didn't concern them, filing petitions demanding information about budget allocations and generally making a nuisance of themselves. But the deputy commissioner, being a pragmatic man, had decided that it was better to try to co-opt a potential problem rather than let it run loose and directionless. This philosophy he'd been in the process of explaining to his friends when Manoj had arrived.

'See, sir, there are two ways to deal with a potential problem. Either you can destroy it or you can absorb it and turn the problem into the solution.'

'What do you mean?' his friend and crony, Ghorpekar, the lawyer, asked.

'I mean,' he paused for effect and lowered his voice, 'do you watch the National Geographic channel? Have you seen the series on killer spiders?'

The others said nothing, waiting for him to continue. If such a remarkable sentence had come from anyone else it would have been ridiculed.

'Spiders do exactly that. Once they catch a creature in their web, they use every bit of their victim's body – hair, bones, enzymes – in the construction of their own proper webs. See, that is smart. That way, no evidence is left.'

'So what exactly do you plan to do with this young man?' the congressman demanded. 'Be careful, his father-in-law donates generously to the Congress party. Questions would be asked if he were to disappear.'

'Oh no sir, nothing like that,' the deputy commissioner replied, looking horrified. 'But if he is determined to do social work then it is better he does what I want him to do so that the government can get the credit. That is all I meant.'

The congressman wasn't completely convinced. 'You should be careful when you go around comparing the government to a killer spider,' he warned. 'People might take it the wrong way.'

Once Manoj had been absorbed into the group, the men

returned to an earlier topic of conversation.

'What makes small towns such as this so special,' the Congressman said, using his well cared-for hands to emphasise his point, 'is that everyone knows each other. So there is no crime.'

'Exactly,' the deputy commissioner agreed, nodding his large head enthusiastically, 'and I want to keep it that way. Do you know that in my three years in the district there has not been a single violent death?'

'Keep it that way,' the politician said. 'We need people like you to guard the real India. The real India is in places such as this, far out of reach of the big cities. Our big cities are ruined; they are no longer representative of India. People cut each other's throats not for money, but for pleasure. Everywhere it is competition, competition. There is no place left for tradition, for the old values of family, respect for elders.' He finished his speech and smiled automatically at the others who were all nodding their agreement.

'Absolutely right, sir,' the deputy commisioner said. 'That is why I chose Madhya Pradesh as my state. I want to live and work close to the real India. So that it doesn't disappear.'

Manoj tried to think of something clever to say. 'But the real India needs to change too, if only to save it from becoming too perfect. Perfect is boring and that can make people stag-nate – if you know what I mean.' He looked intensely at the faces around him and those same faces stared back uncom-prehendingly. 'I mean, it is important to develop, to evolve,' he finished lamely, not sure of what exactly he'd been trying to say.

Luckily no one challenged him on it. 'So you like Khandwa then? That is good, good,' the deputy commissioner said, slapping him on his back.

'Of course, I am very happy to be here and to serve such a fine town,' Manoj replied, thinking of his dairy.

'But what exactly do you propose to do, young man?' the politician asked, his eyebrows raised. 'I know this town and the villages around here. They are not poor.' Manoj looked at him, surprised, wondering if he had been briefed about the dairy by the deputy commissioner.

He cleared his throat which had gone suddenly very dry. 'Not everyone here is rich,' he said. 'This area has its landless, its homeless, its families without livestock or prospects.'

'What are you talking about?' the Congressman spluttered. 'You are seeing poverty where there is none.'

'He has to sir, that's how he makes his living. Like me, I see a court case in everything,' the lawyer said, laughing.

They all laughed, even Manoj. 'No offence sir,' Manoj said more politely. 'I know this may not be the poorest part of the country, not like Bihar or Orissa, more like Maharashtra, yet there are many poor people here too, people whose children don't get milk, or education, or jobs.'

The deputy commissioner frowned, then chose to ignore Manoj's words.

'He wants to start a dairy, sir,' he said, turning to the congressman, 'and give milk for free to the poor. Right now he wanders the villages, inseminating cows while hunting for poor people. Hah, hah, hah.'

The others followed his cue and laughed loudly too.

'As long as he doesn't start inseminating the animals himself, I won't stop him. It is a free country after all,' the deputy commissioner added and they all roared with laughter again.

Manoj refused to join in. Obviously he was to be the evening's entertainment for these people. Well, let them laugh, he thought savagely. Soon it would be his turn. When he had the people on his side, he'd have the deputy commissioner licking his sandals.

'You are from Jaipur University I believe?' the congressman asked Manoj kindly, feeling the joke had gone far enough. 'My wife's uncle taught there for many years.'

'Yes sir,' Manoj replied.

'And what did you study there?'

'History.'

'Oh. That is unusual. No one studies history any more. My wife's uncle was a historian, I think.'

'And what was his name, sir?' Manoj asked curiously, succumbing to the politician's charm.

But before the latter could reply, the deputy commissioner cut in. 'I have been trying to persuade Mishra to start an ice-cream factory here, sir. Khandwa needs decent ice cream. He could start his own international brand, like that American company Baskin and Robbins. You must know the shop in Indore, sir, in Pleasant Mall? That would be a far greater social service to the community.' This time it was the politician who led the laughter.

Manoj was tempted to point out that it was the first time he was hearing of such a suggestion, but he wisely held his peace. He was not brave enough to antagonise a deputy commissioner.

On the other side of the room Pratima watched the men anxiously, her ears straining to catch their conversation. She saw them laugh and felt happy. Her husband was impressing them, without doubt. Then Helen Choudhury leaned over to her and asked her a question, and she forced her eyes away. 'Huh? Oh, I am from Mumbai,' she replied absently, vaguely aware that the subject under discussion had been origins.

'Which caste?' she asked again. 'They do have castes in Mumbai, right?'

'My father is a Kayastha, I think, my mother a Brahmin from Bengal.'

The air seemed to freeze as the women held their breaths,

digesting what she'd told them. 'Oh, an intercaste marriage, how modern of them,' Mrs Ghorpekar, the lawyer's wife, tittered.

'My father was in the army for a time; it was normal not to worry about a person's caste,' Pratima replied casually.

The lawyer's wife looked shocked. 'Thank God the army doesn't rule India,' she said feelingly. 'They would turn it into a mish-mash of people with no proper identity or traditions, don't you think, Mrs Amar Singh?' she asked the politican's wife.

'Of course, democracy is a good thing,' she answered absently, her eyes moving from her hands to the fireplace and back to her jewellery.

The other women stared hostilely at Pratima until Helen Choudhury ended it by saying brightly, 'And what about your husband? Mishras are Brahmins, no?'

'If you say so – I am not sure. We have never really discussed our caste origins,' said Pratima, feeling more and more uncomfortable.

'How modern.' The deputy commissioner's wife gave a tight smile.

'And how did you and your husband meet?' the congressman's wife, Mrs Amar Singh, suddenly asked.

'Well, our parents knew each other, or at least, our mothers did. They introduced us and. . .' Pratima stammered.

'An arranged marriage. How sensible,' Mrs Amar Singh interrupted, nodding approvingly. 'My husband and I were introduced too. And though my parents weren't rich, he preferred me to all the other girls he'd been shown.'

'How very clever of him, ma'am,' the deputy commissioner's wife gushed, 'but how could he not fall in love with someone, if I may say so, as beautiful as you?'

'You are too kind,' Mrs Amar Singh replied, looking pleased all the same.

Pratima's eyes went to her husband, standing a little apart from the others. How handsome he looked, she thought, how different from the others. She hoped he hadn't said anything awkward or rude.

'Have you found a good maid yet?' Mrs Ghorpekar asked Pratima suddenly.

'Yes, thank you. Her name is Anjali,' Pratima replied absently.

The deputy commissioner's wife leaned towards Pratima and said earnestly, 'I hope she isn't a tribal. Tribal girls, you know, have no morals. They come to the city to look for men, they get pregnant and when the men tell them to get lost, they come to you and cry and expect you to help them. They are stupid. They don't understand that they are being punished for having no morals. You should stay far away from them.'

Pratima said nothing.

Encouraged, Helen Choudhury continued. 'They really have no shame, these girls. Little better than savages, they are. I keep telling my husband that if I didn't have two small children to care for I would do something for these tribals, social work you know. They are hopeless, no morals.'

'What does your father do?' Helen Choudhury asked Pratima suddenly.

'He was in the army, but now he has a construction business,' she replied reluctantly.

But Helen Choudhury didn't seem to be listening any more. Her eyes had gone to the door where the white-coated servant was making urgent hand signals. 'Time to eat,' she said brightly. 'You can tell the men, my dear, while I gather the ladies.'

At the dinner table, Manoj was seated between the congressman's wife, Mrs Amar Singh, and the lawyer's wife, Mrs Ghorpekar. Opposite him were the congressman, the lawyer and his wife. The deputy commissioner sat at one end of the table. His wife, Helen Choudhury, sat at the other. For a while there was silence as chicken, fish, rice, puris and three types of vegetables were served. Then the lawyer, who clearly liked to speak, said loudly, 'Have you heard? The young maharaja has decided to turn his palace into a luxury hotel for foreigner tourists. Can you imagine? I think that it is a shame. That fort was where Subhash Chandra Bose and Shivaji were given shelter. Now it is to be thrown open to the very people who sought to destroy them. The fort should be made public, I say. It is an important monument of our struggle for independence.'

The deputy commissioner's mouth twisted into a sneer. 'The maharaja thinks he is still the ruler here, but he will soon learn who really rules the place. For a hotel you need licences, and for that you need the government and the local community behind you. The maharaja has done nothing for Khandwa, he doesn't even spend one month in a year here.' He looked penetratingly around the table. 'Not even one little month out of three hundred and sixty-five days.'

'But they say he has found himself a manager, a south Indian from Bangalore,' the lawyer said.

'A Madrasi? Hai Ram,' the politician's wife said suddenly.

'Don't worry, that won't help him, my dear madam,' the deputy commissioner said reassuringly. 'His manager won't be able to do a thing here; he won't even be able to make himself understood without speaking Khadhi. He will run away in no time at all.'

'But the problem won't go away, even if the manager does,' the politician cut in. 'What we need is a law making all places of historical importance public places, directly under the supervision of the district magistrate. Then no outsiders will be able to get their hands on our national heritage. After all, what are these maharajas if not traitors and lackeys of the British? They should have been put in jail at Independence. And why should foreigners be allowed to live in their palaces when we can't?'

Manoj had heard enough. 'But hotels bring jobs. What is wrong with having a really good hotel here?' he asked innocently.

They all looked at him, as if noticing him for the first time.

'Jobs? There are enough jobs here,' the lawyer said. 'Unlike big cities. Besides, the issue is not jobs. His palace has historic significance. It should not be polluted by foreigners, it belongs to the Indian people. We need to preserve our heritage, and respect the old ways, our traditions and values. It is up to us to protect places like this from outside influences.' He looked around at the others, trying to gauge the effect of his words. But the others, all outsiders to Khandwa, looked down at their plates and either nodded reluctantly or didn't react at all.

The awkward silence was broken by the deputy commissioner. 'It's not just about jobs. It's the kind of jobs a hotel will create. Hotels bring a hotel culture with them – alcohol, pornography, women of easy morality, and money. Those are the things I want to keep out of Khandwa.'

At last Manoj saw an opportunity to push his plan. 'In that case, why don't you help us with our project? There is no immorality in a dairy, and it creates jobs for poor people.'

There was an astonished silence at the table until Helen Choudhury broke it. 'Mr Mishra,' she said sharply, 'let me remind you that you are a guest and a newcomer here. Amar Singhji is the Member of the Legislative Assembly of this district and my husband is the deputy commissioner. Don't you think they know what does and doesn't need to be done here?'

Manoj stared at the deputy commissioner's wife in wordless astonishment. No woman had ever spoken to him like that. He sought Pratima's eyes but she was staring at her plate. The others also wouldn't look at him.

Again it was the deputy commissioner who came to Manoj's

rescue. 'You are a student of history aren't you, Mishra? Do you know how Khandwa came to have a rajah?' he called out from the head of the table.

Manoj looked at him gratefully and shook his head.

'I thought so. Young men today are all the same,' the deputy commissioner announced.

'But I. . .' Manoj tried to say that he had just arrived in Khandwa and had been too busy, but the deputy commissioner cut him off. 'But I must say I am surprised that you never bothered to learn about the history of Khandwa before you decided to change it.'

Manoj felt his face grow hot.

'Anyway, I suppose it will be my job to educate you. The first rajah was an idiot,' he began portentously, 'couldn't even write his name. The real rulers were the merchants. They weren't particularly rich – for the only commerce in the town was of salt, spices and the meagre household and farming goods required by the peasants in the surrounding villages – but what they made was coveted by the useless lot of dirt-poor tribal chieftains in the surrounding area. So the traders approached the cruellest and most bloodthirsty of the local chieftains and begged him to be the rajah and protect them. The man agreed, provided the traders build him a palace – and pay him a third of everything they earned. That is how the first Rajah of Khandwa, the ancestor of this present Rajah who thinks he still rules here, became the king of the region. He didn't even have to fight.' The deputy commissioner paused and looked at the faces around the table before he delivered his punchline. 'And you know the best thing? The man used to break the necks of live chickens to frighten his guests at dinner parties!'

'Thank God we got rid of the rajah-maharajahs sir, and have someone like you in their place,' Ghorpekar the lawyer gushed.

Everyone except Manoj laughed dutifully, though the politician looked a little annoyed.

At last the dinner came to an end and one by one the guests made their excuses. When it came to Manoj and Pratima's turn, 'Sit down and have another drink,' the deputy commissioner ordered.

'Thank you, but I don't drink,' Manoj replied stiffly.

'Ah yes, I remember.' Mr Choudhury didn't look in the least put out. 'But sit down anyway. I want to talk to you,' he ordered, leading the way to the sofas. On the way he poured himself a brandy, and lit a cigar.

'Khandwa is a small place,' he began, when they were all seated. 'I don't think you understand what that means, do you?'

Pratima and Manoj shook their heads like obedient children.

'It means that from the moment you arrived in Khandwa, you ceased to belong to yourselves. You belonged to Khandwa. That is the way it is in these places. Because they are small and not very imaginative, they want you to fit it.'

'But we are trying to fit in sir,' Manoj protested, 'only no one is helping us at all. Look at what the police has done to me. Look at the way I was put in prison for what, I still don't know. Is this the legendary hospitality of small towns? Why have they made it so difficult for me? I only want to help the poor.'

The deputy commissioner raised a hand to stop the flow of words. 'You will get your dairy back,' he said wearily. 'Your wife was most persuasive. She told me about your ideals, your impatience with book learning, and the way you threw up your PhD to do something useful. I must say, although I do not agree with you, I admire you. But your behaviour has raised too many eyebrows. You were too new, too presumptuous. You were still very much an outsider, so the police thought they could prey upon you.

'I have taken up the matter with the superintendent of police. Although we deputy commissioners are technically their superiors, the police have long since become a law unto themselves. But he is a sensible man and I will see to it you will get your equipment back. But you must learn from your experience. You cannot just come here and try to change things. First you have to give yourself to us. First you both have to belong to Khandwa. And that means you must give up your ego and your city ways. Belonging means understanding that your every action is public, even the most private ones. So be aware of it when you walk down our streets. Know that your every move is being watched, judged and reported upon. And remember this also: small places have ways of taking revenge.'

As Manoj and Pratima tried to digest this, the deputy commissioner stood up and put out his hand. The message had been delivered and there was nothing more to be said. They got up too. He waved them to the door where the same white-coated servant was waiting patiently.

CHAPTER NINE

BIRTH OF A CALF

In Nandgaon, the visit of the dusty stranger on the motorcycle was quickly forgotten. In less than a fortnight he'd become a bogeyman to frighten little children into obedience. The village even forgot why he had come. This was neither by accident or design. Nandgaon had cut itself off from the world. The road had taken a turn elsewhere before it came to the village, leaving only the path that Manoj had stumbled upon. Isolation had brought peace and a certain harmony, and any interference from the outside was seen as a threat.

Laxmi's marriage, by contrast, had been discussed for much longer. First, the villagers marvelled at how Ramu, the village idiot, had managed to find himself an intelligent, beautiful bride. When they learnt that she had even been to college they were awestruck and a little pitying. Why, they wondered, had such a woman agreed to marry an idiot like Ramu? But when they came to know that Laxmi's father had killed himself, they stopped inviting her to their homes, lest she infect them with her bad luck. Even the poorer women kept their distance.

But Laxmi did not forget the man on the motorcycle.

Night after night, lying sleepless in Ramu's hut, she thought of what they'd done, and was torn between hope and fear. Her father's cattle had been handpicked Tharparkars. Would this junglee cow be able to give birth to a live calf? And if she did, what kind of an animal would it be? Would it give milk as the man had promised or would it be a parasite like its mother?

Sometimes, when her belly was full, Laxmi would allow herself to dream. But after a few days the unchanging routine of life in Nandgaon and her isolation would drive all hope out of her.

In the end it was Ramu who noticed the bulge first.

'I think the cow is not well, Laxmi,' he told her worriedly one night. 'Though she is getting fat and lazy, I fear for her. Her stomach bulges unhealthily now and it feels hard, almost as if there is something growing inside it. You know so much more about cows than I, can you check her?' he asked hesitantly.

Laxmi opened her mouth to tell him that the cow was his problem not hers, and then bit off the harsh words that came so easily to her tongue. Quickly she calculated the days that had passed since the motorcycle man's visit, and then rushed outside to check.

It was a full moon night and sure enough the cow was standing at the entrance to her shed looking out over the yard towards the house like a mistress waiting anxiously for her lover. The moonlight threw into relief the roundedness of her stomach and Laxmi realised that what she had hardly dared hope for was actually true. She heard footsteps behind her and turned. Ramu had followed her out to the verandah. She smiled at him, the first real smile she had ever given him. But to her annoyance, he was looking at the cow, his face etched with worry. 'I hope she hasn't eaten something bad,' he said anxiously, his face soft with concern.

Laxmi's cheeks burned. 'You are such a simpleton,' she said harshly. 'Can't you see that she is pregnant?'

She would have said more but Ramu was already running towards the cow. 'A child. She is going to have a child,' he shouted joyously. The cow obligingly lay down and showed him her stomach. Laxmi turned away, but not before she saw him place his long, slender-fingered hands on her stomach and start massaging, the way midwives massaged pregnant women.

A strangled cry escaped Laxmi. She rushed inside.

The next morning when Ramu rose early to fuss over the cow, Laxmi got up too and took him a cup of sweet tea. He was cleaning the shelter, talking joyously to the cow all the while. Laxmi let him finish and then handed him the tea. 'My husband,' she said formally. 'While it is wonderful that the cow is actually pregnant, I think you should take care and not let the others know about the pregnancy. We must keep her inside the house and later you must take her back to the forest.'

Ramu stopped drinking his tea and looked puzzled. 'Why? What are you talking about?' he asked.

'When none of the village bulls has mounted her, they will wonder how she became pregnant,' Laxmi explained.

'But we tell them it was the Doctor Sahib's medicine.'

'A cow pregnant from a medicine? They will not believe you. They will say you are lying.'

Ramu's brow clouded over, and then, just as suddenly, cleared.

'They will think that she had been mounted by a bull before she got here. After all, she has only been here a few weeks. And if anyone asks us we will just say that we do not know. After all, she is a gift from the Devi. Why should She not have sent her with a calf in her belly?'

Defeated by his logic, Laxmi tried another tack. 'The cow is very weak. She may not be able to deliver a healthy child. And then just think how silly we would look.'

But Ramu would have none of it. Instinctively his hand reached for the animal. 'She will be fine, she will be a mother,' he said almost angrily. 'I know.'

'You know?' Laxmi shot back bitterly. 'What do you know? You can't even read your own name.' Ramu's hand stopped moving. For a moment he stayed very still. Then he looked up at her. The look he gave her tore at her heart and she wished he'd hit her. Instead he said quietly, 'I cannot read, so God gave you to me. The cow is the gift of the Devi, the calf will be fine too. You'll see.'

God gave her to him? Laxmi couldn't stop. All the pent-up fury against a world that had deprived her of a father and a future poured out of her: 'And how did she become pregnant?' she taunted him. 'They will think it was you.'

At last his eyes grew dark with anger. In one swift move he rose and leaned over her until his face was inches from hers. 'How dare you?' he said through clenched teeth. 'How dare you throw filth on God's miracle?' The fury in his voice brought Laxmi to her senses: she knew she had gone too far. Hastily she stepped back from him and averted her gaze. Pulling the anchal of her sari over her face she turned to go into the house. Her strangled whisper barely managed to float back to him: 'A miracle? There are no miracles in this world.'

In the months that followed, Ramu became both beggar and thief. He begged wheat and crushed oil seeds and gur from the neighbours and regularly stole sugar cane from the headman's field next door to enrich the cow's diet. As the cow's pregnancy advanced and she stopped going into the forest with him, he left later and returned earlier. At home he would spend all his free time with her, feeding her with his own hands, rubbing her expanding stomach, bathing it in cool river water, and endlessly massaging it.

'You're wasting your time,' Laxmi would tell him cruelly. 'There will be no birth. And if there is it will be stillborn or dead within the first month, you'll see.'

'Don't say such ashubh things,' Ramu would scold, turning away. But Laxmi was only giving voice to her fear, for more than Ramu, she feared the reaction of the others.

Nandgaon, even more than most villages, worshipped its

herd. Every time a calf was born, the temple bells rang out and singers were brought to recite the Krishnalila in its honour. The herd was the most beautiful thing in Nandgaon. Even Laxmi had to admit that. Almost four hundred strong, they thundered through the village each morning like an army. In the evening, when they returned, they turned the sky red with the dust from their hooves. They were magnificent creatures, some – the males – nearly six feet tall from horn to hoof. The females were smaller, but their bodies were more rounded, and their skins were like velvet and when they calved every two years, they produced seven litres of milk, a thing almost unheard of in the region.

A good half of the herd belonged to the headman alone. The other forty per cent belonged to the ten richest families of Nandgaon. The leader of the herd was a venerable female called Nandini who belonged to the headman. When Nandini was a child, legend had it, the headman had saved her from a leopard, and thereafter Bhudevi had blessed him. Nandini was partnered by Shankar, a young bull who was in fact her grandson but belonged to the headman's brother-in-law, Vilas Rao. He was huge, and lent muscle power to Nandini's command. Nandini herself looked old, and her soft velvet skin girdled her shrinking body in comfortable folds. Though everyone claimed she was a hundred, actually she was as old as Nandgaon itself. In fact, when the Great Flood of 1979 forced the headman to move the village to its present location and the villagers asked him to give it a name, he immediately chose Nandgaon in honour of Nandini, who had just been born. For a village was more than a collection of houses. It was more even than a temple and a pond. It was a living thing, made up of the intertwined lives of its people, and of all they held dear.

The herd also represented in concrete and quite indisputable terms the wealth of Nandgaon. Cut off as it was from the road, what little cash income Nandgaon earned came entirely from its herd – whose offspring were sold each year at the Dussehra Mela in Mahendragiri. Since Nandgaon's bulls were famous, they commanded good prices. In addition, extra milk from the cows was collected by the headman, transported by his cousin Vilas Rao to the nearest town and sold to the government cooperative. The money from the milk was not distributed like the milk was but was kept to pay for maintaining the village, its pond, the temple, for paying for festivals, pujas, the local schoolteacher, and the medical expenses of any villager who fell seriously ill and had to be taken to the town. No one went hungry in Nandgaon, the villagers were proud of saying.

The cattle of the village were nearly all related, for the headman generously loaned Nandini's male offspring to the other villagers whenever their cows came on heat. Through them, the entire village was related to one another. But the cattle, Laxmi soon realised, were only the physical representation of something far more powerful that tied Nandgaon together, something that made it very different from her own village, and every other village she had known. This was the love that bound the villagers to their cattle and since the cattle were all related, to the headman and to each other, it was as if all of Nandgaon had a single heart and that heart was the herd.

Which was why, day after day, Laxmi held her breath, waiting for the village's anger. For how could they accept a calf with no link to the herd?

But the anger never came. Instead people came and congratulated her.

'Will you be going to your mother's home or will you have it here?' Savitribai, the headman's daughter-in-law, asked her.

'What do you mean?' Laxmi asked, bewildered.

'Your child, of course. We are so happy. Ramu will be a wonderful father.'

That's how Laxmi realised what had happened. No one had

believed Ramu when he said that his cow was pregnant. For a junglee cow was a junglee cow : like the man on the motor-cycle and all things that came from the outside, best forgotten. Only when months passed and Laxmi remained herself but the cow grew hugely pregnant did they finally believe her. But then they quickly recovered, assuring themselves that it was a false pregnancy. The jokes began: Ramu, they said, had lost his way in the dark one night and made the cow pregnant instead of his wife. And they laughed and they laughed and they laughed all the more when they saw poor barren Laxmi walk by.

But Laxmi wasn't the only one who was worried. The cow was as well. Giving up the road had been hard. She'd grown used to sleeping under the stars and eating what she pleased, when she pleased. But the promise of a little two-legs to play with and a herd to be part of had overcome her reluctance when she had least expected it to and she had followed the two-legs with the gentle hands home.

But Nandgaon's herd had not accepted her. Whenever she approached, they turned away, showing her their arrogant well-shaped behinds or chasing her away with hooves and horns if she came too close. The other two-legs in the village seemed to sense that she was different too and avoided her or threw stones. So she learnt to keep away from them as well.

The only one who seemed to understand her was the two-legs with the gentle hands who healed her when she was sick and so, out of love for him, for she instinctively understood that she meant the world to him, she stayed.

Then the other two-legs had arrived and he'd put something inside her that was cold and alien, not once but twice. In the days that followed she thought of the road longingly. But some-thing in her wouldn't budge. A weight had settled like a stone inside her, a stone that grew heavier each day. Until one day she felt the alien thing inside her, tight-curled and hungry, and knew that leaving was no longer an option.

The calf was born on a bitingly cold February night when the moon was little more than a tear in the fabric of the sky. Almost blind and covered in placental fluids, the newborn snuggled up to the familiar warmth of its mother and promptly fell asleep. The cow, though utterly exhausted, cut the umbilical cord with her teeth and licked the calf's little body till it was warm and soft.

Laxmi was already awake when Ramu burst into the hut, but had not yet mustered the courage to get out from under her single lumpy cotton quilt. She had never been so cold in her life. Even at home, where she had had a bed between her and the floor, she had hated winter mornings and had had to be dragged out of bed by her father or her sisters. But here in Nandgaon with no bed, only a thin cotton mattress between her and the floor, and the quilt that let the cold in at unexpected places, she had learnt that even the cold felt different to the rich and the poor.

When she heard Ramu calling her, she groaned and pulled the quilt more closely around her. Then impatient footsteps mounted the stairs and the man she held responsible for her misery was shaking her awake. 'Come, my Laxmi, come and see the miracle,' he said as soon as her eyes opened. 'It's the cow,' he continued excitedly, 'she's given us a little one.' He saw the surprise in Laxmi's eyes. 'Come, get up,' he said excitedly and headed for the door.

Laxmi's surprise related not to the cow but to the fact that it had given birth to a live calf. And, perversely, she was furious with the motorcycle man. If any old cow could be inseminated, why had her father driven himself into debt and then driven himself out of life, to finance his prize Tharparkars? Had he not already been in debt over them, she was sure that the failure of the cotton crop would not have broken his spirit. No, this was an accident. This calf would not live. She was sure of that so she felt no need to share Ramu's enthusiasm. She took her time getting dressed and only when her husband's impatient cries became too frequent to ignore did she go outside.

She entered the shed and stared critically at the little thing. It was tiny, the smallest calf she'd ever seen, half the size of the normal Nandgaoni calf and looking nothing like one. Its white body was dappled with large jet-black splotches and its face was coal black, as if it belonged to some other animal. In addition, its little face seemed rather squashed, the nose squarer and shorter than in normal cows, giving it an oddly quizzical expression as if it were surprised to be alive at all. Because its face was so small and its neck non-existent, its legs looked inordinately long and fragile. But more than the calf's actual proportions, what was disturbing was the impression it gave of being somehow hastily put together, the parts not quite fitting.

As Laxmi watched, the calf's legs began to move feebly, and it started calling out in a thin hungry voice. The cow immediately awoke and though it was exhausted, it began to frantically lick its swollen udders in preparation for the little one's attack. Laxmi looked at the calf. It was still squealing, turning its blind head from side to side and beating its thin little legs against the ground. She turned away. What was the point of helping such a weak creature to live? It would only grow up to be an extra mouth to feed.

Then slowly, reluctantly, she turned back and bent down, gently nudging the calf's head in the right direction. When at last the calf found her mother's nipple its cries stopped and it began to suck strongly. Laxmi stood up and moved back a bit so she could watch as the calf suckled, its throat expanding and contracting like a strongly beating little heart.

As she watched the unlikely pair, her mind seemed to go both forwards and backwards at the same time, seeing both the future and a snippet of the past that had until now seemed opaque.

She was sitting in the biology lab at the government women's college listening to the biology professor. 'There are only two true miracles in this world, asexual and sexual reproduction,' the biology teacher was saying. Laxmi had looked up from her book, waiting for the teacher to explain further. She wrote it down all the same. She always wrote down everything any teacher said. 'Asexual and sexual reproduction may seem to be total opposites, to have nothing in common,' the teacher continued, 'but that is only the maya, the illusion of samsara.' The teacher turned to the blackboard and drew a squeaky white line through the centre of a circle, bisecting it. 'As you can see, sexual and asexual reproduction are in fact but two halves of a single whole – and that whole is the circle of life, of matter, samsara. The two processes have to be present and happening at the same time for life to exist.'

'Why, teacher? How is that?' Laxmi had asked.

'Because they represent the two basic principles of life, sameness and difference. In asexual reproduction what is whole and complete splits itself into two identical bodies, and those two split into four and so on, so that from completeness we get incompleteness and then completeness again – never losing the identity of the parent cell. In the other case, two dissimilar and incomplete creatures come together to make a single complete whole, one that while retaining some of its parents' characteristics is, in its entirety, unlike either parent cell. So what does that tell us?'

There was silence in the class.

'It tells us that homogeneity and heterogeneity, sameness and difference, have to be present in this world for life to exist.'

Now, looking at the calf blindly reach for its mother, Laxmi at last understood what the teacher had meant. There, in front of her, was the principle of sameness and difference at work.

Despite the fact that they looked nothing like each other it was clear that the cow accepted the black and white calf without question and the calf recognised the cow as its mother. A sense of wonder overcame Laxmi, the same sense of wonder she'd always felt when the first cotton pod burst, revealing its tightly-curled silken treasure, or the first tender little shoots of rice poked their green faces out of the black earth and looked innocently at the endless blue of the sky.

And with it, the grey blanket of misery enveloping her had shifted slightly. And hope, like the first ray of dawn, entered her.

The calf, she vowed, would survive.

A few days later, in the house with the eyes that gazed protectively at the village, the headman learnt of the birth of the calf.

'So what do you think of Ramu's latest?' Bicchoo asked when there was a lull in the conversation that evening.

'Why, has he got married again?' Vilas Rao asked in mock surprise.

Bicchoo continued to look at the headman. 'No,' he said, his voice pregnant with meaning.

'His wife has run away?' Govind Rao suggested.

'Not yet, she hasn't,' Bicchoo said again, his face poker straight.

'Where can she go? No one would take the daughter of a farmer who has committed suicide,' the priest growled.

'He has found the sister of the junglee cow, and it also came home with him?' Govind Rao suggested.

Bicchoo sat back on his heels. 'So none of you knows?' he asked gleefully.

'I suspect no one does. So you'd better tell us yourself and be quick about it,' the headman growled.

Bicchoo tried to look aggrieved. 'I just thought that since he works for you he'd have told you himself, that's all.'

'I don't gossip with servants,' the headman snapped.

'Naturally, you have better things to do, Patelji,' Bicchoo said, his voice oily smooth. 'Anyway, I, being a poor man, have few friends and even fewer servants, and so today when I was returning from my fields, I saw Ramu in front of me with the goats, but no cow. I asked him how the junglee was and you know what he told me?' He paused, looking at each of his listeners in turn. 'He said, "She is fine Bicchooji. She has given birth to a calf"'.

There was a long silence, then everyone began talking at once. 'A calf? How can that be? How could that junglee have given birth?'

'That is not all,' Bicchoo continued with a smug smile on his face.

Everyone turned to him expectantly. 'Is there more? What else has Ramu been up to?'

'It is not him but his cow. The calf is like none that I have seen before. Its face is coal black,' he concluded triumphantly.

'Black?' the others almost shouted in their consternation. 'How can that be? Cows are white. All our bulls are white too. How can the junglee have had a calf with a black face?'

'Its body is all splotched with black too,' Bicchoo added. 'And it is huge. It is only a month old and looks like a year-old calf already.'

'That is unnatural,' the priest exclaimed. 'No cow is half black and half white.'

'It must look like a cinema – all black and white,' said Govind Rao sagely, but no one paid him any attention.

'But how can the junglee have a calf at all?' Vilas Rao finally asked the obvious question. 'None of us has allowed Ramu to cross his cow with our bulls.'

Everyone looked blank, for no one had an answer.

The priest tried to have the last word. 'I feel uneasy about this calf,' Saraswati Rane intoned. 'I don't think the animal came from God.'

'Ramu claims its mother was a gift of the forest,' Bicchoo reminded them, poker-faced.

'Then maybe it was impregnated by the forest god too,' said Govind Rao, with a suggestive leer. Everyone cackled, but the laughter was tinged with uneasiness, for no one could really understand where the calf had come from or what made its face black.

'But how do you know so much about this calf?' the headman asked. 'Did you go to his house? Did you see it?'

'No,' Bicchoo replied, 'but I know it is an ugly monster.'

'Of course, and you saw this monster with your own eyes,' the headman said sarcastically. He looked at the others. 'The cow may be a junglee, but to call her child a monster is blasphemy, isn't it, Punditji?'

Before Saraswati Rane could reply, Bicchoo said smartly, 'No, but I sent my son.'

'You believe your son? Children love to exaggerate,' the headman said.

Bicchoo smiled. 'Not my son. He is as honest as Bholu* – I mean, Ramu. Cow and calf were tied to the neem tree outside and the calf was suckling the mother. At first he noticed nothing wrong with it – except that it was a very ugly creature of course, like the mother. Then the calf stopped suckling and turned to look in the direction of my son and my son got such a shock he almost fell off the wall.'

Nobody spoke. They all looked at the headman to see how he would react. But the headman said nothing, staring distractedly at his hookah.

'It probably won't survive, if what you say is true,' Vilas Rao said.

---

* Innocent, often used as a name for someone who is not quite right in the head.

'Oh, leave poor Ramu alone. He has had more than his fair share of bad luck.' The headman was thinking of Ramu's gambler father and his poor mother who had died when the boy was fourteen.

The others all looked at him, horrified.

'Don't take this so lightly, Patelji,' Saraswati Rane warned. 'There are some who will be saying it is a miracle that a cow of the forest could produce a child. Miracles must not be encouraged.'

'Except if they come from you?' the headman said softly.

'Miracles don't come from me, they come from God,' Saraswati Rane replied touchily.

'A miracle could never be so ugly,' Bicchoo said immediately, making the others laugh.

'But this is not about beauty or the lack of it. There is the herd to be considered,' Jaiwant Rane the schoolmaster pointed out, stating what was foremost on everyone's mind. 'This calf is a creature of the village, born on its soil. Does that make it a part of the herd?'

'Something must be done. We cannot have our children drinking the milk of a parentless cow,' Govind Rao added.

The others ignored him, their attention on the headman.

But the headman's mind had wandered. Unaware that the others had stopped talking and were looking at him, Gopal reached for the last pakora on the plate. Waving the pakora in their faces he laughed. 'Let us leave poor Ramu's calf alone and concentrate upon our own affairs, shall we? Most probably, it won't even last a fortnight.'

CHAPTER TEN

SOORPANAKHA

To the village Ramu's calf was an enigma from the day she was born. But to the children she was a source of delicious terror. Seven-year-old Subhash, who felt that he was an authority on all things bovine because he took his father's cattle out to the fields every day, could not get over the calf Kami's eyes. 'Look at those pink eyes, they are the eyes of a rakshas*.'

'What kind of rakshas?' five-year-old Mani asked innocently.

'A forest rakshas,' Subhash replied.

'How do you know what a forest rakshas looks like? Have you seen one?' Mani challenged.

'What do you mean "have I seen one". Of course I have. It has black and white skin, big teeth, and pink eyes. It is as tall as a jamun tree. And it eats human beings.'

'But you never go to the forest,' Mani pointed out.

'Of course I've been to the forest.'

'When?'

'At night, when little boys like you are asleep.'

'I am not little.'

'You are a dwarf, a little dwarf.'

Mani didn't take the bait. 'I don't believe you,' he said calmly. 'Your baba would never allow you out after dark.'

'He didn't know. They were asleep.'

* demon

'Oh.' Mani was unconvinced.

'So how come the rakshas didn't eat you?' Mani asked, remembering the conversation of the previous day. He and the shopkeeper's son were back at Ramu's house, watching the calf tied to the neem tree. Overcome by curiosity, a knot of children had followed them down the lane to Ramu's house.

'Because I hit it and ran away,' Subhash replied.

'With what did you hit it?' Mani asked suspiciously.

'With a stone. You see, he has weak eyesight. Small pink eyes mean weak eyesight.'

'Oh really? Prove it to me.'

'What do you mean prove it? I have nothing to prove to you.'

'Yes you do,' Mani insisted. 'Show me that the calf has weak eyesight and I will believe you about the rakshas.'

Too late Subhash saw the trap that had been laid for him by his little friend. 'OK, I'll show you,' he said bravely. 'Watch.' He picked up a stone and flung it at the calf. It was not a very well-aimed throw and the stone was too heavy to reach the calf. It fell nearby, kicking up a puff of dust. The calf jumped and faced the direction from which the stone had come. The cow turned its head too, bared its teeth at the children and pawed the ground menacingly. The calf looked at its mother in some surprise, then tried imitating her.

A sigh of delicious fear rippled through the children.

'Why doesn't it have a fifth leg?' four-year-old Mukul asked his elder brother Keshav.

'Because you are confusing it with a wishing cow. This is not a wishing cow, this one eats stupid little boys like you.'

'Eats us?'

'Yes – see its red mouth? See how red it is? How do you think the calf became so big?'

Mukul grew pale and his face puckered up in fear.

'Don't cry,' his elder brother warned, recognising the signs.

'Don't cry or it will come and eat you.'

'See, I told you it was the child of a rakshas. Did you see its teeth?' Subhash shouted triumphantly. 'Run, run, run. Before we all get eaten up.' And he dashed off, the others behind him.

Like the children, the adults' reactions to the calf varied dramatically. Some believed that the birth of the calf was a miracle – a gift, as Ramu put it, of the forest – while others believed the calf was cursed, a monster. But they were all agreed on one thing: its unbelievable ugliness was proof that it was exceptional. The upper-caste families, with cows and land of their own, stayed away, fearing that the animal's ugliness might be infectious. But either because they were fond of Ramu or because of the awe that spectacularly ugly things inspire, they did nothing more drastic than hope for bad news. So they asked Ramu each time they saw him how the calf was doing and Ramu, pleased by the interest the calf was generating amongst his betters, glowed as he told them. Afterwards, amongst themselves, they made bets on how long a calf like that could survive. The other group, consisting mainly of the poor and unfortunate, treated cow and calf as divine beings, bringing them small offerings of flowers, beaten rice or gur whenever they could.

The only ones who weren't awed by the creature's ugliness were the thirteen-year-olds. But that was because they were on the threshold of puberty, and matters of sex and reproduction, though still mysterious and monstrous, were never far from their minds.

'Maybe it was one of the goats that did it,' thirteen-year-old Kishore volunteered.

'A goat on a cow? Chhie. No proper cow would take it,' Madhav answered with the certainty of his thirteen and a half years. 'It was a human. A man. That's why the short face.'

There was a shocked silence.

'You can't be serious,' Keshav exclaimed. 'No man would

do that.'

'Why? A desperate man might,' Madhav retorted.

'Even a really desperate man would not stick his flute into a cow that ugly,' Keshav scoffed. 'You are dreaming.'

'If a goat can fall in love with a cow, why can't a man?' Madhav replied, his logic unassailable.

'OK. Which man then?' Keshav challenged. 'Do you know him?'

'A man in love,' Madhav replied.

An awed silence fell over the group as they struggled to picture Ramu atop his own cow.

'Perhaps Ramu knew that his cow was actually a devi in disguise and –'

'But Ramu is married –'

'Exactly. That is why the Devi had to put on a disguise.'

'That's why he doesn't mind the calf being so ugly,' Madhav added by way of explanation.

'But I think those black patches are lovely. I want them too,' a little voice suddenly piped up.

From their superior height, six pairs of teenage eyes looked down at Keshav's little brother Mukul.

'You idiot. Shut your stupid mouth or I will shut it for you,' Keshav said, breaking into a sweat with embarrassment. 'Go home.'

'But I wanted to make a wish.'

'I told you this is the child of a ghost and a rakshas not a wishing cow.' Keshav gave his little brother a push. 'Now go away.'

Laxmi was the only one in the village not surprised by her calf Kami's colouring or shape. She knew how Kami had been conceived. She also knew that hybrid cows came in all colours and shapes. She had read, in her courses in the agricultural college, of the high milk yields the hybrids were capable of, but she was not convinced that a junglee mother would ever produce a profitable calf. Had Kami been male the calf would have been of some value as a draught animal. But a female? Mentally she would shake her head in disbelief. Even if Kami lived, she was unlikely to yield much milk. And, Laxmi was convinced Kami would never bear a viable calf.

Then there was the added complication of her own very mixed feelings towards Ramu and the cow. The solitude she had at first sought, and then achieved, by rejecting Ramu's timid overtures now felt like a blanket that was slowly suffocating her. But there was nothing she could do, or so it seemed. In the village even those she worked for continued to greet her with averted eyes. Certainly they always paid her well for her work, giving generously of their milk and grain. But never had anyone even offered her a cup of tea in their homes, or asked her to stay a while and chat.

Which left only Ramu. But he had eyes only for his animals. If he noticed what Laxmi wore or what food she put before him, he no longer dared to make a comment, for fear of her ever-ready retorts. Once, in frustration, she put too much salt in his food. He ate it without uttering a word, drank a large glass of water, and rushed out to his animals. She blamed the cow for this, for Ramu's fascination with mother and child refused to diminish. Every time Laxmi looked at the cow's soft, milky white skin she herself felt she was growing dark and wrinkled. And whenever she saw Kami suckling her mother's teats, she felt old and barren.

Ramu was the only one who was convinced that the calf would live. He remained convinced that the gods of the forest had sent him a gift. He believed that the cow doctor on his motorcycle, who had never returned, had been sent by them to make her fertile and that the calf would be his salvation. He even dared to hope that it would one day bring Laxmi and him together. He had chosen the calf's name, Kamdhenu, the giver of wishes, and the first of his and Laxmi's future herd.

'Kamdhenu.' He would say the name under his breath, not daring to say it aloud until the pujari had whispered it into the animal's ear. For there was great power in a name. Everyone in the village knew that.

Ramu went to see the priest to ask him to do the naming. 'So soon?' Saraswati Rane asked. 'Don't you want to wait and see if the calf will survive? I heard it was weak and ill.'

'No, no, nothing of the sort, Punditji. Those are just the words of idle tongues,' Ramu assured him.

'But who is the father of the calf?' the priest asked. 'Without a father, no calf can survive.'

Ramu remained unfazed. 'The calf is a gift of the Devi. How can it not live?' he replied.

Ramu's answer surprised Saraswati Rane. He looked at Ramu sharply. Clearly Ramu was smarter than he seemed. For by invoking the Devi, he had put the priest in a tight spot: refuse to name the animal and run the risk of affronting the Devi. Saraswati Rane thought fast. 'I will name your calf once you have collected its weight in rice and given it to the temple,' he said. 'If she is a gift of the Devi, the Devi must be thanked, you understand.'

Ramu's face fell. 'But I am a poor man,' he stammered.

'If the Devi wishes, you will find your rice just like you found your cow,' the priest replied.

Ramu was heartbroken. He went straight to the cow and told her everything. Unable to understand anything except that bare essentials – that her beloved two-legs was unhappy – the cow looked into his eyes with her own liquid kohl-rimmed ones and gently put her head on his shoulder. 'I'm so sorry my friend,' Ramu said brokenly to the cow, stroking its neck. The cow held his gaze for a long moment then licked his face.

Ramu realised he was crying and laughed shakily. 'You're right. I musn't give up hope. The Devi will help us.'

He heard someone come up behind him and turned. Laxmi

was standing in the doorway watching them. She bent down and handed him a glass of tea. Ramu took a quick sip, for he was thirsty, and realised that she must have overheard everything, for the tea was cold. Embarrassed, he turned his back to her and pretended to clean the cow's ears. A little later Laxmi returned and placed a small package beside him. Steeped in his misery, Ramu didn't even look at it. Only when the little calf tried to tear open the bundle with its teeth did he rescue it and look inside. There, in his hand, was a fistful of rice.

Tears came into Ramu's eyes. How hard Laxmi must have worked to save that little packet. And yet, she hadn't hesitated, she'd given it all to him. For Kami, he corrected himself. His fingers closed tightly around the little package. Umno Devi had not abandoned him.

By April, when it was time for repainting the horns of the cattle, the entire village knew that the calf wasn't going to die; though only ten weeks old the calf was already one and a half times the size of any other calf its age. Her stomach bulged with well-being. Her eyes were clear and alert and her skin glowed with health, accentuating the uniqueness of her colouring. And her face stubbornly refused to change, continuing to look as if someone had cut off her snout.

'It may be healthy, but it is still a monster,' Darbari the barber told his clients, with a flourish of his razor, and they all grunted their assent.

'Wonder what he will name it,' Sushilabai remarked, as she and her husband sat together in the shop.

Govind Rao laughed. 'Poor Ramu will never be able to find a name for it. No name exists for an animal that ugly.'

Sushilabai laughed. 'Perhaps, but in his eyes it is beautiful. So of course he will have a name for her.'

Govind Rao sniffed. 'He fusses over it like a mother.'

'Exactly,' she nodded, satisfied, 'which is why he will certainly have chosen a name for it.'

Govind Rao smiled broadly. 'You really are clever, dear wife – how did you know?'

'Know what?'

'About Ramu and Saraswati Rane.'

Sushilabai's face grew intent. 'What do you mean? I was just guessing. Tell me what happened immediately.'

Govind Rao shook his head in wonderment. Women! How did they know things? he wondered. 'Well, you are right,' he said at last. 'Ramu did go to Saraswati Rane and ask him to name the calf. Saraswati didn't say no, he just told Ramu what it would cost him, and Ramu went away,' Govind Rao finished, poker-faced.

'Cost him how much?' Sushilabai asked, smiling.

'Two maunds* of rice. He said that if the calf was a gift from the Devi, then the Devi needed to be properly thanked,' Govind Rao said, chortling with glee. But to his surprise, his wife didn't join him, her face intent, absorbed in thought.

'What? What is it?' Govind Rao asked, somewhat irritated.

Sushilabai shrugged and reached for her knitting. 'Perhaps his wife will help him,' she murmured.

'What? Speak up, will you,' Govind Rao ordered.

'Laxmibai. Maybe she will help him.'

'She?' Govind Rao sneered. 'What has the daughter of a suicide farmer got to sell except her body? And that, no one in this village will dare to touch.'

His wife pursed her lips disapprovingly, surprised that her husband would speak so about another woman in front of her. 'There are other ways,' she said.

'What ways?' Govind Rao asked absently, looking at the

---

* Old-fashioned form of counting grain that dates from the Mughals. One maund is equal to 28 kgs.

clock on the wall. It was almost time to go to the head-man's.

'I heard that she is rebuilding Kuntabai's kitchen.'

'So what of it?'

'Kuntabai pays her too well for it, and sings her praises,' his wife replied calmly.

'Kuntabai,' Govind Rao growled, 'that woman has more money than sense and a son who is a weakling. If Prembhai had not died so suddenly her son would have known how to put her in her place.'

'Krishnabai sings her praises too. Says she is the best needle-woman she's ever found,' Sushilabai added. 'In fact, I was thinking of trying her myself.'

Govind Rao was startled. 'Is she that good?'

'Everyone says so. She even does Kuntabai's accounts, I am told.'

Govind Rao's face grew sullen. He was one of those that had disliked Laxmi from the very beginning, convinced that the daughter of a suicide farmer, and especially one as disturb-ingly tall and beautiful and educated as Laxmi, could only spell trouble for the village. But his wife, for all her tininess, was boss and so he nodded reluctantly. 'Oh, all right. One kitchen or one sari blouse won't be enough to pay for two maunds of rice.'

'Of course not – even if she built twenty kitchens she wouldn't be able to do it.' Sushilabai laughed. 'I was only teasing you.'

Silence descended on the shop, Sushilabai returning to her knitting and Govind Rao to his tobacco.

'We wondered why all of a sudden she had become so helpful,' Sushilabai said suddenly. 'Maybe Ramu will let her name it.' She gave her husband a sidelong glance. In Nandgaon, only the men were allowed to do the naming – unless the one being named was a girl.

'Well, she is smart. Maybe she can come up with a name for such an ugly one,' Govind Rao laughed.

Suddenly an invisible voice piped up from under the counter. 'I know, I know, I can think of a name.'

Husband and wife looked down at their son Subhash and then at each other. They'd forgotten he was there, he'd been so quiet.

'Huh, you, how can you think of a name? It is not yours.' Govind Rao glared down at his youngest child.

'But I can, I have. It's Soorpa. . .Soopannakha,' he stammered.

'What? What kind of a stupid name is that?' Govind Rao told him. He got up. 'Enough of your silly games, go and revise your lessons instead. Or Punditji* will be angry and beat you in front of all your classmates.'

But Subhash was a determined child. He ran after his father and grabbed his hand. 'But I have, I have, and it's a good name. Like the rakshasi in the Ramayana, the one whose nose was cut off by Laxman Bhagwan.'

All at once Govind Rao understood what his son was trying to say. He sat down heavily and slapped his knee. 'Soorpanakha. Of course. What else can you call a creature that has no nose? Why did I never think of that myself?' Laughter like slow thunder rolled out of his ample chest. He picked Subhash up and cradled him in his arms. 'Did you hear that, Subhash ki Maa†? Did you hear what your clever son just said?' He gave his son a last kiss and stood up. Then reached for his wife. 'You have an amazing son, Subhash ki Maa. This I have to tell the others,' he said, and strode out of the house.

When class finished the next day, the entire school ran

---

* Refers to Jaiwant Rane, the schoolmaster. Punditji is an honourific used in villages for the schoolteacher.
† mother

through the village chanting Soorpanakha, Soorpanakha, and down the sugar cane-shaded path to Ramu's hut. Jaiwant Rane the schoolmaster heard them, and laughed out loud wondering which unfortunate child had been so named. The barber under the peepul tree heard it too, and so did a few mothers. All of them crossed their fingers and hoped the child in question was not one of theirs. Laxmi, helping Vilas Rao's daughters-in-law clean and sort their rice, heard the children calling the calf by its new name too. Her eyes fell on Vilas Rao's second grandson. She laughed. Soorpanakha – a good name.

Curious to see how the calf would like its new name the village children climbed on to the boundary wall of Ramu's house and peeked over the top. The calf and its mother were lying in their usual place under the neem tree. For a few seconds the magic of the animal's dappled skin held them. Then one of them whispered the name.

'Soorpanakha,' Mani called softly.

The calf and its mother, both of whom had been sleeping when the children arrived, heard it and woke up. They looked towards the wall and recognised the children. The cow flattened its ears in welcome. She liked children. Their sweet chattering voices brought back earlier, happier times. The little calf, knowing only Ramu's hands, was totally unafraid of the children and reached for its mother's teats.

'Look, she likes her new name,' Subhash yelled.

A murmur of approval went through the line of boys. 'Soorpanakha, Soorpanakha,' they called, more confidently this time.

The cow looked up from the pile of grass in front of her. Something was wrong. The little two-legs voices were too loud, too harsh. A distant memory, one of pain, jogged itself free. She stood up slowly and faced the children, dislodging the calf from her teats. The calf, sensing its mother's disturbance, came out from between its mother's legs and pressed itself against her. Seeing this, the children were greatly emboldened and began to chant even louder. Then some budding poet had a brainwave. 'Soorpanakha, Soorpanakha, show me your teeth,' he sang. In less than a minute the chant was taken up by the entire line of boys.

'Soorpanakha, Soorpanakha, show us your teeth,' they called, laughing and pushing each other in their excitement.

But all the calf did was to stare. 'Soorpanakha, Soorpanakha, show us your teeth,' they chanted, 'sharp as thorns, long as horns.' But now they were laughing as they sang. For the name had robbed the calf of most of its power, and the way it cowered against its mother only seemed to confirm it. Suddenly a stone flew out of the assembled crowd and hit the calf on its nose. It yelped loudly, like a little pig in distress. The assembly of children burst into laughter. Another stone, this one thrown by Subhash, hit the little calf on its hind leg. It jumped and bared its teeth at last. But the children were having too much fun to notice.

Walking through the sugar cane field, a sack of broken rice balanced on her head, Laxmi heard the little calf scream. She dropped the bag of rice and ran.

But long before she saw the children perched on top of the wall she could hear them chanting their cruel song and the words of their song made her blind with rage. Without stopping to consider the consequences, she leapt off the path into the midst of the sugar cane and with her harvesting knife cut herself a long thick stick.

The children were having great fun. They roared with laughter each time a stone found its target and the little calf jumped. 'Dance, dance, little monster,' they called out to the little naked calf, now quite shorn of any vestiges of power and mystery. They didn't become aware of Laxmi until she began to hit them.

'Get off! Get lost!' she shouted, hitting their calves and backs of knees indiscriminately.

Those who'd been hit fell off the wall crying, then picked themselves out of the mud and ran back to their homes. But as soon as they were out of earshot, they took up their song again.

After she'd rid the wall of children Laxmi pushed aside the reed curtain covering the entrance to the angan and entered. Inside the angan everything looked strangely normal. Calf and mother were under the tree. The calf was suckling away, pulling strongly at the mother's teats the way it always did. The mother was licking the little one's face, her own delicately pink ears flicking back and forth as she tried to mask her own fear and comfort her child. Then Laxmi's eyes fell upon the stones that littered the courtyard, encircling the two animals. Some were large and jagged. Some were streaked with a dark liquid. Laxmi gasped. As she drew closer she noticed streaks of dried blood on the calf's sleek black and white coat. She cried out in horror and reached out instinctively to examine the wounds, but the calf uttered a plaintive mewl and cowered against her mother. Then Laxmi noticed that the calf wasn't the only one hurt. In fact, much of the blood on the calf didn't seem to belong to it at all. Suddenly she saw exactly what must have happened. The cow, unable to free herself or her child, had put herself in front of the little creature, directly in the path of the stones. A lump formed in Laxmi's throat. Unable to bear the sight of the blood, Laxmi grabbed a bucket and ran to the well to fetch water.

In a week the wounds healed and mother and calf seemed to forget about their ordeal. But the name stuck. For with its new name, the calf had been given a place in the village, and an identity. It was no longer dangerous, it was an understandable part of their world – Soorpanakha, the ugly one. The one who had tried to be something she was not and had had her nose cut off by the gods.

CHAPTER ELEVEN

RAMU AND LAXMI

When nothing terrible happened, Nandgaon at last accepted the ugly one. Grudgingly and with reservations perhaps, but accept her they did. They had to. For an unwritten rule governed life in the village: all creatures born on its soil belonged automatically to the village, a part of its collective unconscious. The feeling grew, neatly put into words by Darbari the barber, that perhaps the calf's looks were punishment for some crime in a previous life and therefore its bad luck was non-transferable. Nothing bad befell Ramu or Laxmi either, giving further proof to Darbari's theory. So Nandgaon breathed a sigh of relief and resumed its old habits – its preoccupation with weather, politics and the iniquities of the outside world.

As for Ramu and Laxmi, Kami the calf became the glue that bound them together.

In the beginning, Laxmi had kept her distance – repelled by the calf's obvious ugliness, convinced that it had no future. But from the day when she returned to the hut to find the boys pelting the calf with stones and chanting its new name, Laxmi made herself the calf's guardian. A name like Soorpanakha, she reasoned, was too huge a burden to bear all alone – as heavy as being the daughter of a farmer who had killed himself.

Perhaps she wouldn't have felt so strongly had something else not taken place some weeks earlier. The calf had been in its fourth week of life when one day Laxmi returned from the fields to find its mouth tinged with pink. Then she noticed something else. The cow would turn away each time the calf approached its udders. With a sinking heart she approached the pair under the neem tree. As soon as it saw her the little creature began mewling piteously and perhaps because the presence of a human gave her courage, the calf made another attempt to reach its mother's teats. This time, to Laxmi's horror, the cow actually kicked the little one away. Laxmi rushed forward and grasped the cow firmly by its ears, immobilising it. The calf approached once more and this time the cow, unable to do anything else, let it suckle. When the calf had been suckling strongly for some time Laxmi let go, satisfied that the crisis had passed. She knew that it was quite common for cows, like human mothers, to get fed up of having a child hanging on constantly to their teats. Or sometimes calves, in their eagerness to feed, bite their mothers' nipples with their razor-sharp teeth, making feeding incredibly painful for the mothers. In both cases, the mothers refuse their children milk for a few hours or even a day until the wound has closed and they are rested.

The next morning Laxmi rose early and rushed to the animal shed. A reassuring sight met her eyes. The calf was suckling with all her might while the cow stood still, every once in a while bending her head to pick up a mouthful of grass. But over the next few days though the calf seemed to be doing little else but eat, it grew thinner and thinner. By the evening of the third day it was sucking at anything and everything that came within reach – hands, feet, machine parts, even the branches of the neem tree. Laxmi was beside herself. It hadn't taken her long to realise what had happened – the cow's milk had dried up. She tried to feed it some porridge made with their own precious milk. But it was too rich for the poor calf who threw up almost as soon as she ate it.

'Do something,' Laxmi ordered Ramu. 'Go to the village

and beg them to let Kami come and suckle one of theirs. Tell them we will pay them if they want.'

Ramu didn't move. 'Pay them? With what?'

'I'll find a way,' Laxmi snapped. 'Just go.'

Ramu opened his mouth to tell her it would be of no use, but the look on her face made him shut it. He left, despair in his heart.

He went first to Vilas Rao's. In the courtyard was a cow, its teats swollen with milk, and a tiny calf, not more than a few days old. He looked at them in delight and then asked for Vilas Rao. Unfortunately, the latter wasn't in, but his young wife Gauri was. Ramu smiled at her sheepishly. Once upon a time, before he had married Laxmi, Gauribai had been his favourite 'aunt', feeding him and flirting with him in equal portions. But since Gauribai was known to thrust her large breasts at any boy over the age of five, Ramu had never tried to seek her out after his own marriage.

'Gauribai, I am so happy to see you,' he said familiarly. 'Our cow stopped giving milk four days ago. The little one will die if she cannot find a second mother. Could I bring her here?'

'Here?' Gauribai asked frostily. 'Why would you do that? Is that why you came here?'

'Of course. And to see you,' Ramu added hurriedly. 'I'm sorry I haven't been to see you recently. I promise I'll make up for it in the future. Please don't hold it against the little one. She will die if she doesn't get milk.'

Gauribai's lovely face grew sullen. 'You think I care?' she spat. 'Do you think I care that you've forgotten me? I don't.'

'Then let me bring my little one here,' Ramu begged, desperation driving him. 'I'll. . . I'll pay.'

Gauribai's eyes blazed. 'Never,' she hissed. 'I want you to feel what it is to lose something you love.' Ramu, stunned by the venom in her look, fell at her feet. 'Gauribai please,' he begged. 'Punish me, don't punish an innocent.'

'Innocent?' Gauribai sneered. 'Nothing about that fatherless creature is innocent. Better she dies.'

'Hush. Don't. . .' Ramu reached out to touch one of her shapely ankles.

But quick as a cat, she moved away. 'Don't what? Your animal is cursed. The entire village is praying it dies. Now get out. Don't pollute my house any further.'

Ramu stumbled out, avoiding the houses of the wealthy at the centre of the village and heading towards the outskirts where the boatmen lived. But even there, news of his misfortune had preceded him and they all lied, assuring him that none of their animals was lactating.

By the fifth day, the little calf was so weak it could hardly stand up. Laxmi wouldn't leave the little creature's side. She rubbed its stomach with warm mustard oil and tried to feed it through a little tube. Nothing worked. The little one seemed to have accepted the inevitable and lay in Laxmi's lap making sad little sounds every once in a while. Then Ramu, who until then had been paralysed with grief, suddenly had a brainwave. One of the goats, a nanny called Gauri, had lost a child due to a scorpion bite and was equally miserable, her body refusing to accept that her child was gone. He'd been milking her himself in order to ease her pain and they'd even tried feeding some of it to the calf. But the strong sour smell of the goat's milk had made the calf wrinkle its nose and turn away.

Not waiting for the sun to set he drove the goats back to the village and parked them in the sugar cane field outside the hut. He rushed into the angan. Laxmi was sitting with the calf inside the animal shed. She was crying.

'Dry your tears and help me,' he said peremptorily, grabbing the torn blanket the calf loved to worry and rushing out. He dragged the lactating goat inside and tied it to the neem tree. Then he threw the tattered blanket around it and, using the end of the same cord he'd used for tying the goat to the tree, he secured the blanket to the goat's body. Laxmi watched from the doorway of the animal house in growing bemusement. 'Have you gone mad?' she asked.

Ramu didn't answer. His face was set, determined. He pushed past her and heaved the calf into his arms. Staggering under its weight he carried it to the neem tree and set it down beside the goat. Then he stepped back. Laxmi clasped her hands together and found she was praying under her breath.

For a while the calf simply lay there, showing no interest in the goat, but too weak to move away. The goat, after standing stock-still for some time trembling with fear, suddenly decided that the creature beside her wasn't dangerous. She reached across and began to lick the little calf all over. After a little while the calf tried feebly to stand. Ramu rushed to her and lifted her up. He gently guided the calf to the goat's teats. Laxmi held her breath. The calf shook her head, and lay down wearily once more, shutting her eyes. Then, Laxmi caught hold of her head and spoke urgently into her ear. The calf opened her eyes when it heard Laxmi's voice, and then when Laxmi gave her a little push, went up to the goat and began to suckle as if her life depended on it. Over the calf's head, Laxmi looked at Ramu, and in that instant her opinion of him changed forever. Not only was he far from stupid, she realised wonderingly, but he was also brave. For if he could risk the headman's anger for an animal, she reasoned, what would he not do for her?

In the village everyone spoke of the calf's miraculous recovery. 'How can it be? One moment that ugly *rakshasi** is starving to death and the next she is looking fatter than ever?' growled Vilas Rao, glowering at his cronies.

'Some say that it drinks the blood of its mother,' Govind

* demoness

175

Rao put in.

'Perhaps Bicchooji's information is not as reliable as one thinks.' That was the headman. 'Maybe the explanation is not at all complicated – maybe the animal eats daliya.'

Vilas Rao shook his head. 'He is too poor to get his hands on daliya, unless someone's giving it to him.'

'The calf goes to the forest each day, perhaps it eats grass there,' Bicchoo said softly.

'At its age?' Vilas Rao scoffed. 'Have you turned stupid?'

'Maybe this is just a stage in an illness. The calf won't survive, of that one can be sure,' the schoolmaster said soothingly.

Ramu, returning with the goats, overheard Jaiwant Rane's remark and smiled to himself. 'Jai gauri maa,' he said beneath his breath.

Perhaps because of all the goat's milk she'd consumed as a child, by the time it was a year old the calf was incredibly naughty and had a wicked sense of humour. It turned everything into a game: eating was a game, troubling its mother was a game, sleeping was a game, going to the forest was a grand game, even being bathed was a game. In short, every waking minute was a game. But her favourite game was to lie absolutely still and pretend she was dead. Laxmi would then have to pet her and tickle her and sing to her until at last the calf had received enough loving. Then she'd open her eyes and sneeze, a very deliberate theatrical sneeze, and then up she'd get, dashing off into the courtyard to run in mad circles. The game went on until Laxmi pulled a piece of sugar cane from the pouch at her waist and held it out. Sugar cane was one thing the calf loved to the point of madness. Laxmi was convinced this was because her mother had been fed on such large amounts of it while she was pregnant. And so at last the little creature was caught. Though even then, it was the calf who had the last word, looking up at Laxmi with laughing kohl-rimmed eyes and wrinkling her short stubby nose, as if to say, 'Hah, fooled you.' Then Laxmi's heart would melt and she'd hug the little body tightly, as if it held the only warmth in the world she was likely to get.

Laxmi's feelings towards Ramu didn't change immediately, but little by little she found herself beginning to watch him admiringly, liking the strong confident way he handled animals. His knowledge, though he couldn't put it into words and it hadn't come from a textbook, was surprising. One day, as she watched him gently slip the dislocated foreleg of a young goat back into its socket, she found herself wishing her father could have met Ramu. 'How did you do that?' she asked him afterwards. 'Did someone teach you?'

Ramu had looked surprised. 'Teach me? No. I just held her and knew what to do. It was easy.'

'But how do you know what to do?' Laxmi persisted.

Ramu had thought hard. 'I pray to the goddess and she gives me clues. The place feels hard or hot or cold. I touch and a picture comes into my mind, like. . . like a map of where to touch.'

Laxmi shook her head disbelievingly. 'God's gift,' she said to herself proudly. 'Even doctors can't do that.'

Little by little, their conversations grew longer and Laxmi found herself looking forward to their evenings together. She discovered that Ramu knew a tremendous amount about the forest and about healing, stuff that was in none of her college textbooks. And for another matter, he had a way of describing things that made them come alive. So if he was describing how he'd collected the honey from a honeycomb deep in the forest, the lives of the bees in the hive suddenly became a part of the story and one could almost hear them buzzing angrily. Their after-dinner conversations grew longer and longer and they found they couldn't stop sharing – not just their days, but also their memories of the past. And from there it seemed natural for their hands and eyes to meet and hold.

Laxmi's newfound happiness did not go unnoticed in the village. Some, like Kuntabai the widow, were genuinely pleased. Others were relieved. Discord of any kind was considered unlucky in Nandgaon.

'I just passed Ramu's Laxmi and guess what, she was smiling. And then when I turned the corner, guess who I saw holding on to the branch of a chameli tree like a lover? Ramu!' Vilas Rao remarked to his wife Gauri as he entered the angan one evening.

Gauri looked up from the dough she was kneading and scowled. 'And so, what is it to you? Do you think she's beautiful too?'

'So you've noticed also,' Vilas Rao chuckled.

'I notice lots of things, my husband; I don't tell you the half of them,' Gauri replied tartly. Tossing her head so that the loosely-tied hair came undone she added, 'As for that arrogant creature, I wouldn't waste my time noticing her. It would only bring bad luck upon us.'

'Really? Why is that?' Vilas Rao asked distractedly, coming to stand behind his wife.

'The daughter of a suicide farmer is the daughter of a suicide farmer. What can change that? Look at that Soorpanakha. Everyone blames poor Ramu, but I am sure it was Laxmi who did it. She is too clever by half. Soorpanakha was her way of taking revenge on the village.'

Vilas Rao began to knead his wife's shoulders. 'I didn't know you spent so much time thinking about Ramu and Laxmi,' he whispered. 'Come now. Think of your poor husband instead.'

Gauri pushed him away. 'I have work to do,' she muttered.

Gauri was an exception. Most people had already forgotten

all about Laxmi's unfortunate past. For after all, bad luck was something that came to everyone in the end. Just as good luck did. And since no one had committed suicide in Nandgaon, the concept of suicide itself was one that was hazy and distant, a problem for the outside world to contend with.

But Laxmi's ultimate triumph came from an idea she came up with herself. For months she'd walked past the village school and seen Jaiwant Rane struggle to control forty upper-caste boys of all ages. One day, driven by a strange bubble of happiness, she walked inside the yard and asked to speak with him.

'What do you want?' Jaiwant Rane had asked gruffly.

Laxmi hesitated. Jaiwant Rane was a thin, nervous man, slightly cross-eyed and with hands and feet that were too large for his small emaciated frame. Because he was so thin, his head, which he kept shaved except for the Brahmin's little ponytail, seemed too large and heavy for his body. And yet, he somehow managed to make Laxmi feel like she was behaving like a naughty child. Suddenly her idea no longer seemed reasonable, sensible even; rather it appeared vain and arrogant. But she thought of the children and her dreams of being a teacher and the words burst out of her. 'I want to help you teach,' she said in a rush.

Jaiwant Rane had been so surprised by her proposal that he promised to consider it simply because he couldn't think of a good enough excuse with which to refuse. That evening he told the headman of it, expecting the headman to laugh at the idea so that he could then refuse her with a clear conscience. But the headman, to his surprise, was in favour of it. 'You've always complained about how difficult it is for you to manage alone, Jaiwantbhai; take her and use her. It will keep her out of mischief,' he said.

So Laxmi was put in charge of ten naughty little boys ranging in age from four to six. And in no time she had transformed them into model students, awed by her beauty and fascinated by what she had to teach them. For Laxmi was a natural teacher.

Yet she wasn't content. It was the little girls she was after. After a few weeks, when Jaiwant Rane praised her efforts, she felt emboldened enough to ask if she could teach some girls too. Jaiwant Rane looked at her as if she'd suddenly turned into a viper. 'Girls!' he said in tones of horror. 'Never.'

But when Mamtabai, his wife, found out, she argued with him like a tigress. 'And why shouldn't the girls learn too?' she challenged him. 'Do you think they are too stupid?'

'N-no. Of course not. But what will girls do with their knowledge? It is a waste of effort. What use will they have for their learning once they are married?'

'They will teach their sons and save you a lot of work,' Mamtabai replied. 'You think Nandgaon can remain forever cut off from the world?'

'What do you know about the world?' Jaiwant Rane grumbled, not meeting her eyes. 'You tell our Patelji that.'

And so Laxmi began to teach the little girls of Nandgaon as well, giving the mothers of Nandgaon a much-needed few hours of rest, and in the process becoming the most appreciated adult in Nandgaon. But in spite of this, Laxmi remained unsatisfied. For how could a person feel complete, she told herself, without a piece of earth to call their own?

A year and a half passed. Between her work in the fields and homes of Nandgaon and her teaching, Laxmi was soon so busy that she didn't even smell the blossoms of the mango tree, or notice the way the waxy red blooms of her favourite goolar carpeted the ground when spring came around again. She hardly felt the searing heat of the summer, or the rain-heavy breezes of July, the month she had been born. Then one morning Laxmi awoke to feel the cold reaching up through the thin straw mattress again, nestling in the muscles of the small of her back.

She got up stiffly to prepare the tea. Later, as they sat together on the steps of their hut in the early morning sunlight, she asked Ramu, 'How old is Kami now?' Ramu screwed up his eyes, trying to calculate. 'It was winter when she was born and now it is almost Diwali again,' he murmured, 'so that means. . .'

'Twenty months. She is already twenty months!' Laxmi exclaimed.

'Yes, yes of course,' Ramu agreed hastily. Goats he could count quite easily, but months were invisible, complicated things. 'But she is as big as Nandgaoni two-and-a-half-year-olds,' he said proudly, his eyes wandering to the neem tree under which mother and child were tethered.

'That she is,' Laxmi agreed, 'and twice as naughty.'

They said nothing more to each other after that, each wrapped in their own thoughts. Ramu was thinking of the cow, knowing it would be waiting impatiently for him. Laxmi's thoughts were more complex. The time had come to find out if the man on the motorcycle's promise would come true. A part of her doubted very much that the calf when mated would produce either milk or viable offspring. And yet, some part of her believed fiercely, perversely, that it would be so. She'd tried very hard to stamp out that part of herself, believing it was as irrational as Ramu's belief that Kami had been marked by the gods, as irrational as believing that she could restore her father's reputation. And yet, despite her best efforts the feeling had persisted: what if the man on the motorcycle was right?

'It is time to give Kami a child,' Laxmi said at last.

Ramu froze, his glass halfway to his mouth. 'A child?' he spluttered. 'It is too early for that, surely – Kami is but a child herself.'

'No, no, she is not,' Laxmi answered, amused at the fatherly horror in Ramu's voice. 'Our Kami is far ahead of the others in her development. I can tell she is ready.'

'But she is not strong. You know she's contantly getting sick,' Ramu said slowly.

'That is because she eats too much!' Laxmi said impatiently, 'Don't you want to see if what the doctor promised will come true? Why else did you name her Kamdhenu?'

'But she has already given me what I most desired,' Ramu replied, looking at Laxmi in a way that made her suddenly shy. She looked away, her cheeks burning.

For a few moments neither spoke, the air around them electric.

Eventually Ramu broke the silence. 'But why the rush?' he asked.

'Because. . . because. . .' Now it was Laxmi's turn to hesitate. 'Because I am tired of drinking black tea, that's why,' she said in a rush, flinching as she saw the hurt in Ramu's eyes.

Ramu looked away, chewing on a blade of grass. 'Even if we are willing, who will let their bull near her?' he asked in a whisper.

Laxmi looked at him in surprise. 'It's your village. Surely someone. . . We could pay.'

Ramu shook his head regretfully. 'No one,' he said baldly. 'She is a foreigner and will always be one.'

And me? Laxmi wanted to ask, her body going rigid with anger. Am I not one too? And all the wives and mothers of Nandgaon – for didn't the village strictly prohibit their men from marrying within the community? But she knew Ramu was right. Cows and women did not enjoy the same regard. The headman had allowed the cow to remain in the village but it had never been allowed to mingle with the herd. She jabbed her stick viciously into the dying embers. 'We don't need a bull,' she said quietly, feeling once again the need to avenge herself on the world.

'What?' Ramu looked at her in surprise. 'Have you gone

mad?'

'Not at all,' Laxmi replied blandly.

'Then you must mean taking her to a tantric and that I will not have,' he said firmly.

Laxmi snorted. 'You think I believe in that kind of terrible magic? I would never allow it.'

'Then what are you saying?' Ramu asked irritably.

'I am saying we take Kami to the Doctor.'

'To the Doctor? Why? She is quite healthy now.'

'To get her with a child,' Laxmi answered impatiently.

'So that is how. . .' Ramu's voice tailed off as horror crept into his face.

'No, it is not as you imagine,' Laxmi said quickly, catching his face in the palms of her hands. She leaned into it and in whispers explained to him exactly how the insemination was done.

'And it works?' Ramu asked at the end.

'You have seen the results,' Laxmi replied.

'But the headman, what will we tell him? He would never. . .'

'Nothing. . . He needn't know,' Laxmi replied bravely.

Ramu was silent as he digested all that Laxmi had told him. 'But how will we find this doctor?' he asked guardedly.

'I don't know. But Khandwa would be the place to begin to look for him. If nothing else, at least we will find someone who can tell us where we might find someone like him. I remember at the college they talked of an institute not far from Khandwa with many doctors and even foreign cattle,' Laxmi explained.

'I don't like it. Why not simply go to the next village and find a mate for Kami there?' Ramu asked.

'Because the Doctor's medicine will produce an animal that is better than any we would get by crossing Kami locally,' Laxmi explained.

'But how can you be sure we will find the Doctor Sahib?' Ramu demanded.

Laxmi shrugged, 'I don't know. But I feel certain we will. We must. For Kami's sake.'

'And the village? How would we explain it to them? Another fatherless child?' Ramu asked sarcastically.

'When they see the amount of milk Kami produces they will all be begging us to tell them how we did it,' Laxmi answered.

Ramu said nothing and Laxmi watched his face anxiously. 'It means a lot to you, doesn't it?' he said at last, looking sad.

'What does?' Laxmi asked.

'Having a herd of your own,' Ramu replied. 'You'd do anything for it, wouldn't you?'

Laxmi nodded. 'If we don't have land, at least we can have animals. Without either, we are nothing. I am tired of living off the charity of others.'

'But it is the village's duty to look after us. And if they don't, the headman will,' Ramu cried. 'No one in Nandgaon has ever. . .' He stopped, averting his eyes.

'Committed suicide or died of hunger,' Laxmi finished his sentence for him. 'I know, all of you are so proud of that. But I was not born here and I am tired of spending every night in darkness!' she cried. 'And I know there are other ways to live than to always be wondering where your next meal will come from, and other things to eat except other people's broken rice,' she finished cruelly.

Ramu was the first to look away. 'All right, do what you want to do,' he mumbled, getting up and walking out.

CHAPTER TWELVE

THE MELTING LADY

Soon after the dinner at the deputy commissioner's, Manoj had set about applying for the various permissions he needed with renewed vigour. But after eight months of waiting and a pile of letters five feet high, the licensing clerk in the Khandwa Municipal Council (KMC) still hadn't given him the licence to change his plot of residential land into industrial land and so he had been unable to set up his dairy. Then the electricity department had fined him for using personal electricity for industrial purposes, even though all he'd done was install an industrial size freezer for storing semen in the shed, and then to top it all the KMC health inspector arrived and demanded a bribe for not fining him for keeping a non-domestic animal domestically.

He'd refused them all and gone instead to the deputy commissioner again. But the deputy commissioner had laughed in his face. 'I cannot help you,' he'd said. 'Business licences are given by the municipal corporation. I have no jurisdiction over them.'

'But you have influence,' Manoj protested. 'If you told them, they would do it.'

'My dear man, I am a public servant not a raja,' the deputy commissioner cut him off. 'What world do you think we are living in? This is a democracy you know.'

Manoj had uttered a sound that was halfway between a growl and a curse, and left.

He then sold Pratima's jewellery, bribed the health inspector and the electricity department, and applied for a licence to extend the use of his property rather than change it. Broke and sickened by all the bureaucratic wrangling he postponed the idea of giving free milk to the starving and abandoned himself to the nocturnal pleasures that a small town like Khandwa abounded in.

Seeing the man she'd fallen in love with become a stranger, Pratima couldn't help but remember her last conversation with her father.

'I will not say goodbye to you,' he'd said to her, 'for I know you will be back in Mumbai soon. Your husband is an idealist, and no one can live with one. For idealists are worse than madmen.'

'Like Gandhi and Shri Ramakrishna. They were all madmen weren't they, Baba?' she'd replied sweetly, gritting her teeth. 'Then why do you have their pictures on your office walls?'

'Because they are dead madmen,' he'd replied, laughing. 'Maybe you are smart enough to save your madman from his ideas. Wives have great power you know. After I lost my toes on Siachen glacier. . .'

'I know, I know, Baba. You've told me that story a thousand times already,' she'd cut him off.

But though she had tried, she hadn't been able to, she thought bitterly. Her husband had turned away from her and thrown himself into the arms of strange women, returning to her bed in the early hours of the morning, reeking of bad alcohol and cheap perfume. But as she began to think of accepting defeat and returning to her father's home, fate stepped in in the form of the good Colonel Sutcliffe.

Once again it was the deputy commissioner who inadvertently brought this about.

One day Manoj arrived at the deputy commissioner's office to find the latter all alone, balanced awkwardly upon a stool surrounded by dusty leatherbound books.

'What are you doing, sir?' Manoj cried .

'I am spring-cleaning,' the latter replied stiffly. 'Those chaprasis are lazy buggers and the only way to keep them on their toes is to do things oneself every once in a while. Look at these books – they are full of worms!'

'Terrible, sir. Can I help you?' Manoj asked, seeing an opportunity to further his cause.

The deputy commissioner frowned, mentally weighing the consequences of letting Manoj help. 'OK,' he said at last, 'you can throw these away for me. But,' a malicious smile lit up his face, 'read them first and make a summary of what is in them.'

Manoj was struck dumb by the meanness of the man. 'Are you serious, sir?' he'd asked at last.

'Of course I am,' the deputy commissioner had replied. 'The government needs to keep records of what is thrown away.'

That is how Manoj discovered the journals of Colonel Lionel Sutcliffe, superintendent of railways from 1917 to 1925. Lionel Sutcliffe had been sent to Khandwa from Lahore in the Punjab to protect the builders of the British colonial railway from the marauding tribesmen that descended upon the railway from time to time. By the time he came to Khandwa the colonel had already spent twelve years in the country, had two local wives whose colourful fights he duly recorded in his diaries, and spoke Hindustani and Punjabi fluently. He had a cynical view of both the Indians and his British colleagues which surprised and delighted Manoj as he read late into the night. The Indians, the good colonel wrote, were ideally suited to be enslaved because they were idealistic and fond of stories. The English on the other hand were never going to be able to hold Hindustan because they were too interested in making money to bother to really understand the natives. And so the colonel had decided to write down everything he knew about Khandwa and its people so that someone someday would learn what Hindustan had been like before the arrival of the British.

From the colonel's journals Manoj learned that for nine hundred years Khandwa had perched upon the lip of empire and after-empire, never making history but never quite being forgotten either, a frontier town beyond which was only wilderness, animals and forest people. Khandwa's sole moment of glory had been in the thirteenth century when the southern silk route had changed course due to political instability in neighbouring Burhanpur and made Khandwa its rest stop. But then the merchants of Khandwa, resentful at having to part with half their earnings to the king, made a secret deal with the Delhi sultanate to rid them of their king. And so the grandson of the rajah the deputy commissioner had mentioned at the dinner party was in fact poisoned by his own concubines, Manoj read, fascinated, while the army of the Delhi sultanate waited patiently outside Khandwa's fortified walls. After that, Khandwa's history was one Manoj was only too familiar with – a slow descent into abysmal poverty as empire after empire sucked away the peasants' meagre resources in the form of taxes to pay for wars in far-off places and droughts or floods took care of what was left, making the region's farmers deeply and forever endebted. But all that could change, thought Manoj excitedly, with the work he was doing. No longer would the villagers be dependent on kings or the weather, or politicians and their lackeys. He would give them back their independence. He would give them back their pride. And so he vowed to try again.

But Pratima wasn't to know any of this. For it never occurred to Manoj to tell her. In Manoj's eyes, Pratima represented failure with a capital F. He had never told her about his golden-haired Spanish Durga. He had never told her of how he'd betrayed his goddess, leaving her waiting for him in a hotel room while he came to explain to his mother's friend why he could not marry her daughter. And he had never told Pratima that when he chose her he had in fact chosen his mother over the exciting woman with hair the colour of gold. And so, while he holed himself up in the tiny little garage beside Govinda's shed and read and read, Pratima – in ignorance of all that was going on inside Manoj's head – racked her brains for a way to rekindle his idealism.

Every year, around the time of Diwali, the Khandwa Lok Kalyan Samiti*, KLKS for short, held a giant Diwali Mela† in the cricket field at the centre of the town. Walking past the cricket field one day as the traders were setting up their stalls, Pratima had a brainwave. She would bring Manoj to the fair, she thought excitedly, for it would be full of peasants, exactly the kind of people Manoj had come to Khandwa to help. And so one sunny Sunday afternoon, she barged into their bedroom and pulled open the curtains, flooding the room with sudden sunlight.

Manoj groaned and buried his face in a pillow. 'Close those damn curtains and let me sleep. I'm tired,' he mumbled.

'And who told you to go out so late?' Pratima responded. 'Come on, today we will see some real humans for a change.'

Manoj blinked and shut his eyes. But daylight still managed to pierce his eyelids, turning them into curtains of red. 'Humans? I don't need humans,' he croaked. 'Why don't you go and see them yourself?' he muttered.

'Alone?' Pratima's voice rose an octave and opening his eyes a fraction Manoj was obliquely gratified to see the hurt flower on her face. But she recovered quickly. 'Come on, the fair is

* Khandwa people's welfare association.
† fair

starting today. It's what everyone has been waiting for all year. And this year is supposed to be the best ever – let's go. Please, there's a circus, and a death well and a freak show even.'

'What? A death well? Freak show? What are you talking about?'

'The Khandwa Lok Kalyan Samiti's Diwali Mela. You know the big temple on the corner of the cricket ground that we've always found so ugly? That was built from money from the Mela,' she babbled. 'It used to be a very small thing held on the outskirts of the town, shunned by all the respectable people. But then the traders of the town, they decided to build a new temple, and so because they were too cheap to pay for it themselves or it was too expensive or both, they decided to sponsor the Diwali Mela and use the money from it to pay for the temple. The first year alone it made them so much money that they decided to make it an annual event, and that's how –'

'Hold on, slow down,' Manoj cut her off. 'Why are you telling me all this, what has it to do with us?'

'With us? We have to go. The whole of Khandwa will be there, many thousands of farmers too. And. . . and there is a melting lady – I saw her advertised on the posters. Truly horrible.'

'Don't be stupid. There is no such thing.'

'I promise you there is. There was a photo of her too, a truly horrible thing who looked like a partially-deflated balloon, utterly without bones.'

'No. I don't believe that,' Manoj exclaimed. 'Must be something made of butter.'

'Please let's go see it,' Pratima begged.

Too late Manoj saw the trap she'd laid. So he forced a grin and gave in. 'You silly girl. Of course I'll take you.'

The fair was where Ramu and Laxmi came to look for the man on the motorcycle.

They left Nandgaon well before dawn, after giving the animals a full day's ration of fodder. They took a boat to the other side and then walked up to the road head. But the bus either was not going to come or else it had come early and so they had to walk again. Eventually they were picked up by a truck on its way to Mumbai with a container full of furniture. The truck dropped them off at the crossroads to Khandwa. Ramu and Laxmi walked into the town, and stopped at the bus stop for tea.

'So have you come for the Mela?' asked the young boy who served them their tea. He looked at Laxmi's red bangles and sparkling high-heeled sandals, the remnants of her trousseau.

'No we've come to find someone,' Ramu replied.

'To find someone.' A glimmer of interest lit the boy's eyes. 'People come here to lose themselves – how can you possibly find someone?'

'Because he is a doctor, and doctors don't live in villages,' Laxmi answered.

'Which of you is sick?' the boy asked, looking alarmed, his hand reaching out to snatch his teacups away.

'Neither of us,' Ramu answered, holding firmly on to his cracked and filthy teacup. 'Why are you so scared?'

'Because there are strange diseases in the villages these days, things that never existed before,' the boy replied, looking sullen.

'Only because the cities had them first and passed them on,' Laxmi said sharply.

The boy looked unconvinced so Ramu added, 'Look, we are not searching for a doctor for ourselves, we are looking for an animal doctor, one who goes around with milk cans hanging off the side of his motorcycle.'

The boy's face cleared at once. 'An animal doctor! Then you are not sick. You should have said so before.'

'Do you know him then?' they asked eagerly.

The boy's face grew cunning as he perceived a way to extract money from the two villagers. 'Maybe,' he answered non-committally, 'maybe not.' And he moved away to serve two other customers.

When it was time to pay and the boy came around again Ramu gave him a five-rupee note and told him to keep the change. Then he asked again, 'Do you know where we can find the animal doctor?'

The boy pocketed the money quickly. 'It's a big city, this. How should I know all the doctors here?'

'But you said. . .' Ramu said angrily.

The boy gave him a pitying look and shrugged. 'Maybe you can try the fairground. Everyone in Khandwa goes there. You can find everything, even animal doctors.'

But Ramu and Laxmi didn't go to the fairground, they went to the post office first. For as Laxmi pointed out, if there was someone who would know where people lived it would be the postman. But a huge lock decorated the door. Ramu looked helplessly at Laxmi. 'You see? It's useless,' he said. 'Nobody works in the city.'

Laxmi didn't answer, disappointment lodged like a bone in her throat. She turned and stared unseeingly at the teeming Mela ground with its Ferris wheel and circus tent. The noise from the Mela, the hubbub of ten thousand conversations pierced by the cries of vendors and the laughter and occasional crying of children swept over her. She stared at the giant Ferris wheel and felt small, insignificant. Perhaps Ramu and her mother were right. One could not change one's fate. Her feet hurt, the shoes she had brought to come to the city had given her a blister and no one, other than the tea stall boy, had even looked at her and Ramu, much less spoken to them. She turned back to Ramu, her mouth already forming the words, 'Let's go home.' But Ramu, seeing the look on her face, put his hand over her mouth. 'Let's try the temple, the pujari must know everyone,' he said, pulling her by the hand.

So they climbed another set of steps, this time made of cool bright white marble bought by the KLKS out of the money generated by the Diwali Mela and, after ringing each of the seven bells made from a combination of seven metals, they offered the remaining five of the ten rupees that Manoj had given Laxmi and which she'd carefully saved, to the pujari.

The pujari's eyes flickered in surprise when he saw the money. Villagers sweetened their entreaties to the gods with silver, not paper. He glanced at the couple and noted Laxmi's expensive shoes which contrasted oddly with her husband's threadbare dhoti and her own much-washed sari, and his curiosity was aroused. So while Ramu was lying prostrate on the marble floor praying to the goddess Laxmi, the pujari approached the flesh and blood Laxmi who was standing to one side admiring the decoration on one of the marble pillars behind the deity. She didn't believe in prayers any more. Not after what had befallen her. 'Jeete raho beti, what village have you come from?' the priest asked kindly.

'From Nandgaon,' she answered, watching him warily.

'Ah yes. Nandgaon has a very beautiful temple to the Devi, a very old and respected one, is that not so?' he asked. 'Your village is far. I visited it once, long, long ago.'

'The temple is still there, Punditji,' Laxmi answered, and waited for the what he would ask next.

'And what is it you have come here to ask the Devi for? A son, is it?'

Laxmi blushed. 'No, no, not at all. We are looking for someone actually, a doctor.'

'Who has a big black motorcycle,' Ramu added, getting up and joining them.

The priest frowned. He was used to clarifying spiritual and moral dilemmas, or giving hope to the hopeless. 'A man on a motorcycle? Here?' He indicated the steps. 'You have come to the wrong place, you should be looking down there.' And he pointed at the Mela ground. 'There's where you will find your motorcycle. Here only the gods live.'

But Ramu missed the disdain in the priest's voice. 'Thank you, thank you, Punditji,' he said fervently, touching the pujari's feet.

'May you have a long life my son,' the pujari murmured automatically, blessing them before he turned back to his deity.

Grabbing Laxmi's hand, Ramu began to bound down the steps.

'Stop, stop.' Laxmi pulled her hand free and sat down on the steep step.

'What is it?' he asked impatiently.

'There are thousands of people down there. Couldn't you see the pujari was making fun of us?'

'Impossible! Don't talk like that!' Ramu snapped.

Laxmi had never seen Ramu so angry. 'What do you mean?' she demanded.

Ramu's face softened as his anger died. 'Whatever the pujari was thinking or thought he was saying doesn't matter,' he answered. 'The Devi spoke through him answering the question I had asked of her.' He pulled Laxmi up. 'Come,' he ordered.

Ramu imagined that it would be relatively simple to find the man on the motorcycle once they were in the fair-ground, that the man would magically appear before them like the gods in the stories. But once inside, he realised it wasn't going to be like that at all – for the Mela was far bigger, messier and more crowded than it had seemed from the temple. There were literally hundreds of stalls standing shoulder to shoulder selling everything that a villager could ever wish for. From each one, anxious vendors cried out to the passers-by, inviting them to stop and look. Some vendors had even got magicians and for-tune tellers to sit in front of their stalls in order to attract a crowd. Others had contented themselves with big signs gar-landed with flashing lights advertising their wares. But it was impossible to stop. The narrow alleyways were packed with people, entire families, fathers, grandfathers, great-grandfathers, mothers, daughters and great-granddaughters, walking, eating and talking. And amongst them, strolling slowly and aimlessly, looking carefully at the goods on display, were the newly poor who distinguished themselves from the old and established poor by their distant disapproving stares, while the old-timers simply gawped at everything, wanting only to be entertained.

And so Ramu and Laxmi floated on, carried by the wave of bodies pressing against them through row after row of stalls crammed with bright synthetic saris in satin silk and polyester finishes, steel and plastic pots and pans, water pumps, fake spare parts for tractors, bangles, cosmetics, fake lace bras, pet-ticoats and blouses, vegetables, agarbattis, beedis, bindis, rib-bons, medicines, spices, aphrodisiacs, fertilisers and prayer houses. They passed innumerable numbers of children's wear stalls specialising in frilly nylon dresses, cotton vest and shorts and ready-made dhotis for boys, shops selling DVD players, refrigerators, televisions and sofa sets, and dhabas selling hot jalebis, poha and puri channa. At last they arrived at the centre of the Mela, where the amusements were. Here the crowd divided itself into tightly-bunched groups around the different attractions – the circus tent, the rides for children, a giant Ferris wheel, a boat suspended on a pendulum.

'We will never find him, it is too big,' Laxmi said at last, shouting to make herself heard.

'What? No, no. Don't say that. We have just begun to look. He could be inside any one of these,' Ramu replied.

'How do we know he is here? He could be anywhere in this city or in another,' Laxmi cried. 'Let us just go. It was a mistake to have come in the first place.'

Ramu shook his head. 'Have patience, and trust in the goddess Laxmi,' he advised. 'She will send him to us.'

'But we have walked through the entire fair and we still haven't found him. How come your Devi has not shown him to us yet?' Laxmi demanded.

Ramu's eyes scanned the crowd worriedly. He had no answer for his wife and in truth he was beginning to doubt himself too. 'I don't know,' he replied doggedly. 'The Devi works in mysterious ways. Maybe she is testing us. We'll have to be patient.'

'Huh. . . patient indeed. . . You sound just like that pujari of yours,' Laxmi said, referring to Nandgaon's Saraswati Rane.

Ramu blinked nervously. 'Oh no,' he said seriously. 'Saraswati maharaj is an important man.'

'And you, with your direct line to the Devi, what are you then?' Laxmi asked, turning away disgustedly.

But Ramu wasn't listening to her any more. He was looking at the giant Ferris wheel that had begun to turn. 'Come and see all of Khandwa, all of the district and all of Maharashtra from the sky. Feel like a god. See your home from the clouds,' the announcer shouted through his loudspeaker. 'Join the brave men and women who are willing to go up there where before only the gods could go. Your last chance this afternoon. Tomorrow we will be gone. Come one come all, for only two rupees you can be a god too,' he called.

Ramu stared at the man. He was a tiny man, little more than a dwarf, and dressed in the strangest clothes – a long black coat which was short in the front and long at the back, striped trousers that were also too big for him, and a very tall black hat.

'Hey you,' the little man called, looking straight at Ramu, 'you with the beautiful devi at your side. Come up here. The world is not the place for a woman as beautiful as that.'

Ramu didn't know whether to be angry or pleased. He looked

helplessly at the little man.

'Come on. Don't think. Not everyone gets to become a god,' the dwarf urged.

Something clicked in Ramu's brain and the way ahead was as clear as day. Quickly, he grabbed Laxmi's hand and began pulling her towards the Ferris wheel. 'What. . . Where are you taking me?' she demanded.

'Into the sky,' Ramu replied.

'What? No! Are you mad?' Laxmi tried pulling away but Ramu was stronger and held on to her hand. Then the man at the gate had her and was thrusting her into a seat. Ramu scrambled up behind. 'What. . . what are you doing?' she gasped.

'Don't you see?' Ramu cried.

'See what?' The music began and they started to move upwards. Laxmi clutched the arms of her seat, her insides turning to liquid. 'Why are you wasting our money like this?' she cried angrily. 'Do you think money grows on trees? Get me off this thing immediately and let's go home.'

Ramu didn't respond, looking down at the dome of the circus tent as it slowly receded, growing smaller and smaller like a deflating balloon. Beside it, the pointed conical top of the mystery maze looked like a giant breast, with strange-looking men climbing its sides. He looked down at the mysterious amphitheatre from which there emerged a steady rumble and the roar of engines, at the rows of plastic squares in green, red and yellow that sheltered the various stalls.

'Don't you see?' he whispered, awe in his voice. 'We are being tested. To find our doctor it is not enough to look at the world through human eyes. One has to look at it through God's eyes.'

Then, as they rose higher and higher, nearing the top, Ramu took his eyes off the earth and into the burning blue sky. Then he closed his eyes and prayed, his prayer coming straight from his heart, bypassing words. He spoke directly to the goddess Laxmi, begging her to help him find the man the were looking for, to guide his eyes.

Beside him, Laxmi was silent. As they had cleared the forest of tents and telephone poles, her anger had fallen away from her, and she too had stared fascinatedly at the spread of the earth. The Mela which had seemed endless only minutes before was now reduced to the size of a patched and multicoloured bedsheet, the colonial buildings with their tiled roofs surrounding it like the frame upon which the bed was strung. Around it the town opened like a flower – dense, untidy – a mess of blue and green walls and flat roofs with telephone lines and washing. She could see the stepwell, a giant green square cut into the ground, and far on the other side, the royal palace with its enormous banyan tree. Her head grew light. This is what the gods must see, she thought, not just the ugly spread of dhabas and truck workshops, railway repair yards and hardware shops but also the fields and the silence of the mango groves. The Ferris wheel gathered speed and she felt her stomach fall away from her. Like Ramu she looked up then into the merciless blue sky. Higher, I want to go higher, she thought giddily. If only she could get high enough, she would see the future too.

Their car crested the top of the Ferris wheel, paused for a few seconds, and then began to descend rapidly. The earth grew large again and rose up to swallow them. Laxmi was lifted off the seat, weightless, as they fell. Then, all of a sudden, the wheel stopped with a jerk and Laxmi felt the metal of the seat cut into her thighs. They were only a few feet above the top of the tent. She looked at Ramu accusingly. 'So where is he then?' she challenged.

Ramu didn't answer. He was staring fixedly at a tall conical structure that looked like a water tank topped by an onion-shaped dome. 'There,' he answered, pointing at it. 'Look.

Motorcycles. He must be in there.'

Laxmi followed his pointing finger and saw the motorcycles painted on the sides of the structure with film stars riding them. She noticed a small wooden balcony on one side, saw a door open and a man on a motorcycle edge on to the balcony. She held her breath, wondering what he was doing there, certain the rickety wooden structure would collapse under the motorcycle's weight. But the balcony didn't collapse. The man revved up the engine and sailed over the heads of the spectators to land in the midst of the crowd, miraculously unhurt. The crowd roared its approval and there was a rush towards the entrance of the dome.

'Come, we must go. He is there. I am sure of it,' Ramu said leaping off the bench before they had actually come to a stop. 'Hurry.'

'But wait a minute. How do you know he is in there?' Laxmi asked, trying to collect her breath.

Ramu didn't answer. Pulling Laxmi after him, he scrambled and pushed his way to the front of the crowd before the ticket booth.

Trailing behind Pratima as she worked her way systematically through stall after stall of junk, Manoj marvelled at his wife's fascination for rubbish. She was like a magpie, he thought, collecting anything that was bright and flashy. How was it that the daughter of a filthily rich man could like stuff meant for the poorest of the poor? He watched through half-closed eyes as she haggled like a local with a basket vendor selling plastic baskets in shades of mauve, parrot green and mustard. She'd even begun to dress like them, he noted cynically, decking herself in cheap synthetic saris and contrasting blouses, totally oblivious to the fact that that was how prostitutes dressed. Today she was wearing a mauve and pink sari that made her look uglier and darker than usual. He looked away from her at the sea of faces passing by, wave upon wave of them. A giant sleeping sea. He wanted to reach out and shake them awake. But to do that he had to know them. How could one know anything except by separating it into tiny pieces and studying the pieces like a scientist? And how was one to break up an ocean into its individual droplets? One couldn't. It was impossible. But one could join them. The thought came unbidden, giving him an almost erotic thrill. All of a sudden, Manoj felt suffocated by the cluttered disorderliness of the shops. He felt an overwhelming desire to join the flow of humanity passing slowly in front of him, to let them decide where he would go and when he would stop.

And so he plunged into the mass of human debris leaving Pratima to look after herself. Almost instantly he found himself hemmed in on all sides, unable to move an inch of his own volition. Lean smoke-scented bodies pressed into him, absorbing him into the larger body of which they were a part. He let the human tide carry him forward. The din of the fair receded to a gentle whisper in the background, the rumbling of retreating thunderclouds, waves losing themselves upon the still sea-shore. Manoj ceased to think, his brain going limp like an oyster, letting himself be pulled along by the ebb and flow of that giant mass of bodies.

He arrived at last at the centre of the fair. Here the crowd magically thinned, the mass of moving flesh rapidly losing energy and direction, and finishing by forming little islands around the different amusements on offer. He wandered idly from one to the next, marvelling at the giant murals of freaks, ghosts and musclemen, listening to the patter of the hosts trying to sell their shows, feeling oddly free. He watched a group of circus monkeys in crimson jackets leap off each other's shoulders and turn backward somersaults, three or four in succession before their feet touched the ground. He watched the magician stab his assistant twenty times as she wiggled her fat nylon-clad thighs before a group of hypnotised villagers. He almost joined the crowd of people lining up to see the amazing melting woman and the man who ate fire.

A structure caught his eye. It resembled a round water storage tank with a balcony sticking out like a saucer on the top. A wooden wall enclosed the structure and perched on the top of the wall was a young boy in tight acid-washed jeans and long hair sitting atop an Enfield. Beneath him a lackadaisical announcer beckoned casually. 'Only those with two rupees can come up, the others may please stay away. This is not a show for the poor, the faint-hearted or the merely curious. Come quickly before it is too late to see the hero challenge death. Last show of the day, our hero is tired.'

Manoj pushed his way through the crowd, intrigued by the indifference of the announcer and the sheer normality of the adolescent on the wall. Neither seemed in the least interested in the crowd. He looked at the motorcycles painted on the wall, wondering what sort of a show it was.

'Here,' Manoj shouted, holding out a two rupee coin. 'Tell me, what kind of show is this? What does your hero up there do?'

The announcer glanced down, looking supercilious. 'You'll see soon enough,' he replied.

'I want to know first, then I'll decide,' Manoj answered huffily, not used to being given so little importance.

'Why? Can't you wait?' the announcer asked looking surprised.

'No, I can't.'

'Then go,' the latter replied rudely.

Manoj was about to do exactly that when there was a roar from the crowd and he turned – in time to see another young man on a motorcycle leap off the balcony and go sailing over the heads of the spectators to land safely in a little cloud of red dust. The spectators gave a shout of wonder and then they all rushed the gate, clamouring to be allowed in. Because he had been in the front, Manoj was borne along by the tidal wave of eager spectators, up the rickety stairs of the structure, and deposited on a wooden platform that ran around the circumference of the structure covered in wire mesh. He looked through the mesh and found himself looking down into a circular sand-covered pit with high wooden walls that ended at his feet. Behind him, the gallery filled quickly, eager villagers pressing against him so that once more he was immobilised, his body stuck to the wire mesh. He let himself go limp and looked down. It was like looking into the inside of a drum. Manoj experienced a rush of vertigo as he looked down, as if he and all the two hundred people around him were no more than mosquitos suspended on a wire mesh looking into a fishbowl.

In the centre of the pit, looking more like a silly toy than ever, was a battered red Maruti 800. Beside it, wasp-waisted and elegant, was a black Enfield 500 very much like his own.

He waited impatiently for the action to begin but nothing happened. Every few minutes, the door in the side of the pit would open and a young man in jeans would enter, look at the audience and leave. Manoj began to worry about Pratima. He hadn't intended to desert her. But the magnetism of the crowd had been too strong. Now he imagined her turning to ask him something and realising he wasn't there. He pictured her face filling with disappointment and then panic. Mentally, he shook his head, telling himself not to be silly. She would know how to get back to the house. But what if she couldn't? a voice in his head whispered. What if one of those nylon saris she loved caught fire and the crowd began to stampede. It didn't take much to imagine what would happen to a big-city woman like Pratima. Manoj wiggled desperately, trying to dislodge himself from the mesh. But it was impossible and all he managed to do was to draw the ire of his neighbours who in revenge pressed him even more firmly into the wire mesh.

Just then the door at the side of the pit opened again. A young boy dressed just like the others in tight jeans, high-heeled shoes and a checked shirt came in. He had a red bandanna around his neck and an elaborate coiffure held in place by large quantities of hair oil. He walked up to the bike and mounted it with a macho swagger. Then, sitting astride the bike, he took out a comb and proceeded to carefully comb his hair, ignoring the catcalls of the people in the gallery. Manoj felt sorry for the boy, who looked barely fourteen, his skinny frame dwarfed by the giant machine he was sitting on. Using the pointed toe of his boot, the boy gunned the bike, and began to ride it slowly around the ring. Bored, Manoj looked away, staring instead at the faces of the spectators, wondering why they had suddenly gone so still.

Manoj followed their eyes, looking down into the pit, and could hardly believe what he saw there. The motorcycle had climbed on to the wall of the pit, but was moving so slowly he couldn't understand how it managed to remain upright. Then, as the bike circled higher and higher it tilted further and further in until it was perpendicular to the walls, running parallel to the ground. Manoj found he couldn't breathe. For the bike still didn't appear to be going very fast and if the boy fell he would be met by a sheet of metal-hard ground that would almost certainly kill him.

Manoj broke into a cold sweat. The fact that the rider was so young made it somehow worse. Then a second boy came into the arena. He was older and bulkier than the first and dressed like a dandy. Manoj recognised him instantly; he was the one who'd been sitting on the wall behind the announcer. This boy leapt on to the second bike and within seconds he'd almost caught up with the first one. Manoj stared at the faces of the motorcycle riders – so blank, so young and so rural. He wondered where they came from, and if their parents had ever seen them doing what they did.

Then the first boy took his hands off the handlebars of the motorcycle and lifted his legs so that they were perpendicular to the bike. Manoj held his breath, certain the boy had gone too far. Then the second boy did the same. The first boy looked behind him and for a second, an emotion, annoyance, showed on his face. The bike wobbled and the crowd moaned. The boy grabbed the handlebars of the bike and steadied it, then, feeling he'd been outshone, he did something even more daring. He stood up on the bike. Manoj felt his heart clench even as he was filled with admiration for the sheer guts of the boy. One had to be fourteen and totally unaware of death to be able to do something like that. Around him the crowd roared, breaking into a frantic clapping, stamping their feet on the ground. The boy, however, pretended not to hear. He kept going for a few turns more and then sat down again. Then the other boy, not to be outdone, brought his other leg over and stood with both feet on a single footrest.

The two bikes chased each other around the circular walls of the arena, going faster and faster and higher and higher, until they were almost touching distance from the gallery whose very walls and floor trembled, the roar of the motorcycles a deafening thunder.

At each rotation, the onlookers moaned or shouted and so all of them missed the entrance of a third man who slipped silently into the driver's seat of the little red Maruti Suzuki 800 and began to drive it around the pit. In fact, they only noticed the car when it joined the motorcycles climbing slowly but steadily up the sheer walls of the pit. A cry of pure fear tore itself from the throats of the crowd and then everyone went quiet, watching with a mix of fascination and horror the motorcycles and the car chase each other.

Trapped against the wire mesh, Manoj felt suddenly vulnerable. There were too many of them, the walls could not possibly bear the weight of the car, the motorcycles and the spectators. He had a clear image of what the place would become if the walls were to collapse, could almost hear the cries, smell the burning rubber and wood, and see the flames and the blood and the mangled flesh. Suddenly he was no longer a spectator looking at someone else dance with death, he was doing the dance himself. And for him, there would be no escape.

He could no longer bear to look at the young men in the pit. He looked away, staring instead at the faces of those around him. That's when he saw Ramu and Laxmi. For of all the faces in that place, theirs were the only ones apart from his that weren't staring at the vehicles in the pit. They were staring fixedly at him.

Across the pit, over the roar of the crowd and the sound of straining engines, their eyes met.

CHAPTER THIRTEEN

A TASTE OF HAPPINESS

Thanks to Laxmi's careful planning the insemination went perfectly. One Monday they woke Kami up in the early hours of the morning and while it was still dark Ramu, who had borrowed a boat from Kehar Krishna the previous day, rowed them downstream fifteen kilometres to the bridge where they waited until dawn brought an empty truck that carried them the rest of the way to Khandwa.

Ramu returned alone to Nandgaon where he quickly spread the news that Laxmi had returned to her mother's house for her brother's wedding. Kamdhenu, he explained, had gone with her because the animal refused to be parted from his beloved mistress. The latter quickly became the joke of the week. And then Darbari the barber had a brainwave. These usually came to him while he was massaging a head. This time the head belonged to Govind Rao's wife's nephew Prakash, who had only recently come to live with them. 'She must have taken the ugly one with her in order to get rid of it,' Darbari announced. 'As a wedding present for her brother.'

A moment's astonished silence greeted his words, and then his audience burst into delighted laughter.

'Of course, how obvious!' Prakash shouted, clapping his hands delightedly. 'She is a clever woman, that one. I wish I had married her.'

'Then you are either foolish or brave,' Darbari grunted. 'Nothing could be worse than an educated unlucky woman.

She will make you lose your luck and then argue with you while you try to get it back.' The others laughed, happy to have Prakash the loudmouth put in his place.

'Or distract you – if she is as beautiful as that one,' Vilas Rao's son added drily.

And they laughed again.

Laxmi returned with Kami a week later. But since neither seemed changed in any significant way, Nandgaon soon forgot that they'd gone away at all. Life in the village continued at its lazy bovine pace. The days melted into weeks, weeks into months and winter was followed by a short splendid spring. Even Ramu, who had never felt happy about what they had done, stopped feeling that some terrible retribution awaited them around the corner. Only Laxmi, watching Kami slowly expand, secretly rejoiced.

Unlike its mother, Kamdhenu's child was born on the hottest day of the driest June Nandgaon had ever known.

Summer had come early that year, catching everyone by surprise. One moment spring was in full flood, the forest aglow in red and yellow, and the next, the sun had burnt all the flowers away and their shrivelled corpses littered the ground. April then gave way to a furnace-like May and Jaiwant Rane the schoolmaster ended school early, deeming it too hot for knowledge to enter his students' brains. The river shrank to a thin brown trickle, more mud than water, and the once-lush meadows became brown and dead and pockmarked by hooves. The village animals were forced to abandon the river bed and forage in the forest for anything even remotely edible. Many were bitten by the snakes that lay in the mud on the edges of water holes trying to cool off. Others consumed poisonous plants whose enticing green leaves were too hard for hungry stomachs to resist. The herd dwindled by a tenth of its size. But to Laxmi's surprise, no one seemed particularly worried about the drought. There was enough water in the village's two wells, Ramu explained, to see them through until the monsoon. 'By Gaopuja the rains will have come and the river and the herd will be replenished,' he told her.

'But how can you be sure?' she asked.

'It has always been like that,' came the reply.

But Laxmi remained sceptical. She'd never known a summer this terrible in all her twenty years of life. It was as if the gods were determined to stamp out all life on earth and begin the world again. Fires erupted spontaneously in the fields where dry stalks had become ready tinder. Wild animals came right up to the village walls and because they had removed the thorny barriers around the village for fear that they too would catch fire, the villagers took turns patrolling the perimeter, banging their sticks on the ground and blowing on their bamboo whistles to frighten the forest animals away. And though they were quite successful, in the process they also awoke those inside the village who were lucky enough to get sleep in spite of the heat. For the others who lay sleepless in their huts, the guards were human clocks that marked the slow passage of the night.

By early June food became scarce as the previous year's reserves, for humans and animals, began to run out. Those who depended on work to fill their stomachs had to tighten their belts and suffer – for there was no work to be had. The sun had turned the earth to stone. The headman did his best to make work for his labourers, but eventually even he ran out of ideas. And so he gave each family a bag full of rice and one of lentils, and told them to stay home instead.

Like the others without any land of their own, Ramu and Laxmi grew accustomed to drinking watery tea without milk or sugar and eating a single meal in the day. They worried more for their animals. For Kami was at the end of her nine-month pregnancy and looking like the baby would fall out of her any minute. She'd suffered more from the heat than from hunger though, mewling and moaning constantly, looking for all the world as if a demon had possessed her – rolling her eyes in their strange pink-rimmed sockets, twitching uncontrollably. She hardly ate, only touching food when Laxmi fed her with her own hands, though by June she even stopped doing that.

Seeing Kami's suffering, Laxmi was struck by remorse. She thought of her mother's last words to her. 'Don't be greedy,' the latter had said. 'Don't expect too much from life. And don't expect too much from your husband. Obey him and be happy with whatever he gives you.'

She wondered if she'd made a terrible mistake. Who knew what kind of animal she would bear and if she'd be able to feed, it let alone give them milk as well? And Kami was so huge already, if there were complications, where could they take her? There was no animal doctor within miles of Nandgaon. And then, living in Nandgaon where cows were still treated like humans had changed her. The thought of Kami dying filled her with dread. There was the question of the village's reaction too. Because of the heat, people had ceased to move out of their houses and so Kami's pregnancy had gone unremarked, it seemed. But Laxmi knew that the lucky state of affairs could not last. What would happen then? she wondered. How would the villagers react?

Perhaps her mother had been right. She should have tried to be happy with what life had given her. But then, a small voice inside her insisted, she would be betraying her father. Wasn't the education she was so proud of and the furniture her mother had so loved also come out of her father's greed? She thought of her own words to her mother then.

'If you are not greedy, how will you ever get anything from life? How will you make your life better?'

'Better?' her mother had sniffed. 'You think you are better

than me just because you want more? Your father should never have sent you to that expensive school if this is what it taught you, stuffing your head with unsuitable dreams, making sure you will remain dissatisfied until you die.'

Kami's whimpers brought Laxmi out of her reverie and she realised that her fingers had been digging into the animal's flesh. 'I won't let you die,' she whispered into Kami's ear as she stroked her, 'don't worry. I will take care of you and the little one you have inside.'

In mid-June water rationing began. The villagers were only allowed to take two pots of water each, one in the morning and one in the evening. The headman oversaw the drawing of water from the well in the centre of the village himself. Each morning he arrived punctually at six but the line was already quite long by five o' clock. For those who came early got almost a full pot, those who came later got half. By six in the morning his men put a huge iron lid over the well which he secured with locks and those who hadn't managed to draw water within the hour had to go home without.

The twenty-first of June, the day Kami's contractions began, was especially hot. That morning Laxmi and Ramu had awakened at four o' clock, gulped down their tea and rushed out to see the animals. The predawn darkness promised another day of searing heat but Ramu sensed in it something different, something heavier, a whiff of moisture that hadn't been there before. 'The rains are coming,' he said.

'You say that every day,' Laxmi grumbled. 'I don't believe you.'

When they entered the hut the iron rich scent of childbirth filled their nostrils. 'Oh my God, it's here,' Laxmi whispered. 'You go get a light, I will take care of Kami.'

But when Ramu returned with a candle, Laxmi shook her head. 'No, not yet.'

'But the water has burst,' Ramu whispered anxiously. 'What

will happen?'

'Don't worry, the child is alive. It will take time, that's all.'

'Why is she so quiet?' Ramu asked.

'Because I have been rubbing her stomach. The contractions are coming, I can feel them, but the birth will take time – it is her first. You had better go, the goats will be waiting.' What Laxmi didn't say was that a birth without the water could leave the mother so badly torn inside that she would bleed to death.

Ramu opened his mouth to protest but then shut it. Laxmi was right. If he didn't get the cow and the goats out to the forest before the sun rose, they would all return to the village hungry and the headman would give him no payment. For now even the forest had become stingy, its water holes almost dry. And only those who reached them first got anything to put in their stomachs. Those who came late had to fight others to get to the water and many an animal returned from the forest maimed for life. But Ramu's knowledge of the forest had stood him in good stead. He just followed the tracks the wild pigs left. They knew where the Devi hid her water and they dug holes to bring it out. So he always managed to find a little spot that the others hadn't yet discovered for the goats and his cows.

Ramu and the cow left hurriedly, leaving Laxmi with a panting Kami. Alone, Laxmi looked at Kami anxiously. The poor animal was so huge her udders actually touched the ground. How she had managed to hold on to her child this long remained a mystery to Laxmi. For a second Laxmi's blood went cold: what if there were two in there? She sat down and pressed her palms against Kami's stomach. She put her ear to Kami's stomach to see if there wasn't another little heart beating inside there as well. But all she could hear was the restless whoosh of liquid swirling inside.

Water. Suddenly Laxmi realised that they'd forgotten all about it. Usually Laxmi awoke at three and was always close to the head of the line. Now Laxmi looked at Kami, panting loud and fast, and knew she would have to go and beg someone to give her their place. It would not be easy. She swallowed drily. 'I'd better go,' she told the panting Kami. 'Don't worry, I will be back soon.'

When she returned with her half pot, the sun was high. The ground beneath her feet burned and yet she did not hurry, for she was weak with hunger and the half pot of water was both heavy and precious. The sagging walls of their hut looked even sadder and smaller without the cover of the tall lush sugar cane. The headman had sold his sugar cane that spring for an excellent price to a trucker he'd met in Khandwa who took it straight to Mumbai and all that was left in the field was a few cruel spears, hard and sharp as needles. But having decided that sugar cane was too risky a crop and involved too much investment, the headman had removed the pump beside Ramu's hut and transferred it to his other fields on the other side of the village. His were the only fields that had been sown. And almost half the village was employed by him in guarding them from the deer, bison and nilgai* that abandoned the forest each night in search of food. As she neared the hut, Laxmi's ears caught the sound of a long howl of pain and with an energy born of panic she ran inside. Kami's howls filled the little shed. Laxmi knelt down in the mud and slime and held her.

After that it didn't take long. With Laxmi there to play midwife, Kami was able to concentrate on pushing her child out. Three times she pushed, her head on Laxmi's shoulder and then her body went limp and her knees buckled beneath her. Kami fell, taking Laxmi with her. Laxmi looked at the long wet body of Kami's child and laughed in relief. Along with the

* kind of antelope

relief came the thought, inconsequential and yet worrying: how will I wash my sari? There is no water.

It was a large child, jet black in colour. Kami watched it lying there, its legs jerking sporadically, mewling loudly, and wasn't sure what to do. She looked uncertainly at Laxmi and then began to clean herself. So it was Laxmi who cut the umbilical cord and cleaned the calf with the precious half pot of water. And the calf, thinking that the human hands were those of its mother, tried to crawl into Laxmi's lap and find the thing it knew it had to have. Instead all it found were Laxmi's fingers which it suckled desperately until Laxmi pulled her hand away and, gently lifting the little creature, put it beside her mother. Then the little thing instantly found what it was looking for and began to suckle strongly.

How big and black it is, Laxmi thought, awestruck. Another thought struck her and she carefully parted its legs. It was a male. A huge smile lit up her sweaty face.

When Ramu returned, the cow, who had been impatient to return all afternoon, pushed ahead of him and entered the barn first. She went straight to Kami and lowed anxiously. Kami, who was lying down, lifted her head and licked her mother's face. The cow then bent down and began to lick the little calf who immediately woke up and began to search for the cow's teats. The cow moved away and looked at Ramu as if to say, 'Do something.'

Ramu came forward immediately and touched the newborn's nose delicately and then, wonderingly, buried his hands in the little creature's soft, soft fur. Over the two bodies, Kami's and her bull-calf's, Ramu's eyes met the cow's. 'All this is your doing,' he told her gratefully, a catch in his voice. 'I will never forget.' The cow had never come on heat again. She was too old, and too tired. Hearing her beloved two-legs' voice the cow left mother and child and came over to him, licking his face thoroughly as well.

After a few moments, Ramu pushed the old cow away and went to the newborn. He began methodically to massage the new arrival. But Kami, impatient, pushed herself in front. So with one hand he massaged her as well. The cow watched him, quietly chewing away. Despite the impending drought, Ramu was happy. His family was growing, even though around him things were dying. He thought of the flies in the forest – how they flew straight up into the sky just before they died and then fell senseless to the ground.

Then an unfamiliar scent assailed his nostrils. His shrunken stomach clenched, coming wearily to life. He turned around to see Laxmi standing in the doorway, a cup of tea in her hands. But Ramu had eyes only for her face. He had never seen it shine so brightly, like a dark red lotus just awoken from sleep.

'Here. It's made in milk not water,' she said excitedly, holding it out to him. 'Your Kami gave it to us. She also gave us a beautiful healthy bull-child.'

Wordlessly Ramu took the cup from her. He lifted the cup to his lips, then stopped, as if was listening to something.

'What is it? Don't you want your tea?' Laxmi asked, hurt. 'I even begged some elaichi off Sushilabai for it. Won't you even taste it?'

'Of course.' Ramu obediently took a sip of the fragrant liquid and was instantly awash in pleasure. He closed his eyes and the thought came to him that from now on, happiness would always have the taste and smell of a cup of elaichi-flavoured tea.

Watching him drink his tea Laxmi thought of all the times she'd poured her bitterness into that cup, putting salt in it to make him angry, then waking up early and making it for him while he tended to the pregnant cow just so she could repulse him at night. Now, as pleasure suffused his mobile face, she was struck by how handsome he was, and was suddenly proud. No one, not in Khargaon nor in Nandgaon nor even in Khandwa, had a husband as good-looking as hers. She thought briefly of the doctor and his sad wife with whom she had left Kami while she went to her own home. Then Ramu's hands were pulling her towards him. She looked down shyly. 'Are you happy?' she asked. 'We are going to be rich!'

To her surprise Ramu's face darkened and instead of taking her into his arms as she'd hoped, he let go of her.

'What? What is it?' she asked anxiously.

Still not looking at her Ramu said, 'I am scared, that's all.'

'Scared of the village? The headman?' Laxmi cried. 'They have said nothing so far. Now they will all be jealous.'

Ramu's head came up and his eyes were haunted. 'I don't want them to be jealous. It only leads to bad things. I never wanted to be rich. Especially not this way.'

'What do you mean "not this way"?' Laxmi demanded angrily, a lump forming suddenly in her throat. 'What did you want? Someone to come and say, "Here Ramu, you are so good at finding food for my goats, take this land and this lovely house and be happy"?'

'That is not what I meant,' Ramu answered uncomfortably. 'It is just. . . It feels wrong to me, that's all. We are making what was never meant to be. I think the gods never meant for us to be rich this way. They will find a way to make us pay.'

Laxmi felt a shiver of apprehension at his words, but quickly suppressed it.

'Shh,' she said, putting her arms around him. 'Everything will be fine. You'll see. Nandgaon'll be wanting you to be their Patel soon.' And she pulled Ramu towards the hut.

But in one thing Laxmi was wrong. Nearly everyone had known that Kami was pregnant as early as February. Bicchoo had made sure of it.

'Have you seen that Soorpanakha recently?' he asked one evening when he'd joined the others at the headman's house. Everyone had been in a good mood that night. Spring was almost upon them.

'No. But I hear she is looking uglier than ever,' Govind Rao joked. The others all looked at Bicchoo, intrigued. Only the headman didn't look at him, but down at the ground instead. 'Has something happened to her? Did she grow an extra set of horns?' he asked without much enthusiasm.

'I hear she is pregnant,' Bicchoo replied softly.

'What? But that is impossible,' Vilas Rao exclaimed.

Everyone turned to look at the headman but before he could respond, another did.

'That explains it. I wondered why she looks like she swallowed her own mother.'

Everyone looked at the speaker. Jaiwant Rane hardly ever spoke and indeed he seemed equally surprised to hear his voice.

The headman frowned but still refused to give his opinion.

'But how can that be?' Vilas Rao cried. 'No one here would be stupid enough to let. . .' He never finished his sentence, lapsing into a brooding silence, wondering who the traitor could be.

'But she is pregnant alright,' Bicchoo whispered.

'Shocking!' Saraswati Rane exclaimed.

'Perhaps Ramu is trying to make a herd of his own.' This came from Bicchoo, accompanied by a laugh. 'A herd of ugly cows.'

The others laughed too, but their laughter was short, strained. As usual Bicchoo's words, though said lightly, held a grain of truth and it was that which stung.

Still the headman didn't react, his face expressionless.

An uncomfortable silence descended upon the group, the

carefree atmosphere of a few minutes earlier now completely vanished.

At last the silence was broken by the headman. He looked up suddenly and smiled. 'I'm sorry, my friends,' he said, looking completely relaxed, 'but I was just thinking. . .' and here he went into peals of laughter, 'those bulls in Laxmi's village must either be blind or really ugly themselves.'

At first no one reacted. They looked at each other, trying to gauge their neighbour's reaction. Then Govind Rao giggled, Vilas Rao snorted and Jaiwant Rane, usually so dour, put his head between his hands and roared with laughter. Seeing them, Saraswati laughed too, and Bicchoo was forced to join in, though the latter's laughter clearly had a false ring to it.

Satisfied, the headman turned and called a servant to refill his guests' hookahs. Ramu had had enough bad luck in his life, he reasoned – the man deserved to be left in peace.

Night had fallen when Ramu and Laxmi returned to the world. Someone coughed discreetly outside the hut. Laxmi sat up, hurriedly disentangling her sari from Ramu's dhoti.

'Who is it?' Ramu called.

'Is everything all right?' Kuntabai's son replied shyly. 'Maa sent me. She told me to tell you that she had kept a little water for you since Laxmibai hadn't come for the evening line up.'

'Everything is fine,' Ramu replied. 'We were just doing a little puja for the rains. Tell your mother we are grateful for her concern.'

Inside the hut, Laxmi felt an insane desire to laugh and she stuffed her sari in her mouth. In the darkness Ramu put his hands around her and pulled her to his warm hard chest.

Kami's desperate lowing brought them out at last. Lantern in hand, they rushed to the animal house. The cow was awake, solemnly chewing away, the newborn one was fast asleep; only Kami stood at attention looking reproachfully towards the door.

Drops of milk dribbled from her swollen udders to the floor.

'Hai Ram. The poor thing. Heat some oil and get as many pots as you can find,' Laxmi said urgently, sitting down to massage Kami's udders. Milk rained on the ground and indeed it was as if Kami was praying to the earth.

Ramu returned with warm oil and two earthen pots, which was all they had. He sat down beside Laxmi and grabbed two of Kami's teats. They were harder than any he had ever touched and he felt pity for the animal.

Ramu and Laxmi set to work and in no time the first pot was full to the brim and the second almost full.

'Go get another pot,' Laxmi ordered, 'we've only started here.'

'But there aren't any more,' Ramu replied. 'And anyway, shouldn't we leave some for the baby?'

Laxmi flashed him a look of irritation. 'Go ask our neighbours for some pots then. There is too much milk in her. She will get sick.'

Ramu's eyes widened and he turned to go. But at the door he stopped and turned around.

'But then they will all know,' he said.

'They will all know soon enough,' Laxmi replied, pushing back a strand of loose hair from her hot face. Her hands had lost their strength and she was finding it hard to bring the milk out. 'Besides, it doesn't matter now. They will be lining up outside begging for some milk soon.'

Ramu's face mirrored his doubt but he left anyway. Some things could not be controlled. But perhaps, he reasoned, their discovery could be sweetened slightly. He went straight to Kuntabai. As a gift he took her their only cooking pot filled to the brim with milk. Kuntabai wasn't at all surprised to see him. She thought he was coming for the water she'd saved for them. When Ramu presented her with the milk she just stared at it, not quite able to believe what she was seeing. 'What?

What is this?' she said at last.

'Milk,' Ramu laughed, 'for you. Kami has given birth to a bull-child.'

'Is she all right? She didn't bleed too much? Did you have to sew her up?' Kuntabai asked anxiously. 'She was so huge.'

Ramu laughed again. 'No, she is fine. What is more, she is so full of milk we don't know what to do with it. Would you be able to lend us a few pots? I promise you we will bring you as much milk as you can drink.'

'Already?' Kuntabai looked surprised. 'Of course, Ramubeta, and you don't have to give me anything, just your wife's company every once in a while. Go to the kitchen and take whatever you need.'

Ramu thanked her and was about to go when another thought struck him. 'Could I. . . could I have a little rice too?' he asked hesitantly.

Kuntabai's pots weren't enough. Ramu had to return to the village four more times.

Once they were finished with the milking Ramu told Laxmi hesitantly of his idea and for once she didn't laugh at him. For the rest of the night they sat together and made the kheer and then in the early hours of the morning Ramu stole into the village and left the little packages of still-warm kheer in front of everyone's doors.

And so it was that by the time they gathered at the well that morning, the entire village knew that a bull-child had been born to the ugly one and that the ugly one was giving milk just like any normal mother would. But the news was eclipsed by another far more momentuous event. In the night clouds had gathered, heavy rain clouds that withstood the eye of the sun. So when Nandgaon gathered at the well that morning though it was oppressively hot, the sun for once was hidden.

'Obviously the birth yesterday pleased the gods,' the headman joked, in a good mood. 'Let us give Ramu's wife the water first, so that they will add their prayers to the good punditji's and we will have rain.'

Keeping her head well covered, Laxmi went to the front of the line and as the iron lid was hauled off by the headman's hefty servants, Laxmi's earthen pot was the first to go inside. As it descended, Laxmi offered the Devi a quiet prayer: 'Let the little one grow big and strong, make him the village's Kamdhenu,' she whispered. In her mind she had visions of the black one's semen adding fresh vitality to the herd and the entire village transformed by unheard-of wealth.

When the pot hit the water with a dull thud, the villagers cheered wildly, for just then, many of those in the line simultaneously felt on their faces the first few drops of rain.

CHAPTER FOURTEEN
SOORPANAKHA'S CHILD

The headman soon forgot what he'd said at the well. But the others didn't. To them, his words were prophetic. The little one had to be lucky, they reasoned. For hadn't its birth brought the rain that ended the drought? And so the ugly one's offspring was given an identity – and with it, an indelible place in the village; one, moreover, that had been endorsed by the headman himself. Within a week of his birth, Shambhu was being called the 'lucky one', the one who'd brought the rain.

As if eager to make up for lost time, it rained without a break for a fortnight. Humans and animals alike took shelter and waited for the rain to stop. At the beginning the men whiled away their time playing cards and smoking, while the women knitted and sewed, or tried to keep the children amused. The atmosphere in the village was like the afternoon of a grand puja, happy in a hidden sort of way.

Then, as the rain continued to fall, the streets of the village became muddy rivers peopled by the corpses of ants, earthworms, dragonflies and bees. Lured out by the brief periods of intense sunshine between squalls they would be overwhelmed by the next squall. As the rain went on, the villagers stopped going out altogether and sat wrapped in blankets, on their verandahs, staring glumly at the falling rain, the sound of it echoing in their heads, making it difficult to think let alone talk. The village ran out of beedis and matches became too soggy to light. Food had to be eaten half-cooked as wood refused to light and stoves smoked so terribly that the older people begged for them to be put out. And where before people were unable to sleep because of the heat, now it was the damp and the rats that tormented them, for swarms of them had taken shelter in the houses. The children complained bitterly, for the rain meant they were always under the eyes of their elders.

But if the rain was hard on the humans, it was worse for the animals. At first it turned the river bed into the most heavenly of meadows and the animals grew fat on tender new grass. Then, as the river began to swell, the river bed turned into a swamp. And then one day, like rats abandoning a sinking ship, the leeches came out of the mud and each animal in the herd returned home looking like a walking beehive. Ramu was called for and rushed into the forest to collect arjuna bark which when boiled became a thick purplish glue so evil-smelling that even the leeches could not stand it. The animals were kept indoors after that, forced to eat whatever the humans could forage. They lost weight, and developed a fever that spread through the herd, reducing it by a third.

They stopped giving milk. All except Kami, and so those with little animals to rear were soon running through the rain to Ramu's hut with gifts, begging for milk – which they always received. As a result, if there was one topic of conversation that managed to survive the rain, it was the miracle of Ramu's ugly cow. For no one could understand how an animal with no breeding, and no known sire could produce so much milk.

'So will you buy Ramu's milk, Patelji?' Bicchoo asked the headman slyly one evening. He, Saraswati Rane and Vilas Rao were gathered morosely around a lantern on the headman's verandah, watching the rain fall. There had been little conversation that evening so everyone brightened when Bicchoo asked his question.

A hint of a smile turned up the corners of the headman's

mouth. 'He hasn't tried to sell it to me yet.'

'Really?' Bicchoo asked, feigning surprise. 'How is that possible?'

'If he did offer it, I would refuse,' the headman said gruffly.

'Is that so? Why is that, Patelji?' Bicchoo smiled as he sprang the trap. 'The whole village is drinking Soorpanakha's milk.'

Annoyance chased the humour off the headman's face. 'Not the whole village,' he snapped, 'only those who have no other choice. It's this damned rain.'

'It really is a miracle, the way that ugly calf has turned into a real Kamdhenu,' Saraswati Rane gushed, joining in suddenly. He had come late so he'd missed the first part of the conversation.

The others looked at him in surprise and then nervously back at the headman whose brow had darkened like thunder.

'Do you too have to use that word? I am tired of hearing it,' Vilas Rao grumbled. 'Everywhere one goes, Ramu's Kamdhenu is all one hears about. You'd think the Devi had come to live in our village, the way people talk.'

'Well, what other explanation is there?' Saraswati Rao demanded. 'You may not believe in miracles, but then explain to me why that junglee's child can produce enough milk to sustain all the children in the village?'

Vilas Rao looked to the headman for help.

'I think the stories about the cow are vastly exaggerated,' he said slowly. 'You know how people are. And with this rain, their hands and heads are empty. What can you expect? Give it two months, and you'll see – no one will talk of this any more. Besides, bad stock is bad stock. I wouldn't be at all surprised if the ugly one's milk were suddenly to stop. That's what happened to the junglee,' the headman explained.

'What do you mean? How is that possible?' Now the headman had everyone's attention, even Bicchoo's, which was what he had intended. Smiling, he told them about how the young Kamdhenu had been fed on goat's milk. 'Ramu thought I didn't notice but of course I had. The nanny's teats were high and empty every time she returned from the forest.'

'Wah!' Vilas Rao exclaimed, 'you really do see everything. I always thought that Soorpanakha's face resembled that of a goat.'

'But you should have punished him,' Saraswati Rane said angrily.

'The man's a thief,' Bicchoo added sourly.

But Bicchoo had lost his audience, for his story about Kami's mother had had the opposite of the desired effect, and the headman's brow had cleared. He just shook his head and laughed. 'Forget Ramu and his goat – I mean, cow. We have more important things to discuss.'

But the headman turned out to be wrong. The rain did not stop, and interest in Ramu's Kamdhenu did not diminish. For important people had begun to take an interest in it.

The chief source of news about Kami and her calf was Govind Rao's wife, Sushilabai. Overcome by curiosity, she had seized the opportunity provided by a break in the rain to go and see the ugly one's child.

Laxmi had been cleaning the cowshed at the time. When she heard the door open she rushed out. 'Come in, come in,' she greeted Sushilabai, trying hard not to show her surprise. 'I was just finishing milking Kami. Please, why don't you go inside, I will be with you in a minute.'

Inside the hut, Sushilabai's eyes went immediately to the hole in the roof. Ramu had covered it with plastic, but the water still dripped into the room from the edges. So Ramu had dug a drain right through the middle of the room for the water to go out. She shuddered. It was the first time she had come to Ramu's house, and its bareness came as a shock.

Laxmi entered, carrying two large earthen pots in her arms.

She put them down carefully. 'Would you like some tea?' she asked. Sushilabai nodded reluctantly. 'Actually I came to ask for a favour,' she began politely. 'There is something I don't understand in the accounts – can you come and take a look sometime?'

'Really?' Surprise, then worry, tightened Laxmi's features. She had been doing Sushilabai's accounts for a year now and there had never been a problem before. 'I'll come right away,' she said getting up.

'It's not urgent,' Sushilabai hastened to assure her. 'I was coming this way anyway. This rain makes me feel very strange. Sometimes. . . sometimes I just have to get out.'

Laxmi relaxed. 'I know. The rain makes the village seem too small, doesn't it?'

'Better rain than drought.' Sushilabai shuddered. 'We should all be thanking you, it was your Kami's child that brought the rain.'

'The rain? Really?' Laxmi laughed. 'Is that what everyone's saying?'

'That's what everyone's saying. Didn't you know?' Sushilabai leaned forward curiously. 'Can I see it? Is it a male or a female?'

Laxmi frowned. So the business about the accounts had just been an excuse. 'Male,' she said shortly.

'How lucky,' Sushilabai gushed.

Laxmi didn't answer. She stood up, went to one of the pots and took out a cup full of milk. Sushilabai watched her pour the milk into the saucepan and thought, so the ugly one is giving lots of milk. She stored the information away like a squirrel, to be shared later with her cronies.

At last, when Sushilabai ran out of things to say, she got up and made to leave. But Laxmi stopped her, filling an earthen pot with kheer and handing it to her shyly. 'I made this yesterday. Please take it for Mani, Hari and Kusum,' Laxmi said.

'Kheer?' Sushilabai asked. It smelt delicious and envy filled her. It had been several weeks since anyone had drunk tea with milk, let alone eaten kheer. 'You have enough milk for this too?' she asked.

Laxmi could not quite hide her smile of triumph when Sushilabai accepted her gift. Now they were equals. Borrowing a phrase of Ramu's, she replied modestly, 'It is the gift of the Devi.'

Sushilabai lost no time in telling everyone who would listen about her visit to Laxmi. But the story she told was so mean that it only fuelled the village's curiosity. Nothing she said could alter the fact that the Kamdhenu was giving lots of milk and that her calf was a healthy male, already nearly twice the size of other calves its age, and that it had brought the rain. This, along with the fact that Ramu regularly brought gifts of milk, butter and ghee for people in the village, making no distinction between rich and poor, made certain that Ramu's amazing good luck came up again and again in conversation.

'You know, that Ramu isn't so bad,' Bicchoo told his wife. 'He promised to lend me money as soon as the rain stopped.'

'And you believed him?' Parvatibai sneered.

'Of course, a man that stupid cannot lie.'

'Well, if he gives it to you, you bring it straight to me, half-half, remember? Or I will go and see the headman again and have you beaten.'

Under the banyan tree where the barber continued to work under an awning of blue plastic – refusing to give in to the rain – Vasantrao Amrate remarked, a touch of envy in his voice, 'He is a lucky man, that Ramu. Not only does he find a cow in a forest, but that cow has a child that lives and that child has a child too.'

'He is blessed, not lucky. For who can be as lucky as that?' the barber replied.

Vasantrao sighed even as he nodded in agreement. That morning he'd gone to his fields only to find that they had been completely inundated. Though he worked like a slave, he had never had a day's luck in his life.

Seeing the look on Vasantrao's face in his mirror, Darbari remarked compassionately, 'Don't worry. Your turn will come too. Look at Ramu, never a lucky day in his life until that junglee cow turned up.'

'Forget that junglee. You should ask his wife to help you,' Ram Manohar Athare suggested.

'Chhe!' Darbari spat his betel juice into the rain. 'If she was a witch, how was it that her father was so unlucky?'

But Ram Manohar knew he wasn't popular and was used to having his opinions dismissed. He thought for a moment then replied, 'Then it is the Kamdhenu that is the witch.'

'Hai Ram, how can you say that?' the barber said. 'Even the headman has admitted that the ugly one's child is lucky for Nandgaon.'

The headman alone remained unaffected by the gossip surrounding the Kamdhenu. For though the rains brought the new year, the old year sometimes refused to die easily. This year was going to be one of those years, he feared. And as the rain showed no sign of lessening, he became convinced that the river would flood. Though the site of the village had always been spared he was always on the alert because the bank on which the village was now located wasn't as well protected as the one where the abandoned village had been.

'But the river has flooded before and we have been all right. How can you be so certain that this time it will be different?' Saraswati Rane argued.

'Because this year was hotter than I have ever known,' the headman replied. 'I feel it in my bones.'

'But what proof do you have, other than that of your bones?'

Saraswati Rane persisted.

The headman smiled. He knew Saraswati Rane too well to be annoyed. 'In nature everything moves in cycles, Saraswati Rane,' he explained, 'so when you have lived long enough you begin to recognise the patterns. For the last two years we have had good rains; this year should have been bad. Instead, the rains came late and have gone on too long. It is not natural.'

'Well said, Gopalbhai, this year has been different,' Vilas Rao agreed. 'I felt it in these old bones of mine too.'

'A drought and a flood in the same year?' Saraswati Rane cried. 'Impossible! The gods would never allow it.'

'Saraswatibhai, you may think you know the ways of the gods, but I have been observing the ways of nature all my life,' the headman said with some asperity. 'In nature there is always a balance. If you have day, then you will have night; if you have cold then you will have heat. If you have a drought this long, you will have a flood that is as bad.'

Several people nodded, looking scared at the same time. What the headman said made sense to them. Govind Rao, forever the peacemaker, adroitly changed the subject. 'Have you heard the latest Bicchoo story?' he began.

'No, tell us please,' Vilas Rao begged, the beginnings of a smile already in place. The others voiced their agreement, eager to move on to more pleasant topics.

But over the next few weeks, as the rains refused to abate, the headman began to prepare. Together, he and Mahendra looked over the receipts of the previous year, calculating all that had been lent and all that had still to be repaid. Then, from the threads of the previous year he began to shape the year to come, allocating different amounts to a wide number of categories of expenses from well-cleaning to pujas, making lists of those who were likely to pay him in the coming year, and those whose repayments would have to be postponed or written off.

Unlike the government, his was a one-man show. It was his eyes that had to watch and to calculate all that needed to be done in the village, his fields that had to generate the surplus to make sure that the bottom never quite fell out of his people's lives. From the start he had been conscious of the fact that as headman everyone would rely upon him to make sure that the world remained more or less as it had always been: harsh, difficult, but bearable. And unlike Saraswati Rane, he had little faith in the gods. Planning, calculation, anticipation – those were his gods. They were what had kept him headman all these years. 'Me and the gods,' he used to comment jokingly to his wife when she was alive. 'We are what make Nandgaon Nandgaon.'

'Thik hai, thik hai,' she would say drily, 'but the gods are slippery creatures. You shouldn't put your faith in them.'

'Not my gods,' the headman replied proudly, slapping his account books. 'They are one hundred per cent reliable.'

When they were finished with the counting and accounting, the headman had all his grain sewn into plastic sacks, numbered and branded, and then placed in the storage area under the roof.

'Is it really necessary to put them up there?' Mahendra asked, looking quizzically at the headman. 'It will take the men twice as long and because of the rain we only have half the usual number.'

Gopal grunted. 'So you think I am an old fool too?' he asked.

Mahendra shook his head. 'I have seen too many young fools not to respect the old ones,' he answered, making the headman laugh.

Gopal quickly grew serious, looking out towards the gate. 'Much as I hope otherwise, I believe the flood will come, and when it does it will be sudden.' He paused, a note of urgency entering his voice. 'In fact Mahendra, I want you to do one thing for me. Tomorrow you must call the boat people here.'

'The boat people? What for?' Mahendra asked.

'I want them to ready their boats, just in case they have to get us out of here in a hurry,' Gopal explained.

Mahendra was quiet. Then he asked, 'You really believe it will come to that when such a thing has not happened in thirty years?'

'I do,' the headman replied calmly. 'And my conviction grows each day.'

Again, Mahendra said nothing. Then, calmly, he asked, 'And what is your plan?'

'If Nandgaon goes, I want you to make sure that everyone gets to the other side. Take them to the abandoned village, the women and children first.'

'You mean old Nandgaon? None will agree to go there now. It is full of ghosts, they say.'

The headman laughed. 'Why not? As we grow older we all live with ghosts anyway. I think they're quite good company.'

Mahendra shuddered. 'Then I hope that this time you are wrong, Patelji.'

CHAPTER FIFTEEN
THE FLOOD

When they heard the temple bell ring, the villagers were not scared. The bell had been rung in the past – before the Great Flood of 1979 when the old village had been all but destroyed and then again in '84 when the water had come into their homes but hadn't stayed. Laying bets on how far the waters would rise this time, they began to pack their most precious possessions in bundles and placed them high upon the shelves cut into the walls. It was a relief to be doing something at last. Cheerfully they waited for the water to arrive.

But in the end, all their guesses turned out to be wrong. The river first swallowed the marshlands that fringed the water's edge. Then, in the space of a single night, it submerged the long lush meadows where the cattle would graze and covered the ghats where the women would bathe. And after that, as if it had made up its mind that nothing would be allowed to stop it, the river rose steadily up the steep bank to the village's edge. The headman sent word that the old, the sick, the women and the young children should be evacuated. By afternoon only the men and the older boys were left to look after the animals. Everyone else had been piled into boats along with what they could carry and taken to the old village. Except Laxmi, who had insisted on staying behind. 'If something happens to you, I will have no one,' she'd told Ramu fiercely, 'and I would prefer to die by your side.'

'I will not die, buddhooraani. Our Patelji is just being extra cautious. I am staying only for the animals,' Ramu had tried to reassure her.

'Then I will stay too,' Laxmi had said firmly.

'You really think it will come into our homes?' asked ten year old Girish, looking down at the water that lapped the edge of the bamboo cliffs. The swollen river looked like a lake now. The rocks, covered in winter with the chalky droppings of nesting water birds, had long since been submerged. The bamboo bridge they had built the previous year was nowhere to be seen. The house-high reeds along the far bank were also gone. Only the crowns of half-submerged trees marked the opposite bank of the swift-flowing water. There was hardly a ripple on its surface. The eerie calm was deepened by the silent whisper of the ever-falling rain.

'It's so big already, how can it possibly get any bigger?'

'It can't, buddhoo, look at it,' Deepak, all of eleven, replied. 'It has no energy left – soon it will begin to recede. My baba said that Patelji has grown old, old and scared. This water is so calm we could swim in it and nothing would happen.'

'Really, then why don't you try?' eight-year-old Suresh, Saraswati Rane's youngest child, asked. 'Your father is nothing more than a bigmouth, that's what my father says, and. . . and so are you.'

Deepak's face grew dark at the insult. 'OK, I will. But only if one of you "girls" joins me,' he declared.

The others looked at the water and though it appeared quite benign, the sheer volume of it frightened them. One by one they shook their heads.

'Fine,' Deepak shouted. 'Then I'll go alone.' And not waiting for anyone, he rushed down the steep path. Almost instantly the eight-foot-high bamboos closed in around him, whispering their warnings. Deepak hesitated. Through the curtain of rain he could hear the water lapping relentlessly at the foot of the cliff. But he reminded himself of what his eyes had seen and that he was the strongest swimmer of all the boys in the village. And then there was the goddess of the river – she would protect him.

On the top of the hill, half the boys watched the mouth of the path, expecting him to reappear, while the other half watched the tail of the path where it melted into the water.

'Hai Ram. He is mad,' Suresh muttered. The others ignored him, feeling that he was in some part responsible.

'How brave he is, unlike some people here,' one of the boys said.

'Look how big his muscles are – like a wrestler's,' another added admiringly.

'At least he keeps his word,' muttered a third.

'Tell him to come back. The water can rise at any time,' Suresh cried angrily. Why had God not given him muscles instead of brains? He had only been trying to impress the others. 'Come back. It's dangerous,' he shouted as Deepak emerged triumphantly at the water's edge. Deepak pretended not to have heard. Instead he thought of how stupid Suresh would feel when he returned, and how the others would look at him. He thought most of all of how proud his father would be when he told him. So, without looking back, he hurriedly stripped off his clothes and stepped in.

Almost instantly Deepak felt the water fasten on to his feet and so, being the experienced swimmer he was, he flipped onto his stomach and began to swim. Immediately the pull of the water lessened and he was able to cut through the water like a knife through butter. From above the others watched, fascinated and terrified. But Deepak was a strong swimmer and the speed with which he distanced himself from the shore so convincing that none of them thought to run back to the village and sound the alarm.

Only Subhash called out, 'Come back. The flood may come any moment now.'

But all Deepak heard was 'moment'. And anyway, even if

he had heard it all, he wouldn't have turned back. The water, dense with silt, buoyed him up onto its surface. He swam out further, enjoying the feeling of freedom it gave him after the cramped quarters of his family's kitchen. He looked back at the boys on the cliff. They looked tiny and insignificant. He thought of how stupid the headman would feel when he heard of what he, Deepak, had done and all of a sudden felt as big and powerful as the river. He saw the boys on the village's edge wave and waved back. 'You are all a bunch of scared girls. See? It's fine. There will be no flood,' he shouted. 'Look at me.'

But as the words left his mouth he wondered if he hadn't gone too far, and made the Devi of the river angry. He began to swim back. Only now, it was as if a giant hand pulled him back. He kicked out at it wildly. But that only made the hand grip him even harder. He kicked out again and to his horror felt himself pulled slightly upstream. What was happening? Panic brought a fresh burst of energy with it and this time when he kicked out he actually managed to move a tiny bit closer to the bank. He stared at the shore, suddenly noticing others, grown-ups, had joined them. Some were waving at him, telling him to come back at once. Others were pointing at something to his right. He turned his head to the right just as a wall of water crashed on top of him, pulling him into the depths. Though those in Nandgaon would only learn of it much later, far upstream the barrage – made with more sand than cement – had cracked under the weight of the water.

On the river's edge everyone went silent. A few people moaned, others whispered prayers. Subhash blinked away the tears that blurred his vision and searched the churning waters desperately for his friend. 'There,' he cried after a moment, 'there he is by the huge tree trunk. He's OK.'

But Subhash was wrong. Deepak, far from being saved, was actually in terrible danger. For his feet were firmly caught in the roots of the giant tree. He'd tried to kick his way free but the tree had rolled over instead, enmeshing his legs even more firmly under it. Deepak felt bubbles of panic begin to fill his chest. 'Help,' he cried, feeling terribly alone. 'Help me.'

On the banks of the river, the villagers began to cheer, thanking the river goddess for saving their child. Only Deepak's mother was unconvinced. She stared numbly at her son, feeling certain something was wrong. 'Why isn't he coming back to me?' she cried suddenly.

'He will, don't worry – when the river sets him on the shore again,' Darbari Lal reassured her.

Deepak's mother shook her head, trying to find words for the nameless dread that filled her. 'He's too far away,' she said instead. 'He's too far away.'

Just then a fresh wave of water came from behind and made the tree spin like a water wheel. Trapped under the tree, Deepak had a vision of his mother standing on the shore. He waved his arms and opened his mouth to shout his mother's name. Water rushed in, sealing the panic into his lungs like cement. Ghostly arms reached out to embrace him.

Laxmi was cooking when she heard the sound of water outside. 'So it's come,' she thought matter-of-factly, looking at the chapatti in her hands. Five steps led up to the huts, steps she'd cursed when she was tired. Now she felt sure they would save her. The chapatti she was kneading seemed all-important now. And yet she didn't hurry, working the dough with the rolling pin until the chapatti was a perfect round. She threw the chapatti on the meagre flame and began to roll out another chapatti. . . Laxmi made two more, listening to the rush and gurgle of water grow louder and louder. Only when they were done did she get up and go out on to the verandah.

Laxmi had never seen a flood. Her own village Khargaon was too far inland. And yet the scene that met her eyes felt oddly familiar. It didn't take her long to figure out why. Her mind, which seemed to have detached itself from her body the moment it heard the rushing water, was incredibly clear, like a bird that was so high above the ground it could see everything, both past and future.

According to the Puranas, the soul of a dead man had to first voyage through hell before it went to heaven. And that hell, like the world in whose image it was made, had different levels each with its own particular landscape. The seventh level of hell, the priest had explained to her grieving mother, was for those who killed themselves. It was called Vaitarni, the river of pus. The priest had taken great pains to explain exactly what the river of pus contained and how it ate into the soul, causing terrible pain. To protect her father's soul required special prayers, expensive ones. Her mother had sold every last bit of furniture and their house as well to pay for those prayers. So Laxmi had listened carefully, and demanded a translation. What she saw before her exactly matched how she'd imagined the seventh level of hell would look.

The hut had become an island in a seething churning river of angry brown moving relentlessly forward, spitting up bits and pieces of other people's lives, a tiny hand clutched at the verandah and Laxmi gasped. Then the rest of the body emerged, a child's doll, very well made but headless. Other things, a plastic gun, a soap dish, the sodden remains of a filmfare magazine, a child's textbook – all solemnly circled the hut then took shelter under the verandah and then floated away again as the water rose some more, bringing with it fresh debris.

There was a loud crack and the foundations of the hut shook. She clutched on to one of the beams holding up the roof. Where was Ramu? she wondered. Her eyes flew to the door of the animal shed. As if sensing her concern, the door burst open and Ramu appeared, carrying the calf in his arms.

'We must leave now, head for the forest,' he shouted over

the sound of the rain.

'But – but how? And the animals, who will take care of them?' she asked.

'Don't worry about the animals, they will look after themselves. Go. Get out. The roof of the hut will fall any moment now!' Ramu screamed. But Laxmi only stared at him, unable to move. Ramu didn't wait. He threw the little calf on to the roof of the animal house and jumped into the waist-high water.

'Noooo!' Laxmi cried but her cry was swallowed by another sound, many times louder, as with a terrible dry crackling roar, the back wall of the hut collapsed.

Both Ramu and Laxmi watched in a trance as the river ate up their home, sucking huge chunks of the wall into its avid mouth. The sound it made was to haunt her forever after: sucking, chuckling, victorious.

Then Ramu was beside her. 'What are you doing? We have to go,' he said urgently. 'Didn't you hear me warning you?' Laxmi clung dumbly to his hand as he pulled her into the water after him. Immediately a thousand hungry mouths fastened around her ankles. She screamed, kicking out wildly. Ramu immediately lifted her into his arms the way he had done with the calf and carried her out of the ruined yard on to the path that met the road.

'The animals,' she said urgently, when he set her down. 'You must go back, you cannot leave them. I will be fine, go to them.'

'No,' Ramu answered, 'they will be fine.' But the bleak look in his eyes gave the lie to his words.

'You must,' Laxmi insisted, stepping into the water to show she was unafraid.

'Then go towards the forest, not the village, and climb the fattest tree you can find,' Ramu ordered as he began racing back.

Laxmi watched him go. She did not let herself wonder if she would see him again. She promised herself that even if she had to go to the kingdom of Yama* to get him back she would. Then she turned and clambered back on to the path, concentrating on making her way forward, one foot at a time.

Then the path ended abruptly and all Laxmi could see was a vast body of water. She looked around desperately for the road that led from the village to the forest but it had disappeared. The landscape that met her eyes was utterly foreign, another country, made up mostly of water. The once-familiar trees, still clad in joyous new green, looked like medium-sized bushes growing magically in the midst of the lake. On the far side like a shadow painted against the clouds was the forest. Suddenly she noticed small heads bobbing on the surface of the water, swimming for the jungle. Her heart sank. She couldn't swim.

She stared down at her feet, suddenly noticing that the water was no longer reaching her calves, but had come above her knees. She shut her eyes and found herself praying for the first time since her father's death. Then, through the sound of the rain, she heard the splash of hooves and turning saw the cow followed by a scared Kami sticking close behind. When they saw her blocking their path, the cow turned and leapt into the water. Immediately their bodies were swallowed and only their heads could be seen, bobbing solemnly on the surface. 'Kami, come back,' she called desperately, wondering why Ramu wasn't with them. But either Kami didn't hear or she was too terrified to leave her mother's side. Laxmi watched them for a second then jumped in after them. But they were fast swimmers and before she knew it, Laxmi was up to her neck in water and the gap between her and the animals had grown. Then her foot slipped and she went under. When her head re-emerged she tried to paddle to keep afloat but was hampered by her sari,

* god of death

now a dead weight that threatened to pull her under again. Just as she was about to give up, something twisting and snake-like caught her eye, and with her last little bit of strength she grabbed at it.

Kami's rope saved Laxmi. When it went tight and pulled at her she was able to put one foot forward and then the other. At several places the water came up to her chin and once or twice she slipped again and would have gone under if it hadn't been for the rope.

Little by little, inch by inch, she was pulled across the body of water by the animals. But the nightmare didn't end once they were amongst the trees. For the floor of the forest was carpeted in streams, all of them rushing wildly towards the fields, creating currents that could easily knock a man off his feet. The three were quickly separated. Kami fell first, then Laxmi and finally the cow. The force of the water was such that even the surefooted cow was swept along some distance before she found her footing once more. Laxmi was lucky. She was thrown against the trunk of a tree and knocked senseless. When she recovered consciousness it was because the rope that had saved her was wound so tightly around her wrist that it had torn the flesh off.

Groggily she looked around her. Though the landscape was different, each tree a little island in the midst of a thousand raging rivers, the scene was no less hellish. She saw something white in the distance and guessed it was the cow. She then tried to unwind the rope around her wrist and was almost pulled into the water again. She grabbed an overhanging branch, biting her lips to stop from crying out as the rope bit into her again. Then she saw Kami and all thought for herself vanished. The poor animal was struggling to keep her head above water, trapped in the midst of a rushing mini-river.

Laxmi braced herself against a tree and began to pull on

the rope.

'Come, come, come, Kami,' Laxmi called to her reassuringly. 'Come to me.' She pulled on the rope with all her might and felt a large weight suddenly release itself. Kami had found a foothold. Laxmi continued to talk reassuringly to Kami, her eyes locked into Kami's terror-filled ones. Slowly, in spite of the current that continued to bite into the rope at intervals, Kami began to come closer.

When at last they were face to face, the two clung to each other, each leaning into the other, the boundaries between animal and human dissolved. For Laxmi, her arms wrapped around Kami's still quite substantial body, it was as if suddenly a weight slid off her shoulders. Her debt to Kami had at last been paid. Her thoughts went next to Ramu and her heart missed a beat. Had he been able to get out? Kami licked her face and Laxmi realised she was crying. The thud of a branch falling into the river brought her back to the present. She looked up at the overhanging branches of the tree and decided to climb it. There was less chance of Kami being swept away once she had tied the rope to the trunk of the tree. She stood up gingerly and placed her hand on the slippery bark.

The headman was the last to leave the village. He had been sitting, perfectly dry and protected, in the triangular space under the roof between empty bags of grain. From the little window that opened outwards, an innovation for which he was responsible, he'd watched the river slowly swallow the village. He'd had a bird's eye view and felt sorry that he'd never thought of going up there before.

It was only when all that was left was debris floating unheeded through open doors and empty windows that he admitted to himself that the village was finished. The life inside was long gone. He watched a chair emerge from his daughter-in-law's room and remembered it as one of his own that had disappeared during one of his trips out of Nandgaon. He had a vision of his room, the room in which he and his wife had slept for twenty years, slowly filling with water, seeing it from above – the fan and the tubelight that never worked, the photos of his mother, his father and Nehruji, first prime minister, whose words had so marked Gopal over the airwaves in 1947. The water would have eaten away at the faces of those venerable people, wiping out the expression in their serious eyes, taking what meaning was left in them and mashing it into pulp. He imagined the water lifting the bed until it touched the ceiling, swallowing the cupboard, and the square teak box at the foot of the bed in which his wife used to lock away her jewellery and saris. The box had long been empty of course but he hadn't had the heart to remove it, some irrational part of him feeling that as long as the box was there his wife continued to be alive. The idea of water filling its waiting spaces had saddened him, as though somehow he had betrayed his wife yet again.

So lost was he in his thoughts that Gopal never noticed the boat glide noiselessly up what had once been the main street of Nandgaon. When he caught sight of it, his first sentiment was irritation. He didn't want to leave. He saw Jaiwant Rane's schoolhouse crumble, its rain-sodden roof too heavy for the beleaguered walls to uphold. Just before it he had watched Govind Rao's rather opulent structure fall. He wondered if Vilas Rao's house, which wasn't visible, had fared any better.

Suddenly he felt a presence beside him. His father's ghost, looking as he remembered him, only greyer, sat there wrapped in an old blanket. *So this is your perfect village*, he said sarcastically. Gopal looked down, over the gate whose eyes had long since been drowned. The platform below the peepul tree in the middle of the village where Darbari the barber worked was under water. The tree had become a refuge for the egrets and cormorants that normally lived in the river bed. . . It *had* been a perfect village, he thought. There had been no murders, no blood feuds. The drains never clogged, water was plentiful, the fields rich. Few people left the village. The thatch had been a mistake, he conceded. 'I tried to save money – tiles are expensive,' he explained apologetically. 'But then, thatch is what we did in the old days. It is beautiful.'

Are mud walls beautiful too? the ghost of his father enquired sarcastically.

'The plinth is made with cement, it is only the additions that don't have any; the headman clarified. 'Anyway, three per cent cement is enough to withstand any flood.'

Provided the cement is one hundred per cent cement. Did you test the cement before you bought it? his father asked.

'I can't be expected to test everything myself and to be suspicious of everyone,' Gopal answered angrily. His father coughed, a sound eloquent of disbelief. Or perhaps it was Gopal's own cough, grown old with time.

The sound of shouts and splashing drew Gopal's attention once more to the boat approaching him, narrowly missing furniture, beams, tree trunks, cooking pots and chairs. It wobbled drastically, and the four men in it leapt to the sides in order to steady it. What had happened to the others, he wondered. Had they left the village in time, or had the boats rescued them already?

When the boat arrived, he made them take the bags of food first and then come back for him. He waited patiently beside the spectre of his father as the water level kept mounting until only the shikara and the flagpole on top of the little temple were visible. And even when they fell Gopal could not tear his eyes away, feeling as if somehow it was important that someone be there until the bitter end, for the destruction of a world should not be without witness.

CHAPTER SIXTEEN

AFTER THE FLOOD, THE TOWN

The doorbell rang. Another cow for Manoj to inseminate, Pratima thought dully. Since the rains had begun he seemed to have become even busier than before. Pratima opened her eyes a sliver. What time was it? she wondered. The room was in darkness, the heavy curtains drawn. Was it day or night? The television was off which was why she'd heard the doorbell, she realised.

The doorbell rang again. She waited for the maid Anjali to answer it and tell the person to go down the driveway to the back. But instead of the maid Anjali's musical voice she heard the bell ring a third time – a long, irritated sound. She pushed herself wearily off the bed and in the semi-darkness put on her dressing gown.

The rain had stopped, Pratima realised as she went down the stairs. The house was absolutely quiet. Into this quiet filtered other sounds, normal everyday ones – a tap running, someone banging wet clothes rhythmically on the floor, a woman's voice screaming at a servant, a motorcycle refusing to start. Pratima breathed a sigh of relief. She had always thought people in small towns all knew each other. But since they'd arrived over a year ago, not a single neighbour had come over and introduced themselves. The sounds they made were her only companions during the day – and for three weeks the rain had cut her off from them. The doorbell rang again and she hurried to open it, feeling suddenly hopeful.

'Yeh Manoj Mishra ka ghar hai kya?' Mrs Ghorpekar, the lawyer's wife, asked arrogantly. Though her bulbous eyes were masked by a pair of huge old-fashioned sunglasses, Pratima could feel them boring into her.

'Oh-ho it's you, Mrs Mishra! I'm sorry, I didn't recognise you!' she exclaimed. 'You *have* changed.' She stepped inside. 'So hot outside. This terrible rain. You would have thought it would help a little,' she babbled walking into the drawing room, 'but no, it rains and then it is as hot as ever. Who would imagine that not far from here there have been floods. Those poor, poor farmers. Hai, hai, first drought then flood.' She fanned herself vigorously. 'Many more suicides will happen this year I expect. That poor deputy commissioner, not his fault but he will get transferred. Politicians are like that you know, always putting the blame on the bureaucrat.'

Pratima followed Mrs Ghorpekar inside, her mind blank. Where was Anjali? she thought resentfully.

In the middle of the drawing room the lawyer's wife turned and surveyed her slowly. 'Are you wearing your nightie still, Mrs Mishra?' she asked, horror and awe in her voice.

Pratima tried covering her nightie with her hands. 'No – yes,' she stammered. 'I mean, I was about to wash my hair.'

Mrs Ghorpekar looked at Pratima's lank-unkempt hair. 'But there is no oil in your hair,' she pointed out with unassailable logic.

Pratima's cheeks burned with embarrassment. 'Yes, yes, well, yes, you are right Mrs Ghorpekar,' she said, touching her hair and laughing nervously. 'You see, I ran out of oil and have sent the maid to get it. But I was going to oil my hair – well, I mean, wash it,' she corrected herself quickly.

Mrs Ghorpekar looked at her as if she were slightly mad but said nothing. She waddled over to the sofa and perched herself on its edge. 'How long ago?' she asked.

'How long ago what?' Pratima asked.

'How long ago did she go, your maid,' Mrs Ghorpekar repeated herself patiently, primly even.

'A – about fifteen minutes,' Pratima replied.

'Tsk, tsk,' Mrs Ghorpekar shook her head and pursed her lips disapprovingly. 'That is too long. She is flirting with somebody.'

'I doubt it.' Pratima was quick to rise to the missing Anjali's defense. 'She probably couldn't find the right oil in Lalji's shop.'

'She is still tribal, right? We told you they were trouble. Now you will see, you will see.'

Before she could say more on the subject, Pratima interrupted her: 'Would you like some tea?'

Mrs Ghorpekar didn't reply at first. A small smile tickled the edges of her mouth. 'Who will make it for us?' she asked.

'Uh, I will,' Pratima replied. 'I know how to make tea.'

Mrs Ghorpekar gave her an indulgent smile. 'No need. Let us sit down. I have important information to share with you.' She patted the empty seat beside her. 'Has anyone been in contact with you about the flood relief operation?'

'Flood?' Involuntarily Pratima looked at the one window in the room, high up on the south wall, where a chip of milky white sky the size of a bathroom tile could be seen.

Unlike the surrounding villages, Khandwa had barely felt the rain. Its hard cement surfaces gave the water few footholds and so most of it ran off down into the sewers where it decimated the town's rat population. Where the sewers were too shallow or where there weren't any, the roads swiftly became drains upon whose untroubled surfaces bloated and unrecognisable bits of refuse floated solemnly down towards the river.

'This terrible river, she is so unkind. The poor villagers have lost everything. Surely you must have read about it, Mrs

Mishra?' Mrs Ghorpekar sighed exaggeratedly and then looked at Pratima sharply.

'Yes, yes, of course, of course,' Pratima answered, shifting uncomfortably in her nightie, thinking of the rolls of extra flesh that did not belong to her underneath.

'Of course, of course you see. But do you see that these villages, they were made of mud. There is nothing left of them, nothing. The women have lost all their clothes, everything. They are naked practically,' Mrs Ghorpekar explained, pronouncing the word 'naked' with relish.

'Oh.' Pratima could think of nothing to say.

'Indeed. You have no idea, Mrs Mishra, how lucky we are here in Khandwa,' Mrs Ghorpekar continued.

'I suppose we are lucky,' Pratima repeated like an obedient child.

'Terrible, terrible,' Mrs Ghorpekar said, sensing Pratima's resistance falter, 'but tell me, has no one approached you about donating your old clothes and what-have-you yet?'

Pratima shook her head. 'I don't have much but I will do my best to give you whatever I can,' she replied dutifully.

'Everybody has things they don't want in their cupboards. We in the city are so privileged. You can bring your things to the Women's Flood Relief Headquarters, that is WFR HQ, where Mrs Helenji and I are working,' Mrs Ghorpekar said, satisfied. Then, seeing Pratima's blank look she added, 'It is situated in the government middle school, ground floor last room in the left-hand corner.' She got up slowly, looking around the room once more. She gave an exaggerated shudder and turning to Pratima said dramatically, 'Your house makes me feel uneasy. There is no *raunaq* here.' Her eyes narrowed and she looked directly at Pratima's navel. 'Perhaps that is why you haven't been able to have a child yet. You should do something about this place. It is too poor. Too empty. You said your father is rich, no? Why don't you ask him to help? It is not proper for important persons like Manojji and yourself to have to live like this.'

Pratima's head snapped up. 'Why? What business is it of yours how we live?' she asked, eyes blazing.

To her surprise Mrs Ghorpekar didn't react. 'Of course, of course, dear,' she said soothingly. 'You are right of course. But this is a small town and you and your husband are important people. Think of what your neighbours will say. See, I am a modern woman, but others are not so modern and people talk you know.'

'Talk – about what? I don't even know my neighbours,' Pratima said sharply.

'Why don't you have a child? It is natural to have children in a marriage. You want a child, don't you?' Mrs Ghorpekar asked.

Pratima felt something go still inside her. But before she could think of a suitable reply, the lawyer's wife fired another question at her. 'How long have you two been married?'

This Pratima could answer easily enough. 'Three years,' she replied.

'Three years!!!' Mrs Ghopekar repeated in shocked accents. Pratima felt the exclamation marks sticking into her like pins in a pincushion. 'It may be too late then dear.' She shook her head sorrowfully, like a doctor giving bad news to a young patient. 'Hai, hai. Didn't your mother tell you – you have to do it fast after marriage, or they lose interest. Men, they are all like butterflies, going from one flower to another. It is only natural. Where is Manojji, by the way?'

Pratima didn't answer, wishing the woman would go away.

Mrs Ghorpekar meanwhile was staring at Pratima critically. 'Doesn't matter. You are still young. Just wear some silly foreign underwear, tie your sari on your hips and give him some English liquor.'

Pratima felt the blood rush to her cheeks. 'It's not that. I. . . I have too many things to do,' she mumbled.

'To do? What is there to do in this town? Give up this false shyness of yours. You are no longer a girl, you are a married woman now. We know what men are about. If you have a problem you can ask me,' Mrs Ghorpekar said eagerly.

But Pratima was on her guard. 'Thank you, Mrs Ghorpekar,' she said stiffly, 'but we have no problems. My husband and I are very close. I. . . we. . . we don't want children because they would interfere with his – I mean, our work,' Pratima replied awkwardly.

'Work, shirk.' Mrs Ghorpekar pursed her lips and shook her head. 'Look at you, wearing your nightie at twelve-thirty in the afternoon. You should get out of your house more, madam. We never see you two together in Gandhi Park. He comes but you are never there. Or anywhere else. You are like a shadow, madam.' Her eyebrows came together, and she glared at Pratima accusingly. 'You don't believe in God either, do you? You never come to satsang at the temple. If you did, maybe then the baby would come to you.' Her tiny nod and smile seemed to suggest she'd satisfactorily resolved a knotty problem.

Pratima stood up. 'I will send you my old clothes, but you really must leave,' she said as firmly as she could. 'I have to get ready, I have to go out.' But even to her own ears, the last bit sounded unconvincing.

Pratima didn't go to Mrs Ghorpekar's flood relief organisation the next day though the local papers were full of stories of the flood. Her maidservant Anjali had not returned the previous day and that night when Manoj forced open the lock on the servant's quarter, they'd found all her things, including the mattress on the bed, had gone. With Anjali gone and Manoj out all day, Pratima stopped bothering to get out of bed altogether. The house slid into a peaceful semi-slumber. Street vendors stopped coming around to the kitchen, the milkman just left the milk by the door and the dhobi's son left the clothes beside the gate. Sometimes Pratima forgot what time it was and when she opened the door to get the milk it had already curdled. She gave it to the cats that had begun to prowl around the house, sensing the growing wilderness inside. Within the house, the mould on the walls grew to the length of a man's beard, and spiders made their homes in it, their gauzy homes deepening the shadows.

In the end it wasn't the silence that drove her out but Manoj. She was eating a packet of Maggi noodles in front of the television like she always did when she suddenly felt a presence behind her. With some difficulty she tore her eyes away from the screen and saw Manoj standing at the doorway, staring at her.

'You shouldn't stay indoors like this all the time, you're getting fat,' he said coolly.

Pratima's hands sought to cover her offending curves. It was true, she'd put on weight. Even before Anjali had left, most of her clothes had stopped fitting her. Anjali for all her faults had been a good cook and since Pratima's instant noodle diet had begun, nothing fit except the long loose nighties she'd bought in Khandwa. But since she never went out – and at this she looked at Manoj accusingly – why should it matter? 'But you said I wasn't to go out, you said that people would talk because it was such a small town,' she pointed out.

Manoj ignored her remark. 'Choudhury Sahib was asking about you. It seems you promised to help with his wife's flood relief project. It's been three days and you still haven't gone. You'd better tidy up and go tomorrow.' He gave her another disdainful look and left.

When the front door closed, Pratima got up and went to the window. She saw his shadow make its way down the driveway to the 'office' at the back. The light came on, a thin line under the door. Pratima's lips tightened. She knew all about the door at the back of the barn. He wouldn't return before dawn.

But since more than anything she longed for Manoj's approval, the next day Pratima got out of bed, determined to stop by the flood relief office. But by the time Pratima had cleared out her closets, making a huge bundle of her trousseau clothes for the flood relief, since nothing fitted any more, it was already almost evening. She stepped outside hesitantly, like a sick person who wonders if she has the right to wander amongst the healthy. The street gleamed like a giant diseased tongue. She stared at it fearfully, convinced that as soon as she stepped on it, it would swallow her up. She waited for a while. The street remained deserted, no nosy neighbours coming out to look at her. She blinked at the glaring blues and purples of the houses, then steeled herself. One step at a time, she told herself encouragingly. Her legs, greatly weakened from her days in bed and the extra weight, wobbled in disagreement.

Eventually she began to walk gingerly down the street and after a few minutes found her walking legs once more. She passed the now flooded and partly collapsed stepwell then turned on to the main road, walking quickly past the temple where the loudspeakers were broadcasting the latest bhajans in preparation for the evening prayers, past the post office, the commissioner's office, the animal husbandry centre, the high school and the government dispensary, outside which a line of blank-faced villagers waited for the doctor to arrive.

She entered the high school compound, hoping that there would be no one there. But even in this she proved unlucky.

'Mrs Mishra, what a lovely surprise.' The high fluting voice of Helen Choudhury was unmistakeable.

'Are you feeling well, Mrs Mishra?' Mrs Ghorpekar asked solicitously, her hand coming around Pratima's shoulders. 'You look a little pale. Did you walk all the way?' A third woman took the bag of old clothes from her.

'So good of you to come yourself Mrs Mishra,' Helen Choudhury said as graciously as if she were in her own drawing room.

'We were about to leave,' Mrs Ghorpekar added. 'Why come so late?'

'No matter. She is here now, Mrs Ghorpekar,' the deputy commissioner's wife said, and turning to Pratima said kindly, 'You will have tea with us, won't you?'

They insisted she accompany them to the sweet house on the corner, from where the smell of freshly-made jalebis perfumed the entire street. 'It is our ritual,' Helen Choudhury explained. 'Every evening after we close the office, we come here for hot jalebis. It is a part of team spirit building.'

'And it is so clean, so modern,' Mrs Ghorpekar added, 'not like the other places.'

Pratima looked around the sweet house with its McDonald's décor. It wasn't at all the way she expected a sweet house in a small town to look.

'Khandwa is changing, madamji,' the silent little woman called Shalini suddenly piped up, 'thanks to you and your husband's influence.'

Pratima wondered what the deputy commissioner's wife had to do with the décor of the sweet shop. 'Did you decorate this place then?' she asked.

There was a shocked silence. All three women stared at her. Then simultaneously all of them looked away, as if she'd done or said the unmentionable. Pratima stared at them in bewilderment but just as she opened her mouth to tell them she'd been joking, the owner of the sweet shop himself arrived.

'Namaskar, madamji,' he said bending from the waist. 'Thank you for honouring my humble shop. What can I bring you? Chai, jalebis, namkeen?' He ran through the list in a practised way and then even as he waited for the answer, steaming cups of tea and plates of jalebis arrived.

'No. That will be all,' Helen Choudhury replied, barely giving him a glance. Pratima's words hung in the air like a bad smell that wouldn't go away. Colour flooded the deputy commissioner's wife's pale cheeks. She gave Pratima a poisonous look and at the same time shook her head, as if negative thoughts were something thrust upon rather than coming from her. 'And how is your charming husband, Mrs Mishra? Not working too hard I hope?' she said brightly.

'No ma'am. I mean yes, actually he is working quite hard. After the flood, you know, so many people have asked for his services,' Pratima replied awkwardly, glad that the question wasn't a personal one. She wondered if Mrs Ghorpekar had reported their earlier conversation to the deputy commissioner's wife. She must have, Pratima thought glumly.

'What exactly does he do again?' Helen Choudhury asked lightly. 'Something to do with dairy cattle.'

'Yes ma'am, cattle breeding.'

Helen Choudhury frowned delicately. 'But surely he hasn't got any animals?'

'No ma'am, it is done through artificial insemination.'

'Artificial what?' Helen Choudhury managed to look confused and weary at the same time. She was a delicately-made woman, her delicacy enhanced by the smooth layer of fat that sat evenly on all her bones. She enhanced her look by always wearing chiffons and other soft whispery materials in pastel shades of rose, tea rose yellow or pistachio. She reminded Pratima of her own mother, she realised suddenly with a shudder. 'AI – artificial insemination. We inject the subject with frozen sperm from a foreign donor.' Pratima had been a good student of the KIRD brochures.

Everyone waited for Helen Choudhury's reaction.

'I see.' She bit her lip delicately, then took a sip of tea. 'You mean he is a sex doctor for animals.'

The hiss of breath suddenly released from constricted lungs was audible. But Helen Choudhury hadn't finished. 'And so I guess that makes you the animal sex doctor's wife. Like I am the deputy commissioner's wife.'

At last the others could no longer control themselves and several hastily-suppressed titters escaped them. Pratima stood up unsteadily. 'Yes, yes, of course. I am the animal sex doctor's wife,' she said loudly. 'I must go. He will be returning soon and I have to make sex with him – I mean dinner. Sorry.'

'Why? Have you no servant?' Helen Choudhury asked with feigned surprise.

'A tribal girl. She went away.' Mrs Ghorpekar answered the question as if it were a pre-planned exchange.

Helen Choudhury shook her carefully dyed and curled hair. 'My dear, you should tell your husband to find you another one.'

'He is occupied with more important things, ma'am,' Pratima said stiffly. They were in a booth and her way out was blocked by the corpulent Mrs Ghorpekar.

'Nothing is more important than family, my dear.' Helen Choudhury shook her head slightly, as if remonstrating with a teenage daughter. 'Never mind, I will help you.'

'Really ma'am, that is not at all necessary, actually. . .' Pratima licked her lips, she hated to lie. 'I think I may have found someone.'

'Really, who?'

'A good village girl,' Pratima replied, thinking of Laxmi again. 'Now I hope you don't mind, but I really must go, ma'am. Thank you so much.' Pratima wasn't sure what she was thanking her for, but it felt instinctively right.

'Of course, of course.' Helen Choudhury looked a little disappointed and Pratima felt better. At last the others let her leave.

'My dear, you should not let your husband neglect you,' Helen Choudhury advised, as Pratima bade her goodbye from the freedom of the aisle. 'Come and join us again tomorrow, my dear. The villages in my husband's district need not only your husband, they need you.' She added, like a politician, 'There is a lot of work to be done.'

CHAPTER SEVENTEEN

AFTER THE FLOOD, NANDGAON

The first to arrive in the old village were the old women with the babies. Clutching their precious little bundles tightly, they walked unsteadily down the narrow path bordered by giant honeysuckle bushes that had once been a broad main street. Many of them whimpered in fear and mumbled prayers. For like Kuntabai and Shalinibai, Vilas Rao's ninety-year-old mother, most of them had carried away with them memories of the village as it once used to be, throbbing with life. The roofless cottages, crumbling clay walls, overgrown pathways and cracked courtyards that the weeds had reclaimed therefore came as a shock.

Kuntabai was the first to break free. She walked firmly to what had been her in-laws' home and entered the doorless gateway. On either side were mounds of rubble overgrown with giant jasmine bushes. A memory came to her of the night she'd entered that house for the first time. Oil lamps decorated the walls of the courtyard, and through the fumes of clarified butter she smelt the jasmine that grew over the doorway. She'd taken the scent of the tiny white flower into her lungs and held it there for a moment, a little flame of hope in the darkness of her heart as she wondered what the man she now belonged to and his family were like. Then the women's voices singing out their welcome had pulled her inside and the rapid patter of footsteps, as servants unloaded the large dowry she'd brought, followed her. The house had seemed so big then, so powerful, holding tightly to its secrets. Now, the courtyard was swamped by a sea of elephant grass and weeds. The house itself appeared lopsided as one half of the roof had collapsed, taking a good part of the wall with it. Something clutched at Kuntabai's old heart. She wondered if the forest would be as merciless with her own home once the waters of the river retreated. Tears began to run silently down her cheeks as she realised she would never again see the house she had built. But she brushed them aside. Leaning down, she grabbed an offending hemp and heaved mightily, not letting go until she felt the roots give. From the houses on either side she heard cries of surprise and dismay as others, following her lead, reclaimed what had been theirs.

Over the next few days the rest of the village trickled in, bringing with them what little they had been able to save from the flood. By then the women had organised themselves around the headman's house in much the same way as they had in the Nandgaon they'd just abandoned. Savitribai, the headman's eldest daughter-in-law, took possession of the headman's ancestral home, a rabbit warren of a place with a multitude of dank, airless rooms and three separate courtyards in the south, east and north, none of them connected. And though it was by far the best preserved in the entire village, she complained incessantly. Ramabai went back to what had been the priest's modest little house, and began to repair the roof and clear the hearth of weeds and rubble. Jaiwant Rane's wife found that their home, adjoining the old schoolhouse, had literally disappeared under the giant banyan tree that had transformed the centre of the old village into a forest of aerial roots and so she moved into the old schoolhouse which had somehow, miraculously, stayed intact. Others chose the houses that most suited their needs. Sushilabai, who couldn't stop thinking about the stocks that had been stolen from her by the flood, chose one of the newer houses not far from the house the headman had made beside the ruined road. 'Just look at that,' she remarked to Bicchoo's wife Parvatibai who, because she felt ashamed knowing Bicchoo owed the Patel, was also searching for a house beside the road, 'that unlucky house that Gopalbhai built himself is the only house in the village that is intact. I tell you, we should never have come here. This place is unlucky – I feel it in my bones.'

Like everyone else, Ramu and Laxmi were allowed to choose a house in the village. But by the time they arrived all the houses in the old part of Old Nandgaon were already occupied. 'Don't worry, there are still the houses by the road,' Ramu told Laxmi.

'What road? I didn't see any road,' Laxmi replied, looking distractedly about her.

'The road came up to here in the old days,' Ramu replied. 'I'll show you later. Now go. Take the animals with you and find us a place. I'll go and get some fodder for them.'

So Laxmi walked down the little path leading to the line of modest houses by herself. She passed the house that Sushilabai had occupied and the one Parvatibai had taken. The next two were in ruins and then there was a stretch of empty land, now a budding forest. Laxmi hesitated, wondering if there was any point in going further. But just as she was about to turn back she saw the edge of a building protruding through the trees.

The house was in surprisingly good condition, Laxmi realised as she stood looking at it. It reminded her of her father's house, for unlike the others, it was quite modern with a flat roof made of cement over the main building which had survived almost intact, and walls made of real bricks. She was surprised that no one had claimed it already but didn't stop to wonder why, setting to work happily, clearing the hearth. For the first time since the flood, the numbness of disaster began to recede. For she was in a proper house again.

But her joy did not remain unalloyed.

When Kuntabai, searching for her friend, saw Laxmi emerge from her new home, she cried out, 'What have you done? Hai Ram, what have you done?'

Laxmi looked at her friend in astonishment. 'What do you mean?' she asked.

'This house. . . Didn't anyone tell you?'

Laxmi grabbed the empty door lintel protectively. 'What do you mean, "Didn't anyone tell me"? What is the matter with it? It's the best house in the village, and it's got the best location, right by the road. I am surprised our Patelji didn't take it for himself. Just look at how big it is.'

A tremor shook Kuntabai's slight frame. 'Hai Ram, where is Ramu? Didn't that idiot of a husband tell you? This was our Patelji's own house.'

'What?' Now it was Laxmi who moved away from the door.

'You must leave it immediately. Don't let anyone see you in it,' Kuntabai said urgently, the fear not entirely leaving her face.

'But I like it,' Laxmi protested. 'Besides, this is the only decent place left in the village and if Patelji doesn't want it, then why should he care who does?'

Kuntabai was too tired to argue with her friend. So she said, 'You have no idea of what you speak. Ask Ramu. I have to go now.'

When Ramu arrived that evening, his arms full of bundles of rain-slick grass, he stopped at the threshold, looking as if he'd seen a ghost.

'Look Ramu, look what I found,' Laxmi said brightly, pretending not to have seen his expression. She had managed to get a small fire going in the hearth and the room was warm and cosy if slightly smoky and filled with the comforting scent of rice. The rice had come from the headman's house, for the headman had organised everything meticulously, right down to the distribution of emergency food.

'Hai Ram,' Ramu cried, striding up to Laxmi. 'What have you done? The whole village is talking about you. Did no one tell you?'

Laxmi shook her head, tempted to lie. But she knew it would not get her what she wanted, so instead she raised her chin challengingly and said, 'I know whose house this is – so what?'

'So what? Have you no sense at all? We cannot stay here.'

'Of course we can, the Patelji doesn't want it. Why will he care who does?'

'But this. . .' Ramu goggled, 'this is an unlucky house.'

'And we are the unluckiest people in the village,' Laxmi replied. 'Besides, one day, when the road comes to Nandgaon, we can open a shop here, and we will be called the luckiest people in the village. No house is closer to the road than this one.'

'Laxmi!' Ramu exclaimed, grabbing her by the shoulders. 'Have you no heart? I told you what happened, how our Patelji lost his eldest child to the road. There will never be a road in Nandgaon.'

'Who says?' Laxmi asked stubbornly. 'That was a long time ago.'

Ramu was shocked into silence. Then he said quietly, 'Nandgaon decided to break the road for Patelji, out of respect for what Patelji lost. This house is a tomb. It is a memorial to the dead, not meant for the living.'

'All right,' Laxmi pretended to give in, 'you go and find us all a better roof over our heads.'

And so Laxmi had her way. For Ramu knew that though he and Laxmi could have gone and stayed with Kuntabai or any other family in the village, no one wanted to keep their animals.

When the headman arrived he was greeted with tears of

relief but mainly grief, for most of the villagers were still in shock over the death of Ram Manohar's son, Deepak. Gopal didn't wait. He ordered Kanhaiya the boat master to prepare a boat and headed the search party himself.

For two nights and three days, heedless of the driving rain, they searched the banks of the river. The edges of the river were clogged with debris; bodies of dead cattle, their bellies swollen grotesquely by the gases inside, were lodged between the branches of uprooted trees, and tangled, half-drowned bushes hid severed body parts. Every now and again, as the villages searched the debris for Deepak, one of these would rupture and the gas would rush out, as if with a heavy sigh. Then the smell of rotting flesh would overpower the searchers, leaving them gagging and retching, as they pressed the ends of their dhotis harder into their faces.

By the second day most of the men were sick of it and only fear of the headman's wrath kept them from abandoning the search. 'Why is he doing this?' Ganesh grumbled to his fellow oarsman. 'It's not his son. The body could be anywhere – why must we risk our lives looking for it?'

'Because he knows what it is to lose a son, you young fool. Shut up and row,' Kanhaiya replied, hitting Ganesh across the shoulders with his dripping towel.

On the third day, in the afternoon, when the flies and mosquitos began to bite both dead and living, they found Deepak's body. Kanhaiya saw it first, a bloated foot sticking out from under the trunk of a tree whose branches were enmeshed in the suddenly exposed roots of an arjun tree. 'Hai, hai. Roko, roko,' he shouted throwing down his oar. Then he jumped on to the tree trunk which wobbled so dangerously he was obliged to sit astride it and inched his way forward while the others secured the boat to the big arjun tree that had trapped the tree trunk. From the sudden stillness of his back when he got to the body, those in the boat knew they'd found him.

When they returned to the village with the body, the headman took the organisation of the cremation upon himself, sparing no expense even though there was little left of the body. Every day, in spite of the million things he had to attend to, he visited the boy's mother, sitting with her silently as she cried and moaned, hearing in her grief the ghostly sounds of his own dead wife's cries. And when the worst of her grief had been spent, Gopal promised her he would take Deepak's younger brother under his protection. 'Our Patelji is a god,' Deepak's mother told all those who came to console her. 'He cares for us like his own children.'

And for once the entire village agreed.

The entire village was present for Deepak's cremation. Jointly they mourned Deepak, and through him, the life they had known. But the headman didn't allow them to mourn too long. Soon he had them all hard at work – the men chopping trees for the bridge across the river, clearing streets and replanting fields, the women cleaning and repairing houses. Only Saraswati Rane remained in mourning – for he could not forget his beloved statue of Lord Rama, buried up to the chin in silt and rubble.

Eventually the headman noticed his friend's silence and asked him what the matter was.

'I can't sleep,' Saraswati Rane explained. 'I keep thinking of Rama Bhagwan, all alone in the mud, no one to clean him, no one to listen to his cries. I should never have left him.'

'But you have a temple here. And the statue, which you have cleaned so beautifully, is the same,' the headman pointed out. 'In fact, it is even older. For it is the other one that was the copy in 1979.'

'That is what I thought too,' Saraswati Rane cried, tears beginning to roll down his cheeks, 'but in the night, that other one calls to me. I don't know what to do.'

'Then we must go and get it,' the headman said and immediately he called his servants and told them to tell Kanhaiya to take a group of the strongest men across the river and rescue the statue in the temple.

Then, as days melted into weeks and the skies cleared, the mourning turned into a recounting of the lives that had been saved and a festive atmosphere began to permeate the refugee village. The tea stall, established under the village tree, a huge banyan with many supporting trunks thick as columns, did brisk business. On the other side of the same tree Darbari the barber stuck a nail into one of the supporting trunks and hung up his mirror; he soon had no dearth of customers for few could tell a tale better than he did. Before every house and at each street corner people greeted each other joyfully, hugging and tugging at each other's clothes in wonder. Then stories were exchanged. Most people had gone up to Tiger Baba the tantric's samadhi* on the hill and thus been saved. Some, not so lucky or so smart, had fled into the forest and a few, had had miraculous escapes.

'Are bhai, tu kahan tha?' And a story would be told which the other man had probably heard at least ten times already, a story that corresponded closely to his own, and yet, the listener listened patiently and with feeling, nodding at the right moments and exclaiming at the punchline. Each story was a little different and yet because the basic story line was the same, it allowed the listener to once more relive his own escape and be thankful. Then news of the family was exchanged and at last with a final remark on God's mercy the two men would go their separate ways. Those who were good at telling their stories were called upon to tell them again and again, and with time their stories became liberally embroidered with other

* Memorial built over the place where a holy man leaves the world.

people's stories, their stories becoming a tapestry of the village's story to be brought out and displayed as and when it was needed. Eventually the story of the flood would become a single story that would one day be painted on to the village walls. But that time had not yet come.

By the end of the season, out of the ruins of Old Nandgaon, there emerged a living village again. And though it still looked more like a camp than a place that had existed for over a thousand years, signs of permanence had begun to appear – new doors had been fitted into gaping doorways, kitchens had been cleaned and stoves and shelves built. And though many a room still lacked a few windows or a roof, in every yard there were bags of cement and bricks and tiles waiting to be laid. In the main street, not a single bush or blade of grass remained. And at the backs of the houses, kitchen gardens were begun. At the same time, old relationships were renewed and new ones begun. New promises were made, loans were taken, children were given as security and marriages were arranged. But no matter how hard they tried to re-establish old habits, underneath their feet, the ground had changed. And the entire village knew it.

Although Old Nandgaon was on higher land, it was also the side of the river which had borne the brunt of the flood. When the flood waters receded they took with them every recognisable feature of the river that the village had known. Like a mirror that had been suddenly and brutally inverted, where the village had stood there was now a long gentle slope of rich river loam that stretched from the now placid river's edge all the way to the forest. Gone were the meadows and the paddy fields where the Nandgaon cattle used to graze and gone too was the low bluff that overlooked the meadows on top of which Nandgaon had sat. On the other side of the river beneath the ruins of Old Nandgaon, the broad flatlands where the majority of the village's fields had previously been had disappeared. The river had eaten into the bank, creating a steep cliff. Beneath it was only devastation – with untidy driftwood, stone and rubble washed up against it.

The flood also did to the people what it had done to the land. Those who had had nothing to begin with gained while the rich were the ones who lost. For not only had the wealth of many generations been washed away, but the little they had managed to bring with them was soon spent in making a fresh start.

And then there was the treasure trove of free goods left by the river for anyone willing to search. In this too, the poor were finders and the rich had the unpleasant task of proving something belonged to them and not to a dead man from a village upstream. Many a fight broke out when a member of Nandgaon's wealthier classes came across a daily labourer carrying his second-best spade or his wife saw her kitchen helper walking proudly through the village with her pressure cooker. And yet none of these things greatly disturbed the general good humour that reigned – for people were quick to remind each other that the river had been kind, kind to all except Ram Manohar Athare. And so everyone was especially tolerant of him, and Ram Manohar, finding that he wasn't so disliked after all, grew gentler with his wife and surviving children. So at least in one respect, as Darbari never failed to point out, the flood did good to the village.

Everyone settled down to the hectic rhythm of a new year. The rich new agricultural land created by the river was parcelled out amongst the wealthy and the powerful, the headman keeping most of it. Few people grumbled though, for they were all aware that without the headman, they would probably not have survived anyway. And then there was too much work to do. Fields had to be cleaned and re-sown quickly, and fences had to be made to protect them. In this too, hands were required and those with land were forced to sell their lands in order to raise the money needed to clear their fields. In this, like in everything else, it was the headman who gained, for he was the one and only buyer in the village.

One person was not happy with the distribution of the land across the river, and this was Laxmi.

'Why don't you go and claim a piece of the land across the river?' Laxmi told Ramu as soon as the river waters had receded. 'It is excellent.'

'But we have no right to it – it belongs to the village,' Ramu replied.

'But you are a part of the village!' Laxmi exclaimed. 'You aren't going to walk off with it.'

'But we have no right.' Ramu began to look uncomfortable. 'It is for the headman to decide – and those who lost their lands will be offered the land first. That is the custom.'

'To hell with the custom!' Laxmi said angrily. 'Just go and fence off a little bit. I will get you help. We can do it in a night.'

'Oh no!' Ramu held up his hands in supplication. 'The headman would kill me.'

'He won't. He knows he will be put into jail if he did. There is no law saying you cannot claim land that didn't previously exist. All I ask is that you take a tiny piece just on the edge of the water. You deserve it. You work like an ox from morning until night clearing his fields for him.'

'Enough!' Suddenly Ramu lost his temper. 'I didn't know you were as greedy as your father!'

It was as if he'd slapped her. Laxmi's hand went to her cheek but she said nothing. Silently, she got up and left. Ramu called after her weakly, but he didn't go looking for her until much later and by then Laxmi was nowhere to be found.

But Laxmi didn't kill herself. The search party found her

curled up at the base of a tree on the other side of the new fields, at the edge of the forest. The next day the headman called her over.

'Is everything all right? Do you need something?' he asked kindly, and when she didn't reply, he added, 'Ramu is a good man but naughty sometimes. If he troubles you let me know; I will put him straight.'

Suddenly Laxmi looked straight into his eyes, letting him feel the full force of her will. 'Patelji, Ramu has worked faithfully for you all his life. Can you not give us a little piece of land?'

The headman was so surprised by the request he actually took a step backwards before he gained control of himself. Angry that she had managed to make him look foolish, he answered more sharply than he had intended. 'Out of the question! How dare you?'

To his surprise she didn't try to argue or even to beg. Instead she flung him a look of such hatred that he blinked. When he looked at her again, she was already halfway across the field, taking her place amongst the line of labourers.

CHAPTER EIGHTEEN

THREE MEN IN A FIELD

By the end of the rainy season the sky was so clear that when dawn came, it came suddenly. One moment the sky was grey and soft, and the next a deep rose-red flush was climbing rapidly into the sky. The rose turned red, then orange and gold. But in the fields, the labourers were already hard at work.

At the far end of the newly-ploughed fields, close to the river, three men crouched low, as they sowed a late crop of maize. As they worked they talked quietly in voices that rivalled the birds in their sweetness. 'Wonder if we will find anything in this field,' Keshu Khora remarked to his companion. 'Do you remember how Saibu found a statue of the Kamdhenu when he was working the headman's fields last month?'

'Really? What did he do with it?' Ganga Ram, beside him, asked, looking up.

'He gave it to Ramu,' Keshu replied.

A respectful silence followed, broken at last by Madho, oldest of the three and leader of the Khora community who made up the bulk of the agricultural labour force in Nandgaon. 'Hmph. And what did he do with it? Sell it?'

'Are, what are you saying bhai?' Keshu exclaimed. 'Ramu would never do that.'

'He sells her milk,' Madho muttered looking at the earth in front of him, 'to the chaiwala in Kesarigaon.'

There was a moment's shocked silence.

'Who told you that?' Keshu asked sharply. 'Ramu would

never do that. He knows that everyone who owns cows gives their spare milk to the headman to distribute to those who need it. That is why we always have milk for our children, even those of us who don't have cattle. That is the reason why we are content. . . Ramu was born here. He understands, and Patelji treats him like a son. He would never do such a thing,' he repeated.

'No one *told* me anything,' Madho answered angrily. 'I *saw* him going off in the early morning before it was light with cans of milk tied to that new bicycle of his.'

'Maybe he was just giving the milk to someone there,' Keshu suggested. 'The other Brahmins are jealous of his good fortune,' he continued. 'Ramu is the most generous man in Nandgaon. I should know.'

Only three days earlier, he had taken his month-old son to be blessed by the Kamdhenu. The child had a terrible rash and he had asked Ramu to give him some of the the Kamdhenu's milk with which to bathe the child. Ramu had given him far more than the child needed and Keshu had felt quite over-whelmed. When his child's skin rash cleared magically after the milk bath he was so thrilled that he immediately took a three-kilogram Katla fish that he had caught hours earlier in the river to Ramu. Since then, for him, Ramu could do no wrong.

After a while it was Madho himself who broke the silence. 'I knew that Ramu when he used to run around in nothing but his underwear. I picked him up when he fell down, dried his tears. He was a simple fellow. He couldn't plant a field if his life depended upon it. And now, just because he has bought a field full of rocks, he thinks he is going to become a farmer.'

An uncomfortable silence followed his words. 'Whatever the man, that cow of his is a true Kamdhenu,' Ganga the peace-maker said at last. 'Look how lucky he has been since she arrived. A man who had nothing, not even a mother, now has a wife, a cow and land too. Surely he is blessed by the Devi.'

'That's not what I meant,' Keshu disagreed. 'And even if he is selling his milk outside the village, he is right. Last year was a good year for us all, we could have bought land too if we'd wanted, instead of spending it on music and drinking.'

'They'd never have sold it to us,' Madho growled. 'You listen too much to the likes of your Ramu.'

'How do you know?' Keshu challenged.

'Because I have lived twice as long as you, you young fool,' Madho growled. 'Now stop talking and work.'

At noon, when the men broke for lunch, the entire field had been planted and half of the next one too. They stretched their aching backs and walked to the shelter of the trees. A single silent woman awaited them there, her wiry arm hugging a branch from which three three-tiered tiffins hung. As soon as she saw them approach, she threw off the immobility that enveloped her and got down to business. She put the tiffins in a semicircle on the ground and opened them ceremoniously. Then she helped each man wash his hands and served them quickly. The men wiped their faces with their gamchhas, now freed from the trees which had played guardian to them all morning and attacked the food hungrily. Nothing was said. The noon silence was only broken by the occasional distant sound of a truck horn. After serving them, the woman got up and resumed her earlier position, immobility settling over her just as suddenly as it had left. She remained like that, arms wrapped like a creeper around the tree, until the men's lunch was over, at which point she collected the three tiffins, wrapped them in a ragged gamchha and carried them back to the village. Just outside the walls, she sat down, reopened the tiffins and greedily finished what little remained inside.

In the roofless schoolhouse, the end of school was heralded by the sound of metal hitting metal and a tidal wave of shouts.

Under the giant neem tree Laxmi was arguing with six-year-old Mukul. 'No, you cannot come home with me. What will your parents think?' she repeated for the nth time.

'But I want to see her,' he whined. 'I promised her yesterday.'

'But you have to go home first.'

'Why do I have to?' Mukul stuck his little chin out pugnaciously.

'Because,' Laxmi stopped suddenly, seeing where he'd led her. The 'why' game was one they'd all played. It was designed to wear out the adult and never failed.

'Because she's gone out,' Laxmi replied firmly.

'Out? But she promised. . . she promised yesterday.' Mukul's lower lip began to tremble.

'Yes, but she's gone to the forest today,' Laxmi lied. Since the flood Kami had grown fat and lazy. She no longer went into the forest, preferring to graze when she could on fresh juicy river grass or to eat the fodder Laxmi and Ramu so carefully prepared. As she still wasn't allowed to go with the herd, in spite of the fact that the herd had been decimated, Ramu had the unpleasant task of taking her out at night like a thief. Often the two, Ramu and Laxmi, went together, glad of the fresh night air and the freedom that came with being far from the others. All through the fragrant autumn their love had bloomed.

'When will she come back?' Mukul asked sadly.

'In the evening,' Laxmi replied, knowing how hard it was to be in love for the first time. 'You can come then.'

'But the others will be there,' Mukul complained, 'and I am so small she won't even see me.'

Laxmi hugged him tightly. 'Don't worry, Kami will certainly know you are there. I will tell her you are coming in the evening.'

Mukul brightened instantly. 'You will?'

'I will,' Laxmi promised seriously.

Mukul's face brightened briefly then darkened again. 'But evening is so far away,' he complained.

Inside the silent classroom, Jaiwant Rane's wayward mind clung to the image of Laxmi hugging the little boy. Some called her a witch, he reminded himself, others said she made money out of mud. But the girl was good with the children, practical, intelligent. They learnt quickly in order to please her. He had never had such good results. He watched Laxmi leave the compound. Perhaps, he thought whimsically, she really was a goddess.

Walking through the village to her house, Laxmi didn't notice the way people looked up as she walked past. Nor did she hear the buzz of whispered conversation that began as soon as she appeared. Her mind was elsewhere, tossing numbers about as she tried to work out how much money they could make from Kami before she would need to be inseminated again. For though the Kesarigaon tea shop owner paid them well and took all they had to give, she dreamt of taking their milk directly to Khandwa. She knew they'd get double or even triple the amount there. Instead of fifty rupees a day they'd be making a hundred and fifty or even two hundred a day. In a few short months they could buy another cow and get it inseminated as well. In a year they would have a herd of their own and be able to buy two fields!

Buy. The word made her shiver. In the last three years she had forgotten what it was to buy something. Money crackled against her skin, and a surge of joy rushed through her. She paused in front of Sushilabai's provision shop. Everyone knew Sushilabai overcharged her customers. So, like the others, Laxmi made sure Ramu bought what they needed in Kesarigaon. But since he couldn't read, Ramu always forgot something. This time it was tea sugar and cardamom he'd forgotten. She decided to go in and buy it anyway.

Sushilabai was with a customer when Laxmi walked in so it was Govind Rao who rushed to serve her. 'Laxmibai!' he gushed. 'Welcome. Our little Subhash is always talking about you, I mean, your Kamdhenu,' he corrected himself quickly, his eyes moving restlessly from her face to her breasts. 'And Kami's child is growing well, I hear? Subhash can't stop talking of it. He only wants to play with it, none of ours will do. He says they are not as beautiful as your one.'

'I want a pao packet of chai, half a kilo of sugar, one pao of elaichi,' Laxmi interrupted him coldly.

Govind Rao stared. He was not used to being interrupted by a woman. The other customer, Vilas Rao's wife, giggled, hastily turning it into a cough.

Seeing her husband's discomfiture, Sushilabai waddled up, every inch the respectable matron. 'What do you want? You know you are not welcome here.'

Laxmi felt the blood rush to her cheeks. She wanted to protest but found herself at a loss for words. Meekly she repeated her order.

'All right. Here you are.' Stonily, Sushilabai measured out the sugar and elaichi and added the tea to the pile on the counter. She didn't utter a word as Laxmi counted out the money and put it beside the goods.

After Laxmi left, Sushilabai turned on her husband. 'Why are you treating her like a princess?' she spat.

'I. . . I was only trying to help until you were free to deal with her yourself,' Govind Rao stammered.

'Rubbish. You should have seen your face when you were talking to her. You can't fool me. I am your wife. And why did you have to drag our son Subhash into it, asking about her filthy animals? I'm sure Ramu bought his bicycle with the money she stole from us. No one can make that much money selling milk. Why, our best cows only give six litres a day.'

Exhausted by her own eloquence, Sushilabai sat down heavily on the upturned flour tin they used as a stool. Her double chin wobbled and she buried her face in her hands, beginning to sob loudly. Govind Rao bent over to her awkwardly, trying to console her. 'No, no, no,' he cooed throatily, patting her on the shoulder, 'don't cry, everything will be fine.'

'Nothing is fine,' Sushilabai mumbled through her fingers. 'We are so poor. Look at our house, no better than a ruin. And my beautiful shop – gone. I hate this place.'

'Na, na, pugli. Everything will be all right. You'll see,' Govind Rao repeated stupidly.

'And our animals? Who will replace those?' Sushilabai cried, looking up suddenly. 'Don't you see, we have no milk! No milk!' Her voice rose. 'If I didn't have the shop, then we wouldn't even be able to buy enough for the children. And that witch of a woman, making kheer and giving it to me. Do you know I cannot stop thinking of what that kheer tasted like? I am so unhappy.' And she began to cry again.

'There, there, don't cry, you'll get sick,' Govind Rao said, unconvincingly. 'I'll buy you milk from the headman so you can make as much kheer as you want.'

'I don't want kheer, you fool!' Sushilabai snapped, looking up suddenly. 'I want cows. I want cows that make milk like her Kami does.'

As Laxmi passed the old banyan tree, Darbari the barber saw her and waved. 'Are Laxmidevi,' he called naughtily, 'how is that black and white cow of yours? Any more surprise children coming?'

Laxmi shivered inwardly but she said nothing, keeping her chin raised high.

The ring of men around the barber burst into loud laughter, and Darbari touched his palm to his forehead briefly in acknowledgement before he went back to plying his razor.

Laxmi walked quickly, clutching her packages to her chest, eager to get home before Ramu returned. She passed the headman's new house, a far smaller and more modest building from the outside, though on the inside, it was said, the place was huge, a rabbit warren. She came to the lemon grove beside the well. Three heavily-veiled women were sitting in the shade beside the path, their pots beside them. They looked up when they saw her and Laxmi saw they were in fact the headman's daughters-in-law. Laxmi greeted them politely but they refused to acknowledge her.

Savitribai, the headman's eldest daughter-in-law, threw her a venomous glance and remarked loudly to her sister-in-law, 'Some people in the village have no sense of modesty. They bring shame upon Nandgaon.'

Laxmi said nothing, laughing inwardly. Modesty was for rich women.

One day she would bring the road back to Nandgaon, she vowed. That would teach the headman and his proud daughters-in-law! She could see it perfectly in her head, a village transformed, with piped water, lights, television, a proper school, a bank, a medical centre – everything that Khandwa had. Not for a moment did she miss the old village like the others. Once the road was rebuilt the bus would start coming through, bringing hungry people with money in their pockets.

CHAPTER NINETEEN
THE HEADMAN GETS ANGRY

The headman was rudely awoken by the sound of shrill female voices on the other side of the compound wall.

'Did you see how she walked past just now – shaking her hips like a prostitute? Anything is possible with that one. She is a witch and should be thrown out of the village.'

He didn't need to think to know who the subject of the conversation was.

'She has no respect for anyone. Did you see how high she holds her head? It's amazing she doesn't trip and fall,' a second, weaker voice agreed.

'And did you notice how she ignored us?' the first one continued. 'Who does she think she is? Does she think she has become the patel of this village just because she is living in our old house?'

Our house. They really were amazing, his daughters-in-law, Gopal thought. He had built that house, he and he alone. And only he and his wife had ever lived in it. Now that she had gone, he was the only one who could remember what it had been like. Strangely enough, the thought of Laxmi living in it didn't bother him half as much as his daughter-in-law claiming possession of it.

First voice: 'Did you see the sari she was wearing today? Blue and pink with sequins on the entire body of the sari.'

Second voice: 'Where did she get such a thing?'

First voice: 'Huh, that foolish husband of hers must have

got it for her.'

Second voice: 'But why does she have to parade through the village every day all dressed up like a bride? She even wears sandals, did you see them? All pink and gold with beads sewn into the heel? Does she think she is walking the dirty streets of the city?'

Thank God he'd been given only one girl, Gopal thought. How could God have made women so beautiful on the outside and so ugly inside? No wonder parents had to pay to get girls married off. As if to prove his point, Savitri, his eldest daughter-in-law, said spitefully, 'She wears them because she thinks she is too good for the earth of Nandgaon.'

Second voice: 'She has absolutely no shame.'

First voice: 'Someone should tell Ramu to control her.'

Second voice: 'Huh, Ramu. He is blind and deaf now. Dumb he always was.'

The shrill laughter that followed irritated him even more than the remark itself and he sat up wondering what time it was. He looked for the neem tree which had always been his private clock then remembered that he was in another house. At a loss, he looked to see if his glass of milk was waiting for him. It was not. On the other side of the wall the voices had fallen to whispers. But because he could no longer hear their words clearly, the headman's annoyance grew. Of the two, he mused, he'd always liked the second one, Rama, less. But now he felt he'd been mistaken. Savitri the eldest was far nastier. It was her he'd have to watch. Then suddenly he heard his second daughter-in-law say clearly, 'Did you know that Ramu washes her feet at night?'

First voice: 'What? Ramu wouldn't! Who told you that?'

Second voice: 'Sushilabai.'

The headman grimaced. If there was one woman in the village he disliked more than his own daughters-in-law, it was Govind Rao's wife, Sushila. Govind Rao had been a bully, until he got himself a bully for a wife.

'Are Chup kar,' he roared suddenly.

Immediately the conversation on the other side of the wall ceased. Then he heard the tinkle of ankle bells as the women ran away. The headman took a deep breath and looked up at the endless blue sky he so loved. Little by little the peace of the afternoon returned. He wondered if he should try to sleep again but knew almost instantly that it would be impossible. So he got up and went to have his bath instead.

He had the servants open the gates early and a large group of plaintiffs rushed in. He dealt with them as quickly as possible, ignoring Mahendra's increasingly worried look, as to each one he gave a little more than they expected. Then without a word he got up and went to wait for his friends to arrive.

He didn't have to wait long. Vilas Rao was the first to enter, and the others followed soon after. He hugged his old friend tight, relieved to see him. Vilas Rao had returned from the hospital in Khandwa that morning. He had been operated upon for a typical old man's problem. The headman shuddered, wondering if the same thing awaited him. The problem had begun two years earlier and on the headman's advice he'd consulted a doctor, who'd told him that it could be easily fixed with a small operation but it would cost him his manhood. Vilas Rao had returned shaken and for the next two years stubbornly struggled to remain a man. After all, he had a young wife to satisfy. But after the flood the problem had become so acute that he had had no choice but to go in for the operation.

'You're looking well,' Govind Rao said insincerely. 'As. . . as if you've lost ten years.'

Vilas Rao looked at him and scowled. 'You mean I have gained ten years,' he corrected.

'No, no. I mean you. . . you look really healthy,' Govind Rao stammered.

'Really? So what does that mean? Now that I am no longer

a man, I can be a holy man.'

Everyone had burst into laughter then, but it had been the first and the last laugh of the evening – in spite of the potent home-brewed sugar cane liquor that the headman had ordered to celebrate Vilas Rao's return.

But the alcohol relaxed them and Vilas Rao began to look happier as he described in graphic detail how two nurses had undressed him and shaved his private parts and how after the injection, one so huge it seemed made for a bullock not a human, he had felt nothing.

'But the strangest thing came afterwards when they wheeled me into the ward,' Vilas Rao said, pausing and looking at the circle of faces around him. 'Guess who I met in the bed next to me?'

'Who?' asked Saraswati Rane.

'Who indeed?' echoed Jaiwant Rane.

'The Patel of Kesarigaon.'

'The Patel of Kesarigaon? But he is a young man,' Govind Rao exclaimed, his hand going unconsciously to his groin.

'Not that fellow,' Vilas Rao said scornfully. 'He is just the sarpanch. I am talking of the real Patel.'

'You mean Mukeshbhai Kesarkar?' the headman asked frowning. 'But I thought the old man was dead.'

Vilas Rao shook his head eagerly. 'Exactly, so did I. But there he was in the bed next to me. Ninety-three and still perfectly healthy. He didn't recognise me at first. The nurse brought us chai and glucose biscuits and he asked me where I was from. When I told him he smiled and then sighed, "Ah Nandgaon. Your Patel is well?" and I assured him that you were. He smiled sadly and told me his story then.'

'What story? What happened?' Govind Rao asked. 'And why do you say sarpanch and not patel when they are the same?'

'Because in Kesarigaon there are no more patels,' Vilas Rao

answered, not looking at the headman.

There was a shocked silence and Vilas Rao continued, 'No one listens to the Patel anymore. Now everyone wants to be sarpanch, to get himself elected. It seems that is what the government wants. So now the village is divided into parties, political parties, and they fight to get their candidate made sarpanch, just as the government wants it. As a result the village is full of garbage, the tanks have not been cleaned in years and rats are slowly overtaking the human population. That is what Mukeshbhai told me. He said he envied us in Nandgaon, for our Patel had seen what was coming and had done the right thing, getting rid of that road. He wished he'd done the same thing.' Here he looked at the headman. All the others did too, various mixes of shock, surprise and concern on their faces.

'And?' the headman prodded gently.

'The road. The truckers have brought their women and these women, not satisfied with the truck drivers, have seduced the men, married and unmarried, in the village, and now there is a disease for which they have no name; it is a disease of shame, and several families have it. It comes suddenly, often many years after the man has been with the infected woman, but it leaves no one alive, not even children. And the end is so terrible, it seems, that the doctors won't take the patients into the hospitals. They must die in the village, in the family. Mukeshbhai wanted me to tell you to be especially careful of the widows with children coming from the outside; he said you should throw them out of the village immediately.' Vilas Rao stopped and reached for his hookah. No one said anything, careful to avoid looking at the headman.

The headman's eyes went to the servant woman scrubbing dishes in a corner. He didn't recognise her. So many people had come from the drowned villages asking for work, it was hard to remember them all. Now he looked at her closely. She looked perfectly healthy. Should he throw her out? Where would she go? There was no work to be had in the area. To the city? There she would become what she was trying hard to avoid becoming, for she was quite pretty and would surely catch the terrible disease Mukeshbhai had spoken of. His eyes wandered across the compound to a leafy enclosure in front of the kitchen where his grandchildren were teasing a heavily pregnant goat. What unworthy vessels women were for producing God's most beautiful creatures, he thought. Unbidden, an image of Laxmi came into his mind and he remembered the conversation he had overheard that afternoon.

'There are many kinds of diseases,' he said slowly, 'diseases of the body and diseases of the mind. I wonder which is worse.' He looked at each man in the group and they stared back uncomprehendingly. 'These widows have nothing and no one to look after them. I cannot throw anyone out of the village on the basis of a suspicion. Besides, no one has become sick here.'

His words were greeted by silence for though the others respected him too much to disagree with him to his face, they were nevertheless troubled by Vilas Rao's news.

'At least you could send someone to find out more about this disease,' Jaiwant Rane suggested. The others immediately brightened and added their voices to the request.

The headman nodded slowly. 'All right,' he said. 'I will send someone.'

The evening ended shortly thereafter, and no one lingered over the goodbyes.

Apart from Vilas Rao, none of the four friends slept well that night. Vilas Rao had given them too much to think about. A little before dawn, the headman left his bed and began to pace the verandah outside. Though it wasn't cold, he shivered in the grey predawn light. An unknown disease that lived in the blood of healthy men – what kind of a place had the world become? And how was he to protect Nandgaon from it? When the sky began to clear, he dressed rapidly and, not waiting for his tea, grabbed his walking stick and left, walking quickly through the sleeping village.

At that hour, the narrow streets of Old Nandgaon were still dark and not even the dogs were awake. But one person was, and when she heard the headman pass, her tired face broke into a smile. A good omen, Parvatibai thought. Perhaps the gods will listen to my prayers.

She shook her husband awake.

'Gopal Mundkur is awake,' she said. 'Go after him and wait for him at the entrance to the village.'

'What for?' Bicchoo groaned and turned away from her. 'It is too early,' he mumbled.

'No it is not,' Parvatibai replied. 'It is too late. If you don't get that money we will be shamed in front of the entire village.' She pulled their third child, Kishore, towards them. 'Look at him, he has to go to school today and if he doesn't take his fees with him he will be sent back. Is that what you want?'

'He won't be sent back. I will talk to Jaiwant Rane,' Bicchoo said with as much confidence as he could muster.

'That is what you say each time, then he keeps quiet for a month, and then again the threats, the public humiliation begins. Look at this poor boy's face, just look at it.' She grabbed Kishore's sleeping face with ungentle fingers and pulled his chin up. Kishore tried desperately to free himself and then gave up, keeping his eyes firmly closed instead. 'I am a wreck, he is a wreck. He begs me not to send him to school. He says he will work on his baba's fields,' she finished, glaring at her husband.

'But the headman will refuse to see me. You know he won't see anyone before evening,' Bicchoo protested. 'I'll ask him this evening.'

'This evening? This evening our son will have missed a day at school. The whole village will know and we will have been shamed,' his wife cried bitterly. 'If only you were as lucky as Ramu, then I would not grow old worrying.'

'Ramu?' Bicchoo asked, visibly upset. 'You're comparing me to that idiot?'

'Idiot he may be, but look how much money he brings his wife every day.'

'So now you prefer an idiot with money to a respectable Brahmin without money,' Bicchoo snapped, sitting up and looking hurt.

'Ramu works hard,' Parvatibai said quietly, 'while you have never done so in your life.'

Bicchoo pushed away the bedclothes and stood up. 'All right, you want me to work, I will. But don't you complain when you are treated like an untouchable.' He headed for the door. At the entrance he stopped. 'You want money?' he cried. 'I'll get it for you. I'll go and wait for the Patel.'

Knowing exactly where he was headed, his exasperated wife threw the wooden chapatti belan after him. 'Go, go, go, there isn't any food here anyway,' she cried. Burying her face in her hands, she burst into tears.

Parvatibai was right. Bicchoo didn't go straight to the village's edge to wait for the headman. He went to the tea stall instead. If he found someone for a game of cards, he reasoned, he would easily be able to make the money for the school fees in half an hour. But the tea stall wasn't open and so he thought of going to see his field instead. The headman had given it to him as part of the redistribution of land after the flood but he'd lost it almost immediately to Ram Manohar. Since the headman had made it a rule that land could not be sold without his consent, Ram Manohar only had cultivation rights, in theory it still belonged to Bicchoo.

But as he neared the bamboo bridge, he saw the headman at the far end and so he turned back, looking for a convenient tree behind which to hide. But since there was none, the river having uprooted them all, he was forced to go back to the village and wait there.

Bicchoo slipped down the nearest street and half ran until he reached the end where he ducked around a corner and stopped to catch his breath. He looked around and realised that he was not far from Ramu's house. Suddenly an idea came to him and he smiled. Ramu was rich, and he was generous. Before he could finish the thought, Bicchoo heard the sound of empty milk cans and a few seconds later Ramu appeared, his cheeks still faintly pink from his early morning ride to Kesarigaon.

'Are, Ramubhai, how wonderful to find you here. I was just coming to your house,' Bicchoo cried.

Ramu looked pleased. 'You were? What for?' he asked.

Now it was Bicchoo's turn to be at a loss for words. He could hardly ask Ramu outright for a loan. So he said, 'Actually I wanted your advice.'

'My advice?' Ramu looked startled. 'No one has ever asked me for advice. I don't know if I will be able to give you any,' he replied honestly.

Bicchoo laughed. 'That is why I want your advice and no one else's. You are a great man. You don't give any advice and you don't take anyone's advice either. You do what you think is right for you. And look how well you have succeeded. Everyone in Nandgaon envies you, you are rich, you have the best cows in the village and the most beautiful wife.'

At this Ramu shifted uncomfortably from one foot to the other. He wasn't used to flattery. 'You. . . you really think so?' he asked after some time.

'Of course,' Bicchoo replied easily, 'the whole village does.'

A huge smile lit up Ramu's face. 'Really?'

'Absolutely.'

'That is the best thing anyone ever said to me.'

Bicchoo bit back the laugh that rose in his throat. 'Ramubhai,' he said seriously, 'I have a problem. My son is not going to school.'

'Not going to school? Why?' Ramu looked puzzled.

'Because I do not have enough money for the fees.'

'The fees?'

'Yes, fees. All the high-caste boys pay fees. That is why he is no longer going to school.'

'But that's terrible,' Ramu cried. 'Poor, poor boy. Can you not talk to Jaiwant Rane? He is a just man.'

'I have tried. But he won't listen,' Bicchoo replied, trying to look heartbroken. 'He insists on payment.'

'That's terrible,' Ramu said. 'What can be done?'

Bicchoo took a deep breath. The moment had arrived. The thatched roof of the tea stall beckoned. He was lucky today, he could feel it. Only luck could have driven him into Ramu's arms like this.

But before he could speak, Ramu was speaking again. 'I know what,' he said. 'I'll ask my wife to speak to Jaiwant Raneji. He will certainly listen to her.'

'No, no, no. This cannot spread. It is a secret,' Bicchoo said, dismayed. 'You mustn't tell her.'

'But she is very good at keeping secrets,' Ramu replied.

'No, no. I could not bear the shame of knowing she knew. This must be kept amongst men.'

'Then would you like me to come with you to Jaiwant Rane?' Ramu offered.

'No, no, Ramubhai. You are too kind,' Bicchoo said hurriedly. He looked at the two animals sticking close to Ramu's shins. 'Just give me a small loan. I will pay it back by this evening. You are so lucky, the Devi will bless you for helping a poor man like me.'

'But I have no money on me now. I gave it all to Laxmi. Why don't you. . .' He stopped suddenly, his face reddening.

'I can wait with your animals if you want to go get me the money,' Bicchoo offered breathlessly. 'I'll even take them part-way to the forest.'

Ramu looked away and shook his head. 'It won't work Bicchoobhai, she won't listen.'

'Why? What do you mean? Make her listen to you?'

Ramu shook his head, looking embarrassed.

'All right, then give me the money tomorrow.'

Ramu stared even harder at the ground, then looked up sadly. 'I can't,' he said. 'She warned me about you, you see. I promised.'

Bicchoo opened his mouth to say something more then shut it. Though he was an unlucky gambler, he was a shrewd judge of character and he could see that Ramu would not change his mind. Abruptly he turned on his heel and walked back the way he came, leaving Ramu staring miserably after him.

By the time Bicchoo arrived at the tea shop he was full of bitterness, cursing all rich men, all women – especially wives – and children and God too for good measure. He was so full of his own hate that he didn't see the headman coming out of the tea shop.

'You're looking black this morning, Bicchoo,' the headman remarked. 'Were you refused a loan?'

Bicchoo's eyes grew wide. 'Are Patelji, Ram, Ram. I was just coming to find you. The thing is. . . This is the last time I promise, I have a plan, I will. . .' Bicchoo stammered and began to explain.

The headman looked at him with contempt. He knew Bicchoo's ways and he was tired of haemorrhaging money. The man's needs were endless and he was tired of it.

'You want a game?' the headman interrupted Bicchoo. Bicchoo's eyes bulged and he gave the headman a look that was both scared and anxious. 'If you win I will give you your loan. If I win, you will never bother me for a loan again, understood?' the headman said coldly.

Bicchoo nodded, still looking scared.

They sat down at a table and the headman asked for a pack of cards. 'You deal,' he told Bicchoo. 'You're more experienced at it than I.'

'Are you sure you want me to?' Bicchoo asked cautiously. He could hardly believe what was happening.

'Yes, yes, of course,' the headman said impatiently. 'What better person to lose money to than to someone who owes you?'

'Since you and Ramu are the only ones rich enough to have money to lose.' The words were out of Bicchoo's mouth before he could do anything about them.

The air left Bicchoo's lungs and he put a hand over his treacherous mouth. But it was too late, of course, and he knew it. He stared miserably at the headman's feet, waiting for the blow to fall.

But none came. The silence lengthened and became heavy. When the headman still didn't say a word, he fell at the headman's feet, rubbing his forehead against the headman's legs. 'Beat me, kick me, Patelji, but please forgive me, I didn't mean that,' he mumbled into the headman's dhoti.

The headman didn't answer Bicchoo's pleas. 'Tell me about him,' the headman ordered.

'About whom?' Bicchoo asked nervously.

'About Ramu,' the headman replied.

'Th-there is nothing to tell really,' Bicchoo stammered. 'Ramu's wife is a real Laxmi, the whole village is talking of it. They sell their milk in the market and. . . and, well, they are rich. But nowhere near as rich as you are Patelji, I. . . would never compare.'

The headman frowned. 'But how can they do that? The market is miles away.'

'She. . . she pays a man from there. He comes and gets the milk from the bus stop.'

'Which bus stop? There is no bus that comes here.'

'Kesarigaon. Ramu goes there each morning and evening by bicycle.'

'He does, does he? That's a lot of work for a small amount of milk,' the headman pointed out. For an experienced liar, Bicchoo was doing a terrible job.

'But it isn't a small amount. They have so much milk they don't know what to do with it – at least twenty-five litres every day. They sell half and give away the rest.'

A dreadful stillness took possession of the headman's body. Bicchoo stared at him, horrified. What had he said that could have had such an effect? Just then a dog barked and the spell was broken. The headman picked up his cards and looked at him blandly. 'Are you going to play?' he asked.

CHAPTER TWENTY

WINNERS AND LOSERS

They played cards for an hour. The headman lost the first game and the second. Then the tea came and he revived. The third game he played with his customary mix of caution and brilliance. Bicchoo's play, on the other hand, grew more and more erratic. He kept thinking of his son's school fees. Then he remembered the stakes and the ground beneath him would tremble.

At the end of the third game the headman threw down his cards and said, 'I win.'

Bicchoo kept staring at his cards. The air underneath the thatched roof of the teahouse seemed to boil. Beads of sweat formed on Bicchoo's forehead. Word had spread that the Patel was in the tea stall and that he was playing cards with Bicchoo, and people just had to come and see for themselves.

'One more game, Patelji,' Bicchoo whispered through parched lips, 'just one more.'

'And if you lose again?'

Bicchoo moistened his parched lips with the tip of his tongue. 'Just give me one more chance.'

The headman sighed and ordered them both another tea. He began to deal as it was his turn. Bicchoo, staring at the cards in front of him, began to pray, and from deep inside him came the answering tingle of hope. Like all true gamblers, he believed in his luck. The gods couldn't let him down this time, the stakes were too high. He picked up a card, then a second one. The headman did the same.

Bicchoo smiled. He picked up a third card and threw all three on the table, two kings and a joker. 'I win,' he said.

The headman continued to stare at his cards. Then he looked straight at Bicchoo. His eyes were hard, and yet, somewhere in their brown depths, there lingered a tiny spark of compassion. 'No, you don't,' he said and showed his own – three aces.

A collective 'Aah' came from the men collected around them. But Bicchoo was oblivious to them. He leapt out of his chair and grabbed the headman's cards. 'No, no, no,' he moaned, 'it cannot be.'

The headman said nothing. He stood up. 'I will pay for the tea.' He called to the tea stall owner for the bill. Bicchoo, petrified that he'd leave, threw himself at the headman's feet. 'Don't do this to me, Patelji. Don't do this,' he begged. 'I swear I'll never play cards or drink again.'

'Don't do what? You were the one who wanted this. Now you can find someone else to lend you money for your game. Some other rich man, like Ramu perhaps,' he added softly.

'Nahi*, Patelji, nahi,' Bicchoo howled. 'There is only you who is rich and kind and generous. Ramu is not rich, nor kind, nor generous. You are the only one, the only one, I swear.'

'Then you will have to go to the town to get the money, won't you?' the headman said softly. 'Surely there are money-lenders there?'

Bicchoo was thoroughly miserable now. 'Are, Patelji, haven't you punished me enough?' he sobbed. 'I am hardly a worthy opponent for you, poor luckless creature that I am. But I swear on my mother, I have learnt my lesson, please do not punish me any more, Patelji.'

A sigh of agreement, so delicate it could have been mistaken for a puff of breeze, came from behind the headman. But he

* no

289

heard it and a small smile came to his lips. 'Poor Bicchoo. You are indeed unlucky,' he said at last. 'Let us forget this episode. Come and see me tomorrow.'

A murmur of approval followed this and the people gathered around clapped for their headman. Justice and mercy had been served. The world was back on its feet.

Bicchoo meanwhile was crying. His tears soaked the headman's feet until rough hands picked him up and took him away.

Disengaging his feet from the sobbing Bicchoo, the headman walked out. People clapped and smiled but no one stopped him. For there was a look on the headman's face that said, 'Keep away.'

But he stopped at the exit to pay the tea stall owner. 'Bishnu,' he said, handing the man some money, 'your roof is old and full of holes. I think you need a new one.'

'Of course, Patelji. But as you know, times are hard,' the tea stall owner replied. 'As soon as I have the money I will hire some young men and do it.'

'Bishnu, this tea house is the heart of our village. I will send you two young men tomorrow. Don't wait until after the rains. Life is short.'

'Ji Patelji maharaj.' Bishnu's anxious face broke into a relieved smile. 'Please take back your money, maharaj. This place is yours,' he begged.

But the headman shook his head. 'This place is yours, Bishnu. And Nandgaon's.'

As he left, those inside the tea stall cheered.

Leaning heavily on his stick, Gopal Mundkur walked back slowly through the village to his house. His mind was in a turmoil. He felt bad about what he'd done to Bicchoo, shaming him in public like that. He hadn't meant to do it but it had just happened that way. He would send a message to Parvatibai later. The poor woman didn't deserve to suffer, nor did Bicchoo's children. He sighed. Why did children always have to pay for the sins of their parents? His mind went automatically to Ramu whose own father had sold off everything he owned and more, and then run away. Gopal felt a stab in his chest. He had done his best to protect Ramu.

He continued up the village and it was as if he were seeing it for the first time. Instead of the gracious old houses he remembered he saw a jumble of makeshift shanties, many without roofs. Windows had not been replaced; plastic sheets covered the frames still. Entire rooms where the ceilings had caved in had not been rebuilt. He felt angry with himself, suddenly wondering why he hadn't seen all these things before. How had things changed so much? It was the wretched flood, he thought; more things had changed in Nandgaon than just the location of the village. He should have insisted that they return to the old location, no matter what, and start construction all over again immediately. Where had he put his eyes all these months? In his account books, he thought wryly. He should never have let Ramu's woman talk him into selling them that sugar cane field. It had given Ramu a recognition he didn't deserve. And it had let people conclude that he too thought that fatherless cow of Ramu's was magic. He smiled suddenly at the irony of it – the son of a gambler and a runaway, and married to the daughter of a suicide farmer, being given recognition by none other than the Patel of Nandgaon himself. What had he been thinking?

'Nana, nana, nana. Look, I escaped, I escaped,' his grandson shouted shrilly, grabbing Gopal around the knees. The headman looked down into the gleeful upturned face and suddenly time seemed to do a somersault; the radio was on and an announcer had just informed them that the Americans had landed on the moon.

'You mustn't run away, chhota,' he said, picking up his grandson and holding him tight. 'The world is a dangerous place.'

'Why? How can Nandgaon be dangerous? You are looking after it, aren't you?' his grandson asked, looking puzzled.

The headman stared down at his grandson, awestruck. He felt as if he had been hit by a bolt of lightning. 'You are right. Nandgaon is not dangerous. But the outside world is. And we cannot build a wall around ourselves so we must be careful.'

'But nana, you were the one who said –' his grandson said, pouting.

'I am an old fool,' the headman interrupted him. 'Don't listen to me.'

'You can't be a fool,' his grandson answered. 'Ramu is a fool and you aren't like him.'

The headman burst into laughter and hugged his grandson again. 'Clever boy,' he said. 'Now come with me. I will send someone for your sweets as soon as we get home.'

The little three-year-old agreed gleefully, proud to be accompanying his grandfather through the village. But after a few minutes he grew tired and demanded to be lifted up. The headman picked him up and though the child was heavy, carried him all the way back to the house. On the way, his arms aching from the unaccustomed weight, he came to a decision.

When Ramu brought back the goats that evening the headman was waiting for him. 'How is that cow of yours, Ramu?' he called out jovially.

Ramu stopped, giving him a guilty look. 'F-fine, Patelji, just fine. He is growing so fast.'

'I was asking about your ugly cow, *buddhoo*. The one and only Soorpanakha.' He used the name deliberately, making it sound even uglier than it was.

Ramu blinked, looking hurt. 'Oh, you mean our Kamdhenu,' he said at last, sounding on the verge of tears. 'She is fine, Patelji, just fine. A great mother.'

'Cows usually are, unlike humans,' the headman replied drily. 'Come and give my head a massage after you finish putting the animals in.'

But when Ramu returned, the headman had his eyes closed and seemed to be fast asleep. So he waited, not daring to leave until he was given permission. When at last the headman opened his eyes, the shadows had become shapeless and the sun had dipped low in the west. Outside the gate a long line of supplicants had formed, silent and patient. Just inside the gate Ramu sat squirming with impatience. The headman looked at him and clutched his head, pretending to remember. 'Are, Ramu, thank God you are here.' He called, so everyone in the line looked at Ramu too. 'Get me my chai will you? Then you can begin.'

Ramu got up obediently and went to fetch the tea that the headman's daughter was bringing out. He placed the tea respectfully before the headman and went to stand behind him. 'Ramu, you go into the kitchen and have some tea too, you look tired,' the headman ordered.

'Nahi, nahi, Patelji, I am quite OK. Let me begin now, my wife is waiting,' Ramu replied awkwardly.

The headman frowned. The mention of that woman seemed like an act of defiance. 'Do you see that line out there? If they can wait without questions, so can you. How am I supposed to drink my tea with my head being bounced around, can you tell me? Or is your cow's milk so special that you don't want to drink your Patel's tea?'

Ramu looked startled and then his disarming smile appeared. 'Are Patelji, what are you saying? Without your milk I would have remained a little dwarf with stick-like arms and legs. Your tea is what created these muscles of mine, of course I will be honoured to have some.'

The headman's eyes widened and then he frowned. 'No need for speeches,' he said gruffly. 'Go drink your tea quickly, my head aches.'

Alone once more, the headman drank his tea without tasting it. That Ramu was not such a fool after all, he thought. What a clever answer he'd given, as clever as any politician's! Perhaps he had underestimated him. Perhaps the boy had let them all think he was stupid in order to get their sympathy. Had he himself not protected Ramu at every turn – defending his marriage, the arrival of the junglee cow, and the birth of the ugly one? And this was the way he showed his gratefulness, by arguing with him openly and making him, the headman, into a laughing stock before half the village. A slow anger began to burn inside him.

In the kitchen, where the oil for the massage was gently heating, Ramu sat in his usual place with his back to the door, and waited for the trembling in his legs to recede. He refused to look anyone in the eye, though nearly all those in the kitchen were familiar to him. The old mausi who ran the kitchen, after making three attempts at conversation, sniffed loudly as she handed him his tea. 'Look at this boy. I fed and reared him from when his mother died in this very kitchen. Now look, he's too important to talk to us poor servants,' she told the others loudly. Ramu opened his mouth to defend himself then shut it. Did they know he'd been selling milk outside the village? Laxmi had said that the headman wouldn't have wanted it anyway because the doctor sahib's videshi dawai* had changed the taste of the milk. But still, he couldn't help feeling that they should have given the headman the option of buying it first. Milk was still scarce in the village, for a full third of the herd had gone. He finished the tea without tasting it, and escaped.

* foreign medicine

But Ramu was too late. The gates had been opened and the favour seekers had come rushing in. Ramu had to fight his way through the mesh of bodies with the warm sesame oil for the head massage held close to his chest. When he finally got to where the headman was seated, the headman ignored him, forcing him to wait behind him. He took his position beside the headman's chair and stared stonily ahead, pretending not to notice the curious glances being directed at him. By tomorrow he knew the entire village would know that he'd been at the headman's the previous night waiting like a servant to do his bidding. All of them would assume he was being punished for something and the thought made him hang his head in shame.

When an hour had passed and the oil had grown cold he said timidly, 'Patelji, the oil is getting cold.'

'You can heat it up again, I have almost finished,' the headman replied. 'Now I can enjoy the magic of your hands which I have missed since you became an owner of land.'

A sigh went through the crowd and one could have heard a pin drop as all eyes turned on Ramu, standing beside the headman. A surge of anger went through Ramu. What was the headman trying to say? He massaged his legs every morning anyway, in spite of the fact that he was now a landowner who did not have to. Perhaps the headman had found out and was punishing him for selling his milk outside. In which case, Ramu thought miserably, I deserve it. He looked up at the indigo sky, and wondered what Laxmi was thinking and whether she was worried or looking for him already. Perhaps someone had informed her, and she was sitting in their house worried or furious, waiting for him to return.

Once again Ramu went to the kitchen and had the oil reheated, forced to listen to a litany of complaints from the old mausi. When he returned the courtyard was empty. Only Bicchoo remained. He smiled at the man, trying to make up for having refused him that morning. But Bicchoo refused to meet his eyes. The feeling that Ramu was somehow in terrible trouble grew. But there was nothing he could do about it. Nothing had been said. He set the oil down and went to work with sure fast strokes. After a while he felt the headman's head, neck and shoulders relax and, forgetting the lateness of the hour, he lost himself in his work. When he worked on a body, he stopped feeling stupid and lost; he knew exactly what he was doing. Each body was like a house, one had to find the doors and open them, allow the air to get inside and the bad things to escape. He was thinking this and feeling happier when the headman's voice broke into his thoughts.

'So Ramu, what do you think? Bicchoo here wants yet another loan from me. I already own everything he has. What should I make him give me this time?'

Ramu looked at poor Bicchoo who was squirming with embarrassment. 'You don't own his heart, Patelji,' he said sharply, more sharply than he had intended to. 'I mean, I mean,' he paused, fear constricting his chest, 'Bicchooji doesn't mean to gamble, he just can't help himself. You are a great, generous man, Patelji. God will pay you back if you look after his son's fees.'

Silence. Bicchoo looked as if he'd been turned to stone. And as for the headman, luckily Ramu could not see his face. So Bicchoo had asked Ramu for a loan before he'd come to him, the headman thought grimly. He would punish Bicchoo separately for that.

Behind him, Ramu licked his lips nervously. He had never made such a long speech in front of the headman before. What on earth had got hold of him? 'Pardon me Patelji, I forgot myself. You will of course do what is right for us all,' he apologised.

Luckily all three were saved from having to say anything more by the arrival of Vilas Rao and Govind Rao. Just behind them came Jaiwant Rane, looking distracted, and Saraswati Rane brought up the rear, late as usual. They all looked at Ramu in surprise and then pretended they hadn't seen him. The hookahs were lighted and brought to them, and after a while the gentle euphoria that accompanied the tobacco made it easier to ignore the presence of Ramu behind the headman.

'We were indeed lucky,' Govind Rao said, not looking towards the headman. 'We were spared and this year, God willing, with prices so high, we will make up most of our losses.'

'Thanks to the good sense of our Patel,' Vilas Rao added.

'Yes indeed,' Govind agreed quickly. The others all voiced their agreement.

'Look how the river turned other rich farmers into beggars; she can be cruel to some. Cruel and unforgiving.'

'Like all women,' Vilas Rao added. The others laughed. After the flood, Vilas Rao's wife had run away with her own nephew, the fancy young mechanic.

'Don't worry, you'll get a better wife this year,' the headman assured him, as the laughter died down. 'Just don't run off and get married in secret.'

There was a moment's uncomfortable silence and everyone tried hard not to look at Ramu pounding at the headman's shoulders. Only the headman himself appeared to be enjoying himself.

For the headman hadn't lied when he'd said he had a headache. He'd had it since the time he brought his grandson home. But as Ramu's hands worked their magic, the headache disappeared and a tremendous sense of well-being filled him. Time curved in on itself and he began to feel younger and younger by the minute.

'Are, Ramu, you really have magic in your hands,' he said affectionately. 'I think I may have to ask you to do this to me each evening before I sleep.'

'As you please, Patelji.' Ramu replied absently.

'Huh, here is a man who truly loves me, you see that?' the headman said, turning to the others.

The headman's kind words pricked Ramu's guilty conscience and he said quickly, 'You must not take the worries of our poor village into your own body, Patelji. For if your body gets weak, our village gets weak. Then what will we do?'

The air seemed to freeze in surprise. The others stared at Ramu, their expressions ranging from pity to contempt. The headman gave a triumphant laugh. The others looked away quickly, embarrassed on Ramu's behalf.

But the headman, not content with Ramu's own capitulation, decided to continue. 'So Ramu, how is life?' he asked. 'What are you doing with that field I gave you?'

'Ah, Patelji,' Ramu answered, embarrassed. 'I have not had the time to do anything with it yet. But eventually we would like to grow something on it.'

'Grow something?' the headman asked. 'Grow what?'

'I don't know exactly,' Ramu replied honestly.

'You should put in some barley straight-away,' the headman advised, his face carefully blank.

The others exchanged puzzled looks. What was the headman playing at? It was too late to plant barley now; the monsoon was almost over.

'Really? You think so? I will do it next week even though Laxmi says we must wait. You are too kind, Patelji, to take an interest in one as poor as me,' Ramu answered, overcome.

'I am interested in every member of Nandgaon,' the headman said grandly. 'Everyone matters.'

Tea and pakoras arrived and the headman told the servants to bring Ramu some as well. 'Come join us,' he invited, 'now that you too are one of us.' Beaming, Ramu came and sat down timidly at their feet. The others shifted uncomfortably in the seats. They looked askance at the headman, who ignored them. Then they looked at each other, shrugged and continued with the game.

The conversation moved on to other subjects and soon everyone began to breathe more easily. Only Bicchoo, who knew the reason for the headman's behaviour, hung his head, not saying a word the entire time.

After a while Ramu coughed discreetly and the headman turned. 'Are, you are still here? Go, run back to your wife or she will be angry.'

'Nahi, nahi, Patelji, I am here to serve you first,' Ramu muttered, his cheeks aflame.

The headman glanced at the others triumphantly. Jaiwant Rane was looking at him with understanding dawning in his eyes, the others still looked embarrassed. 'You are the best man in Nandgaon, Ramu, don't ever change,' he said as Ramu bent to touch his feet. 'Trust in my love for you, and I will always protect you.'

When Ramu told Laxmi why he was so late she grew furious. 'You fool,' she spat, 'couldn't you see he was humiliating you? You should have stood up for yourself. You are a landowner now – you don't need his protection.'

'But, he is the Patel. He looks after us all,' Ramu replied. 'And look what he sent you.' He opened his gamcha to show her the vegetables lying there.

Laxmi grabbed the cloth and turned it upside down. The vegetables fell to the floor and rolled crazily in several directions at once. 'Feed them to your precious cow,' she said cruelly. 'You were born a beggar and will remain so. But I was not.'

CHAPTER TWENTY-ONE

ABOUT THE WORSHIP
OF COWS

Each time Ramu crossed the headman or one of the headman's friends, Laxmi's words would rattle around in his head like undigested bits of dinner. What did she mean, he had acted like a beggar? Why did she think he didn't need the Patel? Did a creeper need a tree, bees a field, animals a forest? Didn't Laxmi understand that without the headman there would be no Nandgaon? The very idea was so terrible that an image would immediately fill his head, making his blood go cold: an uprooted tree, its roots exposed, trying vainly to find a foothold in the sky. The flood had had many victims but the ones Ramu mourned most were the trees.

Why did a tree look the same on both sides? he wondered. Was it because, as the priest explained, a tree was really a bridge between the earth and the sky? Dead souls needed trees to reach heaven. The good ones got there, the not-so-bad ones got trapped in the branches and the really bad ones, those who'd lost the capacity to distinguish between good and bad, took the roots for branches and ended up in the netherworld. That was why one should never sleep in a tree, the priest had said, looking sternly at the children in the audience. But then what happened to the souls in a tree when the tree fell down? Ramu had wanted to ask the priest. Where did they go? Did they have feet? Or wings? Did they die of hunger and cold as they searched for another home? Ramu knew it took a tree a long time to die. What happened to it once the souls that had lived within it left? Did it weep? Did it feel alone as it died? These were the thoughts that really bothered him, thoughts he shared with no one except his beloved junglee cow.

Laxmi, on the other hand, boiled with anger every time she saw the headman or a member of his family. For the land that the headman had given them was useless without the tubewell to pump the water out of the soil. And even the money they made from the sale of Kami's milk – and milk prices were higher than they had ever been that year – was not enough to buy a tubewell. She imagined how the headman must have laughed when he gave them the now-useless land and her bitterness exploded in a shower of words. But Ramu had refused to hear anything against the headman. 'The headman never hid anything from us,' he said coldly.

'But we paid him!' Laxmi exclaimed, 'at a time when land was so cheap we could have got the best land in the area for what we gave him.'

'You should have thought of that before,' Ramu pointed out, 'but your hunger for land had blinded you then. Be careful, for it will eat you up if you don't control it. Why don't you go to the temple and pray to the goddess? Maybe she will help you find peace.'

When Laxmi complained of Ramu's behaviour to Kuntabai, to her surprise, Kuntabai agreed with him. 'For once, that boy shows more sense than you,' she said approvingly. 'Listen to him.' And so, Laxmi's anger, lacking a sympathetic ear, fed upon itself, turning into a fire that burned within her day and night until she could feel nothing else. If Laxmi had been a religious woman she might have found peace in prayer and left revenge in the laps of the gods. But Laxmi had no faith in the gods and so she planned her own revenge.

In Nandgaon, the village as a whole celebrated all festivals together, for they were the markers of the seasons. The big festivals like Holi, Ganapati, Dussehra and Diwali were celebrated under the guidance of the priest and the headman with a grand puja in which the entire village, including the animals, participated. But only Nandgaon's landowning families were allowed to sit in the headman's house for the actual puja. The others waited outside until the feasting and entertainment began. But since the headman always entertained lavishly, inviting the region's best musicians and cooks and also gave gifts to the poor, those who were excluded from the puja never complained. But the headman wasn't the only to have pujas. Everyone held pujas for deaths, births, name-giving and marriages, and to these the entire village was invited.

'And what about a naming ceremony for Shambhu?' Laxmi asked Ramu over tea one morning.

'But Shambhu is already six months old!' Ramu exclaimed. 'It is too late for that.'

'All the more reason to name him publicly. It is not right that his name was not blessed by a priest. How will the gods know he exists?' Laxmi countered.

'But they already know he exists,' Ramu replied. 'Look how big he is, how healthy!'

'Of course he is. But for the village he has still to be introduced to them formally,' Laxmi sighed, or pretended to, 'or how will he be accepted by the herd?'

Ramu put down his glass and looked at her for a long time. 'What do you mean exactly?' he asked.

'If we do a really big puja on a really auspicious day, followed by the best party the village has ever seen, then they would have to let Shambhu graze with the herd.'

Ramu's eyes narrowed suspiciously. 'Our Patelji would never allow it.'

'Ah well,' Laxmi let her shoulders droop, 'if you are such a coward then I suppose there is no point in having a puja.'

Ramu's hands clenched into fists, but they remained at his side.

Out of the corner of her eyes Laxmi watched him weaken and felt quietly victorious. 'Next month, just before Dussehra, we could do the naming ceremony,' she said softly.

Ramu frowned, but did not argue. 'Oh all right,' he said, 'but let's not make it a very big thing. I'm sure hardly anyone will come.'

'Of course. Leave it to me,' Laxmi assured him.

Of all the festivals, Gaopuja was the most popular because it was the one that celebrated what the people of Nandgaon held dearest – their animals.

'The rainy season has ended, thank God,' Saraswati Rane said one evening at the headman's. He then looked meaningfully at his cousin, the schoolmaster. 'Never has it rained so hard or for so long.'

Picking up on the hint, Jaiwant Rane looked directly at the headman and asked, 'What are you going to do this Gaopuja, Patelji?'

'What is there to celebrate?' Gopal Mundkur growled. 'Almost half the herd is gone. Our homes are gone. People have no money.' Unconsciously his eyes sought the faithful Mahendra, who sat a little to the side. Earlier that evening Mahendra had waved the red cloth-bound account books like a flag, saying, 'You know why account books are bound in red cloth? So you pay attention to what is inside them.'

'All right, all right. I'll be careful,' the headman had promised. He shifted uncomfortably on his seat.

'All the more reason to make it a big celebration this time. People need something big to take their minds off all they have lost,' Saraswati Rane advised.

'And what about me? I have lost more than the entire village put together!' the headman growled.

'Still, you are richer than all the village put together,' Saraswati Rane answered.

The others burst into laughter and reluctantly Gopal joined them.

'Richer perhaps in some things, Saraswati Rane,' Gopal said when at last the laughter had died down, 'but if one were to count brains as well then you would far exceed me in wealth.'

'Wah, Patelji,' Bicchoo said quickly, 'at least you did not lose your wits in the flood. As long as we have those, Nandgaon is safe.'

There was a chorus of agreement and the headman, slightly embarrassed, called for another round of chai and pakoras.

'But coming back to Gaopuja,' he said to the priest later, biting into a crispy pakora, 'you are right, the village needs something to take its mind off the past. It is time we began to look ahead once more. The harvest will be good this year, and prices will be high even in the nearby villages, for others have lost more than we did. We will all not only recover our losses but make a profit I think. And the river was kind to us, look at those fields. I have never seen soil so rich. So let us plan something big.'

Saraswati Rane, lost in the pleasure of the hot spicy pakora, said, 'Hmm.'

So it was Govind Rao who spoke up eagerly. 'Let's have a theatre group, complete with dancers and drummers. I know of just such a one.'

'Dancers?' Saraswati dropped the pakora he was eating. 'What kind of a puja would that be?'

'What's wrong with dancers?' Vilas Rao joined in. 'Dancers are beautiful, they distract people. You do your puja, Saraswati Rane, leave the rest to us.'

'But Saraswati Rane is right, Govindbhai.' Jaiwant Rane

came to the aid of his younger brother. 'Gaopuja cannot be taken lightly. Or Surya* Bhagwan will get angry with us. As it is, there are those who are saying that the drought and flood were caused by the Devi to punish us for the way in which we treated Ramu's animals.'

'Fools spouting rubbish!' Vilas Rao spluttered. 'Why do you listen to such gossip, Jaiwantbhai?'

'Gossip is not rubbish, Vilas Rao, it is what people believe,' Jaiwant Rane answered seriously. 'I listen carefully to what the world says, for words make the world we live in.' He looked at the headman as he said this.

The headman didn't answer immediately, leaning down to relight his hookah. When the hookah was relit and he'd taken a long slow puff he said, 'Since I am the one who must pay for it, I will decide.' One of his rare smiles suddenly lit up his eyes. 'And you can rest assured, it will be kept a secret till the very end.'

But before Gaopuja there came Indrapuja. Saraswati Rane brushed the mould off his prayer books, drying them like chapattis on the tawaa before he sat down and asked the rain formally to go away so that the crops could ripen under the benevolent eye of the sun. 'Though Indra is a lesser god than Surya,' Jaiwant Rane explained to the children in school, 'Surya is afraid of him. For if the clouds come, then the sun cannot penetrate and there will be chaos on earth.' The little boys were made to cover their bodies in palash leaves and the little girls wearing their best clothes put kabelu flowers on their heads with small clay figures of Indra in the centre. Holding hands, the boys and girls went from house to house, singing and dancing. At each door they were met by the eldest woman of the household who sprinkled water and grains of rice on

* Sun God, taken to be a form of Vishnu

305

their heads, fed them sweets and pressed more rice into the school bags slung over their shoulders. And as if in answer to their prayers, the sun shone down from clear blue skies and the crops grew furiously, as if glad to be alive.

After Indrapuja the headman offered a goat at the samadhi of Tiger Baba, the tantric, so that the rain would come again the following year, only not so copiously, and the entire village feasted upon the six-foot kheer that had been cooked for seventy-two hours on six foot poles dug into the earth. Ramu, the strongest man in the village, was the one who was usually sent into the forest to cut the bamboo poles. But this year the headman sent his own eldest son Gajendra to do it. Everyone wondered, once again, what Ramu had done to anger the Patel. Many thought it must be the family. But Ramu was oblivious of the speculation that surrounded the headman's request to take his son with him. Thinking he was being honoured, he went with him, happily showing the way and choosing the bamboos for him. But after the headman's eldest son had made the first notch in a young bamboo, he let Ramu do the rest of the work and sat in the shade eating the lunch his wife had made him. Unfortunately for the headman, the entire episode was seen by Keshav and Mukul, who told their parents. Soon the entire village, instead of pitying Ramu, was praising him instead.

When Laxmi heard this, she quietly rejoiced and quickly put her plan into action. The first thing she did was to go and see the pujari alone. He was busily watering his sacred tulsi plant when she arrived. As she had expected, Saraswati Rane refused to perform the naming ceremony. 'This is a bad season. Too many festivals, too many marriages and I have to do Gaopuja in three weeks,' he explained. 'But if you want to do the puja after Diwali, I would be able to come.'

But Laxmi shook her head. 'It must be done on the very best and most auspicious day,' she insisted.

'But that. . . that is Gaopuja,' the priest answered.

'Impossible.'

'That is the perfect day, don't you agree?' Laxmi insisted.

'But why? Your animal will not know the difference,' the priest asked, looking puzzled.

Laxmi looked apologetic. 'The Devi came to me in a dream,' she lied fluently. 'She asked me why we had not yet named the child. I am worried for my poor Shambhu. Only a day as auspicious as Gaopuja will do.'

Saraswati Rane's intelligent eyes grew sharp. 'I never see you at the temple. Since when has the goddess started paying house calls to those who do not care to come to her?' he asked.

Laxmi shrugged and looked away. She could not meet his eyes, though she would have liked to.

Saraswati Rane grunted, thinking he had won. 'No one will come for your puja on Gaopuja day, Laxmibai,' he explained kindly. 'Choose another day for your puja.'

Her cheeks burning, Laxmi thanked him and left.

The next day she told Ramu that the priest had refused to do their puja and therefore the only option left to them was to get another pundit from another village. 'But why? Why did Saraswati Rane refuse?' Ramu asked, distraught. 'I have never done anything to displease Saraswati Rane.'

'He said he was too busy on the day,' Laxmi replied.

'What day?' Ramu asked suspiciously.

'Gaopuja,' Laxmi answered.

'Gaopuja? Why do you want to do it then?' Ramu asked, just as Saraswati Rane had. Laxmi gave him the same answer she'd given the priest – because the Devi wanted it.

'But that is the day of our Patel's puja.'

'Forget the headman!' Laxmi snapped. 'He has done nothing for you.'

Ramu opened his mouth to disagree. He wanted to tell Laxmi she was wrong, that the headman was the tree under which he sheltered, they all sheltered. The image of the upturned tree filled his head and dried the words on his tongue. 'You want me to become a woodcutter?' he said hoarsely. 'I cannot. Saraswati Rane is right, we should choose another day.'

'And what about the Devi – who gave you your luck, your animals, who gave you everything? Will you make her angry? Do you want to lose it all?'

At her words, Ramu looked up, wild-eyed. 'Take it all away?' he whispered horrified.

'Of course she could,' Laxmi answered. 'Don't worry, our puja will be so small no one will even notice it.'

And so Ramu gave in and went docilely to Kesarigaon to get another priest, and Laxmi herself went to Mandwa to hire the best dance and music troupe in the area and then to Sanawad to get the best cooks.

Perhaps because the priest was so certain that no one, not even someone as stubborn as Laxmi, could possibly go against his advice, he never mentioned his conversation with her to anyone, not even his wife. Laxmi on her part had sworn Ramu to secrecy and Ramu on his side tried hard not to know more than he had to. And so the village too remained largely ignorant of the headman's plans for Gaopuja and of the plans being made by Ramu and Laxmi.

Meanwhile, once he'd made up his mind to have a truly grand Gaopuja, the headman wasted no time. He immediately set about ordering the best the region could provide and soon three bullock carts of food, lights and a mini generator set were on their way to Nandgaon. But when it came to the cooks and entertainment, to his surprise, his plans were thwarted at every turn. In Sanawad, famous for its cooks, the best were already hired and he had to settle for second best. And in Mandwa, famous for its entertainers, the best were also booked and so he was forced to return empty-handed.

'I just don't understand it, Saraswatibhai. The country has

been devastated by this flood and still people have money to celebrate?' he complained to Saraswati Rane one evening. 'Is the Devi trying to tell me she is unhappy?'

Saraswati Rane smiled. 'Not at all. This is fate showing its hand, that is all. Who in this village will know the difference between best and second best when you have such a mausi in your kitchen? And as for the entertainers, the Devi would certainly not have been pleased with dancers. The kirthankaars of Dausa are still free. Remember them? They came here two years ago. I could ask them for you. The leader's wife is Dayawati's sister's husband's mausi.'

'I knew you would say that,' the headman said sourly. 'I remember them; they sang well but half the village left early.'

'That's not true,' Saraswati Rane answered hotly. 'The people only left to eat and then returned. Surely you remember how good the young boy's singing was?' he added slyly. 'You were the one who remarked on how divine his voice was.'

The headman kept quiet. God was not what the villagers needed this year. They needed to be reminded that life on earth was worth living.

The first that the village knew of Ramu's puja was when the invitation, arrived. Every family got one – except for the headman's family and Saraswati Rane's – a card with a picture of Ganesh printed in red on the top. Laxmi had insisted that Ramu get formal invitations made. He'd grumbled that the headman would hear of it, but then pride had won out. For the very extravagance of the preparations made him believe, blindly, that in spite of the invitations, everything would work out all right in the end and the headman would understand. Somehow, if the worst came to the worst, the goddess would protect him.

'So what do you make of this?' Giridhari the painter asked his wife, showing her the card.

'I told you right at the beginning that woman was not good,' she replied. 'And on Gaopuja day, the cheek! What will the headman say?'

'He'll probably make them change their date,' Giridhari answered, trying to reassure her.

'And so you will go there?' she asked, her lips thinning.

'Yes, indeed. For Ramu's cow makes milk like no animal I have ever seen. If that bull-calf of hers was to give our Munni a child, imagine how rich we could become.'

'How can you think that? The headman would. . .' his wife put a hand over her mouth, too shocked even to say the words aloud.

Giridhari scowled. 'Is your fear of the headman so great that you will let our children stay poor?'

Under the banyan tree, Ramu's invitation was being discussed by Darbari Lal the barber and some of his regulars.

'Must be a mistake.'

'They wouldn't dare.'

'What will the headman say?'

'He'll make them stop it, that's all.'

And so, in the days leading up to Gaopuja, everyone promised Ramu they would come, and ate the delicious kheer he brought them, while secretly waiting for the headman to put an end to it so they could all have one more laugh at Ramu's expense. The headman, however, remained unaware of Ramu's plans, for everyone assumed that he knew already, and he in turn was so preoccupied with the complicated state of his finances, which Mahendra had finally managed to get him to take seriously, that he didn't notice the signs.

Kuntabai was the first to see the tents in Laxmi's back yard. She'd gone over to get some milk.

'What are you doing, Laxmibai? Are you really planning to go ahead with this madness?' she asked bluntly.

Laxmi shrugged her shoulders. 'I cannot go against the wishes of the Devi,' she said, 'and anyway, we will begin ours later in the evening. The others can come after Gaopuja is over.'

'But you know that is impossible. Have you gone mad?'

'Why? Aren't we landowners too?' Laxmi snapped. 'If we are good enough to be invited to the headman's puja, why are we not good enough for the others to come to ours? Besides, the headman has not said anything to Ramu.'

Kuntabai said nothing, staring steadily at her friend until Laxmi was forced to look away. Then, and only then, did she get up to leave, saying softly, 'The line between pride and arrogance is thin. Be careful my friend.'

Laxmi caught Kuntabai's hand. 'Wait – take some milk with you,' she cried desperately.

Kuntabai shook her head. 'There is no need. Even poor widows can't always be bought.'

Perhaps out of loyalty to her friend or perhaps because she too assumed that the headman would find out and put a stop to Laxmi's madness, Kuntabai didn't tell the headman either. As for the rest of the village, so certain were they of the headman's omniscience that they assumed that a compromise had been reached and that Ramu had decided to do his puja the next day.

'But why hasn't Ramu said anything about it to us?' Under the banyan tree, one of Darbari Lal's regulars complained.

'Because he is too embarrassed, I guess. What an idiot, printing cards and everything. As I have always told you young men, making money is one thing, keeping it another. Now look at the headman, he knows how to keep money running like a river though his lands. That is wisdom.'

'So when will Ramu tell us then?'

'The day before Gaopuja, I guess,' Darbari Lal answered.

'Well, I for one will be sad when he tells us, for I hear the cooks he has hired are the best in all the district,' Govind Rao sighed.

But to their utter astonishment, two days before the festival a cartful of cooks trundled down the rutted lane to the village, stopping only to ask directions to Ramu's house. And before the villagers even had time to consult each other properly, Ramu appeared apologetically at their doorsteps and told them that the invitation to the naming ceremony remained unchanged. But he assured them that his puja would begin after the headman's so that there would be no clash and finished up his explanation with an account of how the Devi had come to Laxmi and told her to have the naming done on that auspicious day which is why they had changed their minds.

The day before Gaopuja, tensions ran high. The villagers had listened in stunned silence to Ramu's embarrassed explanation the previous night and then, when Ramu had left, had sat up late into the night discussing it. On the one hand, everyone agreed that the Kamdhenu was the luckiest cow in all of Nandgaon and it would be unlucky not to worship her on such an auspicious day. On the other hand, the headman was the richest man in the village and as its Patel was the only one who had the right to celebrate Gaopuja. To go to both would anger the headman even more, for that would put Ramu on the same level as him – which left not going to Ramu's at all. But that, they felt, might anger the powerful Devi that protected Ramu.

People huddled in small groups, talking in whispers and avoiding each other's eyes when they passed each other in the street. Some cast furtive glances first in the direction of the headman's house and then in the opposite direction towards where Ramu lived. Only in one corner of the village, in the line of ramshackle huts where the poorest of the poor lived, was there no room for doubt. There, they waited eagerly for a chance to worship the Kamdhenu on such an auspicious occasion.

CHAPTER TWENTY-TWO

GAOPUJA

Gaopuja dawned clear and unusually cool. In the headman's house, preparations began at sunrise with the men of the household rounding up the cattle and taking them to the river to be thoroughly washed. As they walked down the main street, doors opened and from each house the cattle streamed out, swelling the herd until there was no room to move. At the village's edge the herd was met by the little boys who were the animals' caretakers. The little boys then drove the cattle across the bridge to the meadows on the other side where they were allowed to feed untill the sun grew strong enough to burn away the mist that covered the river. Then the animals were rounded up and driven to the water's edge where they were bathed and their bodies rubbed with fragrant river reeds and mustard oil and their horns polished until they gleamed like newly-forged steel. Finally crowns of river flowers and reeds were placed on the bulls' heads and wreaths of three-pointed kabelu leaves were placed around the cows' and calves' necks and they were driven back across the bridge to the village.

Meanwhile, in the village, the women and girls attacked the cowsheds with pails and brushes, giving them the same treatment that the animals themselves were getting. They sang as they worked and it was their song and the clanging of pails that awoke the headman. He groaned and covered his face with the sheet. It had been a bad night, a strange unease keeping him awake and staring into the darkness until the early hours

313

of the morning. Had they remembered to ask for the river's blessing before bathing the animals, he wondered anxiously? And had the pails of new milk been brought up for the making of the evening's prasaad and for the washing of the cowshed? His eyes went to the window from where thick spears of light emanated. What time was it? he wondered. Had Ramu taken the goats to the forest and had someone remembered to tell him to clean out the goat house too? The headman threw off his sheets and planted his feet firmly on the cold earth. It made Gopal think of the flood, and all that the water had taken from him.

In the headman's cow shed Vaasanti the old cook, who was supervising the washing of the floors with milk, was stopped in mid-conversation, suddenly struck by nostalgia. 'Look what a poky little place this is,' she grumbled to Savitribai. 'How can the cattle be happy here? We should never have left the old village.'

'Hush, have a care of what comes out of that toothless mouth of yours,' her companion whispered looking scared, 'you know the headman had no choice, the river took the village away from us, not he.'

'Of course, but he must have angered Narmada devi for her to punish us like this,' Vaasantibai answered.

But by ten o'clock, when the animals were brought back up to the village, everyone's doubts were silenced. For the little cowherds had done their work well and the animals looked magnificent. Men, women and children cheered as the animals marched solemnly up the main street of the village. As was the custom, the women and young girls rubbed red and green powder on to the animals' bodies as they progressed up the street towards the headman's house and in the hearts of the onlookers hope grew and a feeling of optimism enveloped them all, mingling with the clouds of red and green powder that floated above their heads. Smiles appeared on the villagers' faces and they shouted out their favourite animals' names, as well as the names of those animals that had perished during the long hot summer.

When the cattle reached the headman's house, he was waiting for them on bended knees and seeing him there, looking just as he always looked, but paradoxically even larger and more solid, the villagers cheered even louder, their love for him rushing to the fore as quickly as it had ebbed before. And as each animal entered, the headman's grandchildren garlanded them and smeared rice paste and red sindoor on their foreheads as the drummers, their muscles bulging like hard-boiled eggs, beat the heavy village drums, and the headman solemnly greeted each animal by name. When the last one had crossed the threshold, the temple bells rang out and the villagers assembled in front of the gate shouted, 'Gaomata ki jai, Dhartimata ki jai.' Drums and cymbals were beaten and long horns blown; the villagers cheered until they were hoarse. But unlike in earlier years, this time the villagers did not linger to discuss the parade and the excitements still to come. As soon as the last drum beat died out, they turned and returned quickly to their homes, avoiding each other's eyes. 'I cannot bear this,' Govind Rao grumbled to his wife. 'Surely the headman must know? He should have made Ramu stop or begun his puja earlier. This is going to end badly, I know it. Surely he could have done something to avoid embarrassing us all?'

But Govind Rao was wrong. For the headman did not know until the very end.

Saraswati Rane arrived punctually at three in the afternoon and began to prepare the sacred fire in a businesslike manner. From his charpoy under the honeysuckle bush the headman watched his friend, almost unrecognisable in the bright yellow dhoti which he wore only for big pujas, his head freshly shaved and his forehead ablaze in white and yellow sandalwood markings. Once the fire was lit and the flames rose towards the heavens the headman would cease to be headman and would become the sacrificer instead, the fire symbolising his sacrifice. The priest would be his father and teacher, guiding him through the spirit world in which he must perform the sacrifice. Gopal stared at the square hollow in which the fire would be lit. It was called the mouth of a cow, he remembered suddenly. What did the mouth of a cow have to do with the sacrifice? he wondered. No one had ever been able to explain it to him. Perhaps after the puja this time, he thought, getting up and going to join his friend, he would ask Saraswati Rane to explain it all to him. Saraswati Rane gave him one brief glance and then went back to making his fire. Neither of them spoke. The headman watched Saraswati Rane light the flame and feed it until it was a bush of light illuminating the faces of those around it. The grandness and solemnity of the ritual thrilled the headman. It had ever since he'd been a boy and had watched his father sit in exactly the same place he was now sitting, performing the same actions Gopal was about to perform. Perhaps that's when the desire to become headman had been born, he thought, suddenly seeing how the shadow world of the puja mirrored and also created the real one. Saraswati Rane looked up and nodded, telling Gopal to begin. They fed the fire together; each time the priest threw something into the fire, Gopal leaned forward and poured either ghee or milk into the pit, repeating the words after Saraswati Rane that would appease the giant serpents that held up the earth. The courtyard began to fill with people and the sound of their whisperings was like the ebb and flow of the tide, a gentle backdrop to the fierce beauty of the fire. The sun began to set and the scent of ghee and spices swamped the courtyard.

Suddenly the headman looked up. Something was wrong. He could feel it. He turned his head and his eyes began to scan the crowd. But none would meet his eye. Yet their fingers, he noticed, nervously tapped the ground or fiddled with the folds of their crisp white dhotis. What was the matter with them? he wondered. Out of the corners of his eyes he saw movement, shadows getting up and slinking away. He frowned. What was going on? Did everyone have a problem with their bladder that evening? It happened again, and this time he noticed that the others were aware of it too. Each time someone left a quiver went through the bodies of those who remained. The headman began to watch the edges of the crowd more closely. He waited for the shadows to return, but none came. The gaps in the rows grew larger and larger. Was it because of the food? he wondered. Probably, he decided.

Then his attention was claimed by Saraswati Rane who stood up, signalling the end of the rituals. The headman stood as well and the courtyard was once again home to noise and confusion. The headman was rushed away, bathed, changed and fed – for he had been fasting all day. When he returned the kirthankaars had begun to sing. Gopal sat down in the front row and closed his eyes gratefully. This was the part he'd been looking forward to all evening. The voice of the main singer, a young blind boy, was of such an unearthly purity that it needed no accompaniment. It took control of Gopal's mind, lifting it up effortlessly towards the heavens. Then as the other voices entered into the chorus of the song, the main singer's voice faded and died out. But Gopal's mind, freed of its earthly constraints by the music, remained up there, looking down at the puja from on high, seeing it as a bird might. Suddenly what had been bothering the headman all evening crystallised into an image, a face. He turned to Govind Rao who was sitting right beside him. 'Where's Ramu?' he asked.

Ramu had watched the headman's herd parade through the streets and in his mind he'd imagined his Shambhu leading them, a crown of river flowers on his horns. How proud Shambhu would be, he thought, to lead such a magnificent collection of beasts! How lucky he was to have been born in such a fine village with such a fine herd, he thought, happiness bubbling inside him. How fortunate he was to be married to a woman as beautiful and intelligent as Laxmi. He followed the others up the street towards the headman's, his heart filled with love and gratefulness. How lucky Nandgaon was to have such a man at its head! Ramu had been waiting all week for the headman to call him and tell him to change the date of Shambhu's naming. But the order had not come and as he stood watching the cattle enter the headman's courtyard, Ramu's heart was so full of love and gratefulness that he cheered louder than all the others, shouting the headman's name again and again.

That morning Ramu and Laxmi together had cleaned out the animal hut and then Ramu had taken the animals to the river in the forest along with the goats. When he returned Laxmi had finished milking Kami and together they decorated the animals' bodies and then took Shambhu out to their still fallow field and made him plough a single furrow.

'There,' Laxmi had said, putting a garland of white chameli and orange marigold flowers around Shambhu's large neck. 'Doesn't he look wonderful?'

'He looks like a god,' Ramu had replied admiringly. 'Surely the others will accept him now.' And indeed Shambhu did look incredibly handsome. His muscles bulged with health, his skin shone. The bump between his shoulders was large, a promise of power. And his small suspicious stare was crowned by an impressively massive forehead. He looked the incarnation of power.

Looking at Shambhu, Laxmi bit her lip unconsciously and Ramu, unable to resist, put his fingers on her mouth. Laxmi jerked away, then rubbed at her lips self-consciously. 'Do you think anyone will come?' she asked huskily.

'Did anyone come for Kami's naming?' Ramu answered.

'And what difference did that make? Just leave it to the goddess.'

At noon Ramu went out to the bus stop to receive the priest while Laxmi hurriedly dressed and fed the musicians and dance party, who were complaining of the heat and the flies and the lack of electricity. When she returned, the first guests had already arrived, the clothes clean but not new, the fabric thin and stretched taut like the skin over their bones. They sat quietly in the shade of the house. Laxmi, coming into the courtyard, squinted into the sun. A few of them she could recognise, but there were many she didn't know, people who were obviously refugees from the flood, recent additions to Nandgaon's population.

Ramu returned with the priest and she rushed to welcome him and wash his feet. He complained bitterly about the road and the heat and then ate well, blessed Laxmi and fell asleep. Laxmi went outside. The yard had filled with even more people.

At five the priest came out and, still grumbling, demanded water to wash with. Laxmi hurried to help him. At sunset he began to prepare the sacred fire on which the name would be 'cooked'. The animals were brought out and tethered to the jamun tree. A sigh went through the crowd. Even the priest looked a little surprised at the sight of them. But after a quick second look he fixed his eyes upon the crowd, taking in the quiet air of desperation that clung to those who waited there and his lip curled into a sneer. He looked at his watch, got up abruptly and went around to the back of the house for a smoke. Those who waited barely noticed, for their eyes were fixed upon Kami.

At nightfall, when Venus could be seen shining brightly in the sky, the pujari returned and without giving the crowd another glance began the ceremony, mumbling the prayers at lightning speed. Before any of the onlookers had even realised what was happening he'd sprinkled holy water on the animals, standing as far as possible from them with a look of disdain on his face and asking, 'Which is the animal to be named?'

Laxmi brought Shambhu forward.

'And what is the name?' he asked.

'Shambhu,' Ramu answered, leaning forward and whispering the name into the priest's ear.

The pundit nodded and he in turn leaned forward and whispered the name into the animal's ear. As if on cue, Shambhu snorted and pawed the ground.

'He accepts his name. His name is Shambhu,' Ramu announced. A cheer went up from the assembled crowd and a shower of rice and petals rained down upon them. The crowd rushed forward, clustering like bees around Shambhu's shiny black body.

Suddenly Laxmi found the priest by her side. 'I must talk with you,' he whispered urgently, taking her aside. Then he demanded his payment. 'Won't you eat with us, pujariji?' Laxmi asked, astonished.

He looked uncomfortable and mumbled something about having another puja to attend to.

Suddenly Laxmi understood and her eyes blazed. 'Here, take your money and go,' she cried. 'We don't need your blessings.'

Haughty disdain replaced the apology on the pujari's face. Laxmi knew the look well – all priests she'd ever met knew exactly how to look that way. Condescendingly, he took the money she held out to him, and counted it. Seeing it was all there, he smiled professionally and said, 'Bless you my daughter, bless you.'

But the blessing fell on deaf ears as Laxmi had already stalked away. Anger tore at her insides and her ears filled with the sound of a phantom keening. She stared bitterly at the crowd. A chaotic disorderly scene met her eyes, dwarfed by the large stage that the dance party had insisted on putting up at one end. Most of the guests were still clustered around the animals, but at the other end of the angan, near the stage, Kuntabai and a few other women were beginning to organise the food. Laxmi imagined the scene at the headman's, row after ordered row of important people, the kind of people that a pundit would be happy to sit amongst, all related to the headman in one way or the other.

Darkness descended and a sense of anticipation filled the air. The drummers came out and quietly began to play. Lanterns were brought out and placed around the stage, creating pools of flickering light that transformed the tattered, travel-weary curtain into a rich red velvet landscape. Then with a dramatic flourish the curtains were swept back and the drummers began to play faster and faster until the music reached a crescendo. Then a dancer appeared. Laxmi, stepping out from the kitchen, felt the breath catch in her throat as she watched the crowd so magically transformed – worry and anxiety ironed out of their faces as they devoured the dancer with their eyes. The yard slowly filled with shadows, each one arriving alone and sitting quietly at the edge of the circle of light.

All night the singers sang while the dazzling Chameli pirou-etted and pounded the floorboards, the curls of flesh around her hips and just under her frilly lace and satin-covered breasts glowing with pearls of sweat. Laxmi noticed that the dancer had small rather delicate feet for such a voluptuous body and wondered how those little feet could sustain the weight of the thousand bells tied to each ankle. The answer came later when she went backstage with another round of tea and saw the great Chameli looking small and lost on a little footstool, rub-bing her calves as tears slipped silently down her cheeks. Laxmi immediately called Ramu over and the two of them massaged her legs until the song ended and the other three dancers returned. Then Chameli went back on and the red curtain became a frame for a human bolt of lightning darting across the stage. All night the drummers drummed and the dancers stamped and whirled in their shimmering saris, the sweat rolling off their heavily scented bodies in fat rivulets, flavouring the cool night air with the scent of desire.

And so no one in Nandgaon slept that night. Especially those in the headman's compound, for whom the sound of the drums was a bitter reminder that for once the heart of Nandgaon beat elsewhere.

CHAPTER TWENTY-THREE
AFTER GAOPUJA

Saraswati Rane was not a man to be swayed by dreams. All his life he'd done what he had been trained to do – care for his temple and preside over the births, deaths and marriages of his people. But from the day Rama Bhagwan appeared in a dream just after the god was rescued from the ruins of his old temple and demanded that a temple be built for him, Saraswati Rane was a different man. The idea for the construction of the temple came to him in another dream: just like Hanuman Bhagwan, the monkey god, had carried Rama Bhagwan on his shoulders, the temple would sit on top of his house. Access to the temple would be from stairs that would curve outwards like two giant ears on either side of his house. For a long time he simply contemplated his vision, a temple that would tower over the entire village, dwarfing even the sacred banyan tree at its centre. Then Rama appeared to him a third time and told him to hurry up and begin, or else Nandgaon would be destroyed again.

So, much to the disgust of his wife, he sold all his land except for the two fields that were close to the river and used the money to strengthen the foundations of his house, build the curling stairs and the platform above it and order a brand new statue of Rama. When Saraswati Rane had spent every last penny he went to the others. But no one gave him any money for none believed anything would come of it. In desperation Saraswati Rane had gone to the headman. But the headman had only laughed. 'I have better uses for my money, Saraswati Rane, than wasting it on your temple,' he'd said.

After Gaopuja, Saraswati Rane knew that God would soon have his temple.

After Gaopuja a strange lull descended upon Nandgaon. On the surface, nothing had changed. Everyone still worked together, joked, laughed and gossiped together. But scattered amidst the various conversations of the day were holes, hesitations where there shouldn't have been any, sudden pauses in the conversation that turned into uncomfortable silences until the discussion was hurriedly, self-consciously, taken up again.

For this unnatural state of affairs the villagers blamed the headman. They had all waited tensely for him to punish Ramu or take revenge. But days stretched into weeks and the headman stayed as passive as a rock. 'I cannot bear this,' Saraswati Rane complained to his wife. 'The village is going silent under the weight of its own swallowed words. Why doesn't the headman just punish Ramu and be done with it?'

'Why are you asking me? You are his friend,' his wife replied.

'Because, you silly woman, that is exactly the problem. Because I am his friend I cannot ask him.'

His wife shrugged. 'Then you should punish Ramu yourself,' she said.

Laxmi too waited eagerly for the headman to do something but as time passed and he did nothing, she became furious. For unlike the others, she understood what the headman was doing. He was telling them and telling the village that she and Ramu were nothings, so unimportant that even their misdeeds, like those of children, were not to be taken notice of. Day after day, she thought of how much her revenge had cost them – the enormous amount of money they had paid to entertain the village, borrowing from the tea stall owner in Kesarigaon against future deliveries of Kami's milk – and how no one even spoke of it any more, and her anger grew.

The only one who seemed unaffected was Ramu himself, for the fact that the headman's behaviour towards him remained almost unchanged filled him with so much joy that it kept a smile permanently on his face.

'I told you, didn't I?' he said to the junglee cow. 'Your grandchildren and great grandchildren will be a part of the herd.'

The cow, whose skin had acquired a few more folds recently, stopped eating and looked at him.

'What is it?' he asked her. 'Aren't you happy that they will belong to the herd?'

He scratched her under the comfortable folds of her neck. 'I know, I know, they weren't kind to you and Kami. But you have to forgive them. They didn't know you then. With the herd, as with humans, things don't change overnight.'

The cow shook her head, shaking off a fly that had settled on her nose. Ramu thought of Nathan Lal, the headman's favourite billy goat, who had died last year, bitten on the nose by a viper in his own shelter.

'You don't agree? But you're wrong. They will accept you eventually. But the point is, would you want to leave me and go with the herd instead?'

The cow thrust her head into his chest and kept it there, her cold nose creating a circle of damp just below his heart. Ramu hugged her to him. 'I could not bear to part with you too,' he said, 'not even to the herd.'

Jealous of the attention the cow was receiving, Shambhu, who was almost as big as a normal two-year-old, ambled over. He stopped in front of Ramu, snorted angrily and then thrust his snout into Ramu's shoulder.

Ramu scratched him between the ears as the bull had wanted. 'You'll see how they will love you, the cows of Nandgaon,'

Ramu told him, 'for you are the incarnation of their dark lord.' But after a while Shambhu got bored and went back to eating. Ramu turned back to the cow who had remained quietly at his side. A touch of sadness crept into his voice and he said, 'I don't mind if your grandchildren go to Nandgaon – as long as you remain by my side.'

The cow looked solemnly up into his face and then gave it a lick.

'Aren't you going to punish Ramu?' Jaiwant Rane asked the headman at last, unable to bear it any longer. He, Vilas Rao, Govind Rao and Saraswati Rane were with the headman. A month had passed since Gaopuja.

'Punish him?' the headman asked innocently. 'What for?'

There was a moment's stunned silence. All three men looked at the headman, shock on their faces.

'For his insolence, damn him,' Vilas Rao spluttered.

'And his lies,' Saraswati Rane added.

'His arrogance,' Govind Rao mumbled, looking guilty.

The headman raised an eyebrow and looked at them quizzically. Apart from Saraswati Rane, the others had all gone to Ramu's party. 'What do you want me to do?' he asked.

The headman had thought long and hard about what to do and had come to the conclusion that Ramu would never have done what he had if it hadn't been for what Gopal himself had done to humiliate the man. He, the headman, had not only sold Ramu a useless piece of land but had rubbed salt into the wound by deliberately refusing to recognise Ramu as a landowner. Naturally, any self-respecting man would have retaliated. The fault was his. How could he punish Ramu?

'Punish him!' his friends cried in unison.

'There is nothing to punish,' he answered, much to his listeners' amazement. 'There is no rule or custom forbidding a man from holding a puja when he wishes.'

'But. . . but such a thing has never happened in Nandgaon. What will people think?' Vilas Rao stammered, eyes bulging.

'They will think what they wish and then they will realise that their headman is right as usual, a little puja isn't a very important thing, and if Ramu got his dates all wrong, why should I make it into a big event?' the headman replied, adding with his usual wry humour, 'Do you want me to punish the mosquitos that dare to bite me too?'

After a moment's hesitation, Vilas Rao, Govind Rao, Saraswati Rane and Jaiwant Rane began to laugh.

And the village followed suit. But unlike the headman, they could not forget. For they felt that justice had not been served. Ramu had known about Gaopuja and yet he had stolen the region's best entertainers and cooks. How could such insolence go unpunished? Perhaps if they had talked about it, someone would have come up with an explanation. But out of loyalty to the headman they wouldn't discuss the matter even amongst themselves. And it was this that made the holes – consisting of words unspoken and therefore undigested – in the conversations between people.

But this soon changed – for words once formed in the mind had a way of finding an audience. 'Strange days,' the barber told his acolytes. 'I never thought I would feel this way. As though someone had died or left suddenly in the middle of a conversation.'

'How well you put it, Darbari Lal!' the group of young men who were his loyal admirers said in a chorus. The barber smiled, encouraged, and continued. 'The headman should never have let him keep that junglee cow. You wait and see – that animal will end up turning us all into junglees.'

'I wish the Patel had done something,' Saraswati Rane grumbled to his cousin. 'The whole village feels different, as if there is a bomb under our feet waiting to explode and no one can find it.'

'Ramu should never have married an outsider,' Jaiwant Rane replied.

'Really?' Saraswati Rane looked quizzically at his cousin. 'But I thought you liked her.'

'Like? It is not for me to like or dislike; it is for Nandgaon that I worry now. The headman has made a mistake, I feel it in my bones. Does a good farmer ignore weeds in his field? The headman is a good farmer, that is why he is headman,' Saraswati Rane cried, aghast.

After a moment's uncomfortable silence Jaiwant Rane said, 'It is not for a poor Brahmin to tell our Patel what to do, but I think he will regret his kindness one day.'

'If you really believe that, then you should have the courage to tell him,' Saraswati Rane snapped, going red in the face.

'Nandgaon is already finished, why bother an old man?' Jaiwant Rane replied.

'He is not old,' Saraswati Rane said loyally, 'or stupid. You'll see, he will put that upstart Ramu permanently in his place if he ever gets above himself again.'

And so, what the headman had hoped to achieve – to delegate Ramu's puja to the great dustbin of things forgotten – did not happen. For without their being aware of it, after Gaopuja the people of Nandgaon had begun to see the headman differently and as a result they also saw Ramu and Laxmi differently. The three became intertwined in Nandgaon's collective mind and what the headman lost, Ramu and Laxmi gained. Just as Ramu's cows, each so different from the other, began to occupy centre stage in the life of the village. But of the three, it was the Kamdhenu who was venerated. For Ramu had named her too well, and the belief that she was indeed the giver of wishes spread rapidly.

Thus it was that a few months after Gaopuja, as Ramu entered the village with the cow, Shambhu and the goats one evening, conversations stopped abruptly and several heads turned to watch him go by. 'Ram, Ram,' they greeted him, their eyes on the shining black hide of the animal that walked beside him. As if he knew he was being watched, the way a celebrity knows it, Shambhu inflated his chest and took tiny mincing steps, tossing his head and glaring at no one in particular. Beside him, sticking close to Ramu, the cow looked small.

'Just look how that animal has grown,' Govind Rao whispered to Bicchoo, looking up from his cards. 'It's incredible. Soon he will be bigger than the headman's Mahesh.'

Bicchoo grunted, a sour expression on his face. 'The animal is all puffed up on Ramu's pride. Hit it, and it will become half the size.'

Govind Rao pretended he hadn't heard. 'So how are your animals Ramubhai?' he shouted. 'That Shambhu is the very incarnation of Shivaji's Nandi*,' he called out as Ramu came within hearing distance.

'That is very kind of you, Govind Raoji,' Ramu replied politely, his face glowing with pride.

'And that Kamdhenu of yours, she is still not well?' Bicchoo asked with feigned concern.

'No, no. She is fine. Still giving us lots of milk,' Ramu said proudly. 'But her stomach is delicate so Laxmi prefers to keep her at home.' He nodded once more and continued up the street. The goats were eager to get to their home.

'There goes the luckiest idiot in our village,' Darbari Lal said in an undertone to his clients. 'Not only does the Kamdhenu produce a bull but she also gives him milk. Do you know what the price of milk is in Kesarigaon?'

'No, no, tell us,' his audience cried in unison.

'Fifty rupees a litre. And they say the flood destroyed so many animals it won't go down for a few years.' Then, turning

---

* Shiva's mount, a giant blue-black bull.

towards the street, 'Ramu,' he called out in a falsely friendly voice, 'come and spend some time with us – don't forget your old friends. Tell us about the Kamdhenu. Any new miracles today?'

Ramu paused, looking uncomfortable. 'But I visited you yesterday, Darbaribhai,' he said.

'But between yesterday and today, many things change. Tell us what is new with the Kamdhenu. We are hungry for news of her,' he said, winking at the others.

'Stupid man. Look at the way he stands, as proud as a cockerel,' Bicchoo said, spitting on the ground. His eyes rested jealously on Ramu as the man stood talking to the barber.

Govind Rao smiled. 'So he turned you down again?'

Bicchoo nodded. 'Says it's his wife's fault. That witch. I wish I could get my hands on her one moonless night. I'd show her.'

'But Sushilabai says that Laxmibai gave Parvatibai a loan just last week.' Govind Rao couldn't resist showing off his own superior knowledge of Ramu's household.

Bicchoo spat. 'Huh, a piddling sum. I never saw any of it. Why can't I have a little of Ramu's luck? If only I had a cow like that, I wouldn't need to crawl in the dust before anyone ever again.'

'Well, maybe you could start by whispering Ramu's name before you throw the dice,' Govind Rao suggested playfully.

'Really? You think it would work?' Bicchoo said eagerly. 'You know, I never thought of that. What a great idea.'

'That's quite an animal you have there, Ramu,' one-eyed Giridhari the painter called out from his front doorstep as Ramu passed by. 'I think I'll have to paint him one of these days.' The painter was sitting on his doorstep as usual, repairing his paintbrushes.

'Really? Will you?' Ramu stopped sharply in front of him. 'And will you do the others as well?'

'Certainly, if you'd like me to,' Giridhari replied.

Ramu's face fell. 'But I can't afford you, Giridhariji.'

'You, not afford a poor painter like me? Why Ramuji, after the headman you are the richest man in Nandgaon.'

Ramu blushed. 'Nahi, nahi, baba. You have been misinformed. Look at me, I am still the same Ramu, without even a house to call my own.' He referred to the fact that the house they lived in was the headman's old house, and it was not technically theirs.

The painter laughed. 'You are too modest Ramuji, everyone knows the Devi smiles upon you. It is only a matter of time before you get whatever you want. Even the Patel is not so lucky.'

Ramu could think of nothing to say.

'I tell you what, I will paint Shambhu for you,' Giridhari said, breaking the silence, 'if you let him mate with my Rani. They are the same age, and I would very much like to be the first in the village to own a child of your animal.'

Ramu hesitated, an image of the headman flashing in front his eyes. He would not approve, he knew instinctively, of such a bargain. 'I don't think Patelji would like that,' he said seriously. 'You know how he feels about our herd. And my cows are not a part of it.'

Giridhari laughed. 'Why bring the headman into this, Ramu? Do you not have the courage to say no yourself? Or is it that now that you are rich you forget your old friends?'

Ramu looked up quickly. 'It's not that, Giridhariji, not at all. But the headman. . . Surely you understand? I would have to ask his permission and I. . . I don't think. . .'

'Why tell him? Since when has he become our ruler? His job is to look after us, not to tell us what to do,' Giridhari replied.

Ramu looked down at his feet, unable to think of anything to say.

Giridhari watched the emotions playing across Ramu's transparent face, and adroitly changed the subject. 'Think about it. There is no hurry. Come and have a cup of tea,' he invited.

The dreaminess disappeared from Ramu's face. 'I can't,' he said apologetically. 'I have to get the goats home or our Patel will kill me.'

'Come afterwards then,' Giridhari answered, 'the tea will be waiting.'

Ramu opened his mouth to refuse but could think of no excuse so he nodded reluctantly and after hastily putting the goats into the headman's goathouse, he returned to Giridhari's. 'Just a quick one,' he warned. 'Laxmi is waiting for me.'

While Ramu was with Giridhari, Laxmi had visitors too: Kuntabai, who came almost every afternoon though she had refused to attend the puja, Parvatibai, Bicchoo's long-suffering wife, and Sushilabai, who also came every day, taking advantage of her status as close neighbour.

'Thank God the winter is coming,' Kuntabai was saying. 'As I get older I like the heat less and less.'

'That is because you get fatter with each year,' Laxmi teased her, stoking the fire.

'My rolls come in handy in winter,' Kuntabai replied, fanning herself. 'I don't know how you cope Laxmi, with nothing but bones between you and mother earth.'

'She has Ramu to keep her warm,' Sushilabai interjected, giggling and rolling her eyes.

Laxmi blushed and busied herself with the tea.

'Is it true that you refused to wash Ramubhai's feet after you got married?' Sushilabai asked as casually as she could.

Laxmi looked startled. 'Who said such a thing?'

Sushilabai chortled with delight. 'So it is true,' she said at last. 'You're a brave woman, I can hardly believed you dared to do that. Weren't you afraid of being beaten?'

'Beaten?' Laxmi looked surprised. 'It never entered my mind.'

'But you didn't know him – how could you have dared?' Sushilabai argued.

Laxmi's face filled with shame. 'I was so angry then, so full of pride. There was no place for thought then. Poor Ramu. He was so patient.' She laughed and shook her head.

'Well, things are different now, thank God. Marriage changes a person, makes them wise,' Kuntabai said, her widow's white glowing in the shadows of the kitchen.

'You lucky thing,' Parvatibai said suddenly. She was a quiet dark woman who looked permanently tired, her mouth a crescent moon whose ends curved downwards in perpetual disappointment. Everyone knew that Bicchoo beat her almost every week.

There was a moment's silence. No one met her eye.

'You shouldn't let him do it.' Laxmi's words exploded into the silence. 'You should complain to the headman. He'll have to do something then.'

Parvatibai's mouth turned down even more and she said nothing, then a small miracle occurred, her face softened and her mouth turned up again. 'It's not his fault,' she said. 'He is a doubly unlucky man. First because he is poor, and second because he is weak. But his greatest weakness is love. And that is why I have to forgive him.' She paused and looked from one face to the other earnestly. 'Besides, my mouth is what starts it. Once this mouth opens, evil spills out of it like a river in flood. How else can a man stop a river?'

No one said anything.

'More tea?' Laxmi asked, breaking the silence.

'This tea is so delicious one cannot refuse,' Sushilabai gushed, trying to give a more cheerful turn to the conversation. 'I don't know what magic you do, but I never get tired of your tea, ever.'

Laxmi ignored her. She leaned forward urgently, fixing Parvatibai with her eyes. 'Nevertheless, I think you should do something, Parvatibai. He can't be allowed to get away with it. After all, he is the one to make you suffer and that is why you say terrible things.'

'If I could have such sweet tea every day, perhaps my mouth would not be so bitter.' Parvatibai tried to make a joke of it but her eyes gave her away.

Laxmi swallowed, a lump suddenly forming in her throat. Out of the corners of her eyes she saw Kuntabai surreptitiously wipe away a tear with the tip of her sari. A strange thought came into Laxmi's mind: she was not the most unfortunate woman in Nandgaon, but quite probably one of the most fortunate. And the weight of shame that had been with her since her father's death suddenly slipped away. She let out a sigh, and the beauty of the evening, the sweet scent of cardamom and hot milk filled her heart. Suddenly she felt lucky again. She looked at Parvatibai who was crying silently and felt an immense need to share her luck.

'But of course you could have tea like this. All you need to do is get yourself a cow or two. Then you could even sell the extra and your children's school fees would never again be late.'

'Huh! And where is the money to buy such an animal?' Parvatibai looked angrily at Laxmi.

'All you would need is a small loan.'

'A loan? Which fool gives a gambler's wife a loan?' Parvatibai cried. 'Our Patel is a fair man, but he certainly is no fool.'

'But I wasn't thinking of him,' Laxmi cried, standing up in her excitement. She turned to the others and included them in her blazing gaze. 'I have some money. We all do. If we put it together as in a bank, then you could buy your cow and pay us back later. And Sushilabai could rebuild her shop and. . . and. . .' she faltered, seeing the look on their faces, 'what is it?'

The others didn't immediately respond.

At last Kuntabai said, 'True, but what if someone doesn't pay? Then where will we be?'

'But we are all sisters. We wouldn't do that to each other. Any of us could get unlucky, a child could get sick,' Laxmi answered. 'Don't you see? This way, at least we would not be dependent upon the Patel for everything.'

'But we have always been dependent upon him. Without him, we would be nothing,' Kuntabai said sharply. 'Why can't you accept that?'

The Patel's name brought one of those silences they were all becoming increasingly familiar with, and the visit ended soon after, the women leaving hurriedly, suddenly remembering the work that awaited them.

When Ramu returned he was strangely silent himself.

'What is the matter?' Laxmi asked him.

'Shambhu is a fine animal, isn't he?' Ramu asked looking directly at her. 'The whole village says so.'

'They are right,' Laxmi replied. 'He will fetch us a lot one day.'

'You want to sell him?' Alarm flashed across Ramu's face.

'Not immediately, but eventually yes, why not?' Laxmi answered, looking surprised. 'With the money we get we could buy three cows like Kami.'

'Three?' Ramu asked surprised. 'Then we would be richer than everyone except the headman.' He kept quiet for a minute, his face growing troubled. 'The headman won't like it.'

'He would be able to do nothing about it,' Laxmi answered roughly. 'Already everyone is asking when we will mate Shambhu.'

'Really? To you too?' Ramu exclaimed. 'Why, only this evening Giridhari promised to paint Shambhu if we let him mate with his Rani.'

'And what did you say?' Laxmi asked, going suddenly still.

'I said Shambhu wasn't ready yet,' Ramu lied.

'Good,' Laxmi said, her hands returning to the task of making chapattis. 'If the headman finds out we are finished.'

But it was already too late. For while Ramu had been talking to Giridhari, Savitribai, the headman's eldest daughter-in-law, who had been waiting impatiently to ask the painter to paint the walls of their new rooms, had overheard the entire conversation.

CHAPTER TWENTY-FOUR
THE MOTORCYCLE GOD

'Do you believe in God, Mishra?' deputy commissioner Prakash Choudhury asked Manoj.

Manoj's step faltered. They were walking around the cricket field in the centre of Khandwa, a group of seven men. All either rich or powerful or both – except for him. Well aware of the honour accorded to him in being allowed to join the august group, Manoj took an extra big step with the other foot so he didn't fall back. For to fall back meant to lose one's place to another, a place any member of the group would have killed to be in.

'I'm not sure sir,' Manoj answered hesitantly, unsure of what the deputy commissioner wanted to hear.

'What do you mean you are not sure, Mishra? Either you believe or you don't believe. What is the difficulty in that? Just tell me. Do you or do you not believe in God?'

Manoj looked away. The flood, not God, had put him there beside the deputy commissioner. For Manoj had immediately seen the possibilities inherent in the post flood situations for his insemination programme and so as soon as the waters had receeded he had recommenced his field trips on his trusty Enfield, milk cans filled with vials of frozen semen. This time, no one had shooed him away. They turned to him with tragic faces, shorn of hope, but as he explained that he would do the insemination for free, their faces changed and many fell at his feet, their tears wetting his sandals. As he saw first hand the devastation wrought by the flood, his attempts to aid the villagers expanded to include medicine, basic first aid and the ferrying of the sick and dying to the hospital in Khandwa. In the countryside the villagers began to call him the motorcyclewala god. The name caught on and a roaming journalist wrote an article in the local newspaper about the motorcycle god and one morning he woke up and went out to pick up his bottle of milk and found he was famous. People on the street in Khandwa called out 'Motorcyclewala Bhagwan' as he passed and women touched his clothes to their children's eyes and asked for his blessing. And so it was that two weeks ago the deputy commissioner had rolled down the window of his official car at a stop light and told Manoj to join him in a little exercise around the cricket field.

'Come on, Mr Motorcyclewala God, you of all people should have an answer for me,' the deputy commissioner teased him.

Manoj's eyes went to the temple to his left. Someone on top was cleaning and a shower of filthy water and heavenly garbage fell heavily down the stairs. The flowers and food were a uniform grey, the same colour but a little lighter than the water that bore them earthwards.

Manoj looked at it and a sudden memory overwhelmed him. 'Jaipur has a beautiful temple, sir, on the top of a hill, the only hill in the city. I used to go there often. At night, when the city lights were like a carpet of stars.'

'Aha,' the deputy commissioner exclaimed, 'so there is a poet lurking inside you, is there? How can you be a poet without believing in God?'

'You mean the Birla temple, don't you?' Ghorpekar the lawyer asked suddenly, joining the conversation. 'I have been there too. All marble and gold, na?'

'Yes, all marble and gold. The Birlas are very rich industrialists so spent a lot on it,' Manoj answered proudly.

'So in a rich, beautiful place you can believe in God, but not in a place that is not rich and beautiful, is that what you are trying to say. That God cannot exist in a small town?' the deputy commissioner asked peevishly, annoyed at not being the centre of attention.

Grunts of disapproval came from the others but they kept quiet, secretly enjoying Manoj's fall from favour.

Manoj thought fast. 'Not at all sir,' he said smoothly, smiling ingratiatingly at the deputy commissioner. 'If God exists then of course he can be everywhere.'

'But you are not sure that God exists?'

'No sir, I am not,' Manoj replied firmly.

The deputy commissioner frowned. 'You know the problem with you Mishra,' and here his voice changed, becoming expansive, lecturing, louder as well, 'you are confusing existence with belief. Now take me, for example. I don't believe; my wife, she believes. We don't worry about whether something is true or not, we believe or we don't believe – it is a matter of choice. That is why you are confused. A man doesn't believe because something exists, a man believes and so he brings into existence.'

'I think therefore I am,' Manoj echoed, thinking of his philosophy classes.

'What's that? Don't go English on me, I don't like it. English is the language of money, not of philosophy.'

'Sorry sir, some English philosopher said that, I forget who,' Manoj apologised. Behind him, someone tittered.

They walked in silence after that, the deputy commissioner looking straight ahead, annoyed. But he didn't fall back and begin to speak to someone else. Relieved, Manoj stayed a step behind and let his mind drift. In the distance they heard the clock tower chime. That bell is ringing for me, Manoj thought happily, telling the world about my invitation.

It had arrived that morning, all typed and official-looking.

The paper was so fine that it glowed white in spite of the grime that habitually disfigured all mail. He had turned it over curiously, wondering who it had come from. Then he'd looked at the postmark and been even more confused. The letter had been posted from Delhi. But Manoj knew no one there.

'Don't stare at it like an idiot, open it,' Dr Pandey, who'd dropped in for a short visit from the Institute, had urged.

He'd opened it carefully and read the contents in silence, hardly able to believe his eyes. The letter was an invitation, to a conference on cattle rearing and insemination in Denmark. He'd turned over the envelope when he'd finished reading the letter twice and stared at his name typed neatly and unmistakeably on the front. How had they heard of him? he wondered.

Dr Pandey snatched the letter from him and read it through. When he'd finished he threw the letter in the air and began to dance around the room. 'You've done it man, you've hit the big time now. Say goodbye to financial worries, hello five-star hotel,' he chanted, grinning widely.

'But. . .'

'But what?'

'But who told them about me?'

'That journalist I sent, Mishra. Don't you see? Someone must have noticed that sexy picture of you and the Spanish (Dr Pandey still called Govinda that) in the newspaper. You're famous. C'mon, let's celebrate.' Dr Pandey bent down and began hunting behind the beakers for the 'milk'.

'No, no, not now,' Manoj cried. He wanted to digest the news properly first. 'We'll celebrate tonight. I know a great new place, good home-brewed liquour, one hundred percent safe and great fat women, just as you like them.'

More bells rang out, temple bells this time. Someone was getting married. And Manoj, still caught in his happy haze, thought to himself, this is the happiest day of my life. He looked up at the darkening sky and it felt limitless. This is the beginning, he thought, the gateway to the future has opened.

Suddenly the deputy commissioner burst out, 'You know how many temples there are in Khandwa? Three hundred. Yes, three hundred temples, I had them counted.'

Manoj gasped. 'That many? I could never have imagined that there'd be so many in such. . .' he stopped abruptly, suddenly becoming aware that he'd been about to make a major blunder.

But he hadn't been quick enough. 'In such a small town,' the deputy commissioner completed Manoj's sentence smoothly. 'There are lots of things you cannot even imagine that take place in a small town.'

'Of course sir,' Manoj agreed. 'Like what?'

'Many things,' the deputy commissioner said vaguely. 'You know why there are so many temples, Mr Professor? Because people in towns need their religion more than people in villages. And you know why that is?' The deputy commissioner had a way of turning everything he said into a question or an answer. 'Because they have been squashed in the city, reduced to a fraction of their original size. So they need to go to temples to feel that God still sees them. Bigger the city, bigger the number of temples, you understand.' He spat out a mouthful of paan and continued. 'So tell me, Mr Professor, how many temples in Jaipur?'

'I don't know sir,' Manoj replied. 'There must be many.'

There were more titters from the others.

'Many is not a number, Mishra,' the deputy commissioner said primly.

Numbers made Manoj think of the invitation again. How many miles to Denmark? he wondered. At least it wouldn't be difficult to find out how many temples they had there – did they have temples there? He laughed out loud, unable to stop himself. Who cared how many temples there were in Khandwa? It would still be a dump.

'What are you laughing at, young man?' the deputy commissioner snapped.

'Nothing, sir. I was just wondering if there were any temples in Denmark.'

'Denmark? Are you trying to insult me?' The deputy commissioner stopped short, and his followers fanned out around him, quivering with rage.

But Manoj just looked at the deputy commissioner. He'd said the name out loud. Now it felt real. 'Not at all sir,' Manoj replied calmly. 'I received an invitation today, from Denmark. That is why I have Denmark in my head, sir.'

The deputy commissioner's jaw dropped. 'You? What kind of an invitation?'

'It is an invitation to a conference, sir, on what I do, insemination.'

'Oh yes, insemination. Nice word. Tell me, are cows very different from women – I mean on the inside?'

Manoj stared at him, his mind going blank. 'I don't know what you mean, sir,' he said as humbly as he could.

'You know exactly what I mean, boy,' the deputy commissioner snapped, beginning to enjoy himself. 'You are a married man.' He looked around at the others. 'We all are. Are cows very different on the inside?'

Manoj gave an embarrassed laugh. 'But I wear gloves sir, I don't really touch.'

'You wear gloves?' The deputy commissioner turned to the others, delighted. 'Did you hear that? He wears gloves when he touches his wife. No wonder he can't have any children.' He turned back to a Manoj frozen with embarrassment and anger and said, 'You have to take off your gloves Mr Professor, or else you will know nothing either about cows or about women. Didn't your teachers tell you that?'

'No, sir,' Manoj said peaceably. Very soon it would be night and the deputy commissioner would return to his fat wife and his well-guarded, prison-like house on the edge of the town, open his bottle of whisky and sit in front of the television. And Manoj and Dr Pandey would go and celebrate. For the nights were when small towns like Khandwa came alive.

As if someone had taken a magic broom and swept them all away, gone were the ugly women with hungry-looking children clinging to their saris, gone was the dust, the beggars, the dogs with their weeping sores and tucked-away tails, and the bored predatory shopkeepers. Instead the streets filled with beautiful young men, warriors, adventurers and risk-takers. Faces changed too as the flickering light of gas lanterns and illegal fires burnished tired skin and hair, and made old, much-washed clothes look new again. Even the dogs looked different, healthier and more alert as they moved through the streets in lethal hunting packs, barking in unison, their tails held high, tongues hanging out, mouths curved in a jaunty sneer. The deputy commissioner was wrong, Manoj thought scornfully. Small towns didn't need temples, they had plenty of other entertainment.

'Eh Mr Professor, are you still with us?' The deputy commissioner's voice intruded upon his thoughts.

Before he could answer, an ingratiating voice cut in. 'I think he cannot hear sir, Denmark is very far away.'

A burst of laughter. But the deputy commissioner frowned. Unsanctioned laughter was tantamount to rebellion. They all fell silent. 'So it is serious then, this Denmark invitation?' he asked.

'Yes.'

'But why did they choose you, of all the people in India, for this?' the deputy commissioner asked.

Manoj didn't answer. Denmark had chosen him, not the deputy commissioner, and that, he knew, was what was irritating the other man. But unlike those far away beings who had chosen him, he could not afford to annoy the deputy commissioner, so he said, 'Frankly sir, I am not sure. I assume that the Institute gave them my name.'

'Why would they do that?' the deputy commissioner asked suspiciously. 'No one gives up free trips to Europe.'

Manoj shrugged. He'd wondered the same thing and the answer his heart had given him was one he couldn't share. *She* was calling him, *she* had found him at last, *she* had forgiven him. He wondered if Denmark was where she lived now.

'When will you go?'

'Uh?'

'Stop dreaming, Mishra. You will not get to Denmark by dreaming. When do you have to be there?' the deputy commissioner snapped.

'In March, sir.'

March. There came the silence of indrawn breath. The deputy commissioner was impressed.

'And how long will you be gone?'

'I don't know,' Manoj replied honestly.

'Aha. I knew it. Once you will go there you will never come back. You development types are all the same. You come talk "village village", but actually you are thinking, "videsh videsh"*, waiting for that call to conference.'

'Of course not sir,' Manoj hurriedly reassured him. 'I only meant that I haven't checked when I will have to return. And besides, once I am there, I would like to spend a few more days, travel a little.'

'Teach the women about Indian-semination, eh?' the commissioner added, poking him in the ribs.

There was a dutiful chorus of laughter from the others and then they all looked outwards, indecisive, waiting for the deputy commissioner to leave. Manoj could sense that they were bored of the subject. Denmark or Mumbai, it made little difference

---

* foreign country

to them. None of them would ever get further than Indore, the state capital. But the deputy commissioner was different. 'Very good, very good, Mishra,' he said, rubbing his hands together. 'I would not have thought it possible, but it seems that you fooled us all. Unknown to us all, you are turning out to be one of those young men who are putting India on the map like. . . like a computer software programmer. We are proud.' He nodded to himself. 'Yes, we are indeed proud of you, Mishra.' He began to walk to his car, whose red light was shining like an electric bindi. 'Come walk me to my car,' he invited, putting a chubby hand on Manoj's shoulder.

The others fell away, their faces disbelieving. Manoj felt as if he were walking on clouds as he walked the deputy commissioner to his car.

'Good night, sir. And thank you for being so kind,' Manoj said politely, stepping back.

'Good night? Nonsense. You are coming with me. We will talk properly over drinks. I want to know more about you Mishra, who knows – one day you may be famous.'

Manoj looked back at the cricket field to see if they were watching. No one had moved; they were all watching, their faces indistinct, a mass.

'Come along, what are you waiting for?' From inside the curtained darkness, the deputy commissioner called to him impatiently.

Many hours later, when Manoj got out of the deputy commissioner's bungalow, he was so drunk he could barely lift his feet. The scent of the night-blooming madhumalati assaulted him time and again, throwing him off balance each time, making the road swim and his stomach churn. He controlled himself by remembering what the deputy commissioner had said and what he'd replied in turn. But it was hard work and the conversation ran like the damaged print of an old Hindi film, in bits and pieces, the sequence somewhat garbled.

'So young Mishra,' Prakash Choudhury had said, very much the 'colonial collector sahib' with his plaid slippers and whisky in hand, 'if I were a betting man, I would never have bet that you would make a success of yourself. You don't look the type. But they say you make quite a tidy sum from your work. Is that true?'

'A comfortable living certainly. But I cannot afford a ticket to Denmark.'

Prakash Choudhury sat forward in his chair, the shiny material of his safari suit trousers straining at the crotch. 'What are you saying, Mishra? Just now you told me in front of everybody that you were going.'

'I didn't say I would go, I simply told you that I had an invitation, sir,' he'd replied cow-heartedly.

Prakash Choudhary sat back, digesting this. He took a large gulp of whisky, then said, 'But you must go. How else will Khandwa become famous?'

Manoj tried to look self-deprecating. 'I really would love to make Khandwa famous, and especially to make your work here famous. Everyone knows your contribution to this town is enormous. But I can't. Being illegal, is expensive, sir.'

'Legal-shlegal.' Prakash Choudhury waved his hand dismissively. 'Forget it yaar, you are one of us now. I will pay your ticket. Indian-semination will be supported by the Indian state.'

Manoj couldn't think of what to say. An image of a naked blonde goddess began to dance in his head.

'You will, sir?' he said stupidly.

'Of course. You know what else I will do for you, Mishra? I will organise an in-semination camp in Khandwa, for all the villages in the area. What do you say?'

'A camp, sir?'

'Yes indeed. I will tell the Block Development Officers to

call all those damned sarpanchs tomorrow itself and have them come here. Then I will explain that the camp is free and I will pay for your ticket to Denmark. Is that not a good idea? A developing sort of idea? Everyone happy, see? Sab khushi ke mare pagal ho jayenge.'

Manoj stood up. He felt the urge to sing the national anthem so he stood up and began to sing, only halfway through he switched to 'Sare Jahan se Accha Hindoostan Hamara', as he couldn't remember the end. But it didn't matter, because the deputy commissioner, even more drunk than he was, was impressed. 'Wah, wah!' he cried, 'you are a true nationalist.' Wiping his eyes with his coat sleeve, he took another fortifying gulp of whisky. 'You know Mishra, I was worried about you when you and your wife arrived in Khandwa,' he said suddenly. 'You remember when you came here for dinner that first time, right?'

'Of course sir, first and only time,' Manoj corrected, wondering if it was the English liquor that was making him so brave.

But Prakash Choudhury hadn't noticed. 'I thought you were a troublemaker then. But I see now that I was wrong. I apologise. Let's drink on it.'

Obediently Manoj drained his glass and the deputy commissioner told the butler to get them both a refill. 'In fact, I have to say that you and your wife have fitted in quite nicely,' he continued, his voice somewhat slurred. 'She is a good worker, my wife tells me, in the drought relief committee.'

'Thank you.' Manoj stared at the ceiling, not wanting to think of Pratima at all.

'Now that you are going to be world famous, you should be thinking about producing a child. A man is not a man until he has a son, I can tell you,' Prakash Choudhury advised. 'You had an arranged marriage, didn't you? I did too. Many young people don't these days, but I say it is still the best system. A marriage is a lottery either way.'

'I would really like to go to Denmark, sir,' Manoj said, thinking with a pang of his goddess.

'You would, would you?'

'Absholutely.'

'Then you must go.'

'I must go, sir.' Somehow even in his drunken state he managed never to forget the 'sir'.

'Yes, you must. I will help you. You will put the flag of Khandwa state in the heart of Denmark.'

'I will put the flag of Khandwa state into the cunt of Denmark,' Manoj repeated, laughing until he was breathless. He looked up at the sky. There was no moon, just a few stars twinkling palely. He began to wobble down the street.

As he turned into his road, a stray cow suddenly appeared, coming straight at him from out of the municipal garbage dump. He stared at it as it walked past, acknowledging it with a dip of his head. Another fragment of memory popped into his head, the missing piece in the jigsaw puzzle of the night.

'So you call yourself a modern man, am I right, Mishra?' Prakash Choudhury had asked.

Manoj had nodded his head uncertainly.

'And are you a moral man too?'

He nodded again.

'How can that be? How can you be moral and modern at the same time?'

'Because I want to make others happy,' Manoj had said simply.

'And you think that it is enough to choose to make others happy?'

'It is better than thinking of oneself, no?' Manoj had replied defensively.

'Good answer. You are a clever man, Mishra. Shall I tell you what I think? I think you are a liar. Being modern means choosing and choosing, as our good book the Gita will tell you, has consequences. Not always happy consequences either. Some people will win and be happy, others will lose and be sad. Which is why you are a liar, Mishra. You cannot make everyone happy.'

Manoj had said nothing, heat rising in his cheeks.

'So what made you decide to be a modern man? Do you know?'

Manoj stopped dead in the middle of the street. The cow was gone. There was no one there any more except himself. The giddy effect of the alcohol was almost completely gone and a dull ache had begun behind his eyes. Manoj frowned and rubbed them hard, trying to remember what he'd said. Giving up, he stumbled on home.

CHAPTER TWENTY-FIVE

THE SECRET LIFE

Gopal, Patel of Nandgaon, awoke as he usually did shortly before dawn. He stared up at the wooden-beamed ceiling and frowned. He was worried. The previous night Vilas Rao had come to them, his eyes uncharacteristically bright and a silly smile on his face. He had had a box of sweets in his hand. Opening the box with a flourish, he'd announced that his young wife, Mamtabai, was pregnant. Gopal and the others had been thunderstruck.

'And are you pleased?' Gopal had asked cautiously.

'Pleased?' Vilas Rao had answered. 'It is a miracle. The Devi has blessed us. Nandgaon is indeed lucky to have the Kamdhenu.'

Kamdhenu? The headman had exchanged worried glances with the others.

'What has that animal got to do with you?' Saraswati Rane had asked.

'Ah, that's a story,' he said, laughing merrily. 'That naughty wife of mine went to Ramu's Gaopuja without telling me and ate a piece of prasad that appeared miraculously in her plate. She swears that it is this which has made her pregnant, for she thought of me as she ate it. She's known for four weeks, she says, but was too scared to tell me. Luckily my mother noticed and told me. Silly woman, how could I be angry? Thanks to the Kamdhenu, I will be a father again.'

Gopal had been the first to break the cordon of silence.

'Congratulations my friend,' he said stiffly. 'It is not the Kamdhenu but you who are to be felicitated.'

Vilas Rao had beamed. 'The Devi blesses our village,' he said simply, 'because of our headman who is the incarnation of Lord Rama.'

Who could the father be? Gopal wondered. Probably that damn truck driver nephew of Mamtabai's who'd visited for a week and had ended up staying five months. He clicked his tongue in frustration. Ramu's Kamdhenu and her miracles were becoming a nuisance. Sunshine pouring through the high window above the door made him get up hurriedly. His brass *lota* waited on a low blue stool. As he let himself out of the back door he heard someone bathing in the kitchen and caught sight of his daughter-in-law Savitri. She is awake early today, he noted, somewhat surprised, as he headed into the fields. When he returned, his toothbrush and his clothes along with a fresh towel and soap had been placed beside the bath house. Before long he had washed his hands and face and brushed his teeth. Then, grabbing his stick, Gopal set off on his daily walk, crossing the sleepy village on silent feet, not turning around until he reached the bridge that led to the fields on the other side.

His father had been a walker too, walking religiously every morning. It was from him that Gopal had got the habit. When it was hot he left early, and when it was cold, as it was now, he waited until the sun came up. But he never missed a day. From the bridge he could see both villages – New Nandgaon, now in ruins, and Old, untidy but inhabited. How strange, he thought, looking at the remains of the village he'd built, that he would die in the house of his forefathers and not in the house he himself had built. When he got to the other side, he bent down and grabbed a fistful of rich black earth. At least the land could not be killed, or moved. Embarrassed by the sudden onrush of emotion, he opened his fingers and let the soil fall. After that he walked swiftly onwards, and soon had only maize and millet for company. Then his pace slowed and he turned his head slowly, drinking in the endless expanse of fields, some still a fresh young green, others already a bright ripe gold. Their military straightness was broken here and there by a fallen tree, the only reminder that the fields were new. A sudden gust of cool October wind made the maize chatter, pushing his thoughts to the future. The harvest was almost upon them and soon the unlucky year would finally be behind them.

The headman turned and headed into the forest. Soon he was enveloped in the silence of the trees. A leaf fell, making him smile. When he was a young man, trees had always made him think of women. Now they were just trees. But he loved them even more. 'If you listen carefully,' his grandfather used to tell him, 'you will be able to feel another world, the world the trees hold inside.'

'And what world is that, Grandfather?' the eight-year-old Gopal Mundkur had asked, wide-eyed.

'An unseen world,' his grandfather had answered seriously.

Then he had shown Gopal how to curl his fingers like a doctor's stethoscope and place them on a tree, his ear pressed to his hand. 'You know when a tree is ready to die, for the music inside grows slow, losing its rhythm,' his grandfather had told him. 'Only once you have listened to the music fade should you cut the tree.' The headman shivered now, remembering those words. Some day not so far in the future, the music inside him would fade too. That was probably why Vilas Rao had refused to question that little slut of a Mamtabai, for a child was the best protection against that fading music. Then, in one of those strange jumps the mind sometimes made, it occurred to Gopal that the trees were as much in danger from the Kamdhenu's miracles as he was. For where else would the fodder for those eating machines come from? Bicchoo had told him of how much the Kamdhenu consumed, and how Ramu used to pay for the fodder until the Kamdhenu's devotees grew to be so numerous that their offerings were enough. An image of a forest being cut down as a hundred Kamdhenu lookalikes stared hungrily danced behind his eyelids. His hands curled into fists and he swore to himself that he would never allow it. But the image didn't disappear. So he put his ear to a gnarled old banyan tree three feet in diameter and closed his eyes, hoping the song of the tree would banish it.

As the sounds of the forest retreated he heard the music, faint at first but getting clearer with each passing second, the low-pitched hum like an unending 'Aum' coming from the centre of the tree. 'Imagine the sound of the path cut by a river through a mountain. Listen to that sound. That is the sound of the living soul rushing through all matter. The sound of life. Soma,' his grandfather had instructed him. 'That is what you are hearing.' Gopal, his ear stuck to the old banyan tree, heard nothing at first, and nothing even though he waited for quite a while. Then, as his mind went quiet, faint, barely discernible, he made out the rhythmic vibration of the soma as it climbed from the earth into the leaves. The tree was old but not yet dead. Time was rhythm, he thought, shutting his eyes, and rhythm was life.

'Patelji, Ram, Ram.' His thoughts were rudely interrupted by a familiar voice. The headman stepped quickly away from the tree. 'What, Saraswati Rane, you are following me this early in the day? Has someone died? Or has your precious Ram murthi been stolen?'

'I've been searching for you,' Saraswati Rane replied, 'all over the fields.'

'Well you've found me now,' the headman replied. 'Even in the jungle, I see there is no escaping you.'

'Have you heard the latest?' Saraswati Rane asked, pretending he hadn't understood him. 'A single hair of the

Kamdhenu placed under the pillow can make a man rich.'

'What? Is that what you came all this way to tell me?' the headman asked sarcastically. 'Besides, if Ram Manohar needed something, why didn't he ask me? Am I not good enough?' 'Maybe he doesn't like to pay interest,' Saraswati Rane volunteered, looking satisfied. So the headman had heard that particular story.

'What? Does he think everyone should be as stupid as the government?' The headman banged his stick on the ground. 'No interest means nothing gained. How else do I ensure that they don't waste money on stupid things?'

The headman shook his head glumly, thinking of the waste, not just of money but of a man's hope. Saraswati Rane continued, 'It's sickening. You should see her, fat as two animals put together. She never goes out – except to be bathed in the angan. You should see how the people line up for that.'

'What? People go to see an animal being bathed?' he cried.

'Of course, and they collect the dirty water to take home with them. Some say it cures skin ailments, and coughs in young children.'

The headman groaned. 'Why don't they eat its gobar as well?'

'They collect that too. You know those two rascals, Shyam and Kehar, Bhimrao's sons?' Saraswati Rane paused for effect. 'Well, they clean the Kamdhenu's accommodation, and they made quite a profit selling her droppings until Laxmibai found out and put a stop to it.'

'And then she started selling it herself I'm sure,' the headman muttered bitterly.

'But you haven't heard the worst,' Saraswati Rane continued. 'They say that certain people have had their cows impregnated by that magic cow's son, Shambhu,' he said too casually, flicking an invisible insect off his dhoti while looking at the headman out of the corners of his eyes.

'What!' the headman banged his cane so hard on the ground that it flew out of his hands. 'Who has done this? Which traitor dared to do so? Tell me his name and I will have his house burnt,' he shouted.

'But you are the one who let Ramu keep the cow.'

'That was different. How could I have known? How could I have foreseen this?' Gopal groaned.

'Nandgaon is in terrible danger. And it is all the fault of that. . . that witch,' Saraswati Rane declared softly, a secret smile on his face he couldn't quite hide. But the headman was too upset to notice.

'Mamtabai is hardly a witch.'

'The other one,' Saraswati Rane replied.

'Which other one?' the headman asked, pretending not to understand. 'Have we got two witches in Nandgaon that I know nothing about?'

Saraswati Rane grunted. 'Don't try to ignore the problem before you, my friend. It has already become a mountain.'

'The world is a problem. What do you want me to do about it?' the headman snapped. 'Create a flood to wipe it away?'

'Don't laugh at the gods, Patelji, they may still be of help to you,' Saraswati Rane said sharply.

'The gods have never helped when a human has asked,' the headman shot back. 'Why should they help me now?'

'Gods' ways are difficult to understand, Patelji, that's why you need Brahmins to help you.'

'Really?' Gopal's eyebrows drew together in a straight line. 'And how will you do that?'

'People need distractions, my friend; just now all the distraction is being provided by Ramu and his animals. You have to take the lead again,' Saraswati Rane answered slowly.

'What do you mean? Should I be scared of Ramu's ugly animals? Do you know who you are talking to? I am the headman of Nandgaon, not some ignorant labourer.'

'In that case you have been headman for too long and have forgotten what it is to fear the unknown. . . like a poor labourer.'

'What should I be scared of? You think I can't control Ramu? The man is a simpleton.'

'But your simpleton managed to make a joke out of your puja,' the priest pointed out.

The headman could think of no reply to that so they just stared at each other stonily.

The priest was the first to look away. 'Perhaps you don't know all of it,' he said softly. 'I should have told you this before, but I felt too guilty. Now Vilas Rao's story has made me realise there is no time left.'

They fell into step on the path that meandered through the no-man's land between field and forest, the headman a half-pace ahead, lashing out at the undergrowth underfoot.

'Ramu's wife came to see me before Gaopuja,' the priest began. 'She invited me to come and do the naming puja. At first I said yes. Then she told me the date and I refused, pointing out that that was the day of our Gaopuja. And you know what she said?' He paused dramatically. 'She said that she didn't care. The Devi had come to her in a dream. To her?' he sneered. 'A woman who never has come to my temple?'

'But there are many who don't come to your temple. And she helps Jaiwant Rane with the little girls. So how can she be such an enemy of Nandgaon?' the headman asked.

'That,' Saraswati Rane spat, 'was pure arrogance, to show us she's better than us. Why should girls be educated when they will only become liars and troublemakers like her?'

'But girls grow into mothers. If they are educated, their sons will be better educated, don't you think?' the headman pointed out.

Saraswati Rane said nothing for a while, then he looked up

at the headman and said simply, 'I fear for the future. Bad things are about to come to Nandgaon. The way to evil is always opened by a woman. Remember how Kaikeyi got Rama Bhagwan disinherited?'

But try as he would, the headman couldn't picture Laxmi as Kaikeyi. Instead the one who came to mind was Draupadi. He thought of Draupadi wearing Laxmibai's face, glaring angrily at the Kauravas as they pulled her half naked, hair undressed, before a thousand male eyes. 'You should never have encouraged Ramu to marry her. Outside blood is bad blood,' the priest continued.

'I didn't,' the headman responded. 'I only said that to protect poor Ramu from the village's anger. The truth is I felt responsible. The day the matchmaker came to see me, Ramu was giving me a massage. I must have forgotten he was there. But he was and he'd listened to everything that sugar-tongued matchmaker said. I think he must have fallen in love then.' He laughed a deep belly laugh at the thought then shook his head. 'The world is maya, and that maya is made up of words.'

In spite of himself, the priest laughed too. 'How true, Patelji, you have lost none of your wit with age.' He paused, then added slyly, 'Nor your love of a pretty woman.'

'And you have not lost your powers of persuasion, Saraswati Rane. All right, whether or not Nandgaon needs it, I will make your temple to Rama – for that is what you are really here about.'

'You need it, Gopalbhai, you need it,' Saraswati Rane said fervently, his face breaking into a big smile, 'for Rama is your god, you are his spitting image.'

'Now you flatter too much, Saraswati Rane,' the headman said, shaking his head, but smiling all the same. 'Go start the work, before I change my mind.'

Saraswati Rane looked worried for a second, then laughed. 'All right, all right Gopalbhai. I will go now and you will see, in a week they will all have forgotten about the Kamdhenu and will be singing the praises of Rama, and of you.'

After Saraswati Rane left, the headman remained lost in thought. That people wanted to mate their animals with Ramu's upstart bull worried him more than he dared admit. For one could replace a Kamdhenu with a Rama, but how could one fight greed? Greed was a god that had no face and once it arrived, all other gods died. He said a silent prayer to Lord Rama, hoping he was strong enough to defeat the Faceless One.

As Gopal entered the village later that morning, Bicchoo came up to him in great excitement. 'Patelji, Patelji, guess who have come?'

'The deputy commissioner sahib?' Gopal answered drily, knowing full well it wasn't true. No high-ranking government official had come to Nandgaon since the road had moved elsewhere.

Bichoo shook his head, his eyes widening at the very mention of such a godlike person. 'Are, Patelji, you are making a fool of your poor Bicchoo again. It is the walking people with their goats who have come. Ramu saw them camping in the forest.'

The headman frowned. 'So soon? How is it possible?' Nandgaon was familiar with the tribes that came from the west with their goats and skirt-clad, silver-bedecked women. Various bands regularly came through Nandgaon, once on their way east to the cattle fairs of Benares, Allahabad and Patna, and then on the way back. But it was only January, too early for them to be heading home. And too late for any group to be going to the fairs. Something must have happened. Nevertheless Gopal was pleased. The tribes kept to themselves, rarely venturing out of their camp. And they were excellent workers and great musicians. The headman looked forward to hearing new songs.

That evening, their leader, a tall thin man wearing the high tight dhoti of the Rabari tribe, turban, earrings and a short white kurta tied across the chest, came to see the headman. Night had fallen when he arrived. The courtyard was unusually full, for word of the Rabaris' arrival had spread through the entire village. Saraswati Rane and the others were all there. But when the Rabari leader was led into the firelight, the sight of his face gave all of them a shock.

Gopal was the first to recover. 'My friend,' he said rising to embrace the man, 'welcome to Nandgaon. Whatever troubles you may have had are at an end. You are among friends now.'

The tribesman's drawn, painfully thin face broke into a smile. 'Maharaj, may you live a hundred years. I and my tribe are grateful to you.'

'Have something to eat and to drink,' the headman urged him beckoning to a passing servant, 'then come and tell us how the world is going.'

No one said anything until he left. 'I wonder what could have happened to him,' Vilas Rao muttered. None of the others ventured a guess. The look on the man's face had chilled them to the bone.

'Maharaj,' the leader of the Rabari said when he returned, 'we come with five hundred head of cattle and goats. Our women and animals are tired and in need of food and rest. We beg your highness to give us a little grazing space for a few days where we may rest and regain our energy. And if there is work to be done we will gladly do it in exchange.'

The headman didn't reply immediately; his eyes were on the terrible condition of the clothes the man was wearing. Then he said, 'Weren't you the one who gave me some goats five years ago?'

The tall Rabari frowned, trying to remember. Then his face cleared. 'Indeed Maharaj,' he replied nodding eagerly. 'But it was my father, not I, who gave you those goats,' he said.

'You are right,' the headman nodded, satisfied. The man had passed the test.

'Five hundred cattle, did you say? Just five hundred?' In all his years he'd never heard of such a thing. The tribesmen were rich, they only travelled with thousands of animals.

The man stopped abruptly and his shoulders slumped, his pride slipping away. 'You are right Maharaj. We had many more,' he said, turning around slowly. 'We started with five thousand, Maharaj, but the world is a cruel place.' And then he broke down, blubbering like a child, trying to cover his face with hands that were too thin to hide behind.

For a few minutes the entire courtyard was silent, frozen by the sight of the proud Rabari in tears. Then the headman took charge. 'Send the others away,' he whispered to Mahendra who was sitting behind him. 'I want to talk to our guest.' The headman rose and led the Rabari leader away to another part of the verandah. There he made the tribesman sit down again and talked to him casually of his father. He passed the tribesman his own hookah and when, after taking a long drag, a tiny light returned to the latter's eyes, the headman invited him to tell his story.

'We are a walking people, Maharaj,' the Rabari began slowly, 'yug yug se hum chaletay aye hain. We have never depended on anyone for anything, except our animals. Last April when the grazing in our part of Gujarat was exhausted we set out as usual. We had five thousand head of the finest cattle that we'd ever managed to raise and we looked forward to selling them off at the fair in Benares.

'Our animals were fit and we reached Benares well in time. The fair had not begun but there were lots of buyers there already. With a light heart I paid the fees for one of the best spots at the fair and we set up the enclosures for the animals. A day passed, two days, then a week. No one came to buy. Of course, many people came to see. Our animals were wonderful creatures, their horns larger than any of the others in the market, their skins tight and shining, their eyes clear and fierce. But no one bought.

'We didn't care. The price we asked was high, but our animals were good. We spent our money day after day on food and on fodder, confident that soon our pockets would be full of gold.'

The tribesman gave a bitter laugh. 'But as a man gets poorer his hope grows stronger. Behind every bullock cart, money seemed to be hiding. And as the hunger settles in your belly, your head grows light and you believe that what you are doing is fasting, purifying yourself as you wait for the money to arrive. But what is actually happening, what *was* actually happening, was that we were getting poorer and poorer. Fights broke out amongst us; my people began to steal from one another. A man was killed and I could not stop it.' He stopped, gulped, and the tears began to flow once more. He wiped them away with a practised gesture, as if he'd become used to crying. Then he continued. 'But that was only the beginning. Even while we starved we still bought fodder for the animals. Our women, the holders of our wealth, sold their jewellery for the people they still came to see our animals. Then the fodder became more expensive and our cattle began to lose their flesh. We knew we could not wait any more.

'Maharaj,' he said thickly, 'I would have accepted any price then. But there were no buyers.'

'No buyers?' Gopal repeated, bemused.

The man gave a cry and buried his face in his hands once more. 'I have so much blood on my hands, so much blood, my animals, my beautiful animals. I was wrong, I was too greedy, too arrogant. Oh God,' he mumbled thickly through his fingers, 'forgive me, forgive me, God, let me die too.'

In the courtyard people shuffled uneasily, feeling the invisible hand of tragedy settle upon them.

The headman waited patiently for the man to continue.

At last the man looked up and the headman got another shock, for the man's eyes had become like stones. 'I sold them to the butchers,' he said coldly, 'all except a thousand, the pride of my stock. I sold them for nothing. I sold them for the price of the flesh they carried on their bones. And you know what they said to me, those butchers? They said that they would pay me to carry away the horns and throw them in the garbage. And because our children had no milk, we did it. With these hands I have buried the heads of four thousand cattle. Since then, we have been walking,' he finished expressionlessly.

In the courtyard one could have heard a pin drop. The headman looked up and was surprised to see his friends Saraswati Rane, Govind Rao and Jaiwant Rane standing motionless at the edge of the circle of faces. Many unconsciously wiped at tears with the backs of their hands.

'Why was no one buying your cattle?' The headman asked the question that trembled on many lips.

'Because they all wanted a new kind of cow,' the Rabari leader replied, 'an ugly dwarflike creature with no horns but which produces almost twenty litres of milk a day.'

Unfortunately for the headman, horror and pity at the plight of the tribesmen's cattle so overwhelmed him that he never spared a thought for the new kind of cow in the story.

'Of course you can stay,' the headman said thickly, 'and I have lots of work for you.'

Five months later, the headman was forced to admit that Saraswati Rane had been right. The entire village had cheered up when the work started on the temple. To their simple way of thinking, the fact that the headman had decided to back Saraswati Rane's temple project meant that he had forgiven them. But they didn't forget Ramu. For at last they were able to look each other in the eye and talk about the evening of

Gaopuja. They began by asking each other, 'Where were you on the night of Gaopuja?' And the answer would come, 'I was where I should have been, at the headman's house.' But each one knew the other was lying. Then safe topics such as the beauty of the Gaopuja arrangements and the excellence of the kirthankaar's singing was discussed. Everyone agreed, perhaps a little too readily, that the puja that year had been magnificent, outshining the pujas of previous years; the kirtankaars had been exceptional, the food absolutely mouthwatering and the headman had never looked so well in his role as head of the puja.

Then came the question, 'And where were you for the prasaad?'

And in ninety per cent of the cases the other person's eyes slid away and he shook his head. And then the conversation grew vague and yet animated at the same time.

They talked of the night – of how beautiful it had been, how alive the village had seemed with the drums that had kept them all awake, and the ghungroos* of the dancers, and the song of the young boy with the bell-like voice. And then one of them said, 'And which was your favourite?' By 'which' he meant which dancer of course. And the other would reply, 'Chameli' or 'Noorjehan'. And then an argument would break out about the rival points of merit of the two dancers and others would join in and the conversation grew louder and noisier until at last the topic was exhausted and someone said, 'That Ramu is a good fellow.' For indeed if there was one thing that spread through the village like sugar in tea (as Bicchoo put it), it was the general feeling that Ramu was a decent sort, a man one could trust. For hadn't he spent all the money he'd made from the Kamdhenu on them? Then they discussed the Kamdhenu's latest miracle and all agreed that the animal had

* Chain of hundred bells tied around the dancers' ankles.

to be the Devi in disguise. Laxmi too came in for her share of praise, though less so, for she was still an outsider. And then the talk turned excitedly to the temple.

Dussehra came and instead of holding another big puja, the headman announced that the entire village would work on the temple instead. No one complained. Everyone knew that the making of a temple was expensive and this expense was being borne entirely by the headman. Ramu was forgotten and all anyone spoke about was the headman.

'We are indeed blessed,' Darbari Lal told his clients, 'to have such a wise and generous Patel. Not only did he rescue us from the flood but now he finances Saraswati Rane's temple.'

'They say the temple will be covered in gold. Is it really going to be so?' Prabhu, third in line, asked.

'Gold? Who makes a temple in gold?' Darbari Lal scoffed. 'It will be made of marble tiles, so that it will last a thousand years and never get dirty. And Giridhari is to carve the gate. It is the murthi that will be covered in gold.'

An awed silence followed the announcement.

Then someone asked, 'But where does the headman get so much money?'

'From us,' Prabhu said sourly, 'who else? Why do you think he spends it so freely?'

'For shame, Prabhu! Watch that mouth of yours or the next time you come to me I will cut your tongue out,' Darbari Lal said furiously.

'I was only repeating what I have heard,' Prabhu, the youngest son of Chhannu Mahadev, answered sulkily, looking at the ground.

'Well, you are listening to thieves. For only a thief accuses an innocent man of theft,' Darbari Lal thundered. 'Our headman is a great man, he is like a father to us. Does a child accuse a father of stealing from it?'

'Then why does he keep us cut off from the rest of the

country?' Prabhu asked stubbornly. 'Why can my brother not return to Nandgaon?'

'Because he chose to leave us,' Darbari Lal replied. 'No one is forced out of Nandgaon, but once they leave, they cannot come back.'

'But why?' Prabhu cried. 'Who says so?'

'The Patel,' Darbari Lal replied firmly, 'and if you don't want to join your brother on the outside, you watch your mouth.'

'When will the temple be ready?' Ram Manohar Athare asked, changing the subject quickly. 'Will the headman have a feast to celebrate the installing of the murthi?'

'Of course he will,' Darbari Lal answered, 'and it will be a big one. Our Patel does not do things by halves.'

And so, even after Dussehra, people continued to go to the site and ask to help, and the temple grew so fast that to the crowd that gathered each evening to examine the progress, it was as if God himself was lending a hand in its making. All through winter the temple was all anyone talked about and so involved were the people of Nandgaon in its construction that the Kamdhenu's visitors dwindled to only a handful of the faithful.

But the Kamdhenu wasn't entirely forgotten.

As work on the temple came to an end, one evening a delegation of landless labourers, all devout followers of the Kamdhenu, went to see the headman. The delegation was headed by Keshu Ram, whose child had been cured of the rashes by the Kamdhenu.

'May you live a hundred years, Patelji,' they greeted the headman, one by one touching his feet.

The headman blessed them all, greeting each one by name to which each man bowed his head gratefully. 'To what honour do I owe this visit?' he asked.

'Patelji,' Keshu Ram spoke up at last, keeping his eyes on

the ground. 'Patelji, we have come to ask you to grant us a favour. You are like a father to us; you gave us land to build our houses, fields where our women could go without losing their modesty, and a washing ghat. We, in turn, have tried to be like loyal sons. No work of yours have we left undone. Under our care, your fields have flourished, your animals have multiplied. And we have served your children and their families as well with the same devotion and will continue to do so.'

'A favour? What kind of favour?' The headman sat up. These were not the kinds of men to get into debt or to ask for favours.

'Do you remember after the flood when we moved to this place, how we found a murthi of the Kamdhenu in the field?' Keshu began eagerly.

The headman frowned, then nodded.

'It was in one of your fields, Patelji, the one that gave the record crop this year,' Keshav added.

'Ah yes,' the headman nodded, remembering, 'and I said you could keep it, didn't I?'

'Yes Patelji, you did,' Keshav said, and several voices murmured their approval.

'Then what is the problem? Have you lost it?'

'No Patelji, we have it right here,' and the group parted to reveal a small bundle tied up in a few clean gamchas. 'We want you to allow us to give it to you, Patelji,' they said in a chorus.

'To me?' The headman tried to act surprised, though he knew what was coming.

'For the temple,' they said in unison.

'It will bring the village luck,' Keshu added humbly.

The headman was silent for a long time, studying his feet. The delegation of the Kamdhenu's faithful waited patiently, as was their habit. At last the headman looked up. 'I can't,' he said baldly, 'I cannot do as you ask.'

A ripple went through the bodies of those in front of him, a sigh of disappointment. Then no one moved. Some looked bewildered, a few angry. But no one said a word. Their heads turned as one in the direction of their leader.

The headman looked from one face to the other, begging them silently to understand. At last he looked into Keshu's lined face.

'Patelji,' Keshu said at last. 'Until now we never needed a god; you were ours. Today I see a man, not a god. Come,' he said, turning to the others. 'We must go.'

The headman said nothing as one by one they touched his feet and left. That damned Kamdhenu, he thought savagely. Why didn't someone just get rid of it for him?

CHAPTER TWENTY-SIX

THE TEMPLE TO RAMA

'Gopal Mundkur,' Saraswati Rane announced, turning to headman standing beside him, 'this temple is your temple. Every stone you see here is yours. And though the temple is big and dominates the village and all the surrounding countryside from here until Khandwa, this giant construction is only a shadow of your own greatness.'

'Nice words, Saraswati Rane. But I will only believe you when I see the results,' the headman replied, eyeing the giant structure towering over Saraswati Rane's house with doubt. 'Meanwhile, every day that damned bull sires a new child.'

Saraswati Rane smiled. 'Don't worry, Patelji,' he promised, 'very soon it will be as if she had never existed. When shall we do the murthi sthapna?*'

When the headman announced the date of the murthi sthapna the villagers cheered the headman and Rama Bhagwan in the same breath. 'Jai Shri Rama, jai Patelji,' they shouted so that the name of the headman of Nandgaon would be forever joined with that of Shri Rama, the god king, incarnation of dharma and of good governance. Their cries ringing in his ears, the headman began at last to believe that Saraswati Rane was right.

The announcement threw the village into a frenzy of preparation. Women spring-cleaned their homes, and after they fin-

* Establishment of the statue in the temple.

ished they gathered under the direction of the headman's daughters-in-law to sing and prepare the food for the feast. The men worked on the village. They repaved the main street and tidied the drains. Not a single door or window was left unrepaired. Fresh glass was put in windows and paint on walls. Holes were dug on either side of the two main streets where the procession would pass and fifteen-foot bamboo poles were stuck into them. From these poles silver and gold tinsel streamers were hanging, specially ordered by the headman so that the village looked like a true 'Rama Rajya' – clean, wealthy and happy.

The establishment of God's image in a new temple is the second most difficult thing in the making of a temple. The most difficult is the trapping of the living spark within the breast of a brand new deity. For a god that had no home was considered to be like Rudra-Shiva, a wanderer, one who had turned his back on the world and was as much at home amongst the dead in the burning ghats and cemeteries as he was upon the highest mountain top where the air was so thin it hurt to breathe. To bring such a one back into a world limited by four walls required extremely strong prayers and there was only one god that could give the Brahmins the strength to bring the wandering heart of Rama back, and that was Rudra-Shiva himself. And so, the pundits had declared that before the murthi sthapna, they would do a Soma Yagna* necessary to find the statue's wandering soul and transfer it into the cold unmoving stone. Then, and only then, could the statue be installed in its new home. Trembling, Saraswati Rane went and informed the headman of their decision. But to the priest's surprise the

---

* One of the oldest and most complicated of Vedic rituals dedicated to Rudra-Shiva, the Soma Yagna was believed in its original version to take a thousand and one priests a thousand and one days to complete.

headman only sighed and went inside his room. He returned shortly thereafter, a cloth-wrapped bundle in his hands. 'Here, take my wife's jewellery, and sell it. It is all that I have left,' he said, thrusting the bundle into Saraswati Rane's hands. The priest didn't wait, almost running out of the gate for fear of the headman changing his mind.

When the long-awaited day finally arrived, Saraswati Rane awoke from an uneasy dream-filled sleep to the sound of water splashing somewhere deep inside the house. He listened to the unfamiliar sound and frowned. Why was there no sound of banging and hammering, no patter of feet over his head? he wondered. Then he remembered what day it was and smiled. He wondered if he should offer his assistance to the Brahmins in the hall downstairs. Not yet, he decided. First he would go and see his beloved. The statue of Rama was lying on the bed in solitary splendour in his old bedroom. 'This is the last time you will be a guest in my house, Ramaji,' he whispered, caressing the statue's stone hand. 'I just want you to know how honoured I feel to have had you here.' He wiped a tear from his cheek. 'Even when they move you into your new home I won't be far. In fact, I'll be just beneath you. You have only to call me, Ramaji Bhagwan, and I will come to serve you.' In the darkness a few more tears fell on the cold stone statue and then he got up and went to the river to bathe.

By the time Saraswati Rane had bathed, though it was still dark, all the Brahmins had come to the river's edge too. When dawn arrived, silvery grey and shy, the pundits were all ready, sacred threads and tikkas in place. As the sky lightened they began the all powerful gayatri mantra, the most sacred of all mantras. 'Om bhurbhuvasva, tat savithur varenyam. . .' they chanted sonorously, calling to the sun's rays to answer them. Then, as the sky blushed in response, they started the recitation of the thousand names of the sun, the vishnusahasranamam.

By the time the sun had peeped over the horizon, no one in the entire village remained in ignorance of the tremendous importance of the day, for the voices of the chanting pundits, magnified a hundredfold by the loudspeakers Saraswati Rane had secretly hired, reverberated in every house and every street of the village.

The chanting of the Brahmins continued without pause through breakfast, making children so excited that they barely allowed their poor mothers to wash and comb their hair and dress them in their festival finery. By ten o'clock in the morning a crowd had gathered in front of the temple, chattering excitedly as they waited for the prayers to end.

But the prayers continued through the morning and at last when the palanquin bearers arrived and the statue of Rama was taken first to the headman's where it was ceremonially welcomed to the village and then paraded through the streets beneath showers of rice, flowers and cries of 'Jai Shri Rama', everyone was relieved and ready to go home for a good lunch and an afternoon's sleep. The statue was then taken into the temple, introduced to its new home, bathed, fed and put to bed.

By five o'clock, everyone was thoroughly bored and impatient for the festivities to begin. They gathered at the tea shop across from the temple, pointedly ignoring the temple entrance which was all muffled up in haldi-coloured* cloth.

'I'm tired of waiting all day, I wish they would hurry,' Sushilabai complained.

'Can't understand what they've got left to do, they've been praying since dawn,' Govind Rao added sourly.

'Hardly matters what those Brahmins do, as long as they make people wait. It makes them more expensive,' Darbari Lal explained slyly, making those around him burst into laughter.

---

* Deep ochre, colour made from turmeric/haldi.

'I'm glad I am not paying for the puja,' Govind Rao said. 'It must cost a fortune.'

'You never pay for anything anyway,' Darbari Lal shot back instantly, 'which is why you will never be headman.'

Govind Rao glowered at him, his hands curling into fists.

'Poor Patelji, the pundits have been here for a week, all fifty of them,' Sushilabai said quickly. 'Just in food alone he must have spent the equivalent of two prime bulls. And then there is the question of their fees, not to mention the gifts he's going to have to give them afterwards.'

Everyone's eyes grew round as they contemplated the enormity of the expense the headman had incurred.

'At least two lakhs this will cost him,' Bicchoo said importantly. 'Those Brahmins are expensive.'

Everyone turned to look at Jaiwant Rane, the only Brahmin in the shop. 'Expensive? Your child has been studying for free from me for years,' Jaiwant Rane countered. 'Besides, that's what Brahmins are for – to receive gifts. Yet no one gives me any.'

'We give you our children masterji, and you make them work hard for you,' Darbari Lal responded amidst more laughter.

'What do you think Giridhari has painted on the entrance?' Darbari Lal asked seriously, once everyone had stopped laughing.

'Village scenes – like he usually does,' someone suggested.

'Pujas.'

'The making of the temple.'

Darbari shook his head. 'Not at all, he has made gods and goddesses of such beauty that if you look at them before the murthi sthapna has been completed, you will go blind.'

'Impossible. How do you know this?' Prabhu, the angry young man of the village, challenged.

'I know it because I am triple your age you idiot, and I have seen it happen with my own eyes,' Darbari Lal answered. 'Our

Giridhari is no ordinary painter, he is a magician. But you, Prabhu, are too young and foolish to know of it.'

Sensing a story in the making, those in the vicinity crowded around Darbari eagerly. 'Tell us, tell us,' they cried. Darbari was Nandgaon's best storyteller.

'Oh it is too old and too long a story to be of interest,' Darbari answered airily, still glaring at Prabhu.

'No, no, no. Please tell us,' the others begged, those on the edges crowding in, adding their voices to the chorus of entreaty.

'Come on, Darbari Lalji, one little story to put us all in the mood. You know your stories come straight out of heaven,' Govind Rao said flatteringly.

'Yes, do tell it again,' Jaiwant Rane laughed.

'Even Tulsidas didn't tell stories like you do,' Bicchoo added, wanting as usual to have the last word.

'Oh well, if you all insist,' Darbari Lal said at last, looking around in a satisfied way.

Everyone clapped again and Darbari Lal, pleased, puffed up his chest and waited for silence.

'This is something that happened a long time ago,' he began, 'when I was just a young man.'

'When were you a young man, Darbari Lal? You are too wise to have ever been young, and too rich,' Bicchoo called from the back of the crowd.

'Shut up Bicchoo,' Jaiwant Rane muttered roughly, 'you go too far always. Let us hear the story.'

Pleased, Darbari Lal continued. 'Giridhari was only slightly older than me, a wild youth if ever there was one. I was no less wild but I lacked his courage. We used to tease the girls together. No one was safe when Giridhari had a sling in his hands.

'Eventually the entire village got fed up and went to the Patel – not this one but his father – and complained.

'The Patel, our Patelji's father, who was also tired of Giridhari's pranks, summoned Bechain Kashle, Giridhari's father, and told him to occupy his son. Incensed at having been publicly shamed, Giridhari's father sent Giridhari to work in the Patel's fields. Giridhari worked hard but he was very unhappy and shortly thereafter fell sick. At first Bechain thought it was one of Giridhari's childish pranks, gave him a sound beating and sent him off to the headman's fields. For a few days everything was all right, but then one day Giridhari fainted in the middle of a field, just like that – he crumpled up like a scarecrow without a stick. Giridhari was brought home on a stretcher and his mother wailed and tore her hair. But Giridhari's father was not convinced. He thought it was another one of Giridhari's pranks. So he dragged his only son to Tiger Baba and vowed in front of Mata Kali's murthi that he would keep beating his son until sense entered him.

'And so he began. Giridhari screamed and screamed and begged his father to stop. Giridhari's poor mother, hearing what had happened, rushed up the hill and she too begged her husband to stop. But Giridhari's father pushed her away and continued to beat his son. At last the screams of Giridhari and his mother brought Tiger Baba out of his meditation and he came to see who had dared to disturb him so rudely.

'When he saw what was happening he opened his left hand and said a mantra and Giridhari's father was frozen, his hand drawn back to hit his son. Then Tiger Baba put a paintbrush in Giridhari's hand and asked him to paint what he saw before him. For with his third eye Tiger Baba had seen the magic in Giridhari's finger tips. Giridhari stayed with Tiger Baba for five years and when he was ready to return Tiger Baba blessed him and gave him some advice. He told Giridhari to paint but never to look at what he'd made.

'And that's what Giridhari did, faithfully following his guru's advice, and becoming famous throughout Nimar. Then one day the inevitable happened.' Darbari Lal stopped and looked at the faces around him.

'What happened?' several voices prompted impatiently.

'Giridhari fell in love. But the girl he loved was the daughter of a rich high-caste farmer and he was painting her portrait. Knowing his love was hopeless, when he'd finished the portrait, impatient to see if the likeness was correct, he forgot his guru's words, and turned and looked at what he'd made.' He paused dramatically. 'And what do you think happened?'

No one replied.

'Giridhari went blind in one eye. For as his other eye was about to fall upon the work he remembered his guru's words and covered it with his hand. That is why we call him one-eyed Giridhari today.'

There was silence when he finished, the respectful silence that followed all tales of magic.

Then Prabhu said mockingly, 'Wah, wah. A good story, Darbari chacha. But it is just a story. A painting cannot make a man go blind.'

The barber turned in Prabhu's direction and scowled. 'A story? What I just told you is the truth. If you don't b –' The rest of his words were drowned in an ear-shattering battery of drums and trumpets. Everyone in the tea shop left their drinks and rushed into the street.

On the terrace of the temple the pundits who had actually been conducting the puja, were standing in a single line, identical in their haldi coloured dhotis. Some were playing the instruments the villagers had heard in the chai shop, others were chanting the last few prayers, and still others were busy preparing the huge seventeen-branched lamps that were to be lit later for the aarti*. The crowd around the temple thickened

* Evening lamp/lighting ritual.

as from the lanes on all four sides more people arrived.

When at last the entire village had gathered before the temple, the Brahmin musicians suddenly went silent. The village stared at them expectantly, wondering what would come next. Then someone at the back of the crowd shouted, 'Look, look, the gate!' and all eyes went to Giridhari's gate.

'*Hai Bhagwan*, I don't know how they can stand being so far away from the ground,' Govind Rao said loudly, putting words to the fear in everyone's hearts as Giridhari's two assistants, Madho and Hari, untied the rolls of cloth at the top of the gate.

'Amazing how those monkeys never fell off all these months,' Vilas Rao muttered into his moustache. 'They must have been under the protection of Rama Bhagwan.' Those near him nodded in agreement and whispered 'Ram, Ram' softly. The rest of the village just watched silently as the two boys, their legs wrapped around the fragile bamboo sticks, slowly unwound the cloth. Suddenly a sweet lisping voice piped up, 'Maa, Maa, don't look, don't look, or you will go blind,' making all those who'd been present in the tea shop while Darbari told his story laugh. Even before the crowd's laughter had fully died the gateway stood revealed in all its glory. At first no one spoke. Then an awed murmur began.

'It is the best thing he has ever done,' Jaiwant Rane whispered to Vilas Rao beside him. 'To this work he has given his soul.'

And indeed that is why the crowd had sighed all together. For as they had looked upon the gate, they'd forgotten it was a gate and had found themselves transported to their old village again. For only Giridhari with his artist's eye was capable of capturing that lost world, the Nandgaon that for so long had been the source of their pride and which had been eaten up by the river. At the foot of the gate was the river which wound around the foot of the temple in the form of Saraswati Rao's famous ear-shaped stairs. The two pillars upon which the gate stood were the cliffs that rose from the river up to the village. From the base, round and round the pillar in a thin line there mounted the village herd, so lifelike that you could actually distinguish each animal by its idiosyncrasies. Leading them, right in the front, towards the top of the left pillar was the headman's Nandini, the leader of the herd, and beside her was Mahesh, the headman's first bull, his hump huge and horns menacing. The rest of Nandgaon stretched over the arch of the gate, with the main street running through the bottom centre.

'Look, there's the headman's old house – see the gate with the eyes,' Sushilabai whispered to Kuntabai who was standing beside her, 'and see, that must be your house with the flour mill next to it.'

'And there's your shop,' Kuntabai replied, smiling delight-edly, 'and look there you are serving a customer, and little Sushil is reading a book sitting on the floor beside Govindbhai.'

'And look, there's Bichoo playing cards,' Parvatibai exclaimed, laughing.

'And Darbari Lal, with his customers in a circle behind him – see, his mouth is open, he's talking. And those listening are openmouthed too,' Prabhu added naughtily.

'Are, there's my tractor, and me in it!' Vilas Rao exclaimed.

'And there's Mahendra,' Bicchoo cried, 'with his red book.'

And indeed, Giridhari hadn't forgotten a soul. Not even the peepul tree that had fallen down just before the flood, struck by lightning. But just as marvellous as the people was the forest behind the village. Giridhari had turned the forest into a magic one, painting each and every flowering tree irrespective of the season, the ashok and the mahua, the mango tree – its flowers like Kama Deva's arrows – the dhak – looking like Shiva's sacred flames – and the tall ghostly goolar.

The crowd broke into excited chatter as they spotted much-loved corners of the old village. Many had tears in their eyes. For not only had the river taken away the village, it had also forged an entirely new landscape, so that if it hadn't been for Giridhari's work, it would have been as if the village had never existed.

'Look, there's Ramu's hut. He hasn't forgotten even that,' Kuntabai cried. And sure enough, nestling between village and forest was the headman's sugar cane field and the tiny tubewell hut in which Ramu had stayed all his adult life.

'With Ramu coming down the path between the sugar cane. And there on the other side of their wall is Laxmi with the Kamdhenu,' Sushilabai added, clapping her hands in delight. She and Govind Rao had been one of the first to have their animals impregnated by Shambhu and they now went around boasting about it.

Savitribai, the headman's daughter-in-law, standing silently on the other side, followed Sushilabai's pointing finger and felt a surge of anger. How had Giridhari dared to put them in the painting when it was her father-in-law who had paid for the temple? 'That's the only bit of ugliness in an otherwise charming picture,' she said loudly, pointing to the image of the Kamdhenu and her mother. 'Of course, it's nothing compared to the pictures in my own dear father's house. Why, he had one made of me too that he sent around and so many offers came for me he didn't know what to do. . .' Her words tailed off as she realised no one was listening to her. Furious, she glared at the image of Laxmi with the Kamdhenu, noticing how cleverly Giridhari had highlighted Laxmi's beauty simply by placing her beside the ugly animal. 'I will put them in their place,' Savitri promised herself. 'I will not let that woman win.'

Then the crowd fell silent again, for bit by bit as their amazement had worn off they'd all come to see the huge hole in the centre of the work – the headman was missing. Giridhari, seeing the discomfort on their faces, turned to look and all of a sudden his face paled.

'Hai Rama,' he whispered to himself, 'what have I done?' He thought fast and turning to the others, 'I know what you are all thinking,' he announced loudly, 'but believe me, Giridhari never makes a mistake. Our Patelji is like Rama Bhagwan, and like the eyes on his gate, he is everywhere. My entire painting is but a portrait of our Patelji, for Nandgaon is nothing without him.' Raising his hand he shouted, 'Patelji zindabad!'

At first no one reacted and fear flashed across Giridhari's face. Then, from several different corners came the cry, 'Patelji zindabad, Giridharibhai zindabad.' Others took up the call and suddenly all eyes were on the headman standing amongst the priests under the gate. The crowd cheered madly again, clapping and stamping their feet. The headman stepped forward, raising his hand for silence. The crowd grew instantly quiet.

'Friends and relatives,' the headman called, 'I feel full of pride as I stand here. This temple is big, it is beautiful, a fitting home for Shri Ram Bhagwan and I am proud to welcome him to his new home. And yet, for me, this temple is not half as beautiful as what I see before me.' He paused and looked at each of the faces gazing up at him from the front of the crowd. 'For me, each of you is a temple. You have been created not just from the milk and the ghee of Nandgaon, but also from the love between man and man, and man and animal. Remember this when you look upon this temple. Every one of you is a temple and the soul of Nandgaon lies not in there,' and here he pointed to the temple behind him, 'but in your hearts.' At this the entire street erupted in applause so loud that the rest of the headman's words went unheard. So the headman just lifted his arms once more and blessed the upturned faces.

On the platform the pundits began to sing Tulsidas' Ramayana, starting from the very first verse which everyone knew by heart. The others fell silent, their eyes fixed hungrily upon the temple. Then as the evening star became visible, the temple doors were opened and the murthi was revealed bathed in the golden light of a thousand ghee-filled lamps. On the street a cry of such joy broke out that even the headman found himself smiling and cheering with the others.

No one had imagined the temple would look quite so grand. Because it was built on top of Saraswati Rane's house it towered over the rest of the village, visible from the furthest field. The shikhara* was painted a deep, sunset crimson and rose to the sky like a flame and on the top of the shikhara was fixed a bright golden trident and a saffron flag. In front of the shikhara, almost dwarfing it but not quite, was a large rose-coloured dome, the roof of an entirely separate mahamandapa with a brand new puja space. The dome of the mahamandapa was supported by eight pillars, their sides decorated with mirrors and interspersed with painted tiles of other temples. The rest of the courtyard too was paved in pink and white tiles which gleamed in the sunlight, brand new and unforgiving. Behind the mahamandapa the actual room where the idol was to be installed was quite small. But it looked big as it was also mirrored from floor to ceiling and in between, tiles of beautifully painted devatas and devis had been inserted to keep the main murthi company. In the end, the only dark thing was the statue itself, carved out of black Kalinga stone.

Afterwards everyone said that it had been the finest night Nandgaon had ever known, a night when every man and woman in the village felt their hearts fill with hope. And such

* High pointed roof; the head, or top of the temple.

was their joy that they had all talked, danced, eaten, laughed and hugged each other a thousand times, each time experiencing the sameness that united them. Involuntarily their eyes would go to the temple, dressed in its robe of golden light, and their eyes would brighten as they saw that essence that was common to them all reflected there. And then, feeling even happier than before, they went off in search of more food or music or other friends.

Towards the end of the night when the stars were at their brightest, just before the arrival of the dawn, the headman gave Mahendra the signal to set off the fireworks. The air rang with cries of 'mharo patelji ki jai ho' and everyone turned to look for their beloved Patel, calling out his name, unable to stop, telling the stars of their admiration, their love for their headman. And when the headman appeared at the top of the temple stairs, the crowd cheered madly once more, stamping their feet so hard that the ground shivered like the skin of a drum. When they finally grew silent again, the headman spoke some more. He talked of life and God and destiny; he talked of the future and what the future meant for a village such as Nandgaon. Then he informed them that they would no longer celebrate Gaopuja after Indrapuja as they had been doing, but instead the headman would have a brindavani puja every year on the third day after Divali. This, he said, would be the best way to celebrate their miraculous escape from the wrath of the river and to mark a new beginning for Nandgaon. Everyone cheered wildly again, welcoming the new, and happily relinquishing the past.

Only Laxmi, standing silently at the back of the crowd, understood what the headman had done: how with one stroke he had made irrelevant all that the Kamdhenu had achieved. No one would remember their Gaopuja. Soon no one would even remember the Kamdhenu. For how could a mere animal compete with a god? A cold wetness on her cheeks made her realise she was crying. The Patel had outsmarted her. Perhaps the village was right. She should have accepted how others saw her and not tried to make a place for herself that fitted with how she saw herself. She should have accepted the destiny the gods had made for her.

CHAPTER TWENTY-SEVEN
THE END OF GOOD LUCK

The cow awoke suddenly from a deep sleep. She looked around the barn, wondering what had woken her up, but saw nothing unusual. On her right Kamdhenu, her daughter, was eating her way contentedly through a giant heap of chopped hay and grain. On the other side Shambhu, Kamdhenu's son, was lying down, but with his back to them in order to assert his budding independence. He was so still it was obvious he was deeply asleep. Reassured, the cow put her head on her forehooves and tried to sleep. Perhaps it had been nothing more than a lizard falling off the wall or a stone dropped on the roof by a bird in flight. But sleep eluded her. The something that was stalking her felt close now. She shivered, wishing Ramu or Laxmi or any of the little two-hands who generally hung around the Kamdhenu would return. But instinct, the same instinct that had always told her exactly where each member of the herd was, told her that both Ramu and Laxmi were far, far away.

That morning they hadn't gone into the forest but for once she had been glad. The forest no longer felt safe to her. For several weeks now strange images had been coming into her head, causing her to jerk to attention, every nerve in her body alert. She would tremble violently, a feeling of nameless dread hitting her so strongly that she would suddenly stop eating and walk off in the direction of the village, propelled by a sense of urgency that was stronger than her, stronger than anything she'd known since she gave up 'going somewhere'. But before she'd gone more than two steps her beloved Ramu would catch up with her, place his hands on her shoulders, talk to her in his familiar voice, and the feeling of terrible danger would pass, leaving her nervous and confused.

The sound came again, a gentle scratching sound, louder this time. Her ears flicked forward and after a short pause the sound came once more, ending in a click. She turned her face towards the door and waited. After a bit, the door swung open, framing a star-studded night sky. Silhouetted against the sky was a two-legs. The cow grunted in relief. She was used to them constantly coming to see the Kamdhenu and knew they meant no harm. Beside her, Kamdhenu stirred, sensing the arrival of more food.

In the distance the sound of fireworks was heard and the two-legs stepped quickly inside the barn and shut the door. The smell of sweet laddoos filled the air and the cow's mouth watered. Now even Shambhu noticed and in his sleep he grunted and turned. The two-legs lit a match and held it up above her head. It looked at the cow and the stone feeling of dread that had been living inside the cow suddenly came alive. She flattened her ears pleadingly, hoping the two-legs would understand and leave. But the two-legs, though she did turn away from the cow, didn't leave. Instead she turned towards the Kamdhenu who was looking up interestedly, trying to see what food the two-legs held in her hands.

Unlike her mother, Kamdhenu was used to the two-legs bringing her food. She expected it. This two-legs was no different. It knelt before her and gently put the food down on the ground, considerately keeping at just the right distance. There came a disturbance from the stall next door where her mother was, but Kamdhenu thought it only natural. Obviously her mother wanted the food too. She hastily bent her head and swallowed and swallowed, not waiting to chew. The food disappeared into the giant digestive machine that was her stomach, and there it waited to be slowly chewed and disposed of, safe from the eyes and mouths of the other two. The Kamdhenu relaxed and lay down again. The laddoos had been very, very good and she'd eaten them all. Only then did the two-legs turn and go away.

The door clicked shut and they were on their own once more. But this time the cow did not lie down. She remained standing, watching the door anxiously. Until well into the night, long after the two-legs had left, the cow remained like that, her mouth dry, skin in a cold sweat. For, she realised, the thing that had been stalking her was none other than the place that cows went to alone. But it hadn't come for her, it had come for the one she held dearer than the herd, dearer than her own life – her strange, ugly child.

The next morning the headman awoke early. He had slept well, undisturbed by dreams, and he was in an excellent mood. He dressed quickly and let himself out of the house. The street was silent and only debris from the previous night's party tenanted the street. Later he would have to tell Mahendra to organise a cleaning party, he thought. Before the brand-new temple he said a little prayer. 'Let the future of Nandgaon be as bright as its past,' he begged the gods. 'Let the herd be restored and the harvests be generous and let there be no more miracles.' He nodded at the deity hidden behind wooden doors and continued on to the fields. Here, amidst the heavy heads of wheat, he thanked Lord Rama and Sitadevi again. In his ears echoed the cheers of the villagers still. Gaopuja, he thought, taking a deep breath of the sweet air, was at last behind him.

But when he returned from his morning walk, Mahendra met him with his usual look of disapproval. 'Didn't you sleep well?' the headman asked jovially. 'It's a beautiful day today.'

'Not so beautiful from my point of view,' Mahendra replied dourly, pointing at his account books. 'Will you stop this madness before you are utterly ruined?'

The headman stared at the red cloth-bound books sourly. 'You call it madness. I call it an investment. Go for a walk. The fields are looking beautiful today.'

'You spend your money so fast I don't have the time,' Mahendra muttered grumpily. 'Do you know how much you owe?'

'No, and I don't want to,' the headman snapped, frowning. 'Ramarajya has arrived in Nandgaon. This year's harvest will be even better than last year's.'

'And you will need twenty good harvests to pay all you owe,' Mahendra replied sourly. 'I have borrowed from every bank, every moneylender in the district.'

But the headman refused to be deflated. 'My dear Mahendra, there are some things you just won't find answers to in your books. Wait until the gifts start arriving and Saraswati Rane gives us his temple donations. Then the smile will return to your face.'

Mahendra grunted. 'We'll see,' he said, 'but in my experience, people have very bad memories when it comes to giving.'

The cow was the first to hear the sounds of discord coming from the Kamdhenu's stomach. It was pitch dark inside the barn. She looked over the partition at the immense form of her sleeping daughter and wondered what the sounds could mean. After a while, a watery grey light penetrated the barn. The cow waited for someone to arrive. Beside her, Kamdhenu suddenly turned over and moaned. The cow looked at her daughter and then at the door, straining to catch the sounds of her beloved two-legs waking. But the morning was unusually silent and still. The village, exhausted by excitement, sated with good food and music, its anxieties momentarily put away, was fast asleep.

A few hours later the sun rode arrogantly across the sky and still no one had come to see them. The rumbling in the Kamdhenu's stomach grew louder and louder. Her loud panting and increasingly frequent moans filled the barn. The cow watched her daughter helplessly, calling to her in a low voice to come close to the partition so she could lick her face. But her daughter was in so much pain she couldn't even stand. The cow tried to break the wooden partition that separated them, but failed. Her daughter continued to make mewling sounds of pain and fart constantly.

Close to mid-morning Kami stood up and then almost instantly fell heavily on to her forelegs, spewing vomit all over herself. Panicked, the cow got up too and bellowed her fear. This woke Shambhu up as well who, sensing his mother's distress, added his own very deep male voice to the chorus. But no one came. In desperation the cow rushed towards the door. But long before she could get there the rope which her two-legs tied to her legs bit into her, making her fall. But Kamdhenu's distress was too much to bear so she rushed at the door again, bellowing loudly. Shambhu joined her, troubled by the fear he felt around him.

By the time her two-legs came, the cow felt numbed by her daughter's pain. Rivers of brown had begun to flow from her daughter's rear. A bleakness filled the cow. All she could do was watch as her daughter tossed and turned on the mud floor, trying to find a position that eased the pain.

The Kamdhenu tried to get up when she heard Ramu and Laxmi enter. But she slipped in her own body fluids and fell heavily to the ground. Her eyes fixed themselves upon Laxmi's as once upon a time Laxmi had stared into the cow's eyes, seeking refuge from the flood. That time, it had been the Kamdhenu who had pulled Laxmi to safety. This time those same eyes begged for Laxmi's help. Only Laxmi could do nothing except force drops of water into the Kamdhenu's mouth as the life leaked out of her faster and faster. Until the very end, the Kamdhenu's eyes remained fixed upon Laxmi's, always in hope, always patiently, until the light went out of them.

News that the Kamdhenu was very ill spread fast. By mid-afternoon a steady stream of visitors were jostling each other at the barn door trying to get a glimpse of the Kamdhenu. But one look was usually enough to have them backing away, hands over their mouths. After a while Laxmi wedged the door shut to protect the Kamdhenu from curious eyes. Still people came and waited in the house for news. So Kuntabai and Sushilabai took charge of making cups of tea for those who waited. As the visitors waited they looked around Ramu's house, admiring the new furniture, the radio and the bicycle that Ramu had bought. Then someone voiced the opinion that it was hardly surprising that the Kamdhenu was dying. After all, humans were not born to be lucky but to suffer. Then Keshu, always the Kamdhenu's staunchest supporter, suggested that the Kamdhenu had fallen sick because the Devi was angry with them for not putting the Kamdhenu's statue in the temple. Since most of those who waited were the Kamdhenu's devoted fans, the majority agreed with him. 'Nonsense,' Kuntabai snapped when she heard this, 'the Kamdhenu will be fine. It is just that she must have eaten something bad yesterday. People will feed her all sorts of things and then blame the gods when something goes wrong. Now why don't all of you go and pray at the temple for the Kamdhenu's health to return quickly.'

A low murmur came from the crowd. Then slowly one by one they filed out. By late afternoon the temple bells were ringing constantly, much to the delight of Saraswati Rane.

By teatime the headman was in a thoroughly bad mood. No one had come to visit. All morning they'd waited: he, Mahendra, and the entire household. But the gifts – the chickens, eggs, fruit and vegetables that should have come pouring in – never arrived. In the village the temple bells rang incessantly, the only sign that Lord Rama was being given his due. Just after noon, his eldest daughter-in-law appeared with a visitor. The headman brightened. The sight of the man behind her always cheered him up. He looked up into the tribesman's face and smiled in welcome. The tribesman smiled back. In the harsh sunlight, his gold earrings gleamed like mini suns against his dark face. He was a different man from the one who had first come to see the headman and though his clothes were still patched and poor, he bore himself with pride, with no sign of the defeat that had characterized him then. He folded his hands and bowed before the headman. 'I have come to take my leave of you, Maharaj,' he said in his deep, musical voice.

'Leave? How can you leave?' the headman exclaimed. 'Savitribai, bring some chai and pakoras for us,' he shouted.

But the tribesman shook his head. 'No, there is no time. We must go now. The pundit has said so.'

'Saraswati Rane? Don't listen to him, he knows nothing. Besides my fields have still to be harvested. There is at least a few weeks' work for you. Come, sing me that song you sang last night about the princess who fell in love with the moon and let us forget about this talk of leaving.'

But the tribesman shook his head firmly. 'No Maharaj, not your pundit, ours. He says we are to leave now or our cattle will begin to die.'

A cold fist clutched at the headman's heart. 'And our cattle, what will become of them? Is there some disease that will strike soon? If so, then you must tell me,' he said.

The tribesman shook his head. 'The pundit wouldn't say what it was. He only said that the good luck was leaving this village.'

'The good luck? But you were there last night, you saw with your own eyes the temple we have built. How can the gods abandon us now? There is no finer temple in the entire area!'

the headman exclaimed.

The tribesman shrugged helplessly. 'Maharaj, I myself don't understand it. But we cannot go against our pundit's wishes. I am sure you understand.'

The headman scowled. 'Have I not taken care of you, given you work and shelter and fodder?' he demanded. 'If something terrible is to happen, then surely I have a right to know?'

The tribesman looked embarrassed and wouldn't meet the headman's eyes. At last he said, still looking down at the ground, 'I think it is more because of what you have done, Maharaj, that our pundit wants us to leave,' the tribesman said apologetically.

'What I have done? But I have done nothing.'

The tribesman looked full into the headman's face. 'Of course, Maharaj, you are a good man and a fair one. Our quarrel is not with you, or with anyone in your household. But our pundit believes that some of your people worship that devil's cow, a sister perhaps of those that caused the death of our herd. Therefore the pundit says we must leave.'

'What are you talking about? A devil's cow? There is no such thing here, only our Nandgaonis which have been with us for generations. He must be mad. How dare he insult our herd? I would get rid of him if I were you.'

The tribesman frowned and opened his mouth to say something, then thought better of it and shut his mouth firmly.

'Stay, please stay,' the headman cried desperately. 'We must have a feast for your departure, see you off properly. Next week if you like.'

The tribesman shook his head firmly, regretfully. 'I cannot, Maharaj, though I would very much have liked to sing for you once more. But our elders have decided. I only came for your blessing and to give you this, a gift from us.' From inside his blanket he pulled out a tiny jet-black goat and placed her in the headman's lap. 'Her name is Sapna. She was born here in Nandgaon one week ago. May she bring you good luck.'

Realising he would not be able to make them change their minds, Gopal nodded. 'All right then, if your mind is made up, I will not stop you. May Lord Rama guide you on your journey and the goddess Laxmi bring you success.' The little goat began to nuzzle the folds of the headman's dhoti, searching for milk. The headman stared down at it in dismay. 'Where's Ramu?' he asked.

No one answered him.

'Where's Ramu?' the headman repeated. 'Why didn't he come and take the goats out?'

After a few minutes Savitribai replied, 'He didn't come, Father.'

The headman's eyebrows came together in a terrible frown. 'What? Send someone to call that lazy good-for-nothing,' he roared. 'Who does he think he is?'

Immediately a servant boy was sent running to find Ramu and the headman sat back, drumming his stick on the floor in irritation. 'Here,' he called out to Mahendra, 'take this goat and give her some milk in the kitchen.' When Mahendra, his head bent over the account books, didn't answer, the headman's irritation grew. 'Yes, yes, I know what you are thinking, more expenses now that the tribesmen are gone. But so what? I will get a share of the donations that go to the temple. That will more than cover the extra expense.'

Mahendra said nothing.

All afternoon the headman was prevented from sleeping by the temple bells – and grew angrier.

Who had saved the village from the flood?

Who had built the temple?

He had.

And had they given him anything in return?

Nothing.

No more giving, he vowed. He would make them respect him the way they had respected his father.

Just before three, Kuntabai put Sushila in charge and went to the animal shed herself to see if she could relieve Laxmibai. But one look at the Kamdhenu was enough for her to know that things were very serious. She knew the smell of death only too well. It was a smell that had followed her ever since her husband had fallen ill, a smell that even haunted her dreams. She put a hand on Laxmi's shoulder and Laxmi looked up. The latter was crying. 'You have to take her to a doctor,' Kuntabai said gently.

'How?' Laxmi asked. 'In what? She is too ill to walk. If I could I would have carried her. And if I send Ramu, by the time he returns with the doctor she will be dead.'

'I will go and speak to the Patel,' Kuntabai answered. 'He will help.'

'Help?' Laxmi laughed. 'He won't help. He will be only too happy to have the Kamdhenu out of the way.'

And so Kuntabai rushed through the village as fast as her tired legs would carry her and threw herself at the headman's feet.

'What is it?' the headman snapped when he saw her. 'You smell worse than a butcher. How could you come before me in this condition.'

'Patelji, he... she, the Kamdhenu is very, very unwell,' Kuntabai stammered, tears beginning to course down her cheeks.

The headman noticed sourly that the tears were not new.

'Please, you must help.'

'Help?' the headman sneered. 'Help who? I spend my entire day helping the people of Nandgaon. Who saved it from the flood? Who built the temple? Who paid for the murthi sthapna? And now you say I must help an animal too?'

'It is very ill,' Kuntabai repeated uncertainly. She wasn't scared of the headman; her husband had been his closest friend and she knew him to be a fair man. 'It isn't natural,' she continued. 'Something has to be done. You are the headman – if you don't help, who will?'

The headman was tempted to accept. After all, it was a small enough thing and he hated to think of a cow, any cow, dying. But then the temple bells rang out again, and their arrogant chimes made his heart harden. 'I am not giving my cart for a good-for-nothing cow right in the middle of the harvest time. Let Ramu cure her himself, or if he can't, let him ask one of those friends that came for his Gaopuja,' he said.

Kuntabai's face fell. 'So you will not help?' she asked quietly.

'I will not,' the headman replied, 'not for that ungrateful man and his arrogant, stuck-up wife.'

Kuntabai looked shocked, then she said stiffly, 'You forget, Patelji, that this is not about Ramu and Laxmi, it is about your duty to the village.'

'And what about the village's duty to me?' the headman cried. 'After all that I have done, here I am, sitting alone all morning.'

Kuntabai said nothing, backing away silently until she was far enough away to be able to turn her back to him. The headman watched her leave with some satisfaction. It was time the village stopped taking him for granted.

Kuntabai didn't go back to Laxmibai's. She was too shocked by the headman's words. How could a man who represented everything that was right and kind and just suddenly become so deaf? He's changed, she thought sadly, which meant Nandgaon would change too. She stared at the familiar street unrecognisingly, feeling abandoned. Then she went home and hid in the darkness of her kitchen until she heard the cries that told her that the Kamdhenu was dead.

Even as inside the barn, the Kamdhenu's life slipped away, word spread amongst those waiting outside that the Kamdhenu was gone. At first there was silence in the yard. Then a sigh went through the crowd and a quiet sobbing began which grew louder and louder as the minutes went by. Inside the barn Kuntabai and a few others pulled a screaming Laxmi off the Kamdhenu's filthy body and then the women cleaned it and decorated the corpse with flowers. Then four men lifted it on to a bed of reeds and carried it out of the house. The others fell in line slowly and the Kamdhenu was taken into the village for the last time. The temple bells rang out as the procession turned on to the main street, and people lined either side of the street to watch. Some threw flowers and others rushed up to the byre to steal a final blessing.

At sunset the procession reached the river. Nearly everyone was there. Saraswati Rane, Vilas Rao with his youngest child in his arms, Mamtabai, Govind Rao, Sushilabai, Parvatibai, Bicchoo, Darbari, Kanhaiya, Keshu, Madho and all the name-less others whose lives had been touched by the Kamdhenu. Only four people were missing – the headman, Mahendra, his eldest daughter-in-law, Savitri, and Laxmi herself.

Just before sunset the headman awoke from a troubled sleep. All was silent. He cursed under his breath. So the animal was dead. It couldn't have chosen a better moment, he thought furiously. Now they would talk of nothing else for weeks to come. He sat up wearily and Savitribai came forward with his evening glass of milk. It was barely cold, he noted sourly, taking the glass from her. She watched him anxiously as he took a sip and put the glass down with a grimace.

'Father, is it all right?' she asked nervously.

He ignored her question, noticing all the same that she looked pale. 'So it is dead, is it?' he asked.

She nodded, biting her lip.

'Everyone gone to the cremation, have they?' he asked, looking around the empty courtyard.

'Yes Father.'

His eyes swung back up to her face. 'So how come you didn't go to see it?' he asked. 'I would have thought you'd have been the first person there.'

Savitribai looked frightened. 'I. . . I stayed here for you,' she said.

He didn't completely believe her; still he said, 'Good. Clever girl.' Then his eyes fell on Mahendra waiting patiently by his chair, the red account books open in front of him even though it was almost too dark to read. He grabbed his stick and pulled himself up. Savitribai rushed to help him but he pushed her away roughly. 'I'm fine, just leave me,' he growled and she backed away immediately, looking scared.

He walked over to where Mahendra sat on his stool and stood towering over him. For a while he just watched Mahendra's face. After a minute, the other man averted his eyes.

The headman said gruffly, 'So you think I made a mistake?'

Mahendra said nothing, looking calmly at the red account book open in front of him as if deep in prayer. 'It is not for me to judge your actions,' he said at last.

Bang went the headman's stick, making the ground shake. 'Answer me,' he said.

Mahendra looked up. 'The animal is dead. You could have saved it,' he said simply.

'I could not. It might well have died on the way to Khandwa. And anyway, that animal was a nuisance.' Bang. The stick came down on the hard packed earth once more.

Mahendra blinked. He said nothing.

'You dare to judge me?' the headman asked, his voice dangerously calm.

Mahendra looked down, still saying nothing.

'So how come you haven't gone to see the animal?' Gopal demanded angrily.

'My place is with you,' Mahendra replied, 'whatever you do.'

'Liar.' Suddenly the headman's anger and sense of hurt found a focus. 'You are nothing better than a dog, how dare you judge me? You, who I pulled off the streets. You would have been dead a long time ago if I hadn't saved you.'

Mahendra said nothing.

'Tell me, where would you have been without me?' the headman asked, banging his stick on the ground.

Again Mahendra kept silent, but this time he looked up into the headman's eyes, his own patient and full of understanding.

The look almost cost Mahendra his life; for the headman, weighed down by guilt, raised his heavy silver-topped cane, determined to strike the look out of Mahendra's eyes.

Snap went the cane across Mahendra's face, narrowly missing his eyes. Mahendra fell off the stool sideways.

Again the cane rose into the air; it hovered weightlessly for a moment above Mahendra's head, a snake about to strike, and then came crashing down on the man's still body.

Again and again the cane rose and came down upon human flesh. Savitribai tried to grab the headman's arm but he threw her off easily. Eventually servants came running from all directions and pulled the headman away. They gave him a glass of milk laced with opium which sent him into a long, untroubled sleep.

Laxmi had also been given opium after she'd been pulled away from the Kamdhenu's corpse. She awoke after dark, alone in the house. For a few seconds she couldn't remember where she was, or why she had been sleeping at all. Then it all came back and she let out a sob and struggled to her feet. Shakily, for the drug was still affecting her system, she made her way down the verandah steps and into the courtyard.

It was a clear night and the stars lit up the sky. The barn was a solid dark shape silhouetted against the stars. She walked slowly towards it, hoping wildly that it had all been a dream. But she knew it was not so.

Laxmi stared dry-eyed at the barn door and then carefully pushed it open.

It was empty. The cow and Shambhu had been taken away earlier in the day to Govind Rao's place. All that remained was the undignified mess of Kamdhenu's illness. Laxmi sat down on the soiled straw pallet and thought of her dreams, and all that the Kamdhenu had meant. A memory, now mercifully distant, but still burned into her brain, flashed before her eyes: a similar scene, that of her own father, lying on the floor of the animal house. She wrinkled her nose instinctively, remembering the smell. Then her hand, her entire body, grew still. How long she remained like that she never knew. For suddenly, an avalanche of memories overwhelmed her, a house of cards slowly falling, memories confronting and confounding each other, the past mingling with the present. But the smell, she realised, was the same. Kami had been poisoned, she felt sure of it. Her mouth opened and she tried to scream. But no sound emerged from her throat. It was too late. Just as it had been for her father. Then the tears came, rushing silently down her cheeks, and Laxmi fainted.

In the kitchen of the headman's house, Savitribai sat hugging her knees to her chest. When she thought of what she had done, or of it becoming known, her blood went cold. Then she calmed herself by picturing the future, a future that was bright and meaningful. A future in which everyone got what they deserved and Nandgaon was saved.

Mahendra left the next day, his meagre belongings rolled into a single blanket. People watched him leave with red eyes. No one said goodbye. The village was preoccupied with the

Kamdhenu and since Mahendra had never bothered to befriend anyone in the village, no one was really sorry to see him go. And then there was another thing. Mahendra was the one who kept the accounts of who owed what to the headman, and so the people were afraid of him. Because the headman was one of them, the village had long since transferred their sense of resentment on to Mahendra's shoulders and since he never bothered to talk to any of them except when it involved what they still owed, the resentment had festered. So no one was sorry to see him go. And they were all too stunned by the Kamdhenu's death to wonder why he was leaving.

CHAPTER TWENTY-EIGHT
THE VOID

'I tell you the Kamdhenu's death was no accident,' Keshu told the others as he got his head shaved out of respect for the departed cow. 'There were those who were jealous of Nandgaon's luck, so they killed it.'

'You are mad, no one kills a cow – who could even think of such a thing?' Darbari Lal, who was doing the shaving, disagreed.

'I am not mad,' Keshu said violently. 'You are the ones who are blind. The Kamdhenu was an incarnation of the goddess Laxmi herself; she could not have died by any ordinary means. Powerful magic was used by powerful people.' He looked meaningfully at the circle of faces reflected in the barber's mirror. 'People who were jealous of Nandgaon's good fortune.'

'He is right. Only someone who really hates Nandgaon and wants to see us ruined could have done it,' Bicchoo added knowledgeably.

The others nodded slowly.

'But who could that person be?' Darbari Lal asked.

There was silence. The world outside Nandgaon reached in its giant hand.

'Must have been someone from Kesarigaon,' Govind Rao muttered weakly. But no one believed him.

Laxmi thought otherwise. She was convinced that it had been someone from Nandgaon itself. 'They are jealous of us. That's why they killed her,' she told Ramu fiercely.

'Impossible.' Ramu refused to hear of it. 'No one in Nandgaon could even think of killing a cow. Maybe where you came from such a thing may have been possible, but not here, not in Nandgaon,' he said emphatically.

'You think you know Nandgaon just because you were born here?' Laxmi replied angrily. 'Shall I tell everyone how the Kamdhenu was made? Then we'll see if you really know your village.'

'She was never very strong, Laxmibai,' Ramu said awkwardly, 'and what the gods give they also take away.'

'Rubbish. She was perfectly fine just the day before. Why don't you open your eyes rather than putting everything on the gods. What have gods ever done for humans except make problems?' she demanded angrily.

'Hai Ram,' Ramu exclaimed, shocked. 'What are you saying? Have you lost your mind, cursing the gods so?'

'I am telling the truth. That headman spends huge amounts of the village's money on pujas, yet did that stop the flood, or the drought for that matter? Do you think the gods care what happens to Nandgaon? Why, you all are as poor as mice. You fight for scraps off the headman's table and never think of the future.'

'Hush,' Ramu put a hand over her mouth, 'or people will say you have gone mad.'

Then an empty packet of pesticide was found on the bathing ghat and reluctantly people began to believe that Laxmi had perhaps been right and that the Kamdhenu had been poisoned by someone from Nandgaon itself. For the location of the empty packet of poison made it clear that the poison had been bought by someone from the village.

'Now do you believe me when I say that you don't know your village?' Laxmi asked, waving the packet in front of her husband's face.

Ramu's face went pale. He grabbed the packet from her and stared at it closely. 'I don't understand. Who. . .Why?'

Just as a herd of cows feels the void left by the death of one of their own, so did the people of Nandgaon. The Kamdhenu's departure left a hole so big that no amount of talking or crying seemed to fill it. To whom were the unlucky ones to go? Into whose ears would they pour their troubles? Where would the childless women go for comfort, and those who needed milk for a sick and fretful child? With what promises would mothers put their little ones to sleep?

Two months after the Kamdhenu's death, the village still hadn't forgotten her.

'Since the Kamdhenu's been gone, nothing goes right here any more,' Vilas Rao grumbled to his ninety-year-old mother Shalinibai.

'What?' she said, 'speak louder, can't you?'

'I said that since the Kamdhenu died, no one has any luck anymore,' Vilas Rao shouted.

'What work have you not done?' Shalinibai asked, mis-hearing him. 'Why do you mumble when you speak? Have you lost your teeth too?'

'Not my teeth, my wife, Maaji.'

'Your wife? Where is that stupid child?'

'She's run away. Gone. With that truck driver of a nephew of hers.'

'Gone?' Shalinibai shrugged. 'Then get another one, beta. And be quick about it,' she advised. 'There is a lot of work in this house.'

And at the other end of the village: 'I dreamt of her again last night,' Keshu was telling his wife as they drank tea one morning. 'She looked so beautiful. So real. As if she wanted to be alive. I think she misses us too.'

'Who wouldn't?' his wife replied. 'Didn't we love the

Kamdhenu with all our hearts? The gods were jealous of our good luck.'

'And now they've taken it away,' Keshu added.

The headman couldn't understand why the villagers refused to forget the Kamdhenu.

'The way they go on, you would think I had died,' he complained one evening to the others.

'Don't say that, Patelji,' Bicchoo said unctuously. 'You are the soul of Nandgaon, you mustn't compare yourself to a mere animal.'

Only the headman smiled. The others looked at Bicchoo in dislike. But he was a permanent fixture now at their nightly meetings. 'Wah, Bicchoo. I wish others thought like you,' the headman said gratefully. He looked at the priest. 'This has got to stop, Saraswati Rane,' he said firmly. 'You are the pundit of this place – tell people enough is enough. Do another puja or something.'

'I try, I try,' Saraswati Rane said defensively, 'but the truth is that since the Kamdhenu's death. . . well, all kinds of things have gone wrong. People say the luck has left the village, that the gods have abandoned us. It is going to take time to win them back.'

'What? Win them back?' the headman exclaimed. 'What are you talking about? When did you fall under that cursed animal's spell? Not when it was alive, I know.'

'I have not come under any spell,' Saraswati Rane answered stiffly, glaring at Bicchoo, 'but I am realistic. And I only report what I see.'

'Perhaps you could organise a bullfight,' Jaiwant Rane suggested suddenly. 'That will distract people.'

'A bullfight? Jaiwant Rane, that is the last thing I ever imagined you would say. Be realistic, I will not allow the best bulls in the herd to be wasted in such a way. Tell the people to pray to Rama Bhagwan instead. Isn't that what they are supposed to be doing?' He glared at Saraswati Rane as he said this.

'The Kamdhenu and Lord Rama are two entirely different things,' the priest said primly.

'Of course they are. One is a god, the other an animal! How is it that people can be so silly as to worship an animal over a god?' the headman cried.

'But Hanumanji Bhagwan Hanumanji was a monkey,' Saraswati Rane pointed out coldly.

'The Kamdhenu was no ordinary animal,' Vilas Rao spluttered angrily, suddenly entering the conversation. 'You did not benefit from its miracles, because you were jealous of its power. Now it is too late, there will never be any more miracles for any of us. Not even you.'

'Thank God for that,' the headman answered, glaring at him. 'Thank God for that.'

Shortly after the cremation the Kamdhenu's ashes had been buried in Ramu's angan and a small neem sapling planted on top in memory of the neem tree in the other village under which the animal had so loved to sit. After a few months a statue, the same one that had been found in one of the headman's fields and which he'd refused to have installed in the temple, was put beside the neem sapling and every day the Kamdhenu's devotees brought fresh flowers to decorate it in the mornings and incense in the evenings. Afterwards, they sang and told stories about the Kamdhenu, remembering her many miracles. On one such evening, Keshu told those gathered there the story of how the headman had refused to let the statue of the Kamdhenu be put inside the temple. Many knew the story already, but they enjoyed hearing it from Keshu. 'If only he had agreed, perhaps the Kamdhenu would still have be with us,' Keshu ended, tears rolling down his cheeks.

'The Devi must have become angry with us for insulting her creature, and so she took her away from us,' Madho added, completing Keshu's thought.

The others nodded, their cheeks wet with tears also.

'How could our Patel have been so cruel?' a woman cried piteously.

Laxmi, coming out of the house with a tray of fried pakoras overheard her and demanded to be told the whole story. 'Of course,' she cried when Keshu finished telling it again, 'he is the one responsible for the Kamdhenu's death. He must have planned it. For didn't he refuse Kuntabai when she went to him for help? Am I not right, Kuntabai?' she asked, turning suddenly to her friend.

Reluctantly Kuntabai nodded.

'But he was with us at the temple. We all saw him,' Parbatibai pointed out. 'How could he have done it?'

'He didn't, he made someone else do it,' Laxmi said impatiently, 'someone like. . . like that man of his with the account books, the one that went away right after.'

'You mean Mahendra?' Kuntabai asked shocked. 'He would never. . . He was a Brahmin.'

'Then why did he leave so suddenly?' Laxmi demanded wildly.

Kuntabai couldn't answer.

Perhaps because everyone knew Mahendra and yet none had known him well, the rumor that Mahendra had been responsible for the Kamdhenu's death spread like wildfire. For like Laxmi, Mahendra had been an outsider, and was close only to the headman. To the rest of the village, he had been the man who called in their debts. Which was why he was the perfect person to blame. And he had left suddenly and inexplicably. Everyone began to remember instances of Mahendra's cruelty, things he'd seized in lieu of payment, pleas that he had ignored. Then Bicchoo pointed out slyly that it had been the headman who had brought Mahendra to Nandgaon and put him in that very powerful position over the rest of the villagers, and that it had been for the headman that Mahendra had collected the payments. Then the people were filled with anger against the headman. They forgot the temple had been built with the headman's money. They forgot that he'd been the one to feed the village after the flood and to rebuild the herd each time it had been decimated. They only remembered all that the headman had not done – the loans he hadn't given and the favours he had not granted and the harshness of the punishments he had sometimes given to defaulters. Bicchoo encouraged the others to remember, for it covered the fact that he himself was one of the biggest defaulters. The stories of the headman's cruelty grew with each repetition, and one after the other, those who had sworn by the headman's fairness only months ago began to look for someone else to turn to when they had a problem. They didn't have to look far. For Ramu, as the owner of the Kamdhenu and the one who had been hurt the worst, was the obvious choice. And he now had money, for the demands for Shambhu's services had increased after the Kamdhenu's death and Laxmi insisted on being paid.

Laxmi was at first worried when she saw that people had begun to approach her husband for loans. She knew that Ramu was unable to say no. But then she saw an opportunity to repair their damaged finances and encouraged Ramu to give them loans, telling him that he should simply ask them to give him their spare milk instead. This milk she made Ramu mix with the headman's goat milk and sell to the restaurant owners in Kesarigaon. But because Ramu was an honest man, he told those who borrowed from him that he was selling their milk, and to both Laxmi's and his own great surprise, soon nearly three quarters of the village was selling its extra milk through Ramu.

The headman pretended not to notice that no one came to see him any more and that the amounts of milk he received had gone down. Lost in thoughts of Mahendra, tormented by guilt and regret, he withdrew into himself, spending longer and longer periods alone in the forest. He also ignored or pretended to ignore the fact that no one was bringing him gifts or repaying their loans any more. But one evening, when only Saraswati Rane and Jaiwant Rane showed up for the evening game of cards, he was startled into saying, 'Where are the others? They're very late tonight. Has something happened?'

Saraswati Rane and Jaiwant Rane looked at each other worriedly. 'Maybe they went to Khandwa and haven't returned,' Saraswati Rane suggested.

'But they should have told me that yesterday,' the headman pointed out.

'Perhaps they forgot,' Saraswati Rane suggested uncomfortably.

Just then Bicchoo arrived and they turned to him in relief. 'So what fresh news do you bring today?' Jaiwant Rane asked Bicchoo, causing the latter to look at him in surprise.

'Why, nothing, all is well in the village,' Bicchoo replied.

'Come, let's start; the pakoras will get cold,' the headman said impatiently.

But the next night, Govind Rao didn't come again and neither did Bicchoo. Saraswati Rane and Jaiwant Rane looked nervously at the headman when it became clear that the other two weren't coming. They said nothing. Neither were good liars. But the headman didn't ask where they were this time. He stared at the empty places in front of him. 'It seems I have been sleeping for too long,' he said cryptically.

To Saraswati Rane and Jaiwant Rane's immense relief, both Vilas Rao and Govind Rao appeared on the third night. They never gave an explanation as to why they hadn't come the previous two nights and the headman never asked, talking and joking as if nothing had changed.

But things had changed. And, as many people began to say, some things had even changed for the better. For thanks to

Ramu they were getting more money for their milk. And the sudden increase in their income made them want to spend. Keshu went and bought a goat for his wife and a watch for himself. Madho, after thinking a great deal about it, decided he'd wait and buy a bicycle instead. Then he would be able to go into Kesarigaon and look for work or even to Khandwa, where he felt sure he would get paid double. Parvatibai dreamed of a bed and secretly began to hide money in the hole at the base of the jamun tree behind their house. Sushilabai planned to build a pukka shop in cement and brick. But Govind Rao, her husband, persuaded her to give the money to Laxmi instead along with the gift of a female calf in exchange for mating Shambhu with their prize cow, Gayatri. After that, Govind Rao felt it was important to be seen every other evening at the gatherings in Ramu's courtyard.

This, and other information, was given regularly to the headman by Bicchoo. For soon after the evening when Govind Rao and Vilas Rao had not come for the evening game of cards, the headman hired Bicchoo to do the accounts. The headman was aware Bicchoo didn't know very much about account keeping, but he did know everything that went on in the village. In the evenings after the favour-seekers had left, Gopal would turn to Bicchoo and say, 'Now tell me, how are things in the village?'

And Bicchoo would reply, 'All is well, Patelji. With you watching over us, how could it be otherwise?'

'Then why are there not more people coming to see me?' he would demand.

'Because you are in their hearts, Patelji, and your eyes follow them wherever they go,' Bicchoo would reply.

Defeated, the headman would ask directly, 'And how. . . how is everyone – Ramu, for example?'

And Bicchoo would smile and say, 'He is well, Patelji, very well. He has lent Kanhaiya the boatman money to buy a new kerosene stove for his boat.'

'He has, has he?' the headman would say, grinding his teeth. 'If Kanhaiya wanted a new stove, why didn't he come and ask me?'

Or Bicchoo would tell the headman about how Laxmi was teaching the women arithmetic and how to write their names.

'Impossible. Women cannot learn to work with numbers. It is not in their blood.'

'But she does,' Bicchoo pointed out.

'She is not a woman. She is a devil,' the headman replied.

'Patelji, she is talking of a bank only for women. That is why she wants them all to learn how to read and write.'

'A bank for women? She is a fool,' the headman scoffed. 'No one trusts anyone else with their money.'

'But ten women have agreed, and they have each promised to put in a hundred rupees,' Bicchoo replied. 'She tempts them with her learning, teaching only those who promise to join.'

'Chut! Women should not be allowed near money, it makes them mad. Why do they want to bother with that stuff? Let the men handle it and be driven crazy. Look at the mess I am in!'

Bicchoo did not answer, having the grace to look embarrassed.

Then one evening when the headman asked his usual question, some evil spirit prompted Bicchoo to say, 'Why? Have you not heard? Everyone is saying the Kamdhenu was poisoned by someone from Nandgaon.'

'What? From Nandgaon? Impossible. No one would kill a cow.'

Bicchoo smiled cruelly. 'Are, Patelji, you know that Laxmibai has been insisting the Kamdhenu was poisoned since the cremation? No one believed her until a packet of pesticide was found on the women's bathing ghat. Now people are wondering who could have done such a thing.'

'Are you sure it was a packet of pesticide? Did you see it, the packet?' the headman asked.

'No, but Kuntabai was the one who found it,' Bicchoo replied, 'and you know she doesn't lie.'

The headman went quiet. Then he asked, 'And who do they think did it?'

Bicchoo pretended to be extremely nervous. 'I. . . I can't tell you,' he whispered.

'But you must,' the headman insisted.

'I can't, it's too awful,' Bicchoo said dramatically, 'and. . . and untrue. Please don't make me tell you.'

'You must, you must,' the headman insisted, beginning to suspect the worst.

Bicchoo tried to move away from the headman, remembering what he had done to Mahendra. 'N-no one. I mean, I don't know,' he lied.

'Oh yes you do,' the headman said gently. 'You know everything that Nandgaon thinks, Bicchoo. Come on, don't waste our time.'

Bicchoo gave up. 'They think it was your Mahendra that did it, and that's why you sent him away.'

'Mahendra? Me?' The accusation was like a slap in the face. 'After everything I have done for Ramu?' The headman shot out of his chair, thumping the cane so hard on the ground that clods of earth flew like missiles in all directions. Bichoo cowered against the chair, shielding his face. 'Did that stupid animal take away everyone's brains or did they not have any to begin with?' the headman raged, pacing up and down in front of the terrified Bicchoo. 'Why would I do such a thing? How could I do it? Would I bring bad luck to my village? Would I risk eternal hell by killing a cow? Have they lost their minds?'

Bicchoo risked a quick look at the headman's face and nearly cried out in fear. The headman's eyes were bloodshot and bulging, and thick knobbly veins encircled his forehead like the aerial roots of a giant banyan tree. 'Patelji, Patelji, don't. . .' Bicchoo cried despairingly. Then, to his own surprise, he fell at the headman's feet and grabbed him around the knees. 'Patelji, Patelji, forgive me,' he cried. 'I should not have told you.'

That stopped the headman. 'Of course not, you did the right thing. I am not angry with you.' Bicchoo tucked his head as far as he could between his scrawny shoulders, expecting the cane to land at any moment. But instead gentle hands clasped him around the shoulders and pulled him upright. 'It's all right Bicchoo, get up. I want to know everything,' the headman said. Turning to a servant he ordered, 'Get us some more tea and something to eat.'

As soon as the servant had served them, the headman lapsed into silence, staring frowningly into the darkness. Bicchoo stood up, making one final attempt at escape. 'I should go, Patelji, I have bothered you enough.'

'Huh?' The headman looked up and stared unseeingly at Bicchoo for a moment before his expression changed and a smile, somewhat weary but without malice, swept across his face. 'No Bicchoo, you have not bothered me at all. On the contrary, you have helped me. Listen.' The headman bent down and looked full into Bicchoo's eyes, fixing him with the full power of his gaze. 'You must find out who did it, who killed that animal. You alone can do it, Bicchoo.' The headman put his hand on Bicchoo's shoulder and squeezed it gently. 'And when you find out, tell no one but come straight to me and I promise I will punish that person. Will you do this for me?'

Dazed, relief filling his chest and rising up into his throat, practically choking him, Bicchoo stammered, 'Of course, Patelji.'

'Good.' The headman sat back in his chair. 'You can go now.'

After Bicchoo left the headman called for his son. 'Where's my son?' he shouted to the servant fetching water at the well. 'Call him immediately.'

But instead of Gajendra, another servant appeared bringing Jaiwant Rane, the schoolmaster.

The headman stared at Jaiwant Rane in astonishment. 'Are, Jaiwantbhai, are you alone tonight?' he said bitterly.

Jaiwant Rane did not mince his words. 'Indeed I am. Saraswati Rane has gone to bless someone's new bicycle,' he answered, 'but that is just as well. This way we can talk without fear. You see, I want to help you.'

'Help me?' the headman laughed bitterly. 'So now I need help to resolve my own affairs, do I?'

'Your affairs, unfortunately, are the village's affairs. You have let things go too far,' Jaiwant Rane said brutally.

'You are worried for Nandgaon?' the headman said sarcastically. 'Isn't that supposed to be my job?'

'Of course. You *are* Nandgaon. Which is why I am worried,' Jaiwant Rane replied. 'Ramu is getting too powerful. I have come to ask you what you are going to do about it.' He paused, then added more quietly, 'and to offer my help.'

'So now you think I need help too?' the headman asked. 'Are you going to offer to hold my hand as well?'

'Yes. If need be, I would be honoured,' Jaiwant Rane replied, his teeth flashing whitely in the lantern-light.

The headman found himself smiling too. 'As bad as that?' he asked in a milder voice.

Jaiwant Rane nodded and sat down. A servant brought him a hookah and for a few minutes they sat in silence as Jaiwant Rane lit his and had a quick smoke. The headman waited politely, wondering what would come next.

After he'd taken a few puffs, Jaiwant Rane looked the headman full in the face and the headman was surprised to see love and pity there. He looked away, embarrassed.

Then Jaiwant Rane spoke, his words sounding stilted and old-fashioned. For he was not used to showing his emotions. 'Gopal Mundkur,' he declared. 'It is rare for a Brahman like myself to love a tiller of the soil. Our love, we are taught to reserve for God alone. Until recently I was no different. It is true that over the years I grew to respect the way you governed the village. You always kept God's laws in your heart and performed all the pujas with unfailing attention to detail, irrespective of the cost. The good of the village was always in your mind. Even your biggest mistake, allowing Ramu to keep that junglee cow in his house and letting that fatherless calf live, came out of your genuine love for the people of Nandgaon.

'But even then I did not love you. Not until you got rid of that fatherless cow did I come to see you as the incarnation of the Rama Bhagwan I loved. For in killing that creature you damned yourself to eternal hell but you saved Nandgaon. Therefore I salute you. Did not our own good Lord Rama not abandon his wife and unborn children for the sake of the kingdom?'

The headman opened his mouth to tell Jaiwant Rane that he was wrong, he hadn't killed the Kamdhenu, but the latter would not let him. 'No, I have not finished, Gopal Mundkur, hear me out. You are a great and courageous man, there is no one in all of Nimar like you. I will not let Nandgaon lose you.'

Lose me? the headman wondered. How could Nandgaon lose him? He was the Patel. As surely as the sun rose and set, he would always be the Patel – until he decided otherwise.

'They are talking of elections in the village,' Jaiwant Rane continued. 'Bicchoo, the one you so depend upon, was the one who started it. Every evening after he has come here and filled your ears he goes to Ramu's courtyard and talks against you.

And the others listen.'

The headman grunted. But the news wasn't really a surprise. Somewhere inside him he'd known it was so. Jaiwant Rane waited for the headman to say something but when he didn't, he carried on. 'I wish I could have said that that is all, but there is more bad news. Since the death of the Kamdhenu the entire village has gone mad. Other than your own herd and mine, there are almost no families left who have not had the monstrous bull climb atop their best Nandgaoni cows.'

'My god, what on earth for?' the headman cried. 'Surely they don't really believe that that will bring the other one back?'

'Because they all have been bitten by the demon of greed. Ever since they too began selling their milk elsewhere and receiving money in their hands, their hands itch to have more,' Jaiwant Rane replied. 'Now they are even talking of rebuilding the road so they can get their milk to the market faster.'

'Rebuild the road?' The headman clutched the head of his cane in shock. 'But that is the stupidest thing I have ever heard. They can't rebuild that road. It will cost millions – and I will not have it.'

'But the woman wants it, and she has convinced them it can be done,' Jaiwant Rane answered.

The headman didn't respond. He thought of how he had first met the demon of greed. The truck that had crushed his four-year-old son had been overloaded and at the crucial moment its brakes had failed.

'Come back to the present, Gopal Mundkur. Your work is not finished,' Jaiwant Rane continued, reaching forward and grabbing the headman's hand. His voice fell to a whisper. 'You must kill the bull and kill Laxmi and Ramu too – just as you did the cow. Then and only then will Nandgaon be saved.'

'What are you saying, Jaiwantbhai?' the headman cried, shocked. 'I am no murderer! Haven't I seen enough death in my own life? My child, my own wife? How could I kill another?'

'You would only be doing your duty, Gopal Mundkur. Is the life of one, or even three, more precious than the entire village? You cannot allow Nandgaon to be destroyed like this; you are the headman. Nandgaon is your responsibility. Not Ramu, not Laxmi, not even their cow. The soul of Nandgaon is your responsibility. You must look after it.'

'But for me Nandgaon is Ramu and Laxmi and Govind Rao and Keshav and Madhav and Bicchoo,' the headman said sadly. 'I cannot kill, not cows nor humans.'

'But everyone thinks you did, Patelji, everyone thinks you did,' Jaiwant Rane interrupted him, looking disappointed and relieved at the same time.

'I know,' the headman replied, smiling sardonically, 'but they are wrong.'

And there was nothing more to say. The two men looked at each other, each seeing clearly into the other's heart. They looked away after a moment and each reached for their own hookah, smoking in silence. Then, as the silence lengthened, Jaiwant Rane got up to leave. 'Think about it, Patelji,' he advised. 'People can be made to disappear more easily than animals.'

After Jaiwant Rane left, the headman sat immobile in his chair for a long time. His head spun, Jaiwant Rane's words ringing in his ears. First he was accused of being a criminal. Now he was being advised to become one. He stared blindly at the lantern by his elbow, a red fog dancing before his eyes. Around him the angan slowly filled with the scent of food cooking but the headman was oblivious to it all. All he saw was the lamp's flame, growing and diminishing and then growing again. After a while he began to feel strangely detached. What a strange gift power was, he mused – when it came to you it was small, then it grew big, and then when you really needed it, you found it was too small to be useful, and you had to give it away.

But give it to whom? a tiny voice inside him asked. His son Gajendra was hardly a fit candidate – too weak, too easily influenced and a coward. But at least he was of the same blood, the voice whispered back fiercely, that had to count for something. He wished he had someone to turn to for advice, someone with the unshakeable convictions of his father or with a plentiful supply of good sense like his wife. But they were both gone, turned to smoke long since. He sighed heavily, feeling old age stir in his bones.

'Dadoo, Dadoo, is Ramu's Shambhu the strongest animal in the herd?' His grandson's piping little voice easily breached the wall of his thoughts.

'Huh?' He looked up and saw everyone in the angan watching him tensely. They all knew, he thought.

'Nana, you are dreaming again. Why can't you listen to me?' his grandson complained. 'Is Shambhu the strongest bull in the world?'

'Shambhu? That clown is afraid of his own shadow. You can see it in his eyes,' the headman replied. 'No the strong ones are the cows, for they are the smart ones. Our Nandini is the strongest in the village. That's why they all follow her and not Shambhu.' Clapping his hands in delight the little boy turned to the rest of the room. 'There, I told you so,' he said, sounding very grown-up. 'Why don't all of you ever believe me?'

Everyone laughed. Even the headman, though his laughter was cut short by a thought that brought a frown to his face. Why hadn't Bicchoo told him what people were thinking earlier?

He returned to his thoughts. What disturbed him most was the fact that someone like Jaiwant Rane, a decent sensible man, could have felt that things in the village had gone so far wrong that it would require multiple murders to set them right! But how else was one to fight a magic cow? His mind shied away from the word. Why did it have to be born in his village? he wondered. His mind went back to the day Ramu came to him with the news that he had married. He should have thrown him out then, he thought ruefully. Now he had Ramu, Laxmi and the legend of the Kamdhenu to contend with.

A gentle cough interrupted his thoughts. He looked up. His son was standing before him. 'Father,' his son began nervously, 'what can I do for you?'

The headman said nothing. He stared at his gentle indecisive son and wished for the thousandth time that it had been this one that the gods had taken instead of his eldest one.

'They are saying I killed it,' he said shortly.

His son said nothing, hanging his head.

'So you knew?' the headman asked, surprised.

Again his son said nothing for a long time. Then he lifted his head and asked baldly, 'What are you going to do, Father?'

The question came as a shock. The headman realised suddenly that he hadn't really been thinking at all; he'd allowed himself to get lost in the past. 'To do? What should I do? I have done nothing to be ashamed of.'

'Of course you haven't,' his son said quickly, 'which is why you need to create a distraction, something that will give the village a new direction to their thoughts.'

'Rubbish. You talk just like Saraswati Rane!' the headman snapped. 'A distraction. That was what he said the temple would be – and look what happened! Has anyone forgotten that damn animal? They are talking of building a temple to it now. And my temple? Who talks of it any more?'

His son didn't reply, sitting with his head bowed respectfully. And yet there was something in his posture that told the headman that his son wasn't finished, and that he would remain there until his father had let him say what he had come to say.

'All right, all right,' he said gruffly, 'tell me, what is it?'

A cautious smile broke out on his son's sweaty face. 'Baba,' he said using the familiar form of address he used only when they were alone, 'forgive me for this stupid idea of mine.' He stopped, head bowed, waiting for his father's permission to continue.

The headman grunted and so Gajendra continued.

'You may remember the letter we received last week from the deputy commissioner's office,' he began carefully. 'It was an invitation to come to Khandwa for an important meeting of all the sarpanchs.' He stopped and looked hopefully at the headman.

The headman frowned. 'I don't go for meetings with any sarkar* officer, you know that,' he snapped. 'I know them, they only call you when they want something. Bloodsuckers, the lot of them. They give you electricity and then make you pay. They give you piped water which doesn't work properly and still they want you to pay.'

His son waited diplomatically for his father's temper to cool. 'The deputy commissioner sahib is a good man, Baba. He has called the meeting because he wants to give us a lot of money. It is a very important meeting. All the other sarpanchs will be there.'

'So what? Why should I go? I am a patel not a sarpanch. We have never taken government money and we have been fine without it.'

'Yes we have, so far. But the flood washed away most of our money, and the temple used up the rest. Soon there will be nothing left. I heard that the government is giving a special relief package, worth at least twenty thousand rupees, to

---

* government

everyone in the villages that were washed away.'

'They will give money to us a year and a half late?' The headman glared at his son. 'And you believed it, these rumours?'

The corners of the headman's son's mouth turned down in silent defeat. He looked away, preparing to go. Then suddenly he turned and faced his father, anger blazing in his eyes. 'What choice do we have?' he demanded. 'We have to do something. Even as we speak Ramu is plotting against us, promising those who support him a chance to have the children of Shambhu. They all want a Kamdhenu, you know. And they are willing to pay for it. How do we fight that? I ask you, father.'

The headman opened his mouth to tell his son how wrong he was, but no words came out. His son was right. They had to do something, even though in his heart he knew that the government was hardly going to help them. He held out his hand to be helped up instead. 'Come, take me for dinner. I'll do as you say,' he promised gruffly, 'even though I know it will be a waste of time.'

CHAPTER TWENTY-NINE

KAMDHENU AGAIN

Sitting sandwiched between a man who couldn't stop coughing and a heavily pregnant woman who moaned each time the bus hit a bump, Gopal Mundkur wondered why he'd accepted to make the journey to Khandwa. Nothing good could come of it, he felt sure. The bus laboured along the road, swerving dangerously in order to avoid the craters in the middle. The pregnant woman moaned again. An aid package worth twenty thousand rupees! It was just too good to be true. The headman grunted as he righted himself and waited for the next bump or hole. How could one trust a government that couldn't even build a decent road?

The bus picked up speed as they turned on to the highway and cool fresh air managed somehow to find a way through the wall of bodies filling the aisle. The bus grew quiet as people ceased to fight for space. But just as he began to relax the pregnant woman on his right leaned across him and was violently and noisily sick. Though the tubercular man was the one to get the brunt of it, the headman, who was only lightly sprinkled, leapt up and, clambering over the prone woman, forced his way into the crowded aisle. As he tried vainly to find something non-human to hold on to, he cursed his son, Ramu, Laxmi and every living soul in Nandgaon. Fickle, stupid people. How could they listen to a man like Ramu who knew nothing of the world outside? An image of Laxmi danced before his eyes and he felt a surge of hatred for her. She was the cause of his misery; he should have thrown her out right at the beginning. His head pressed against the burning tin roof, he wondered idly what was worse, the killing of a cow or of a woman.

As he was thinking this, the pregnant woman looked up and there was such misery in her face that he knew that nothing he did to her could be worse than being born a woman. He gave her a small smile and her face lit up in spite of the pain it held. Gopal looked away hurriedly, wishing he could change the world. Instead the world, he thought wryly, was destroying everything he had created. Suddenly he remembered something his wife used to say: 'Don't try to take the place of the gods,' she'd warned him, 'only they have the right to live in heaven.' But in spite of what his wife had said, he had created a kind of heaven on earth, he thought proudly. Nandgaon had never suffered the random blows of fate that others had had to deal with. No one had had to run away in the middle of the night burdened by a debt he could not repay. He'd given them a village they could be proud of, he'd given them the herd, he'd given them security. He'd even protected them from natural disasters like droughts and floods. What more could he have done for them?

And because of all he'd done, there was kindness in Nandgaon still, he thought, for the people's hearts had not been blighted by misery. Yet they were willing to throw it all away. The thought was like a stab in his heart.

Eventually the bus pulled into the main bus depot at Khandwa. When the headman stepped off the bus he felt lost, disorientated. It was twenty years at least since he'd come to Khandwa and he was surprised at how different it looked. Everything seemed bigger and noisier than he remembered, and smelled worse too. As his eyes got used to the changes he saw that things weren't really all that different. It was just that everything had multiplied, the cement and fertiliser shops reproducing themselves again and again down street after dusty street as far as the eye could see. After he realised this, the headman stopped using his eyes and allowed his memory to guide him. He soon found himself before the collector's office, now renamed the 'Deputy Commissioner's Office' in shiny brass letters. And the same faded yellow paint covered the walls and the pillars, the same hard brown benches decorated the deep verandah. Men sat or lay prone on them, half asleep in the heat. The old wooden fans whirred noisily, drowning out the sounds of the insects busily chewing away at the woodwork.

As he climbed the stairs, he was besieged by memories. This was where he had fought his first great battle – against the government of Madhya Pradesh, and against the government of India – and won. He remembered how he and Mahendra had pored over the law books in Khandwa Public Library. He remembered how excited they'd been when they found a ruling that said that it was for the people to decide whether they wanted a road or not, except if the road was in an area of strategic importance to the integrity and unity of the country. And how happy they'd been when the government, on the advice of the collector of Khandwa, had decided to reroute the road. He remembered walking down the very same steps he was now climbing, feeling invincible. Perhaps it had been inside these very walls that he had first dreamt of creating a village that was different, that would be immune to hazards of fate, like the deputy commissioner's office.

The sense of familiarity left him by the time he came to the door of the office. The high-ceilinged hexagonal ante chamber was crowded with men, sarpanchs like himself for the main part, he guessed. He felt rather surprised by the number that had come and by their youth and their restlessness. The headman took off his slippers and sat on a chair by the door, in order to better study them. Most of the other sarpanchs he noticed, lip curling scornfully, wore shirts over their dhotis and a few even wore trousers. But it went deeper than their clothes; it was in their bodies and faces, in the nervous way they carried themselves and the childish expectancy upon their faces. They did not simply look young – they did not look like men. Even the few that did have the look of farmers seemed to shrink into themselves before their more citified brethren who strutted around the waiting area like peacocks, talking in loud voices, and looking at their watches.

Eunuchs, he thought scornfully after he'd studied them for a while, castrated by their own greed and the government machinery that propped them up. He remembered the sarpanchs he'd known when he was young, adversaries like the sarpanchs of Kesarigaon, Telgaon and Khanaur, and allies like sarpanchs of Saasagaon and Mirpur, men whose presence filled a room, men who would have scorned standing for election. They had been men who knew how to stand firm. These men, he thought scornfully, in spite of their ceaseless motion, couldn't make the room feel full.

The door of the deputy commissioner's office opened and a man wearing the khaki uniform of a government underling appeared holding a register. 'Village, name, number of years in your present position,' he snapped, thrusting the register at the man nearest him. When at last the register came to the headman, he noticed that the longest-standing sarpanch apart from him had only been in the position for eight years. Then the door opened again and the same peon came and grabbed the register out of his hands. 'Come,' he ordered imperiously, walking through the door. The sarpanches jumped to attention and, patting themselves self-consciously, one by one they went inside.

Gopal was the first to enter and so he had ample time to examine the room.

The deputy commissioner's office was in fact divided into two sections, an octagonal meeting room and a rectangular office dominated by a desk on which the deputy commissioner was expected to work when he wasn't listening to people's problems. The two areas were divided by a shabby velvet curtain, torn in places and hastily repaired. Gopal was surprised by the shabbiness of the meeting room. The heavy teak furniture, lovingly polished until the surfaces shone like mirrors, was gone and in its place was aluminium and plastic furniture that gave the room a feeling of emptiness, just like the men that were slowly filling it. The rest of the meeting room was more or less as he remembered it, except that there were now a row of chairs lining the wall where once there had been bookshelves. Portraits of the chief minister, Indira Gandhi and Nehru decorated the east and west walls. Mahatma Gandhi was nowhere to be seen. Beneath the photos there was a refrigerator with a clock on top and in another corner of the room there was a television covered primly with an embroidered lace cloth. A wide screen occupied one end of the room and in the centre a young man was fiddling with a square metal box on a small table. He had thick framed glasses and wore a khadi kurta over his trousers. The headman wondered who he was. He couldn't be a government servant, for he wasn't wearing the uniform. Tea was served and the headman noticed that the young man was served last. Then the curtain separating them from the deputy commissioner was drawn back noisily and the man himself entered, flanked by his staff, a Block Development Officer and the peon who had handed out the register.

The headman stared at the current deputy commissioner curiously. It was the first time he was seeing him and he couldn't help feeling a sharp stab of disappointment. How different this man looked from the tall, lean, soft-spoken one he'd known thirty years ago. That one had kept no television and no refrigerator and no fancy clock for company. All he'd had were books, walls and walls of them. He forced the thirty-year-old image aside and tried to concentrate on the man before him.

Where the other had always been impeccably dressed in a suit, this one was short and plump and wore a brown-coloured safari suit with short sleeves and the top two buttons undone, showing a ruff of hair at his neck. Gold chains gleamed in that thicket of hair and on his thick fingers were a ruby, a diamond and the navratnas*, all of them set in gold. At last the deputy commissioner began to speak. To the headman's surprise, he addressed them in fluent Nimari. 'My colleagues. Thank you for coming here at such a busy time of year. I am indeed grateful,' he began politely. There was a sprinkling of polite claps.

'This year has not been an easy one for any of you. First there came the drought, then the flood and then the failure of the cotton crop itself. I understand what you must be going through, the despair you must feel. I am the son of a farmer myself,' he said smoothly.

A few more clapped at this and two or three even cheered. But the majority sat silent, waiting. They'd heard such speeches before.

'But natural disasters are nothing new to farmers and we farmers are survivors,' the deputy commissioner continued smoothly. 'Only this time, the flood came on top of high input prices and drought. Naturally many of you were devastated, destroyed by the flood and by your loans.' The deputy commissioner paused and looked at his audience meaningfully. He is a politician, Gopal thought in disgust, not a bureaucrat. And the deputy commissioner's next words seemed only to prove him right. 'I believe that it is the duty of a government to help those of its people who are in distress. And it is especially so in the case of farmers. For without you, a country is weak. Hungry soldiers cannot fight, hungry scientists cannot think, hungry workers cannot work.'

This time most clapped enthusiastically.

* Nine jewels of good luck.

The deputy commissioner smiled. 'Your strength is a country's strength,' he continued fluently. 'And this is as much true today when the country is becoming an economic power as it was when we were struggling to find adequate food for all our people.' The deputy commissioner paused, waiting for more applause. But none came so he continued. 'Which is why I have called you here today. Listen, and watch carefully. I am about to unveil a plan that will make all of you so rich that you will never need to take out a loan again.'

They all clapped and he acknowledged them with a satisfied nod of his sleek, well-fed head. He is like one of those noisy city myna birds, Gopal thought suddenly, all glossy brown and black and gold, full of his own importance and never tired of telling everyone who he is.

After the applause had died down the deputy commissioner turned to the young man in the kurta and then pointed to the screen. 'Now pay attention all of you. Dr Manoj Mishra here, who, some of you may already know, will explain how the package works.'

The headman looked at the kurta-clad man in surprise. How had one so young become a doctor? he wondered suspiciously. He looked at the others. He could see from their faces that none were familiar with the young doctor. Suddenly Gopal felt certain they'd walked into a trap. He looked at the kurta-clad man again and bitterness filled his throat. There was going to be no relief packet. For a relief packet of twenty thousand would have had a politician to announce it, not an unknown man.

But before he could act, the lights in the room dimmed and the deputy commissioner went and sat at the back of the room. Looking at the blank white screen Gopal suddenly found himself thinking once again of the other collector, thin, tall and dark, who had ridden for three hours in the hot sun to come and pay his respects at the headman's father's first death anniversary. Would this man do the same for any of the men present in that room? He somehow doubted it. As memory engulfed him, the young man in the kurta began to talk earnestly, explaining, pointing to the screen, but his words no longer made sense to Gopal, they were drowned out by the sound of ghostly brakes screeching.

As the room was gradually steeped in darkness the headman stopped listening to the kurta-clad man. He was behind a barricade again.

It had been surprisingly easy. While he had watched the women bear away the remains of his son, Vilas Rao had grabbed the ladder leaning against the chai shop wall and rushed into the middle of the road. Then he came back and grabbed the table around which they'd been sitting. 'I won't let them come through, I won't,' he shouted, his eyes red and bulging with grief. A truck appeared on the horizon, and they all watched it get bigger, frozen. The truck driver didn't notice the barricade at first or maybe he simply didn't pay attention, imagining it to be a mirage. Then, as he got closer he saw that the obstacle was real and opened fire with his horn. Vilas Rao rolled a bundle of fodder on to the road which he swiftly set alight. The truck blew its horn again. They watched it approach in a squeal of brakes and burning rubber. The truck driver's face was clearly visible in the light of the flaming haystack and the headman could still see the disbelief on it when he realised it was too late. The truck swerved one last time, teetered undecidedly on its left axle before slowly toppling on to its side in front of the barricade.

Everyone rushed onto the road and just as they pulled the stunned truck driver's companion out and were about to go for the driver himself, they heard a muffled boom like a tyre exploding. Then a giant tongue of flame shot out from beneath the bonnet. The villagers fell back to the safety of the restaurant and from there they watched the truck burn in shocked silence. The truck had been carrying steel pipes and rubber tyres, Gopal remembered, which didn't burn but which filled the air with an acrid smell that remained for the rest of the month, the time it took to persuade the government that they were indeed serious, that the road was no longer welcome in Nandgaon.

Suddenly Gopal was shocked out of his memories by a sight so familiar it made no sense.

The Kamdhenu, looking larger than life and twice as alive, was painted across the white screen. He blinked and looked again. It was the Kamdhenu, all lit up and unmistakeable in her black and whiteness. Stunned, he began to listen very carefully to what the young doctor was saying.

'The idea is to help you all to achieve a quantum jump in milk productivity. With this technology cows that gave ten litres of milk will give twenty-five litres, those that gave twenty-five litres will give thirty-five. A litre of milk sells at nine or ten rupees at the government dairy, more if you sell to a private dealer. Which means that you could earn two hundred and fifty to three hundred and fifty rupees a day. With the money you will make you will not need loans or moneylenders.' He stopped suddenly, looking embarrassed, for he must have realised that most of his audience were moneylenders themselves. 'The idea is that your people will no longer have to depend upon the weather for their income,' he corrected himself. 'They will get their livelihood from dairying. Any questions?'

There was silence. None of the sarpanchs looked convinced.

'And what about the money you promised? The twenty thousand rupees?' the headman found himself asking even though he knew there would be no money coming.

There was pin-drop silence. Then the deputy commissioner spoke up from the back. 'Who said that?' No one answered. Those near him looked at Gopal accusingly.

As Gopal was about to raise his hand, the deputy commissioner burst out, 'You greedy lazy lot. You think the government is here simply to forgive your loans so that you can borrow some more and get your daughters married? That animal there is your Kamdhenu. She is your twenty thousand rupees, more even. Not one of you deserve her, but she is yours. For free. I will be paying for it. You people will never have to take another loan in your lives.'

The lights came on and the picture on the screen became no more than a dim outline. The commissioner stood up, clapping. At first no one joined him. Then his two secretaries and the Block Development Officer began to clap and then a few of the sarpanchs, eager to ingratiate themselves with the commissioner, joined them.

But most of the men gathered there didn't move a finger. The headman tried to get a glimpse of their faces but they were all looking down at their hands, as if mesmerised by the emptiness there. Or perhaps they were saying goodbye to the twenty thousand rupees they had imagined in their palms, the headman thought drily.

'Any more questions?' Manoj asked uncomfortably, once the clapping had ended.

No one answered. He waited, then he cleared his throat nervously and said, 'Well, let me tell you how it will be done. You must be wondering about that. It is very simple. I will come to your village on a day of your choosing by motorcycle. In these milk cans,' and here the lights dimmed once more and a picture came on to the screen, 'I have injections of the semen of the world's most productive stock. This will be put into your cows and the result, as you will see,' and once again the picture of the Kamdhenu reappeared, 'will give you a miracle cow that produces two hundred to three hundred times the amount of milk its mother produced.'

How had Ramu met this 'doctor'? the headman wondered. Or were there more? Another thought struck him, one that made him even angrier – why had Ramu lied to the village, letting them think his cow was magic?

'And what will we have to pay for this?' a sceptical voice asked. 'I know all about you, how much you charge poor farmers.'

'You will have to pay me nothing. It is free. The government pays,' Manoj answered.

'But who will pay us to keep the cows?' someone else asked.

Manoj felt confused. 'Pay you?'

'Yes. For our participation,' a fox-faced sarpanch in tight jeans and a t-shirt replied.

'Ah, huh. You will have to ask the commissioner sahib about that. I can only tell you what I can do,' Manoj answered uncomfortably.

'We don't have enough to feed ourselves, what will we feed them with?' a tired-looking sarpanch in a threadbare dhoti cried. 'My village is filled with widows and old men, we have no crops and no fodder. Who is going to look after the animals?'

Manoj looked helplessly at the man. His mouth opened, then shut again. 'Fodder is easy to find, in the forest. . .' he tailed off weakly.

'The forest went a long time ago. Now there are only fields. And those fields are barren,' the sarpanch replied patiently. Manoj turned to the deputy commissioner for help but the deputy commissioner only shrugged. He, too, seemed at a loss. The silence emboldened the others.

'We want jobs, not cows,' another dhoti-clad sarpanch with angry eyes cried.

'We want fair prices for our cotton.'

'We want the interest on our loans to be waived.'

'We want water.'

'We want seeds.'

'We want the road rebuilt. The governor promised us.'

As he listened to the chorus of angry voices Gopal suddenly realised that he wasn't so different from the others. They were also here not because they wanted to be, but because they were desperate. He glared at the picture of the Kamdhenu that was still faintly visible on the screen. That was no devi, nor was it a magic cow. It was a devil created by the same evil forces that had tried to carve a road through the centre of Nandgaon thirty years ago. Nothing had changed.

CHAPTER THIRTY

WHAT HAPPENED NEXT

The return seemed even longer than the way there had been. Though the headman had a window seat this time he barely noticed when they finally fought free of the city. The sight of open fields did nothing to calm him. His mind kept returning to the scene at the deputy commissioner's office, and he swung between elation and despair.

'That is not a cow, that is a monster,' Gopal had announced, standing up and pointing his finger at the screen.

The deputy commissioner had looked surprised.

'Who are you?' he'd demanded. 'I don't like troublemakers. Don't think I can't handle people like you.'

'I am the Patel of Nandgaon, not a troublemaker,' Gopal said proudly. 'And I know that what you propose will be the end of our cattle. And without our cattle, our villages will die too.'

'Rubbish. You talk like the ignorant villager that you are!' the deputy commissioner spluttered.

The headman bowed his head mockingly. 'I may be an ignorant villager, Sahib, but I know some things about cattle. This land is a hard land. The soil is not rich, the rock lies close to the surface. In winter icy winds blow, carrying away the topsoil; in summer the hot winds take away our water. Yet our cattle survive.' Gopal turned to look at the others. 'Why? Because they belong to this soil, they come from it. And just as each village itself is different, so are its cattle. They may not produce much milk, but they can bear the incredible heat of the summer, and the terrible cold of the winter nights. Where else in India are there such extremes except in this madhya desh*? They can eat junglee herbs, grass that is old and withered or nothing at all – and yet plough an entire village's fields. They can go without water for a day and a half at a stretch and still give us milk. That is what our cattle are made of. It is their milk that gives us men the strength to plough our fields. Once mixed with foreign stock, will our animals milk retain that power?' he asked finally.

'Milk is milk,' Manoj lied glibly. 'The animals you will have will be of better stock. They will give you so much milk, you will be able to sell the surplus and become rich. Why, one cow could give you as much as a lakh of rupees per year.'

'How do you know what is better and what isn't?' the headman cried, turning on him. 'Our herds are our village. I would not trade who we are for a fistful of rupees.'

'So you prefer to remain poor?' the deputy commissioner jeered. 'That will make the government very happy.'

'If being poor is what it takes to remain who we are,' the headman replied fiercely.

'I doubt if the rest of your village feels as you do,' Manoj sneered. So this was the headman who had refused to meet him!

'What do you know of my village?' the headman answered, turning to him.

'I have been there,' Manoj replied. He added cruelly, 'It is a very poor village.'

The blood filled the headman's head so fast he thought it would burst. How dare the young doctor make disparaging remarks about Nandgaon! How dare he sneak into it like a thief without even having the courtesy to ask permission first.

* middle country

He took a step towards him, raising his fist.

But immediately the peon who'd passed around the register jumped up and grabbed his hand. 'Don't you dare. You will be put into prison,' he hissed.

Gopal stumbled and fell against the kurta-clad man's knees. Immediately two policemen who had been standing on either side of the door rushed forward and grabbed him.

'That's enough now, get out,' one growled as they pushed him out of the room.

Gopal's mind went dark as he remembered how they had hustled him out. In the old days, no policeman would have dared to touch a patel.

The two policemen had thrown him roughly on to the pavement and for a long moment he had remained there, too stunned to move. The other sarpanchs had filed past, careful to avoid him. He would never forget the sight of those feet, the paan-stained pavement and the stray cow that watched him with a faint astonishment in her eyes. Then he'd heard someone say, 'Dada, are you all right? Let me help you.' A hand grabbed him firmly by the elbow and pulled him up. He turned to see who it was and was surprised to find that it was the rat-faced young sarpanch who had wanted to know if he would be paid for attending the meeting.

'I am fine,' Gopal had said stiffly, pulling away.

But the young man refused to let go. 'Where do you have to go? I'll take you,' he said.

'Why? Why would you do that?' the headman asked, surprised.

'I admired what you said inside there. No one tells the government they are wrong.'

'That is not true,' the headman replied. 'I did, thirty years ago.'

'You did?' The young sarpanch looked sceptical. 'But times have changed now. You should be careful.'

'Careful of what? I don't need the government.'

'To farm you need money these days. And they are the only ones that have any to give.' Seeing the headman's face, he adroitly changed the subject. 'You must be going to the bus stop, Dada. Let me drop you. My motorcycle is parked just around the corner.'

A motorcycle! Gopal had never ridden on one. But he let himself be led away by the younger man all the same. 'Are they paying you to take me away from in front of the building?' he asked suspiciously as they turned the corner.

The young sarpanch laughed. 'Dada, what are you saying? I would never accept that. You are like my grandfather. A man of courage. I could never have done what you did.' He climbed astride a large black Enfield, somewhat battered, and invited Gopal to sit behind him. The headman did so, feeling both nervous and excited.

'You cannot say what you want because you like money too much. All you young men have that problem. It is the sickness of the city. Come to my village and I will cure you,' the headman said.

The sarpanch laughed again. 'What can one do, Dada? The world is made of money these days, either you have it or you don't. The politicians won't let us farmers have it. They want to keep the countryside poor so that they can keep the money for themselves.'

'Forget the politicians, beta,' Gopal snapped. 'The world is made up of soil and water. Those are the only things that matter. We farmers are the guardians of the earth. Nothing can take that away from us.'

The young sarpanch chuckled. 'Are, Dada, you are too much, you really do remind me of my grandfather. I am so happy I met you.'

'Is your grandfather dead?' Gopal asked.

'Yes. How did you know?' the young man answered.

The headman didn't reply. He looked at the shops that lined the street, at the people crowding the pavement, at the over-flowing gutters beneath their feet, and was glad to be leaving it all behind. He did not belong to the pushing, impatient world of the young sarpanch, a world that turned men into pup-pets.

At the bus stop the sarpanch had insisted on buying his ticket for him and getting him a window seat. Overwhelmed, Gopal leaned out of the window to thank the young man.

'Don't mention it,' the sarpanch replied, waving. 'I would have taken you back to your village if I could. But it is too far away for me; I have things to buy in the city before I go back to my village.'

'You have already done too much. Thank you,' Gopal said awkwardly. He was not used to thanking others, especially those half his age.

'It was nothing,' the young man answered. 'It was a pleasure to serve someone so like my grandfather. By the way, please don't try to oppose the deputy commissioner. This time your white hair saved you. Next time he will have you thrown out and another man elected in your place in no time, and then you too will be drinking milk made in Khandwa. That is devel-opment for you.'

'Not while I live,' the headman said grimly. 'I will never drink foreign milk. And neither should you, or you will forget who you are.'

The bus set Gopal down in the middle of the road. He got down stiffly, his knees obeying reluctantly and began to walk the last three kilometres to the village. By the time he got there a late sun was setting over the fields, turning the heads of late ripening wheat a dull red-gold. Gopal stared at the endless expanse of fields and felt his body grow big again. The differ-ence between city and country was brutal, he reflected. In the country the eye could travel freely for miles. In the city, space was gobbled up by the many needs of the humans that occupied it. And yet it never truly seemed to belong to them, gobbling them up instead. How grateful he was that he didn't have to live in a city.

At last the tall spire of the temple came into view. Inside the temple, the children would be waiting impatiently for Saraswati Rane to arrive, so they could blow the conch and ring the bells and sing 'Om Jaya Jagadish, Hare'. Then Saraswati Rane would light the lamps and offer aarti to the Lord, and afterwards give the children the sweet prasaad they'd been waiting for. Tears came into Gopal's eyes but he blinked them away hastily. Nandgaon would be saved, he vowed.

When he entered the village, he found the place strangely quiet. Children stared at him with frightened eyes and ran away. Women quickly disappeared behind closed doors. Only the old men with watery eyes greeted him. No one stopped him to ask how his trip had gone. Gopal hurried on, ignoring the hurt that pulsed within him. Soon the village would be set to rights. He passed the new temple, shining in the twilight, the children a dark mass at the door. He noticed Saraswati Rane climbing the stairs with his puja tray.

'Saraswati Rane,' he called out.

The priest turned around, squinting into the dark. 'Patelji, how was it? Did you get anything?' he asked.

'Enlightenment,' Gopal replied cryptically.

'In Khandwa?' Saraswati Rane asked quizzically.

The headman gave a short bark of laughter. 'Indeed. I received it from none other than our commissioner sahib.'

The priest looked mystified but smiled nervously at the headman all the same. 'Then you are as usual luckier than I am. I'd better go and ask the gods for enlightenment. Maybe today they will be kind to me.'

'You should not ask for enlightenment, Saraswati Rane, you

should steal it from them. Your problem is that you are without courage,' the headman said.

Saraswati Rane bowed his head to hide his surprise. The headman never spoke like this usually. He wondered what it was that the headman had learnt in Khandwa. 'Do we come to see you this evening as usual?' he asked, looking up once he'd mastered his surprise.

'Yes,' the headman replied, 'and make sure everyone comes. I have news for you.'

Gopal then went by Govind Rao's shop, tucked into the side of the temple. Govind Rao was sitting outside.

'Are, Patelji, back already?' he squeaked, getting up hastily.

'Of course. The city seems to get closer each time I go there,' the headman replied.

'And was it a successful trip?'

'Oh yes, old friend, very successful,' the headman replied, staring hard at Govind Rao. 'Come up this evening and I will tell you all about it.'

Govind Rao nodded, but without any enthusiasm.

But this time Gopal didn't care. By tomorrow everything would be different. He remembered the words of the pant-clad sarpanch who had dropped him to the bus stop. 'Thirty-one years!' he'd exclaimed when Gopal told him how long he'd been headman. 'Do you have people or animals in your village?'

'Why?' Gopal had asked, bridling. 'You think that just because we don't dress like monkeys, we are animals?'

'No, not at all. I was complimenting your village. In my experience, only animals are that loyal.'

Turning a corner, Gopal came upon the heavily-pregnant Laxmi leaning against his compound wall. He stopped short, not knowing what to do. 'You!' he exclaimed.

'Patelji!' Laxmi straightened hurriedly.

'You,' the headman hissed. 'Don't call me Patelji. I know what you've been up to. I know everything. And by tomorrow so will the village. Your power over Nandgaon is over.'

To the headman's surprise, Laxmi looked unsurprised. 'Perhaps it is your power that will be finished, Patelji,' she said quietly.

Astonishment deprived the headman of words. No one had ever spoken to him like that. Then the ugliness of the Kamdhenu flashed before his eyes. 'You stupid bitch, do you think insulting me will get you anywhere?' he said harshly.

Laxmi didn't answer, staring down at her feet. But the headman wasn't fooled.

'Did you think you could fool us forever?' he continued. 'By tomorrow you will be the most hated person in Nandgaon. If I were you I would leave quietly tonight. And take the animals too.'

At the mention of the animals he saw fear enter her face but she overcame it. 'I will not leave, Patelji,' she said quietly. 'I will tell the village my side of the story.'

'And what is that? That you allowed a stranger to come and pollute your animal with foreign sperm?' In spite of himself he was intrigued. Did she really think the village would forgive her so easily?

'No. I will tell them that it's because of you that we lied. We never wanted to but you forced us to with your rules – "nothing must come from the outside and nothing must go out" – you made things impossible for us, just as you do for everyone else.'

Suddenly Gopal lost his temper. 'Don't try to put the blame on me,' he roared. 'You had no business allowing that doctor to do his dirty work. As for letting everyone think that that ugly creature was a goddess, do you think anyone will forget that, let alone forgive it? And what about when they realise that you have corrupted the herd with impure, foreign blood.

How do you think they will swallow that?'

'Corrupt? We have made the herd better,' Laxmi replied haughtily.

'Better? You don't know what you have done, you foolish woman,' Gopal exclaimed. 'You have planted the seeds of greed in every household. Nandgaon will never again know peace.'

'Peace?' Laxmi sneered, her face twisting into a snarl. 'I have freed Nandgaon from your tyranny, Patelji. That is what I have done.'

'Brave words, Laxmibai,' the headman answered calmly enough, though inwardly he was seething. 'You would make a good sarpanch, but never a good patel. For to be a patel you must have honour. And honour is something no woman can understand. Your kind always sacrifices everything to necessity.'

'Honour?' Laxmi's eyes flashed. 'You call the murder of a defenceless animal honourable? You call keeping an entire village poor and isolated honourable? You call depriving people of a road, a proper school and electricity honourable? You made sure that you were the only employer, the only source of money for people's children's weddings, the only person who people could turn to when they were hungry or their children were without milk. You made them your prisoners, Patelji. Now they will be able to be free. What you cannot bear is that a mere woman and a junglee cow could destroy your power.'

Gopal was silent. For the second time she had surprised him. Finally he said, 'You who come from another village, have you not seen how different Nandgaon is? Have you ever known anyone say no to another? Have you ever seen a man look at someone else's wife? Have you ever seen anyone steal from another's field?' he asked quietly. When she didn't answer he continued, 'You are clearly no ordinary woman, Laxmibai, I admire you. But have you in your freedom stopped to consider what Nandgaon will lose?' He paused to let his words sink in.

Then he continued.

'Imagine that your plan succeeds and everyone in Nandgaon has lots of extra milk and sells it outside. They will use their money to buy radios and TVs and motorcycles. And they will spend their time counting their money. The women will have to work even harder cutting grass for their animals – you know how much one Kamdhenu eats – and they will have to spend longer going further and further into the forest to find it, and they will be exhausted, losing their youth and their looks even faster. While the men – money burning in their pockets – will do nothing but drink. Just as it has happened in the other villages. No one will help each other, no one will share milk with a neighbour or be with them when their mother dies. Instead of laughter in the streets, you will have silence, instead of love between husbands and wives, there will be bitterness, and instead of compassion there will be envy. That is the Nandgaon you will make.'

When Laxmi still didn't say anything, he continued, 'Surely you remember? After all, you grew up in such a place, Laxmibai. Or did you love those who tortured your father so much that you wanted to remake Nandgaon in their image? If you have any love for this village, take your animals and go away.'

At last Laxmi looked up and stared into his eyes. 'Time will tell, Patelji, whether you are right and I am wrong,' she said slowly. 'But what I do know is that your days in this village are numbered.'

She spoke with such conviction that in spite of himself the headman felt a chill hand clutch his heart. Then the anger came. His hand itched to hit her, but he could not bring himself to touch a pregnant woman. 'We shall see, Laxmibai. We shall see,' he said briefly, walking past her.

Gopal was still trembling when he entered his outer courtyard. To his amazement there was no one there.

'Savitri, Gajendra,' he called. 'Subhadra, Ganesh,' he called his second son and daughter-in-law. Nobody appeared. Not even Kalyanbhai, his personal servant.

At last a menial came rushing out from the kitchen, wiping his hands on his dhoti.

'Patelji, you are back so soon!' he stammered.

'Where is everyone?' the headman snapped.

The servant didn't answer, looking scared.

'Call them here now,' the headman ordered, then changed his mind. 'No, wait! First get me water and a fresh set of clothes!'

The servant scuttled away. No one else arrived. The same servant returned with water and proceeded inexpertly to wash his feet. Irritated, Gopal took the brass lota from him and washed his face and hands himself. The dust of the city washed away, the headman felt slightly better. The house, though empty, was the same. Somewhere inside the house he heard a child cry out and a woman hurriedly hush it. A servant, probably one of the new ones he'd hired after the flood. He stared critically around the courtyard. It looked as he had left it that morning. Nothing had changed. He stood up and let the servant help him into his clothes. Then he carefully applied a fresh tikka on his forehead. The thought of a doctor putting his hands into the sacred interior of a cow, fooling the poor animal into thinking that he was going to bring her comfort and then infecting her with the seed of a foreign breed, made him feel sick. No one in Nandgaon would allow it. How was such a doctor different from a thief and a cheat, stealing first from the bull and then cheating the cow? He shuddered, feeling somehow unclean. 'Wash my feet one more time,' he ordered the servant, 'The dirt of the city is not so easy to remove.'

After he was ready, the same servant led him through the house to the grain yard at the back. This was where in his father's time, the grain had been brought, measured, sorted and dried before it was stored. In the covered passage-way leading to the yard there had been a giant set of weighing scales suspended from the ceiling. On this the children of the house had swung. Gopal remembered how sometimes his father would come out of his room at the end of the afternoon and give a delighted Gopal a few mighty pushes.

The door at the end of the passageway was slightly ajar, but when he went through he almost fell backwards in surprise.

There they all were. Not just the household but half of the village as well. But they had their backs to him and so none noticed that he had arrived. He pushed his way through the press of bodies till he was in the front.

'What is happening here?' Gopal asked when at last he was so hemmed in by bodies he couldn't move.

He got no answer. Everyone was listening intently to the noises that were emerging from behind the cow shed.

'What is happening there?' the headman demanded, tapping his neighbour on the shoulder.

'Shambhu,' Darbari Lal the barber replied absently, not turning around.

'Shhh,' someone whispered warningly, as those around Gopal realised who was amongst them.

'Are you mad?' the headman demanded. 'Has everyone here gone mad? No one in my household would allow that father-less creature to mount Nandini.'

At this Darbari Lal turned and his face froze as he realised who he'd been talking to.

'Patelji!' he exclaimed. 'Forgive me, I did not know it was you.'

'What is that dreadful animal doing in my cowshed?' the headman demanded.

Darbari Lal looked ashamed. 'He is mounting Nandini,' he answered, staring at the ground. Unable to bear the headman's scrutiny he turned and he tapped the man in front of him on the shoulder. 'Are, bhai, make way, let our Patelji through.'

People took up Darbari's call and the press of bodies parted to let the headman through.

When he got to the front the headman saw that a cordon of jute bags had been created around the cow shed and the earth within the cordon was scarred with hoof marks and streaks of something wet and dark and suspiciously like blood. But the space itself was empty.

'How long has this been going on?' he demanded.

'Since this afternoon. Then not half an hour ago, they came out and went behind the cowshed. They had been fighting,' Bicchoo answered, coming around behind the headman's left shoulder.

'Bicchoo? What are. . . Why?' the headman choked in his rage.

'What am I doing here? Maharaj, I have come to witness the marriage of earth and heaven. Like everyone else, I came to celebrate. Congratulations, Patelji. Your cows will soon be the best in all Nimaar.'

The headman's head spun. He looked around at the press of faces staring eagerly at the cowshed and said, 'Tell them to leave. Tell them all to leave at once. I want this madness to end. You have all been made fools of! That is no child of a devi but the bastard son of a foreign bull.'

No one said anything. They looked at him with concern in their faces, as one would look at a man gone mad with grief. No one moved. So the headman said less self-assuredly, 'Where is Gajen? Where is Gajendra my son? He will listen to me, he will understand. Find me Gajendra.'

No one moved.

'What is going on? Find my son, and get that bastard animal away from Nandini,' he cried.

Still no one seemed prepared to move. At last Bicchoo said, 'Patelji, why don't you sit down? I will send someone to find

him. You must be tired. We didn't expect you back before
nightfall.'

'A chair, a chair.' The call went down the line of onlookers
and like an answer a chair suddenly appeared and was passed
solicitously from hand to hand. The headman sat down uneasily.
He looked around. Where was his son?

'Here they come, here they come.' The cry flew from mouth
to mouth as the two animals suddenly burst from behind the
shed. In the lead was the headman's own Nandini. She looked
terrible. White froth flecked her chin and cheeks and dribbled
out of a corner of her mouth, touched here and there with
pink. Dark red blood oozed from scratches on her sides and
she panted loudly as she ran. Behind her came Shambhu who,
though twice her size, was in no better condition. His chest
heaved, his stomach and chest bled in several places. Dark
patches of perspiration covered his skin.

The headman would have liked to cry out like the others,
but horror numbed his mind, stilling his tongue. Seeing the
two together in that limited space, both outlined starkly against
the mud walls of the cowshed, they looked like mirror opposites, black versus white, evil versus good, a portrait of the epic
battle being waged in Nandgaon. Nandini with her enormous
hump and queenly dome, her gently tapering nose with the
elegantly flared nostrils, her long sleek back and endless legs
looked noble, elegant, as finely crafted as a statue. Compared
to her Shambhu seemed crude and brutish, a hastily executed
sketch of blind muscle-power, drawn by a roadside artist. Where
Nandini's legs were slender and shapely, her knees gently
rounded, Shambhu's fore and hind legs were as thick and knobly
as tree trunks and though not short, not very long either. As
for his head, set upon his massive shoulders (undoubtedly his
best feature, along with his muscular rear), it looked tiny, an
unformed lump that seemed scarcely capable of thought. His
eyes, inflamed with lust, looked particularly inhuman, only

serving to draw attention to the largeness of his sex, which stood ridiculously inflamed and ready, even though the object of its attentions was unwilling.

Suddenly Nandini stumbled. A sigh of anticipation came from the onlookers. The headman leaned forward tensely, willing her to get up. Shambhu, sensing victory, paused uncertainly.

Then Nandini became aware of her audience and, raising her chin, came on to her feet. A sigh escaped the audience. The headman sat back, relieved. Shambhu, confused by the sudden change in his victim's position, first hung back and then, as if regretting his lost opportunity, rushed pell-mell at her. But Nandini was too quick for him. By the time he'd got to where she'd been, Nandini was already halfway across the yard. He stopped at the fence not far from where the headman sat, shuffling his feet undecidedly, clearly distracted by the crowd. Seeing her chance, Nandini turned abruptly and ran straight at him, her small horns pointed squarely at Shambhu's side. Hearing her approach, Shambhu turned at the last moment but not quickly enough. An ugly red gash appeared on his jet black skin.

The crowd gasped. 'Look how smart she is, our Nandini!' someone cried.

'Of course she's smart, she's a woman,' another added.

Seeing the damage she'd inflicted, Nandini did a quick about-turn and came to a stop not far from her opponent, her body angled diagonally to his. She looked up, her head at an angle, watching him. Then, spotting a tiny bit of green that had somehow managed to grow in the dry desert of the yard, she trotted over and caught the plant neatly in her mouth. The headman, leaning forward in his chair, could feel her satisfaction, and felt elation well up inside himself. There was a goddess protecting Nandgaon after all. Surely the whole village could now see the inferiority of Ramu's animal. It was not made to be leader. As for Nandini, though she was half his size, she had proved her superior skill as a fighter and her intelligence too.

They all watched Nandini, wondering what she would do next. She didn't move. Her large almond eyes glazed over. Her jaw moved.

Move, move, the headman urged silently.

Shambhu took a few undecided steps towards her and snorted threateningly. His chest heaved; he panted as loudly as a steam engine. Blood from his wounds snaked their way down his stomach and made puddles on the beaten ground of the yard. He banged his massive foreleg on the ground once, twice, then he too suddenly lost interest and turned away. The onlookers sighed, sensing the fight was over.

'Water, water, they must be given water,' the headman shouted suddenly, realising that both animals were exhausted.

'Water! Water for the animals.' Others took up the cry.

Water was brought and both animals drank long and thirstily. Then they looked around expectantly, searching for their owners, keeping their backs carefully to each other. The mating contest was over for the day.

Not waiting for the gate to be opened, Ramu vaulted over the fence. The headman almost didn't recognise him. Gone was the skinny boy with arms and legs too long for his body, and in his place was a tall handsome man radiating that special something that made one instinctively trust him – contentment. Then, through the gate, the headman's own son appeared. Short, skinny and self-effacing. He went up to Nandini and grabbed the short rope dangling from her neck. The cow, angry at being interrupted while she was drinking snorted and tossed her head, one slim horn slicing Gajendra's dhoti. Gajendra ran undignifiedly towards Ramu, taking shelter behind him. The difference between the two men could not have been greater.

The headman shut his eyes. He knew what the others were

seeing. Suddenly he wished that it had been the other way around, that Ramu with his fine shoulders and open face had been his son. He opened his eyes. Gajendra, much to Gopal's annoyance, had disappeared. A servant entered and led the now docile Nandini away. Gopal got up and pushed his way through the crowd.

As he walked past the familiar faces, he was careful not to look at any of them. He didn't want to see the pity in their faces, or the glee. What had possessed his son to arrange such a comedy? The thought of that black devil's spawn entering his lovely Nandini made him feel sick. Thank God his Nandini had had more sense.

Out of the corners of his eyes he saw Ramu leading his bull out. The giant animal was following him with his head down, as meek as a lamb. They were followed by a swarm of adoring supporters. 'Ramu,' he called out, unable to stop himself. 'Come here.'

Ramu was still anxiously examining his animal's wounds and so he didn't immediately register that it was the headman himself who was calling him.

But Bicchoo, who had appeared magically beside Ramu, prodded the latter and whispered into his ear.

Ramu jerked to attention, his eyes widening in surprise. He handed Shambhu's rope to the man nearest him and ran to the headman. 'You called me, Patelji?' he asked hesitantly, forgetting in his anxiety to touch the headman's feet.

'So now you have even forgotten how to greet your Patel, Ramu?' the headman asked, looking at him quizzically.

Alarm and embarrassment flooded Ramu's face. He tried to touch the headman's feet but the headman moved away. 'No, stop,' the headman said. 'You don't know the meaning of respect, so why pretend? I am sure this. . . this tamasha* was your idea,

* spectacle

447

your way to shame my family while I was far away.'

'Patelji, what are you saying?' Ramu cried. 'You are like a father to me. How could I ever think of doing something like that? I thought. . .' He shut up suddenly, realising that anything he said would only get him into more trouble.

But the headman wasn't going to let him off so easily. 'You thought what? Tell us.'

Ramu flushed but said nothing.

'Come on. Tell everyone here what thoughts light up that peanut-sized brain of yours.' Gopal taunted.

'All right, I'll tell you what I was told.' Ramu stood up straight and faced the headman. With a sense of disbelief, the headman realised that Ramu was taller than he was.

'I was told you wanted this, Patelji. That's why I agreed. In spite of what you have done to me.'

'Done to you?' the headman's eyes bulged. 'What haven't I done for you? I gave you shelter, food, clothes, I brought you up. And even when you disobeyed me and married that outsider, I stood by you. I let her stay, I made her welcome. And when you foolishly brought home that junglee cow, I supported you then too. I was your only friend then. But you forgot that, you forgot that everything you are is because of me. That you can stand before me today, even that is because I protected you all this time. And this is how you repay me?'

'But I have done nothing, Patelji. I have always loved you,' Ramu protested.

'Liar.' Gopal cut him off. 'You have lied to me and to the village.'

'Patelji!' Ramu fell to his knees and grabbed the headman's hands. 'Patelji, what are you saying? What have I done?'

'Done?' the headman roared. 'What haven't you done? First you brought that troublemaker, that unlucky star into our village as your wife. Then you go and pick up a junglee cow.' He turned to the others briefly and then looked at Ramu again.

'And then . . .you tell them what you did. I find it too horrible to speak of. Tell them with your own mouth how you have brought shame on our village.'

He stopped, waiting for Ramu to speak.

But instead of Ramu, it was Govind Rao who spoke, Govind Rao who had been standing discreetly on the edge of the crowd. 'Patelji, you can hardly hold Ramu responsible for marrying,' he protested. 'Or for wanting to keep cows. Isn't rescuing a cow like rescuing someone's mother?'

The headman could scarcely believe his ears. Govind Rao, his childhood friend, was taking Ramu's side in front of half the village!

'Tell them,' he hissed at Ramu, refusing to look at Govind Rao. 'Look at them in the face, all these newfound friends of yours, and tell them the truth about the Kamdhenu.'

When Ramu said nothing, looking steadfastly at his feet instead, the headman elaborated. 'Tell them about the doctor then. How did you meet him? Tell them what he did to your junglee. Tell them about how the doctor injected the seed of an unknown foreign animal inside your junglee. And tell them how you lied to the village, how you went back to the same doctor and made him create yet another monster, this one.' The headman stopped, panting. His heart felt as if it would burst out of his chest but at last he felt clean. He wiped his sweating forehead with the edge of his towel and then stared deliberately at each of the faces present there. At last his eyes returned to Ramu. 'Isn't that right?' he asked softly, then added, well aware that everyone who could was listening, 'I know everything about what you did.'

Suddenly an anonymous voice piped up (later the headman was certain it had been Keshu Ram's), 'Is that why you killed her then?'

'I did not kill the Kamdhenu,' the headman replied truthfully, turning to the others. 'I don't know who did. It may have been

449

an accident. But you are all better off without that creature. She was no devi but a devil.'

Too late he realised his mistake. This was not the way he had meant to tell them.

'Enough of this madness!' he roared, banging his stick on the ground. 'Do you really think that I, your headman, would stoop to such a thing?'

'But, Patelji, who else would want to kill our Kamdhenu? No one else in the village is so fortunate as to be able to do without luck,' Bicchoo said smoothly, appearing suddenly beside Ramu also. 'Isn't that why you built the temple, in order to make sure that God forgave your sin?' he continued, his words filled with venom. 'We may be poor but we are not fools, Patelji.'

'Don't call me that!' the headman spat, looking with scorn at the hate glittering in Bicchoo's eyes. 'You are wrongly named, oh Bicchoo. A scorpion is far less dangerous than you. You should have been called a viper.' Then the headman turned and looked at Ramu and to those watching it seemed as if his face grew gentler, almost sad.

'Ramu,' he called, 'do you remember when you were a boy, how I beat those boys who dared to tease you because you had no father? Do you remember what I said to you then?' When Ramu didn't answer and it was clear from the expression on his face that he remembered well, the headman continued, 'Do you think I could kill something you loved?'

Around him, Gopal could hear the sigh of indrawn breath. 'Tell us Ramu, tell us what you think. You are the best judge.' He ignored Ramu's mute plea for help and looked instead at the crowd, trying to sense their feelings, wanting to catch the instant when the tide would turn in his favour.

'Tell us, Ramu. The whole village is waiting,' the headman taunted.

But Ramu simply continued to look beseechingly at the

headman, and then fell at Gopal's feet. Suddenly the crowd parted and Laxmi came to stand beside Ramu, helping him get to his feet.

Suddenly resolution filled Ramu's face and he said slowly, clearly, 'Patelji, even if it was you, I don't care, you are still my Patelji. Please punish me as you will.'

For a second those gathered there were speechless. Even Laxmi was momentarily deprived of words. She looked at her husband, shock and horror in her eyes. Then cheers burst forth from the crowd. 'Wah, wah, well said, Ramubhai,' they cried, crowding around him and cutting him off from the headman.

Out of pity or out of a nagging sense of guilt, no one watched the headman as he turned and walked away, his body shrinking into itself. If only Ramu hadn't been so idiotically noble, if only Ramu had shown some spite, Gopal thought regretfully. He paused at the door that led into the house and looked back. The grain yard still seethed with bodies but he could not make out their faces. In the gathering darkness, he thought he saw a flame leave him and float into the crowd, towards where Ramu had been standing and where the crowd was thickest. The battle was over and he, surprisingly, was the loser. Soon there would be nothing left of the Nandgaon he had made. He hurried into his house.

The headman found his son hiding in the kitchen.

'What have you done?' he demanded of his son. 'Have you gone mad? Or have you no respect for your father?'

His son turned around immediately, spilling some of the lassi he had been drinking on his immaculate silk kurta. 'Of course I respect you Baba, but there was no other way,' he said calmly, wiping away the liquid with his handkerchief.

'What do you mean. no other way? What are you talking about?' the headman demanded.

'How else was I to convince the village that you had not in fact poisoned the Kamdhenu?'

The headman felt betrayal whisper in his ear. Obviously his son had planned it this way well in advance.

'You call allowing that hideous monster to put his seed in our Nandini a solution?' he demanded. His eyes narrowed and he looked at his son in disbelief. A thought struck him: his son was too weak to have planned this himself. 'You know who did it, don't you? You are protecting someone, aren't you?'

His son looked up, surprise and alarm in his eyes. Then he looked down again and refused to say anything. 'It's someone from this house, isn't it? Who is it?' he demanded, stepping up to his son and grabbing him by the shoulders. 'Tell me at once so I can clear my name.'

Gajendra said nothing, staring at the ground between them as if the answer was written there.

'Tell me. At once,' the headman said again, thumping his stick impatiently on the ground.

His son continued to say nothing.

'You won't tell me?' Gopal's eyes narrowed. 'It must be someone important. Someone of our blood.'

When his son still wouldn't say he banged his stick on the ground again. 'You don't have to speak, just nod your head, Gajendra,' he shouted.

And when his son still wouldn't answer, he added cruelly, 'You probably killed it yourself,' though he knew it wasn't true. His son's problem was that he was too gentle, too kind. And loyal. It was the latter that hurt the most, seeing what was best in his son used against him. All of a sudden the mystery ceased to be unsolvable. 'It was her, wasn't it?' he said quietly, seeing in his mind's eye the worried face of his daughter-in-law.

His son fell at his feet, his shoulders shaking with unshed tears.

'She didn't know what she was doing,' he whispered. 'She is only a woman.'

Gopal said nothing. He put a hand on his son's head and stared at the wall in front of him, at a calendar picture of the goddess of wealth, Laxmi, hanging there. When had it come into the house? Why hadn't he noticed it earlier? He'd make them get rid of it tomorrow. He didn't want any more money-worshipping in his house. 'She did the right thing,' he whispered. 'She didn't know it perhaps, but she did the right thing. The one who is at fault is that witch Laxmibai.' He looked down at his son's bent head and put a hand on his shoulder, 'Do what you have to do, my son,' he said wearily.

CHAPTER THIRTY-ONE

THE END OF THE ROAD

The next day the villagers woke earlier than usual. Few had slept well. Half the village was angry with Ramu for having lied to them about the Kamdhenu. The other half had already forgiven him. A few still couldn't believe what the headman had told them and stubbornly clung to the belief that it was the headman who was the liar.

Either way, all of Nandgaon was united in their conviction that the fate of Nandgaon would be decided that day. For somehow the word had spread that the 'mating' would continue, only everyone knew that it was no longer a mating, but a contest in which the prize was Nandgaon itself. If Nandini prevailed, then the status quo would remain. If, on the other hand, Shambhu won, then everything would change. So that morning, mothers hurriedly prepared their children for school, rushing through their tasks. The men went early to the fields or not at all and all morning the chai shop was busier than it had ever been except on festival days, people huddling in small groups, talking in whispers about the fight to come. Then after lunch, the villagers bathed and dressed with care and then one by one or in groups of three or four, they made their way to the headman's grain yard.

The grain yard filled up quickly. There was much talk and nervous speculation about the outcome of the fight. Some, die-hard followers of the Kamdhenu, believed Nandini would give way that day. Others were sure she wouldn't. Ramu arrived first. A cheer went up in parts of the crowd when they saw Shambhu. He was an impressive sight. His jet black coat gleamed, his muscles rippled beneath their silken covering, the very foreignness of his body shape inspired confidence. Shambhu let out a high-pitched squeal when he saw all the people. Ramu sought to calm him, but Shambhu, sensing the tension in the air, wouldn't listen. He pawed the ground with his giant hooves and swung his head from left to right, as if he were impatient to impale some poor creature on his horns. Someone had repainted them red and sharpened their ends, and so, though they weren't very long, they looked cruel.

Ramu, feeling the rope in his hand jerk and pull, also grew nervous. He gripped hard and shortened it quickly. Shambhu turned his head and gave him a cold look. Ramu stopped, the rope almost slipping from his hands. This was not the animal he knew. He also recognised that Shambhu was sending him a message: once the fight was over, Shambhu would give the orders. Shivering, he led Shambhu into the centre of the field. A gasp of awe went through the crowd. Someone shouted 'Long live Shambhu' and others swiftly took it up. A wave of excitement swept the crowd, who began clapping their hands and stamping their feet as they chanted Shambhu's name. Like Ramu, a few moments earlier, it was as if they were seeing another animal, not the lovable but useless bull-child of a much loved cow, but the incarnation of man's power over nature.

Perhaps the crowd was so blinded by the alien magnificence of Shambhu that they never saw the headman's servant enter the arena with Nandini. So to many of the onlookers, when Nandini appeared, haloed by afternoon sunlight, she seemed a shining white angel at once fragile and filled with the strength of compassion, a vision of feminine endurance and grace.

The animals surprised them, the match lasting all afternoon until sunset. Nandini, as if responding to a threat that was primordial, fought with courage and brilliance, as well as guile. Shambhu, for his part, fought well too. Gone was the diffidence, the youth. In its place was mature power and a concentrated fury. But Nandini countered each attack. Then she would wait, barely out of breath, as Shambhu, flanks heaving, came at her again. For though he was the more powerful, she was lighter and faster on her feet, and each time he rose up on his hind legs and tried to push her down, she neatly side-stepped, coming at Shambhu from the side with her much longer horns. Shambhu howled in pain and his audience gasped. He turned around and his face seemed to swell, his eyes retreated further into the prehistoric folds of his face. But the pain made him more cautious. He moved away from Nandini and turned away from her. At first she watched him tensely, her ears twitching at the slightest sound. Then after a while temptation got the better of her and she bent her head to nibble the fresh grass at her feet.

Shambhu pretended to be disinterested and began to nibble at the grass himself. The onlookers let out a long sigh of disappointment. For a while neither animal took much notice of the other, and the onlookers grew bored. Conversations sprang up like weeds and no one noticed how Shambhu inched closer to Nandini, pushing her inexorably towards the corner. Suddenly he rushed at her and knocked her over, then stepped back and let her find her feet. But before she could regain her composure, he rushed her again, giving her no choice but to press herself against the fence and stare at him defiantly.

That was the image that everyone in the audience went to bed with that night, Nandini pressed against the fence, helpless and vulnerable, as Shambhu ran at her again and again, taking with him little bits of white skin as souvenirs. But to everyone's secret relief, he did not gore her to death. When Vilas Rao, after being roughly reminded by his nephew, blew his whistle with shaking hands, Nandini's body was no longer white but rose.

That night to Laxmi's surprise, a crowd gathered at their house. Passion filled her voice as she took in the host of faces before her. She spoke of the future of Nandgaon, one in which they all had Kamdhenus and electricity and a road, where their fields produced double their present yield with the careful use of fertiliser. She talked of petitioning the government for a proper school and a teacher and a primary health centre with a resident nurse. And though the people there that night were familiar with all Laxmi had to say, this time they opened their hearts to her words. For once the shock had worn off, the headman's revelation had made them see that the outside world was not such a terrible place, for it had created the wealth that Ramu and Laxmi enjoyed.

The next day the two animals were brought together again. This time everyone in Nandgaon was there. Even the half-deaf grandmothers had come, curious to see what everyone was so excited about. Shambhu pawed the ground threateningly a few times when Nandini was led in, made a half-hearted attempt at a charge and then stopped short right in front of her, glaring at her. He drew himself up to his full height and pawed the ground majestically, snorting at the same time. Then and only then did Nandini deign to look at him, and in the long elegant lines of her head was such disdain that no one could fail to see it. Then she turned and walked away to the other side. The crowd sighed in disappointment. Many had even brought their children. 'Sow your seed Shambhu, sow your seed,' someone called and the others took it up. A drum began to give accompaniment until the call became a roar. But the two animals ignored it.

And they ignored each other, keeping to their sides of the fence and staring majestically into the middle distance.

'She's making a fool of him,' Laxmi told Ramu. 'He will not touch her as long as she is standing still.'

But Ramu pretended he hadn't heard.

The previous night they'd had a fight and it had been such a bitter one that for the first time in a long time, when morning came, they still hadn't made up.

Eventually Laxmi picked up a stone and threw it at Nandini, shocking the animal out of her stillness. Nandini yelped in a rather undignified way and turned around, baring her teeth. That was enough for Shambhu. He rushed at Nandini, head down, horns pointed at her stomach. 'Oh, oh. He will skewer her now,' Govind Rao whispered to Sushilabai, 'then it will all be over.'

'And glad I'll be,' Sushilabai replied. 'Each day the shop is closed we lose money.'

But Nandini surprised them, moving away at the penultimate moment and allowing the bull to crash into the fence post.

'Clever, clever thing,' Jaiwant Rane muttered.

A groan went through the crowd as Shambhu, falling to his knees by the shattered post, tried to get up.

'Come on, get up, get up,' Govind Rao muttered, biting his lips.

'Now she'll get him, watch,' Sushilabai whispered, nudging him in the ribs.

Others thought the same and a tentative clapping had begun.

'Now he is finished,' Sushilabai whispered. 'Look at Gajendraji, how can he look so calm?'

Nandini ran towards the bull, then stopped two feet away.

'Finish him, finish him,' came the call from the audience.

'Look, she is waiting for him to rise,' Kuntabai whispered. 'What a kind creature!'

'Foolish thing. He will eat her alive now for she has seen his weakness,' Parvatibai, Bicchoo's long-suffering wife replied, biting her lip.

And indeed, it seemed as if Parvatibai was right. For Shambhu suddenly struggled to his feet and stood wobbling slightly, a dazed look in his eyes.

Jaiwant Rane, on the other side of the shattered fence, shut his own eyes, praying that the end for Nandini would be short and not too painful.

Shambhu ran at her slowly. Nandini waited. Blood streamed down Shambhu's chest, a red cloak. The crowd held its breath. The two animals faced each other – Shambhu, his face puffed and bleeding, looked the picture of rage. But just then the sun slipped behind the trees and Vilas Rao blew his whistle, signalling the end of the session. Ramu rushed into the enclosure to examine the bull's wounds and the headman's servants led Nandini away while others began to repair the broken posts.

That evening as the villagers huddled around their kitchen fires they talking in subdued voices of the day's combat. Bets were laid amongst the younger men about who would win. Most still favoured Shambhu, but a few, Vilas Rao's nephew being one of them, bet on Nandini.

'Our Patel is a very clever man,' Darbari Lal said, 'look how well he understands us. Even though he no longer has his eyes watching over the village, he can still see into our hearts. Whatever the outcome, this is not a mating but a match that no one will ever forget. Which one of us will ever forget the sight of Nandini coming alone into the arena? Already my mind plays out her death in a hundred different ways. Who will remember what Shambhu looked like in victory?'

No one went to see the headman – not even Gajendra, his own son. So Gopal spent the evening alone in the cowshed, tending to Nandini himself, feeding her with his own hands, cleaning and massaging her body until it relaxed and she went to sleep. And even after the animal had fallen asleep the headman remained there, taking comfort in the presence of the other animals, in their similarity, and the beauty of their long slim faces. And yet, as he watched over them, he couldn't shake himself free of the feeling that their faces had become less solid, less real. As if they were all becoming a part of the past even as they lived and breathed.

The next morning the headman was surprised to receive a visit from Vilas Rao.

'I cannot bear it any more,' he said. 'Please end this slaughter.'

The headman shook his head. 'It is too late for that. If Krishna Bhagwan could not stop the Pandavas and the Kauravas* from going to war, how can I stop this battle?'

'But your beloved Nandini may die. And Shambhu too. Do you not care?' Vilas Rao cried.

The headman didn't answer immediately. Of course he cared for Nandini. Wasn't she the symbol of the herd and of Nandgaon and therefore of him too? Hadn't he seen her death a million times in the last two days? But in the last two days he had also understood that some things went beyond death. And so he said, 'There are more important things at stake than the life of a cow. Go, let destiny do its work.'

Once more the two animals were brought together and the village gathered to watch. But there were no calls or cheers, and no drums. And there were almost no women in the audience. This time Shambhu wasted no time, going straight into the attack. But Nandini seemed to read his mind and each time she danced away. And so the epic battle raged on. Sometimes it seemed Nandini was winning and at other times the advantage was clearly Shambhu's. Sometimes it seemed that the two animals would kill each other. And yet neither was quite able to get the better of the other. Each day the village gathered around the enclosure and yelled encouragement at both Shambhu and Nandini. Each day the two animals fought and

---

* The two opposing sides in that epic tale of war, the Mahabharata.

feinted. And only six-year-old Deepak noticed that each day the distance between the two opponents grew smaller, more intimate – as though the animals had grown to know each other, and to look forward to their encounters. And then, on the sixth day, when Shambhu charged Nandini, instead of raising her head, she turned and coyly presented him with her passage.

CHAPTER THIRTY-TWO
THE MODERN MAN

Two years later, election fever had gripped Khandwa once again. The streets were ablaze in orange and green. Hands, the symbol of protection, and lotuses, emblems of the goddess of wealth, decorated the walls of every house and every public building, public toilets, lamp posts and hoardings. The streets were crowded and cacophonous, with official-looking cars with flashing red lights on the roofs honking self-importantly at cycle rickshaws, tractors and bullock carts. Autorickshaws with huge megaphones on their roofs blared patriotic songs and slogans at full volume, inviting people to vote for one or the other party. The atmosphere was electric. The Raja of Khandwa's son was fighting the election for the first time – on a BJP* ticket. As the deputy commissioner had predicted, the Raja's hotel project had fallen through and so the Raja's son had turned to politics instead. Amar Singh, the seasoned congressman who had been elected from Khandwa for the last ten years, was worried – so worried that he had called deputy commissioner Choudhury to the Public Works Department guest house, his temporary headquarters, for an early-morning meeting.

'Have you seen him campaigning?' he demanded of the deputy commissioner. 'I hear he pulls in crowds of fifty thousand each time.'

* Bhartiya Janata Party, the Hindu Nationalist Party.

462

Prakash Choudhury raised an inquiring eyebrow. 'All exaggerated, sir. I was at one of his rallies two weeks ago; not even five thousand were there and they'd all come to see the foreign-educated launda* struggle to speak their language.'

'That doesn't mean anything. I couldn't speak Nimari properly to begin with either,' Amar Singh replied. 'The fact is he is new, he is fresh. People believe him. My people tell me that the local BJP cadres are going from house to house, promising people that if they vote for him he will turn Khandwa into another Delhi. And that he will give them all computers, televisions and the like. Can you not put a stop to it?'

'What? You mean arrest them for making false promises? Then one would have to arrest everyone from the prime minister downwards,' Prakash Choudhury replied.

'Stop playing dumb, Prakashbhai. Don't think that just because you are a civil servant you will be safe. He will transfer you to a hell worse than this,' Amar Singh said irritably. 'I wish you hadn't blocked his hotel project; by now he would have been rich or bankrupt. Either way, he'd have kept far away from politics.'

The deputy commissioner said nothing, looking steadfastly at his ruby ring instead. 'I keep telling you, you have nothing to worry about, sir. I am in charge here.'

'But what are you going to do? In an election no one is in-charge, it is the people that decide,' Amar Singh snapped.

'But there are ways to make them make the right decision. That is what I am here for.'

'What is it? What have you planned?' Hope appeared on Amar Singh's face for the first time.

The deputy commissioner sat back in the uncomfortable Public Works Department guest house armchair. His fingers tapped out a one-two one-two beat on the cheap wooden arm-

* spoiled rich boy

rests. Amar Singh looked at him and thought of how much he disliked the deputy commissioner, especially his fat grabbing fingers that were always reaching for more money.

'So hurry up and tell me what you have in mind. I don't have all day,' Amar Singh snapped.

The deputy commissioner smiled and continued to tap his fingers, enjoying the politician's helplessness. 'I have just the thing for you, don't worry,' he said.

'What is it?' Amar Singh asked, striding up to him eagerly.

The deputy commissioner looked up at him. 'Do you remember the young fire-eater I introduced you to a couple of years ago, the social worker?' he asked.

Amar Singh frowned as he tried to remember. Social workers were nosy pests. What on earth did the deputy commissioner want with one of them? Then his face cleared. 'The one who didn't drink anything except milk and water? Mishra, I think his name was.'

'You are mixing up what he does with what he drinks, but yes, that is him,' Prakash Choudhury said, laughing. 'He is an animal breeder and from what I can tell, an amazingly successful one.'

'You said he was trouble,' Amar Singh said impatiently, 'but you had some crazy theory about neutralising him using spiders or something. Is he still here?'

Prakash Choudhury smiled indulgently. 'Yes, sir, very much so. In fact, if I may say so myself, my theory was very sound. He has been safely neutralised and spends his time doing rather good work for us. He has inseminated several cows in the area.'

'So what good will that do me? I don't even own a cow,' the congressman said peevishly. 'Really Choudhury, I am surprised at you. One would think the Raja had bought you as well, sitting around talking about cows when I have an election to win.'

The deputy commissioner's face darkened but he maintained his calm. 'That is my point. The Raja offers televisions and computers, you – a man of the people – offer the people cows that can produce twenty litres of milk and make them richer than their wildest dreams. Who, do you think they will vote for?'

'Rubbish,' the congressman stamped his foot, 'utter rubbish. I come from a farming background; no animal can produce that much milk. Farmers aren't fools.' He resumed his pacing up and down the worn carpet of the VIP room. 'A promise like that will not even convince my party workers. Besides, the Raja is going about painting himself as a foreign-educated, entirely modern man. He says I am an old traditionalist, incapable of taking Khandwa into the future. Just like the party to which I belong. You want me to confirm that in people's minds? Huh, cows! Can't you come up with something better, Choudhury? I must say, I am disappointed in you.'

Prakash Choudhury said nothing, letting the congressman pace up and down the room. After a while, when the silence had become almost unbearable he said calmly, 'Sir, you want to be different from this Raja with his mad ideas, you want to show the people that you have something concrete, something tried and tested and true to offer. This young man Mishra, who is already very well known all over the countryside, is your truly modern man, a man of the people, willing to use his knowledge to serve the people. And he is producing a truly modern cow that will make gold for everyone. You can use him to make the Raja's son seem like an arrogant, elitist pig – just like his father and all the Rajas before him.'

Prakash Choudhury allowed his words to sink in. The cogs in the congressman's brain, he knew, turned slowly.

Amar Singh's steps slowed and then he stopped pacing altogether and turned to face the deputy commissioner. He was smiling. 'You know, Choudhury, I think you may be right. They will not buy me, but they will buy him. We will give the people their True Modern Man and destroy that upstart Raja.'

Not far away, in the quiet street where he lived, the True Modern Man had just woken up to a glorious hangover. The hangover had been preceded by an equally glorious dream, one in which he was with his blonde princess again and the gateway to the future stared at him welcomingly. Modern life was a series of gateways, he reflected philosophically, simultaneously wondering whether his wife had prepared his breakfast yet. Either one got through them or one was left behind. His mind turned to the conversation he'd had with the deputy commissioner the previous night and a surge of excitement went through him.

'So Manoj, I hope you are ready,' Deputy Commissioner Choudhury had said.

'Ready for what, sir?' Manoj had asked coyly.

'Ready for fame.'

'For fame? What do you mean, sir?' Manoj had felt a thrill of pleasure at the sound of the word.

'Your insemination programme will be inaugurated by our own Congress MP Amar Singhji himself. You remember I introduced you to him the first time we met? His father was a minister in the cabinet.'

Manoj had felt torn between gratification and annoyance. It was his special moment, his hard work. He didn't want a politician stealing the limelight, getting the credit.

'But there is no need for an inauguration,' he had protested. 'I have been doing this for three years already; everybody knows me.'

'Rubbish, every good work needs a proper inauguration. There will be many press people there – this is an election year, remember? Your face will be in all the papers holding the minister's hand. How proud your parents will be.'

The latter remark had taken care of any residual resentment Manoj may have felt. Suddenly he had wanted to celebrate – to get drunk with his friends on the street, to visit his favourite whorehouse, and to see Govinda.

Seeing the look on Manoj's face the deputy commissioner had smiled. 'OK, come to the office tomorrow at noon and we will begin.'

Letting himself out of the back door, Manoj took a deep breath of crisp morning air, fragrant with the scent of jacaranda and madhumalati, and tried to fight the headache that threatened to overwhelm him. Last night he'd celebrated exactly the way he'd wanted to, collapsing in his front garden at three in the morning, unable to reach for his key. Now he hurried down the driveway and opened the door to the barn. Govinda, now enormously fat and beginning to go grey around the mouth, looked up, a blade of straw sticking out of his mouth. The sight of Govinda's immense black bulk reassured Manoj. The headache retreated. He walked around the barn to the other end and pulled the rubber collection bag out of the pail of water in which it was kept. He then took the large oval bag shaped like a womb to the sink at the opposite end and washed it in warm water. Then, armed solely with the rubber womb, he opened the gate of Govinda's stall, calling to him softly. The cow blanket which he'd used in the beginning to disguise his smell and evoke Govinda's desire had long since been discarded. They were long-standing partners and needed no disguises.

Used to his entrance, Govinda didn't move. His right eye fixed itself balefully upon Manoj, informing him of his utter inconsequence. When Manoj was almost within touching distance, the animal turned his back on him humiliatingly. The cold gleam of the tubelights reflected off the shiny darkness of his skin, breaking into pools of quicksilver every time an insect landed on it. The rest blended into the darkness of the stall, so that it seemed to Manoj when he entered that Govinda was all around him. He touched Govinda at last, politely, delicately at first, and Govinda snorted his welcome, turning quickly and demanding his sugar. As Manoj fed him with one hand he began patting the animal's stomach with the other, the collection bag clutched firmly between his own chin and neck.

The strong sulphur smell of the animal invaded his nostrils and his hand moved quicker, stroking long and hard, but avoiding its target. Govinda's skin shivered with pleasure breaking into liquid ripples that ran into each other as one wave succeeded the other. When all of Govinda was trembling in anticipation Manoj slipped under the giant beast and grabbed his red-tipped member with both hands. It didn't take long. When the first drops began to glisten on its surface, Manoj leaned in, and inhaling the sweet scent deeply, fixed the bag around it and squeezed with all his might. He took the other end of the bag in his mouth and blew into it so that the bag inflated quickly, increasing the pressure on the animal's straining member. Govinda grunted twice and it was over. The bag felt warm and full and Manoj retreated victorious, clutching his treasure. He resolved to do it again in the afternoon, after he returned from the meeting at the deputy commissioner's. He would be needing a lot of semen in the future.

The ex-Patel of Nandgaon awoke as he usually did shortly before dawn. He stared up at the wooden-beamed ceiling and out of habit began making a list of the things he had to do. The list was a short one for everything had been prepared well in advance. His son was now in charge of the house and the land. Their dairy was the largest and most profitable in the village. His son had bought all sorts of machines for treating the milk and two milk trucks. And his son had made himself the head of the Nandgaon milk cooperative, a position of immense power and riches. He was also the government's village development officer and regularly filed false reports about Ramu's corruption. Gopal's lips twisted as he thought of his last conversation with his son.

The latter had looked relieved the previous night when Gopal had handed him the keys to his room. Though the room no longer held anything of value, his son had smiled. 'So you are going after all, Father?' he'd asked taking the keys. 'You won't change your mind?'

'But of course not. I had always promised your mother I would take her to Kashi*,' Gopal had replied.

Now Gopal's eyes went to the small wooden box lying on the bedside table that guarded his wife's ashes. Nandgaon had been his excuse for never fulfilling her dying wish. Now that Nandgaon no longer had any use for him, at last he could grant her wish. He got up and slipped his feet one last time into the worn wood of his chappals. Today he would not be going for his morning walk. Instead he took out a brand-new white dhoti from the canvas bag that had been packed for him the previous day and went for a bath.

The courtyard was silent except for an occasional snort or grunt from the sleeping animals and humans. Gopal entered the bath enclosure and worked the hand pump until the bucket was full. After he had finished his bath, he wore his new dhoti, slipped on his sacred thread and wrapped another length of coarse cloth, the dress of the pilgrim, around his shoulders. Then he clumped his way to the puja room for the last time, said his prayers and painted the three vertical stripes of the devout follower of Shiva, lord of all changes, on his forehead. The god had been a wanderer all his life, he reflected – until they built him his Kashi. That was probably why Kashi was also called the home of the homeless. He got up heavily and went down the verandah steps to where the tulsi plant was. He watered it with the water from his puja, thinking of the Ganga all the while and wondering what that mighty river would look like in Kashi.

* Varanasi

The cow awoke well before the first ray of dawn managed to penetrate the dingy grey cement building in which she was housed. The barn where she had lived with her beloved last child had been torn down and a far grander building made of cement had taken its place. Other animals had come to occupy the new space, animals who made her feel alone in a different way. Her beloved two-legs no longer came to take her to the forest and even Shambhu she hardly ever saw, for he was now the leader of the herd.

But she herself never went with the herd. For the herd itself had changed. The animals seldom went out together to graze. Instead their two-legged keepers or the little two-legs would bring them food that smelled of the big smelly things that she'd met so often on the road. In fact, the whole village now smelt of the road. Perhaps that was why the cow felt it was time to move, why she dreamt about that place where the cows went alone. Only now she knew she would not be alone.

Dawn had turned the sky a silver-grey when the headman set off on the road. It was difficult to walk. Close to a century of being attached to the same ten square miles of land had made his feet heavy. But he moved forward determinedly, not looking back. It took him a long time to realise he was being followed. As he was unaccustomed to walking on the hard surface of a road, shortly before Gopal reached Kesarigaon, his knees had already begun to ache. The presence of a piece of gravel in his shoe made things worse and he was limping by the time he reached the edge of the village. He sat down on a milestone and removed the shoe. A blister had begun to form on the side of his heel. He looked about him curiously. He had not visited Kesarigaon for at least twenty years. A giant sun was rising out of the mist that cloaked the fields and he watched it turn the morning mist to rose as it climbed. It had taken only ten years for the forest around Kesarigaon to disappear, he reflected.

How long would it take in Nandgaon?

The sun was a bright yellow disc by the time he felt able to move. In the distance he could make out the first of the day's traffic, three giant and unwieldy trucks weaving their way between the potholes. He glanced back down the road towards Nandgaon, towards the familiar trees topping the proud crest of the river bank, to him the most beloved silhouettes in the world. He knew he would not be seeing them again.

That was when he saw the old cow.

It did not take him long to recognise her as Ramu's junglee cow. She too was leaving, he realised, feeling strangely unsurprised. A smile, the first in a very long time, appeared on his face. He reached into his bag and took out a handful of grain, then sat back and waited for the cow to catch up.

When Ramu arrived at the barn later that morning, he was surprised to find the barn door open. As he entered a feeling of dread took hold. The animals raised their patchwork faces to watch him but he ignored them, searching for the milk-white form of the one he loved more than he did any human being in the village. Her flesh had melted away in the last two years and she no longer went out with him to the forest. He himself, he admitted reluctantly, rarely went to the forest. The affairs of the village kept him busy. And then there were the constant summonses to the deputy commissioner's office in town. Still, his mornings always began with a visit to the one who had made it all happen, the one he knew was the real Kamdhenu. But as he moved through the semi-darkness to her stall at the end of the long hall, his heart felt empty. He heard no sound, no welcoming grunt, no hurried scraping of hooves as a frail body rose eagerly off the ground. The stall, when he got there, was open. He let out a strangled cry.

For days the villagers of Nandgaon combed the fields and forest around the village, but the cow was nowhere to be found.

Ramu was inconsolable. He blamed himself. After a week of fruitlessly searching the fields and nearby groves, he left the village and went to stay in the forest clearing where he had first met the cow, convinced that if she were to return she would first come there. For in his heart he felt certain she wouldn't return to the village. Things had changed. The herd had changed. The coming of the road had brought everything that the headman had warned them about: theft, alcohol, fights. Ramu spent all his time trying vainly to resolve disputes. Let alone sharing food with those who had none, people barely greeted each other as they passed each other on the street. Thanks to the road Nandgaon was filled with strangers, and almost every second house was also a shop to feed and house those strangers. And the nights were noisy with radios and television sets. In contrast, nights in the forest were tranquil, and he slept better there than he had slept in months.

A week passed and Ramu did not return. The villagers grew nervous. Ramu was their headman, after all.

'I cannot understand Ramubhai,' Bicchoo, grown rich and plump, said to Darbari Lal as he was being shaved. 'How can he go off and leave us to the mercies of his wife like this? She isn't even from Nandgaon.'

Darbari Lal didn't reply for a moment. 'He has so many animals,' he said at last. 'I can't understand what he saw in that bag of bones.'

'His luck,' Keshu replied. 'She was his luck.'

'Rubbish,' Madhav spat, 'the Kamdhenu was the lucky one.'

'The Kamdhenu was Nandgaon's luck, the junglee was his,' Bicchoo added. 'Naturally he wants her back.' In the barber's mirror Bicchoo watched them digest the implications of his words. A satisfied smile flitted briefly across his face. Govind Rao would be glad.

Only Laxmi knew why Ramu didn't want to return and she lay awake night after night, worrying about it. So twice a day

she crossed the bridge and walked the one and a half kilometres into the forest on the other side of the river with a hot
meal for her husband. Sitting down in silence beside him, she'd
undo the coarse napkin and open out the tiffin carrier, laying
out the many containers in a fragrant semi-circle. Then she'd
tell Ramu about the previous day, bringing him up to date on
all that had happened in the village.

A fortnight passed this way. And still Ramu showed no signs
of wanting to return.

'If she chooses to return one day,' Laxmi asked Ramu one
afternoon, 'she will find you, don't you think?'

'Perhaps,' Ramu's jaw set stubbornly, 'but I like being here.
I feel close to her here,' he replied. What he didn't add was
that the forest reminded him of the old days when life was
simple and all he'd received from others was kindness.

'But the village needs you,' Laxmi pointed out.

Inwardly Ramu shuddered. 'They have you,' he replied. 'You
are the one who decides. You are the intelligent one.'

Laxmi's heart clenched. She wanted to tell him that he was
wrong, that she lacked his instinctive kindness. And without
it, no decision could be just. But the words stuck in her throat.
Instead she said lamely, 'There is still Shambhu.'

'Huh, Shambhu is different.' Bitterness flooded Ramu's
mouth. 'I wish he had never been born. I wish. . . I wish the
doctor had never come to our village. If only Patelji had found
him first and turned him away.' Thinking of the headman
brought a sharp pain to his chest. 'I wish Patelji were still here.
Then maybe she would still be here too.'

'No, never,' Laxmi cried. 'Don't talk like that.'

Suddenly Ramu threw his flute into the middle of the clearing
and stood up to face Laxmi. 'Then why did she leave?' he
asked, turning and looking directly at Laxmi for the first time
since the cow had disappeared. Laxmi swallowed. She'd known
the question would come and she had an answer ready. But

now she hesitated, not sure if he would understand. 'It wasn't because you did something wrong,' she said slowly, clearly. 'I think perhaps it is not really in the nature of cows to stay in one place.'

'Lies,' Ramu snapped. 'Everyone knows that cows have always stayed in one place; they are part of a herd, they are the soul of the village.' His voice growing heavy with sarcasm, he asked, 'Have you ever met a cow that travels?'

Laxmi felt her knees grow weak at the hardness of his gaze but she kept her own steady. She swallowed, her throat suddenly dry. 'Travelling is what the cows forgot when we brought them into our homes. We made them forget. And we turned them into something else. But the junglee was special. Because she was from the forest, I think she understood a lot more than most animals.'

'Understood what?' Ramu demanded.

Laxmi took a deep breath. She had thought of the answer to this question for many nights. 'In Sanskrit class they taught us that gau has many meanings. Gau is cow, but gau is also the soul. And gau is also the name given to the first ray of light that moves out of the sun to touch the earth.' Laxmi paused, letting her words sink in. Then she asked softly, 'Is it not the nature of the soul to move on? Perhaps the cow felt the need to move; perhaps she understood that her work here had ended.'

Ramu looked at her, and the pain in his eyes as his heart struggled to accept what she had said almost broke Laxmi's heart. She touched her stomach and thought of the new life slowly blossoming there – and prayed to the junglee to heal Ramu.

'Let her go, Ramu,' she begged hoarsely. 'Come back to Nandgaon. We need you. Your son needs you.'

For a long time neither moved. Then slowly the lines of torment on Ramu's face eased. He stepped towards Laxmi and took her in his arms.